Maneater

www.penguin.co.uk

Maneater

ELLIE GRAVES

bantam

TRANSWORLD PUBLISHERS

UK | USA | Canada | Ireland | Australia
India | New Zealand | South Africa

Transworld is part of the Penguin Random House group of companies
whose addresses can be found at global.penguinrandomhouse.com.

Penguin Random House UK, One Embassy Gardens, 8 Viaduct Gardens, London SW11 7BW

penguin.co.uk

First published in Great Britain in 2026 by Bantam
an imprint of Transworld Publishers

001

Copyright © Claire Waller 2026

The moral right of the author has been asserted.

This book is a work of fiction and, except in the case of historical fact, any
resemblance to actual persons, living or dead, is purely coincidental.

Every effort has been made to obtain the necessary permissions with
reference to copyright material, both illustrative and quoted. We apologize
for any omissions in this respect and will be pleased to make the
appropriate acknowledgements in any future edition.

Penguin Random House values and supports copyright.
Copyright fuels creativity, encourages diverse voices, promotes freedom
of expression and supports a vibrant culture. Thank you for purchasing
an authorized edition of this book and for respecting intellectual property
laws by not reproducing, scanning or distributing any
part of it by any means without permission. You are supporting authors and enabling
Penguin Random House to continue to publish books for everyone.
No part of this book may be used or reproduced in any manner for the
purpose of training artificial intelligence technologies or systems. In accordance
with Article 4(3) of the DSM Directive 2019/790, Penguin Random House
expressly reserves this work from the text and data mining exception.

Typeset in 12.8/16 pt Dante MT Std by Falcon Oast Graphic Art Ltd
Printed and bound in Great Britain by Clays Ltd, Elcograf S.p.A.

The authorized representative in the EEA is Penguin Random House Ireland,
Morrison Chambers, 32 Nassau Street, Dublin D02 YH68

A CIP catalogue record for this book is available from the British Library.

ISBNs:
9780857508324 hb
9780857508331 tpb

For my mother, the main reason I'm not squeamish

ONE

There's a particular knack to jointing a chicken carcass. The chefs on TV make it look so easy, but if you don't know what you're doing, it's pretty easy to fuck up.

Thankfully, Renee Landis knows exactly what she's doing, given how many chickens she's dismembered in this job already. She plucks one from the bucket and slaps it onto the table. The slick flesh wobbles as she digs her fingers into its sides, feeling for where the rubbery cartilage meets bone. It only takes a couple of seconds; there's not much variation in chicken anatomy. She slices through the joint as easily as through butter. Behind her, someone turns on the radio.

Pop. First leg out.

'Today, on the first anniversary of the disappearance of Frank Mercer, his wife makes a fresh appeal for any witnesses or sightings that may uncover the truth of what happened to the television presenter. Frank Mercer, best known for his role in the BBC show *I Wouldn't Want to Eat That*, vanished after accusations of improper conduct against contestants – allegations that were later confirmed when chef Bethany Jacobs called for his resignation after he referred to her as a "stupid woman" and told her she "needed to go back where she came from".'

Clack. Second leg comes loose.

'Many, including both his ex-wives and three of his five children, believe Mercer – who would be fifty-nine now – is most likely dead. His first wife, Elena, said that he "hated being questioned", and would "never take responsibility for his own poor conduct", while "expecting others to fall over backwards for him".'

Renee's about to disjoint the wings when she notices three white stalks protruding from the raw flesh. No one talks about this part of the job. She grabs her tweezers and pulls at the stems – because no customer in their right mind wants to look into their bucket of wings and see pinfeathers. Renee extracts the final feather as the news bulletin finishes.

'According to the former Mrs Mercer, her ex-husband never took criticism well. She believes he could be living somewhere remote under an assumed name, or took matters into his own hands . . .'

The radio drones on, cycling through one disaster after another. With the back of her wrist, Renee pushes a dark curl that's escaped her messy bun up out of her face, careful not to touch her skin. It was a habit drummed into her in culinary school, along with no nail polish and how to scrub up as well as any surgeon. Not that anyone would care about that here. The only reason Chickadees has anything approaching a half-decent hygiene certificate is because of her.

Clive, her boss, is far too stingy to spring for prepared meat. He buys the carcasses wholesale and lets her sort them out. Not that she minds too much. Renee has always found the soft *pop* when dislocating the leg, thigh and wing joints oddly comforting. Every now and again, though, she comes across a bad carrion. The meat itself isn't rotten, but some corpses are covered in sores or have hideous deformities from the conditions they were raised in. These are the kinds of chickens customers never see, let alone think about, when they bite into their Nice 'n' Spicy burger.

Working with these chickens used to really bother her. Not because she's particularly squeamish, but because she knows it's not right, even at a cheap chicken shop. People, and the animals they eat, deserve better. But when better costs too much, bargain-basement, bare-necessity-only becomes the norm.

Before Chickadees, Renee trained in high-end restaurants, working with the best ingredients money could buy. Not any more. Now she rummages through a bucket, picking out the carcasses she hopes won't poison someone. She has a clean record, but that doesn't stop the creeping feeling that it's only a matter of time.

She plucks another chicken free and slaps it onto the table. The raw meat quivers as she digs in, feeling for the cartilage, slicing through the joint. First one leg, then the other. Next come the wings – little scraps of gristly meat that are, for some reason, so highly prized by the connoisseurs of chicken shops.

God, I'm bored.

The phrase runs like a litany through her head. She tries to ignore it, but lately it's been deafening. She initially took this job as a stopgap, but now she's been here two years. She's one of yesterday's brightest culinary stars – a once-lauded trainee chef, now forgotten. She runs her knife down both sides of the breastbone and slices off the breasts in one practised cut. She used to do this to duck, pigeon, quail and grouse. Now it's just chicken.

It's always just chicken.

She separates the tenders as the news bulletin ends, then dumps everything in the large steel bowl beside her. What's left of the carcass goes in the bin. She wrinkles her nose at the tangy smell of rotten meat. It doesn't matter how much bleach she uses, the kitchen always stinks.

But she doesn't have time to worry about that. The shop opens in a couple of hours, and she still has around thirty kilos of meat to prep. She reaches for another dead bird, trying to ignore the suffocating monotony of this dead-end job.

Hours later, the carcasses have all been jointed, and the resultant cuts are marinated and ready for cooking. There's already a good number of people waiting for their food, and she's the only one working the baskets and grill tonight. Sweat streaks down her face, threatening to salt the meat even more, forcing her to wipe herself with a questionably clean tea towel. Even though this isn't where she planned to end up, she still takes pride in her work. The chicken isn't of the finest quality – far from it – but that doesn't mean she allows herself to serve low-quality meals. There's a reason Chickadees is now one of the most popular chicken shops in Brixton. But as much as she tries to stay on top of the grease and the grime and the stench, she's not exactly working with the best tools for the job. There's a reason fast-food joints don't get Michelin stars.

'Two Nice 'n' Spicies, a BBQ sandwich and triple fries!' Renee calls out.

A man saunters over to the counter and nods. She wordlessly hands him the already greasy bag. He doesn't even acknowledge her.

'Enjoy your food,' she says with a sigh, mentally adding a well-deserved 'asshole'. Don't these people even realize how much trust they put into her, a complete stranger, only for them to treat her as if she's beneath them? The old joke about spitting in burgers really is just the tip of the pissed-off food worker's iceberg. She knows. She's seen workers do things that are borderline criminal – and she'd be lying if she said she hadn't been tempted herself.

Not that she would. Ever since she was a kid, watching *Ready, Steady, Cook* while sitting on her father's knee, she'd been obsessed with food. Susie Salt and Percy Pepper, learning how to season, understanding the role of flavour, texture and spice. Her parents did everything they could to scrape together a decent life for her and her brothers, but after a while even fish fingers and chips lose their charm. So she taught herself how to get creative with limited ingredients. As her skills grew, she decided to train properly: Food

Tech at school, followed by Catering at college, then proper culinary school after that. She was consistently top of her class, the one to watch, Top 25 Under 25—

'Did you get that, Renee?'

She gives herself a little shake and refocuses.

'Sorry, Adele. Was a million miles away.'

'Yeah, I could tell. Anyway, jerk chicken special extra hot, slaw, small fries.'

Renee retreats into the relative safety of her kitchen. Well, not *her* kitchen. Her kitchen has more vegetables and a lot less cheap cooking oil. She'd asked Clive to order in some rapeseed, but he said it was too expensive. She said the difference would be worth it – her food would taste even better. Clive just shook his head and laughed. Like he gave a crap how the food actually tasted. He just wanted to make as much profit as possible, and better oil didn't feature in that plan.

The jerk chicken is one of Renee's specialities. She'd learned to cook authentic Jamaican jerk from Granni, who had her prepping scotch bonnets from the age of four. 'So you learn, one way or another,' she'd said. No grandchild of Granni's was going to cook without chilli. God, Renee misses her.

It doesn't take long to assemble the order. She'd made sure the thighs were already on the coals before they opened; good jerk can't be rushed. It feels sacrilegious as she shoves two of them into a polystyrene box, oil pooling the moment the meat touches the surface. She doesn't have time to worry about presentation – three more orders are already racked up and, judging by the chatter outside, there's quite a few people waiting to be served.

Out in front, it's obvious Adele is swamped. A party of lads are swigging from lager bottles, a couple of young suits eyeing them nervously as they wait. Outside, a couple peruse the menu. A typical Thursday night.

In the corner sits an elderly Black woman. She looks a little out of place among the young people, and she beams at Renee when she spots her.

'Hi there, Mrs Delaney,' Renee says in a sing-song tone. 'Got your chicken.'

'You remembered to put in extra chilli?'

'Do you seriously think I'd forget?'

Mrs Delaney's laugh sounds more like a cough, but Renee's pleased she's made the old lady happy.

'Oh, you . . . You're a good girl, Renee. Best jerk outside of my own kitchen. Not even my daughter-in-law can get it right these days. But you . . . you know. You understand.'

'It was my grampa's favourite,' Renee says. 'I had no choice but to get it right.'

Mrs Delaney rumbles out another laugh and shakes her head in amusement – just like she does every Thursday.

There's a yell, followed by a chorus of 'Oi! Oi!' The lads are getting louder, and Renee can't help but glance over at Adele. Her co-worker is a fearsome woman in her thirties – a former club bouncer who took this job 'for an easier life'. She usually holds the fort with ease, but these young men are giving even her a run for her money. Mrs Delaney purses her lips at their antics, clearly unimpressed.

'I'd get out while you still can,' Renee says, only half joking.

'Why do they have to do this?' Mrs Delaney mutters. 'No manners.'

'They're young and drunk. Honestly, they're not the worst.'

'They aren't?'

'Nah. Just give them their chicken and they'll go away. It's all bravado. We'll be fine.'

TWO

What Renee didn't tell Mrs Delaney was who the worst types are.

And unfortunately, they've just walked in.

It's eight p.m. – peak hours. Adele is shepherding customers with the weary, if practised, air of an expert sheepdog working with a particularly recalcitrant flock. But it's clear she can't take orders, give them out *and* wait on tables. So if anyone wants to eat outside, it's down to Renee to take their meals directly from the kitchen.

This was one of Clive's great ideas. Other chicken shops only did takeaway, so he thought he'd branch out – corner a part of the market rarely exploited in the fast-food industry.

Outdoor table service.

The only problem was, they didn't have any space to create seating. And he point-blank refused to employ anyone else to help wait the tables, so it's up to the current staff to muddle through. Every night they all prayed for rain.

Too bad it's a real July scorcher – hot enough that Renee wonders what, exactly, she's done to deserve this. Must have been a complete prick in a former life, because it definitely feels like she's being punished.

She risks leaving the kitchen to take four orders to the seating just outside the shop. They're literally on the pavement; she's surprised the council haven't been round to tell Clive to knock it off. But until that happens, she's resigned herself to battling through not only customers but also the poor pedestrians who clearly just want to get home.

There's a lot of people around tonight. The good weather and proximity to Friday means waves of bodies, but even taking that into consideration, she can tell exactly who this food is for.

Her stomach sinks.

There's five of them, all clustered around one table that usually seats three – four at a push – braying at each other. They've got floppy hair and are wearing pastel polo shirts, jeans that are a bit too tight, and expensive trainers. While Renee doesn't like to judge, she can't help the way her hackles rise. Because she knows why they're here. They're not hungry. They're slumming it. Having a laugh.

'Is that for us?' one of the men calls over. 'Because we ordered, like, twenty minutes ago or something.'

'Yeah, sorry, we're really busy and it's just me in the kitchen tonight.'

Defuse before they get riled up even more.

'I see. Well, it's not cold. Nothing worse than cold wings.' The disdain in his voice makes Renee's already fake smile turn even glassier.

'Yeah, Rupes,' another chimes in. 'Cold wings. Almost as bad as cold women.' He leans over the table and leers at Renee. She can feel their eyes on her – tight and suffocating, like a serpent coiling around her body.

'They've just come out of the oven, and I'm a bit busy, so if I can just leave these with you—'

'Oh, come on, sweetheart. You can do better than that. Give us a smile.'

All five of them smirk.

'OK, I have two portions of wings, extra hot; a crispy tender burger with extra crispy onions; four jerk thighs—' They all snicker at this, but Renee simply ignores them. It's not like they're the first to make this tired joke, and the sooner she can get rid of them, the better. 'And six Nice 'n' Spicy drummers.' She waits for the men to move so that she can put their plates down, but they all stay in her way.

'What about the skin-on seasoned fries?' one of them asks, clearly annoyed.

'And the slaw,' says another. 'Like, bro, come on. We've heard good things about this place, but quite frankly, it seems a bit shit.'

'The fries and slaw are coming. I couldn't carry everything at once. I'll be back with those in a minute.'

They still refuse to give her space, so she's forced to lean over them, nearly elbowing one in the face as he grins up at her. That's when she realizes exactly what they're doing.

'Nice breasts,' he says.

'Pardon?' Renee straightens up quickly, almost knocking over one of their beer bottles.

'In this burger,' he continues, lifting the bun – as if that makes his lie more believable. 'Cooked to perfection.'

Before she can gather herself, Renee feels something snake up the inside of her leg. She jerks back with an involuntary cry. Off balance, the first guy grabs her and yanks her down onto his lap.

'Way-hey, Rupes! Ride him, cowgirl!'

Renee has no idea who says this. She can only focus on how this guy – this *Rupes* – is forcing her to straddle his lap. He's holding on to her arms, and he's *strong*. Like, doesn't-actually-have-a-job, just-spends-all-day-at-the-gym strong. For a split second, she's caught perfectly between overwhelming panic at her vulnerability in this situation and blind rage, because what the fuck?

Rage wins.

'Get the fuck off me!' she yells, struggling to break the vice-like grip this man has on her.

People are watching now, and a couple of the posh boys are telling people, 'It's OK, she's just overreacting, just a joke, nothing but banter, bloody hell, women today, am I right?' Finally,

Rupes releases her. She all but leaps off him, turns around and, before she can stop herself, slaps him.

It isn't a hard slap. More of a reflex than anything. But despite being the one who was assaulted, the part of her that was always told to be nice and not make a scene immediately regrets it.

'You bitch,' Rupes snarls, while his friends holler around them.

Much to Renee's shame, tears spring to her eyes.

'Don't touch me.' She tries to sound brash, to show she's a force to be reckoned with, but there's a slight quaver in her voice.

'Come on, love. It's nothing,' Rupes says, spreading his hands in front of him like he's an innocent man. Like he didn't just have pure hatred in his eyes. 'It's just banter.'

'Banter?' Renee almost chokes on the word. 'That wasn't banter. You have no right to touch me, and you did more than just that—'

'Oh my God, you fell over and I caught you. And if we want to talk about touching people, you actually hit me, so . . .'

'Oi, now what's going on here?' The voice is wheezy – its owner a lifelong smoker despite his doctor telling him to quit years ago. 'Renee?'

'Clive. I'm sorry, but these guys—'

'Are you the manager of this establishment?' One of the posh boys drops the mockney and switches to his do-you-know-who-my-father-is voice. To Renee's disappointment, Clive shrinks away from him.

'Yes?' Clive says.

'She assaulted my friend. That's what's going on here.'

Renee's jaw drops. Before she can gather her wits, Mr Proto-Lawyer jumps back in.

'Yeah, you see, we came here to eat because we'd heard the food was good, but this . . . *waitress*' – he puts as much disdain as possible into the word – 'came out with only half our order, then got shirty when Tristan complimented her food. Next thing we know, she's falling over, Rupes catches her, and now she's saying it's all his fault.'

'Oh, oh . . . I, er, see? Umm . . .' Clive trails off, clearly wishing he'd stayed upstairs.

'Clive, that's not what happened. I brought out most of the order and was going to go back for the rest of it, but then he' – she jabs her finger in the direction of the one Mr Proto-Lawyer called Tristan – 'made a really unpleasant remark. Then I felt someone . . .' She catches herself and takes a breath as the memory of someone's hand touching her inner thigh ripples through her body. 'Someone touched me. I was so surprised I jumped. Then he' – she jabs at Rupes – 'pulled me into his lap—' Her voice catches a little.

'He didn't pull her into his lap. She stumbled, then slapped my friend. He should sue. Plenty of people saw it.'

'That is not what happened!' Renee protests. 'They were harassing me.'

'Look, no – don't get angry, but . . . he didn't hurt you, did he?' Clive is stuttering, clearly trying to keep the money on his side. 'It's not that bad in the grand scheme of things, is it? Just one of those things, you know. Japes. Banter. Just apologize, Ren. I'm sure that'll be fine.'

Renee stares back at him, dumbfounded.

Clive simply shrugs.

The men grin. One whoops. They know they've won.

'What—' Renee starts, but Clive interjects.

'OK, lads – that's enough,' he says as the group cackle like hyenas. 'Maybe you should just say sorry to each other. Everything kind of cancels itself out at the end of the day. No use making a scene. Right, Renee?'

Renee stares at the table in front of her. It still has the food she cooked on it – growing cold, all uneaten. All that potential, wasted on a bunch of juvenile pricks who will never know struggle.

She looks up at the sky. It'll be pitch black by the time she has to walk home.

The hyenas are still cackling, making comments about women in general – and women like her in particular. Rupes is still going on about how he could press charges if he wanted to. Clive, standing next to her, is grinning, obviously hoping these animals think he's cool with it all. Other people – passersby and customers alike – just watch. No one comes to her aid. No one defends her. Not a single person tells them to pack it in – that she was just defending herself.

A little girl, around eight or nine years old, peers out from behind her father, her eyes wide. Renee remembers being that age. Being told to be quiet, to be good, to not outshine anyone – especially the boys. She locks eyes with the girl, and something strikes within her like a match.

'Clive?'

'Uh, yeah?'

Renee's heart races as she reaches behind her back to untie her apron strings. Is she really going to do this? Maybe she should just go back inside, get on with her job. It can't have been that bad if no one is willing to defend her—

The little girl looks up at her father, as if seeking reassurance. She doesn't get it. He's too busy watching the drama unfold. A man next to him has his phone out, clearly recording – undoubtedly hoping to catch a woman acting hysterical over nothing so he can farm a few likes on TikTok.

The girl, realizing she isn't going to get any answers out of her father, buries her face into the side of his leg.

Renee takes a long, slow breath. Usually, she lets it slide. This isn't the first time a customer has been rude to her – or about her. But this isn't just about her. If she does nothing and scuttles back into the kitchen, what does that show the little girl watching?

She pulls the strings free, then yanks her apron over her head and balls it up into her fists. 'I can't do this, Clive.'

She chucks the apron at her manager. He fumbles it. Typical.

'Renee . . . What do you mean? What are you saying?'

Renee gives the little girl an almost imperceptible nod, then turns from them all, ignoring the cat calls and Clive's exasperated cries of 'Lads!' and 'Ren, what's going on?'

She swallows hard, hoping it might calm the butterflies in her stomach. It doesn't, but it's too late now. She's made her choice.

She walks away.

THREE

The night bus is full, so Renee decides to walk home. At first, she uses the walk to shake the adrenaline from her body, but around the halfway mark, the doubts really start to set in.

Shit. Has she overreacted? Maybe it was an accident. OK, so they were being awful, but she's supposed to be the professional one. People face worse every day. If only she'd taken the fries with her. Maybe they were just mucking around.

Her phone buzzes. She glances at the screen. Clive, again.

She doesn't answer.

Adele has also texted her, asking what the hell happened, but she can't answer her either, because Renee isn't sure herself. All she really knows is that Clive did nothing to defend her. If anything, he made matters worse. Maybe she wouldn't be so pissed off if this had been the first time. But it wasn't. Far from it.

The ghost of Rupes' hand strokes her thigh. Renee feels bile rise in the back of her throat and desperately swallows it until she gets home.

By the time she reaches her road, the butterflies have transformed into a full cocoon of anxiety. She's gone from doubt to actual worry, because whether it's crap or not, she needs a job. It's why she hasn't quit yet. She glances up at her building – a testament in concrete and glass to the Brutalist style that was so popular when it was originally built as social housing in the 1960s. Now, its soot-streaked exteriors and piss-drenched stairwells speak of a creeping urban decay no one seems to have the energy – or the will – to halt. They are, after all, the have-nots.

The lights in her flat are on, meaning Lola is home, which instantly makes Renee feel better. Lola used to work at Chickadees, so she knows exactly what Clive is like. If anyone's going to understand, it's Lola.

'Hey, hey! The lady of the house is in!'

Renee marvels at Lola's supernatural ability to make people feel better, no matter the situation. She knows they make a strange pairing – one, an outgoing local with a wicked sense of humour and an even more wicked tongue; the other, an introverted incomer, prone to self-doubt and overthinking – but it works.

'Heya, Lols,' Renee says, leaning in to Lola's hug and burrowing her face into her shoulder.

'You're home early. You all right?' Lola's tone has just the right amount of concern in it.

'Not really. Stupid customers.'

'Bad night? Who do I have to kill?'

'Five posh white boys?'

Lola makes a face. 'Ugh. I don't envy you. Don't get them much, but when they do turn up . . .' She straightens Renee up, which is no small feat given Renee has about half a foot on her. 'Come on, let's get you properly inside, and out of those greasy clothes. You have a shower, and I'll get the wine in. Trashy white or red?'

Renee can't help but smile.

'Trashy red.'

'*Oh là là*, how very *français* of you. Turning into a posh bitch.'

'I like the good life.'

'Oh, love . . . when the good life is a bottle of El Plonko from the SPAR down the road . . .' Lola shakes her head in mock disappointment.

'Just get me my wine, not-as-posh bitch.'

Lola cackles as she kicks off her slippers and shoves her feet into a pair of battered trainers. She's wearing pyjama bottoms and her blonde hair is in a high ponytail, making her look as if she's just rolled out of bed, but Renee doesn't say anything. It isn't worth it. Because if there's one thing Lola doesn't give in this life, it's a fuck. She's a self-described street-urchin-made-good, and Renee loves her for it.

'You want any snacks?' Lola asks before she opens the door.

'I dunno . . . Something sweet?'

'Sugar therapy. Got it.'

And with that, she's gone, leaving the flat feeling strangely hollow.

'Oh my God, babe.' Lola drops her jaw and shakes her head to show how shocked she is. 'I can't believe it. Well, I can, but, you know. Fuck those pricks.'

She hands Renee another glass of wine. Allegedly, it's a 'full-bodied red with a berry finish', but in reality it tastes exactly how she imagines vinegar mixed with antifreeze might. Still, it's only a fiver a bottle from the corner shop. It's not like they're going to stock a nice Château Lafite or anything. Not that she's ever tasted a Château Lafite. For all she knows, it could be expensive vinegary antifreeze. It's amazing what a hefty price tag can do to some people's sense of taste.

Renee takes a sip and the alcohol hits her system immediately, making her cheeks flush.

'I know, right?' she says. 'The fact that they did it in broad daylight, too. There were, like, twenty people around. They saw it happen. And even if they didn't see the one who slid his hand up my inner thigh . . .' She shudders at the memory.

Lola takes a sharp breath and squeezes her eyes shut in sympathy. She doesn't need to imagine what that feels like. Just like every woman in existence, she's experienced it first-hand.

'Anyway,' Renee continues, 'they definitely saw the other one grab me and make me sit in his lap.'

'Girl, I admire your restraint,' Lola says, topping up Renee's glass. 'And I take it no one did the right thing?'

Renee snorts into her glass, not gracing that particular question with an answer.

'Fucking typical. And they wonder why we choose the bear.' Lola sets her glass down, a crafty look on her face. 'Why don't I delve into the freezer and see what beige delights I can find, then we'll stick a movie on, drink the rest of this awful wine and, I don't know, put a curse on all men?'

Renee grins. Now *this* is more like it.

Despite her ambitions, Renee is no stranger to the delights of British tapas. Mini hash browns, vegetable samosas, onion bhajis and a Day-Glo bag of hot and spicy wings – they even rustle up a few spring rolls from the back of the freezer. God only knows how long they've been there, but they seem fine once their frost-jackets are scraped off.

Renee usually cooks, but tonight Lola insists she can manage. She shoos Renee out of their so-called kitchen – not because she wants her to relax, but simply because there isn't enough space for them both at the same time.

'I know how to operate an air fryer,' Lola says. 'You don't need a fancy food education to work one of those.'

Renee can't deny she has a point.

The living room is cramped, barely big enough for their couch. They had to choose it carefully and ended up settling for an IKEA special because it could fit through their building's lift doors. Renee picks her way past their generously named 'coffee table' and does her best to ignore the musty smell that emanates from the couch when she sits down. She glances over at the wall, and an ever-present ball of anxiety tightens within her. Even in this heat, the dark stain is getting worse.

'We should probably nag the agency about that patch of damp,' Renee calls to Lola. 'I'm pretty sure it shouldn't be that bad in a heatwave.'

'You think?' Lola deadpans, poking her head round the door.

'They can't ignore us for ever,' Renee says.

'They can and they will,' Lola snorts, her voice ripe with disdainful humour. 'Mate, unless one of us makes it big, we're just another rental statistic. But I'll give them a call in the morning. Give them something to be scared of. Last time, you were way too nice to them.'

'I just felt bad for the poor bastard on the other end of the phone,' Renee says. 'He sounded like he was twelve.'

'You know who says that kind of thing?' Lola points a perfectly manicured talon at her. 'Old people.'

'Shut up.' Renee laughs and chucks a cushion at her. Lola ducks back and picks it up, but before she can throw it back, a shrill alarm goes off in the kitchen.

'Oh, quit your whining,' Lola yells at the air fryer.

Renee smiles as she settles back and switches on the TV – more out of habit than a desire to watch anything. Eventually, Lola enters the room, plates stacked expertly on her arms. She grins as she offers one to Renee.

'*Et voilà!* Beige freezer bounty – the perfect cure for the worst of days.'

Lola flops down next to her, and they both spend a moment piling up their plates. The food is both over-salted and bland – Renee isn't quite sure how the manufacturers manage to pull off both at once – but it's crunchy and comforting. The food of childhood and nostalgia.

'OK,' Lola says through a mouthful of samosa. 'So, we've got that stupid movie with that guy – you know, the one you like who looks like he's made of cheekbones.'

'Timothée Chalamet.'

'That's the bunny. So there's that one' – she continues to flick – 'or there's *MasterChef Australia*—'

'No!' Renee groans. 'No cooking stuff.'

Lola cackles as she moves on to her favourite category: reality TV.

'This is more like it,' she says, popping a mini hash brown into her mouth. 'So, we've got terrible people at the beach, more terrible people in a château, even more terrible people in the jungle—'

'Terrible people in a château,' Renee says, stripping a chicken wing of its meat with practised ease.

Lola clicks the button and settles herself back. They munch through more of their comfort supplies as the usual cast of moral vacuums are paraded on screen.

'No, I don't like him,' Lola says, pointing at an incredibly muscular man. 'He's got cruel eyes. No, thank you, sir. And what's going on with her? Babes needs to ease up on the fake tan.'

Renee smirks and nudges her friend in the ribs.

'Bit rich, coming from you.'

'Oh, so *that's* how it is, is it? My fake tan is a subtle but effective honey colour. Hers looks like she's been creosoted.'

Renee laughs and snuggles down into her blanket, grateful for the distraction as Lola continues to rate the contestants. Her friendship with Lola really is the only good thing that's come from her time at Chickadees. At first, she'd been a bit intimidated by Lola's confidence and her uncanny ability to read people within five minutes of meeting them. Lola had sussed out Renee by the end of her first shift, before taking her to one side and giving her the pep talk she definitely needed but wasn't ready to hear: 'Yeah, I get it. You could've been a contender. Well, that's in the past. This place is shit, but it's better than nothing. Work your way up, girl. That's all any of us can do.'

They became flatmates a couple of months later, saying it was a temporary measure until they both sorted their lives out. That was two years ago.

'So . . .'

Renee tenses. 'So' is Lola's favourite word, and you can tell exactly what mood she's in by the way she says it. In this case, she's using her this-isn't-going-to-be-easy-and-I-probably-shouldn't-be-asking-you-this-but-I'm-going-to-anyway tone.

'Hmm?' Renee replies, as neutrally as she can.

Lola pauses. Another bad sign. Usually, she just says what's on her mind. If she's having to think about how to phrase something, you know it's going to be unpleasant.

'Are you going to tell Graham?'

'Tell Graham what?'

'Don't play dumb with me, girl. You know exactly what I mean.'

And she does. She just doesn't want to think about it right now.

'No, I'm not going to. At least, not yet. You know what he's like. He'll try to fix it and end up making it worse.'

'Oh my God, do you remember when I bought him that "I Identify as a Feminist" T-shirt?'

'Ugh, how could I forget?'

Lola snickers and stuffs a veggie samosa into her mouth.

'That was cruel, you know,' Renee says.

'Not my fault. I thought he'd take the joke. I didn't think he'd wear it unironically.'

'He was so proud,' Renee says with a sigh. 'His smile as he paraded around the South Bank . . .'

Lola laughs into her wineglass before taking a long swallow and looking serious. 'Stop trying to derail me. I'm just wondering what you're going to do next?'

Renee sighs again. Her stomach flips, making her feel a little nauseated. 'I don't know. I didn't actually quit, but I'm not sure I can face going back. Hell, there's a good chance Clive's going to fire me anyway.'

'Oh right, like Clive's going to shoot the goose that lays his golden eggs. You're the only reason anyone eats there. When I first joined, that place was dead. I mean, pure ghost town. You put Chickadees on the map, girl. We went from scorched drummers and bland burgers to gourmet shit within three months, thanks to you.'

Renee knows Lola is only being nice, but she feels herself blush anyway. She chases it with a huge gulp of wine.

'You know your problem?' Lola continues. 'You don't know your own worth. You're like some mad genius in the kitchen, right? You take all that traditional shit your granni taught you and spin it into something fresh. And those taste buds of yours? You should insure them. You are wasted on Clive. *Wasted.*'

'Oh, right, yeah, because everyone's beating a path to my door. Like, I'm awash with job offers.' Renee picks at her samosa, her appetite now gone.

'There you go again! Ren, I love you and all, but you have got to get yourself out there. Show them what you're made of. You're so talented. Someone will see it. I'm sure of it.'

'Look, I appreciate the sentiment, but if that's the case, why won't anyone take me? I graduated top of my class. Three years later, and I'm a fry cook in a chicken shop. No one cares. The culinary world . . . it moves fast. Too fast.'

Lola shuffles up the sofa and drapes her arm around Renee's shoulders.

'Now, that kind of talk is why we're here,' she says. 'And I get it. Rejection . . . it hurts. And the world you want to be a part of? Cutthroat. Those bitches – they're not going to run after you. You've got to chase them, shake 'em, make them pay attention to you. Hell, you think I had the training to do proper restaurant service? Fuck no! But I still tried. And yeah, sure, it took a while. I had a lot of rejection. But it only takes one "yes" to change your life. Just one.'

Renee sniffs back her tears and downs her glass.

'Yeah,' she says. 'Yeah, you're right. Just one yes. That's it.'

'If you don't try, you'll only ever get nos by default,' Lola says.

Renee straightens up and sets her glass down on the table. 'Yeah. You're right. What's the worst that can happen? They say no. And that's it. Nothing else. If you don't ask . . .'

'You don't get. That's my girl. Now, I'm just going to go and get us another bottle, and when I come back, I want to see that phone open and on the poshest, most top-end restaurant recruitment website you can find. Because we don't do things by halves. We want the whole cake – and you'd better be sure we're going to eat it too.'

'What about this one?' Lola is scrolling through Renee's phone. 'They recruit for restaurants and private chefs.'

'No private-cheffing.' Renee wrinkles her nose.

'And why no private-cheffing? You could end up being some Hollywood star's personal chef and travel around the world with them.'

'Yeah, and make nonsense meals with kale, always worrying about macros and whatever fad ingredient is trendy at the time. Granni might have taught me the secrets of jerk, but Nanna taught me that everything tastes better with butter.'

'All right, you've got a point,' Lola says. 'Your pasta in brown butter is to die for.'

'You know it. OK – Vendredi is looking for a commis chef.'

Lola sighs and rolls her eyes. 'See, this is your problem, Ren. Commis chef? Are you having a laugh? You may as well come work with me at Carluccio's.'

'There's nothing wrong with Carluccio's—'

'No, there isn't, but that's not the point. Although I would relish the thought of us working together again, you need to aim higher.'

'I dunno. I can't see Antonio Delucca or Brent Mavel wanting to hire a washed-up chef.'

Lola puts the phone on the coffee table and gives Renee one of her scathing looks.

'Now, this is what I'm talking about,' she says. 'Girl, stop rejecting yourself before you've even tried!'

'I'm not self-rejecting, I'm just being sensible.'

Lola picks the phone back up and makes a *psht* sound through her teeth as she resumes scrolling through the vacancies.

'Aha! Here we go,' she says, a little bit too triumphantly for Renee's liking. 'Chef de partie. Small team. High-end.'

'Chef de partie, though . . .'

'What? You're more than qualified. No, you're applying for this. Money's good, too. Look.' She turns the phone towards Renee, showing the listing. But Renee doesn't take in the job description. All she can focus on is the name of the restaurant.

'Oh my God. NOVA,' Renee gasps. 'I can't apply for that. The executive chef is a genius – Gracie Fitzgerald. They say there isn't an animal out there that she can't turn into a five-star dish. Hell, according to the *Michelin Guide*, she made *sea cucumbers* taste good, and it's pretty much agreed by chefs worldwide that they taste like rubber bands, no matter what you do to them. She's, like, *pfffft*.' With her hands, she mimes her head exploding. 'Top of the top of the top, Lols. There's no way she'd be interested in me.'

'Yeah, no, I'm not taking that. I'm going to send your CV.'

Renee lunges forward to grab the phone, but Lola holds it up just out of reach.

'Lola, stop it!' Renee implores. 'I don't want to ruin any future chances I might get!'

'Forget the future. It's already too late. I've sent it.'

'What?'

'Oh yeah.' Lola waves the phone screen in Renee's face.

There's a message on it that reads 'Thank you for submitting to NOVA.'

Renee flops back onto the sofa, snatches up her wineglass and drains it in one gulp. 'Shit.'

'No, girl. *Yes*. This is a good thing. Get you on some radars. You've had enough time slumming it. Now it's time to put that fancy education of yours into practice.'

Renee holds her now-empty glass out, and Lola dutifully refills it, draining the bottle. She immediately leans over the side of the sofa and recovers yet another bottle, which she opens and uses to top up her own glass.

'Shit, how many of those did you get?' Renee's eyebrows shoot up to her hairline.

'Hey, it was a two-for-three offer—'

'Three-for-two.'

'Yeah, whatever, don't care. Stop trying to change the subject.'

'I'm not trying to change the subject—'

'Liar.' Lola takes a good swallow from her refreshed glass, then gives a little shudder. 'I don't think letting this one breathe is going to do much. Wow.' The phone buzzes in her hand. As quick as a snake, she scans the message. 'Ha!' She holds the screen out so Renee can read it. 'Says your application has been noted.'

'My application has been . . . what? Who the hell is reading CVs at . . .' She checks the little time display on the phone. 'Bloody hell – quarter to midnight.'

'Probably just an automated reply.'

'Except we've already had one of those,' Renee says. 'This means someone's noticed it and, I dunno, put it in a queue?'

Lola grins widely. 'See? Told you it was a good idea. This is fate, Renee, and it's knocking on your door. All you've got to do is answer it.'

Renee groans and shakes her head at her friend. 'Jesus Christ, I can't actually believe you said that out loud.'

FOUR

It's been three days. Three days of anxiously checking her emails. Three days of self-doubt and recrimination. Three whole days of the universe proving her right.

Nothing at all from NOVA, except that weirdly quick notification. Most of the other fine-dining establishments have already rejected her from her CV alone, so logic dictates that she's probably going to hear the same from NOVA.

Everything's not completely lost, though. In forcing her to look at the job market – something she's been studiously avoiding for the last year – Lola did prove one point: there are other jobs out there. She doesn't have to stay at Chickadees. She can apply for some of the more mundane opportunities, then quit if she gets a yes.

It's not much of a plan, but it's better than nothing.

That's if she still has a job at Chickadees.

Renee hasn't been back there since the incident. Hasn't called them, nor accepted any calls or read any of Clive and Adele's texts. This isn't down to anger or stubbornness. It's down to anxiety, pure and simple. If she avoids the issue, it ceases to be an issue – at least in the very short term. Unfortunately, the fact it makes things harder in the long term is a lesson she's never really been able to internalize, and she's now racked with a mixture of guilt and apprehension. For all she knows, she's already been fired. At the moment, she is in this strange, Schrödinger's cat reality – both employed and unemployed at the same time –

and the only way she'll know for sure is if she actually looks in the box.

As she walks past a newsagent, she can't help but catch the headline dominating the front pages.

> *Where Is Jeffrey McAdams? Wife and Son*
> *Say, 'He Had No Reason to Leave'*

Renee counts to herself. Jeffrey brings the total to four missing. All rich men with a reputation for behaving in less-than-stellar ways towards women. It was the same with that Frank Mercer guy – someone finally had the guts to air his dirty laundry, and then he went missing. The more cynical part of Renee thinks that if anyone has the cash to move to Fiji and live a comfortably anonymous life, it's these guys. But then again, everyone knows that Jeffrey McAdams was up there with the best of the bastards. On his third wife, with a whole gaggle of kids who regularly reported how much they hated him. In a way, it's a miracle he'd lasted this long without someone pushing him over the side of his mega-yacht.

Whoa. Dark much, Renee?

Her phone buzzes in her pocket, snapping her out of her reverie. She sighs and considers ignoring it. Probably Clive, or maybe Adele. But it could also be one of the places she applied to, asking her to interview, so she feels compelled to at least check.

She glances at the screen and almost drops her phone as she reads the number.

It isn't Clive. Nor Adele. Not Lola or Graham, either. And it's not one of the smaller restaurants she's applied to.

It's NOVA.

Her hands are shaking as she answers.

'Hello?'

'Hello? Is this Renee Landis?' It's a woman on the other end.

It can't be . . . can it?

It takes Renee a couple of seconds to speak. 'Um, yes. Yes, it is.'

Oh, for Chrissakes, at least try to sound like a professional and not a starstruck child.

'Excellent. My name is Bethany Jacobs and I'm calling to ask if you might be available for an interview for the chef de partie position at NOVA?'

Renee gawps and narrowly misses the lamppost she's about to walk into.

'Hello? Is it a bad line? Can you hear me, Ms Landis?'

'Uh, no – sorry. I mean, yes. Yes, of course. Definitely. Whenever. I can come whenever. You tell me, and I'll be there. Come rain or snow or whatever.'

Stop babbling . . .

'Good.' Renee is sure she can hear the smile in Bethany Jacob's voice. 'How about we say Thursday at ten?'

'In the morning?'

Bethany chuckles. 'Yes, we wouldn't interview at night. We're too busy.'

'Of course. I'm sorry – just clarifying.'

'It's all right, Ms Landis. Ten a.m. This Thursday coming.'

'Right. Ten a.m., this Thursday. Will it be at NOVA, or . . .'

'It'll be at NOVA. You'll have to use the bell by the main entrance as we won't be open at that time.'

'Right – use the bell. Do I need to bring anything? Certificates? References?'

'They would be helpful. But apart from that, no – just your good self. See you on Thursday.'

'Uh, yeah. See you on Thursday. And thank you!'

The connection goes dead.

Renee stands in the middle of the high street, staring at her phone.

NOVA. NOVA called her back. And not only that – they offered her an interview.

NOVA, one of the most exclusive restaurants in London, looked at her CV with all its gaps and still thought she was worth interviewing. This can't be real.

'Oi, love – watch it!' a man snaps as she accidentally walks out in front of his bike. Renee jumps back.

'Oh, sorry. I didn't see—'

'Stupid cow.'

He cycles off. Usually, such an altercation would sour her mood, but not today. No, today is the day she takes action. Screw waiting. Screw being cautious. What was it Lola had said? *We want the whole cake – and you'd better be sure we're going to eat it too.* And she was damned if she wasn't going to start now.

'Oh . . . you're here!' Renee is sure Adele doesn't mean to sound quite so surprised. 'I wasn't sure we'd see you again.'

'Well, I wasn't sure either,' Renee replies. 'Is Clive in?'

'He's out the back. Look, are you OK? I'm really sorry about the other day.'

'It's OK. It wasn't your fault.'

'I would have come out, but I was swamped—'

'Seriously, Adele – I don't blame you in the slightest.'

'Hey, what's all that jabbering— Oh. It's you.' Clive is standing in the doorway that leads to the kitchen, his folded arms resting on his gut.

'Clive.'

Renee's stomach sinks slightly. She's spent the last couple of days rehearsing exactly what she wants to say in this moment, but every single one of her arguments flees – leaving her with nothing but shame, with a side order of panic.

'Well, look who the cat dragged in. You've got some stones, wandering back like this.' It's clear that Clive is annoyed. 'You've missed two shifts and haven't replied to any calls. You're damn lucky you've still got a job, after all you've done.'

'After what *I've* done?' Renee doesn't want to bite, but she can't help herself. 'That man assaulted me, Clive. In front of a lot of people.'

'Yeah, well . . . Those lads – they're just playing.'

'No, they weren't. And you did the square root of jack shit to help me. If anything, you made it worse.'

'Come on, now – that's not true. I came out and stopped them, didn't I?'

'No, Clive, you didn't. You appeased them and humiliated me.'

'That's unfair. They were just being lads – totally harmless—'

'Harmless?'

'All I'm saying is that lads like that . . . they're just having a laugh. It's just a bit of fun – they don't mean nothing by it. That's the problem with you Millennials. You're all so sensitive. Can't take a joke. And let's not forget – you did hit one of them, and that's more of assault than what they did to you.'

'I didn't hit one of them. It was a defensive reflex.'

'Well, that's not what they're claiming. They threatened to take us to court. Had to give them their money back, and you know how much I hate doing that. You've worked in this industry long enough – you know what it's like. The customer's always right. We all have to deal with arseholes, Renee – not just you. I should fire you, after the way you left me in the lurch.'

'I left you in the lurch?' Renee starts laughing, because it's either that or start screaming. At least now she knows – even if she doesn't get the NOVA job, she's making the right choice. She will not let this pathetic excuse of a man make her feel guilty any more. 'Clive, I was coming here to tender my resignation. As of now. This minute.'

There's a sharp intake of breath from Adele, while Clive looks at her blankly, as if he can't comprehend what she's saying.

'You . . . what?'

Renee stays quiet, desperately holding her nerve, fighting down the desire to apologize and take it all back.

Stay steady.

'Look – OK. Let's not be hasty. We can work this out. I can put up a sign saying that kind of behaviour isn't tolerated, and if you need some time off, we've probably got enough prepped in the fridges to cover tonight—'

'No, Clive. I don't want a sign, nor do I want time off.' She takes a deep breath. 'I quit.'

'But . . . you can't do that! You can't just waltz in and say you're quitting. You've got to give me notice. And you don't want to piss me off – I could give you a bad reference.'

Renee laughs again. The weight off her shoulders is instantaneous, like coming out of a dark cave and into blinding sunshine.

'Do you seriously think that bothers me? Everyone knows this place is only good because I prep all the food. Good luck finding someone with my skills who's willing to work for almost nothing.'

'OK, let's all calm down,' Clive says, holding his hands up like he's trying to soothe a jittery horse. He's put on his disgusting appeasing voice – one he thinks makes him sound reasonable, but lands squarely on Sleazy Uncle at Christmas instead. 'That shift was unpleasant for all of us. I'm sorry it happened. But let's not make irrational decisions. I'm sure we can work something out. I mean, I'd like to offer you a pay rise, but you know what this place is like – margins are wafer-thin. But maybe an extra day off? That might sweeten the deal?'

'Really?' Renee snorts.

It's almost depressing how Clive sincerely thinks that would compensate for anything. She could take the time to explain how she felt betrayed; how, after two years of graft, she helped turn this place around. That it was her food people came to eat – not his. When she first started, he bought everything frozen and chucked it in a fryer that hadn't had an oil change in years. She could also mention how he chose to side with those men not just because they were customers, but because their comfort mattered more than her dignity. *Boys will be boys.*

Fuck that.

But she isn't going to tell him any of that. She's been managing the mental load here too long. Let him figure it out.

She turns and waves.

'I expect my last pay packet in my account by tomorrow morning at the latest. If I don't, I'll take you to a fucking tribunal.'

FIVE

She manages to hold it together until she rounds the corner. A heady mix of exhilaration, rage and abject terror race through her, making her shake.

She's done it. She's free.

Renee glances up at the sky. She's not particularly religious, much to her late granni's dismay, but you'd have to be a hardcore atheist not to offer up a little plea to someone in times like this.

'Please don't let this be a fuck-up,' she whispers. 'Please let this work out.'

A clock chimes in the distance. Quarter to eleven. She pulls out her phone and texts Graham, warning him she'll be over soon.

She has news.

Let's just hope it ultimately turns out to be good news, she adds to herself.

Renee always feels a little bit uncomfortable in Chelsea.

It's as if she's constantly waiting for someone to stop her and tell her she isn't allowed here.

She stops in front of a smartly painted terraced house. Over the years, it's been split into three flats. She presses the buzzer for number three.

'Hello?' The voice that answers her is soft, with the tiniest hint of silver spoon.

'Hey, Graham – it's Ren.'

'Hey there, gorgeous. Let me buzz you in.'

As promised, the intercom buzzes and the door latch releases. The air that wafts out smells of polish and expensive air freshener, with no trace of mould nor damp. How the other half lives.

She all but skips up the stairs. She thought she'd feel terrible after technically making herself unemployed, but she doesn't. In fact, she feels more optimistic than she has in months.

Graham is waiting for her on the landing in front of his flat.

'Hello, babe.' He leans down to kiss her. 'You seem in a good mood.'

She beams back at him. 'I am. I've just quit my job.'

Graham looks a little shocked. 'But . . . why? I mean, I know I've been asking you to do that for months, but why the change of heart?'

Renee takes him by the hand. 'Let's go inside, get a nice glass of something fizzy, and I'll tell you.'

'Something . . . fizzy? It's only just gone three—'

'I know,' Renee says, grinning. 'Come on.'

It's always funny to Renee how no one seems to understand why she and Graham are together. She's inner city; he's posh leafy suburb. Her dad worked in a factory; his was a stockbroker. She went to the local state school; he attended an expensive prep followed by an exclusive grammar. Technically, they shouldn't work, but despite their differences, they have done for the last three years.

'So, let me get this straight,' Graham says as he cracks open a conveniently chilled bottle of champagne. Different indeed. 'You have an interview at NOVA on Thursday morning?'

'Yep!' The news sounds even more exhilarating coming out of Graham's mouth.

'Wow. That's, well, amazing! Everyone goes on about how great the food is there. Nightmare to get a booking if you're not in the know.'

'Right?' Renee says, unable to hide her excitement. 'Of course, I still have to get through the interview, but even getting asked to come in is a massive deal. I couldn't believe it when I saw the ad. I wasn't going to apply, but Lola said that those who don't ask, don't get – and she was right!'

Graham pours two glasses of champagne – proper flutes, not plastic on-offer ones from Asda – and hands her one with a grin.

'This is great. I'm so happy for you. Just . . . so happy. This is exactly what you wanted. I know it's taken you a little longer than you'd like, but I knew you'd get there in the end. And NOVA's nearer here, so . . .'

'Graham.' Renee's mood drops a notch.

'Look, all I'm saying is, you don't have to struggle—'

'I'm not struggling! I'm fine. You don't need to give me hand-outs. I can do it by myself.'

'Poor choice of words. I'm not saying I think you're incapable or anything like that, but, love, maybe this is a sign? You know there's space here. You could move in. I could help. And if, God forbid, you don't get the job, it'll be OK because you won't have to worry too much about financials.'

'Graham, it's not that I don't appreciate the offer—'

'Ren, you're making it sound like I'm trying to sell you something. I'm not. I just . . . I want to be there for you. Want you to be here, with me, you know – full time. I want to wake up next to you, drink coffee on Sunday mornings, maybe go for a nice stroll somewhere. We've been together for a while now. Even my folks are asking what's going on between us.'

Renee sighs. It's not that she doesn't want to be with him. She does. But it has to be on her terms, otherwise she's just going to end up feeling like a charity case. Some of Graham's family are already outwardly suspicious of her, undoubtedly wondering what a nice boy like him is doing with the likes of her. She's watched them introduce some soft, cookie-cutter potential wives with names like Camilla and Verity enough times to know they're hoping she's just a phase.

'G, please . . . Can we talk about this another time? Let me see if I get the job, then maybe, later, once I've settled in, we can revisit.'

'OK. You win.' Graham sighs and pulls Renee into a one-armed hug. 'We'll do this later. But in the meantime' – he holds up his glass – 'to Renee, my beautiful and talented girlfriend.'

'You forgot clever.'

'Oh, I did, I'm sorry. My beautiful, *clever*, talented girlfriend, Renee.'

She smiles. 'That's more like it.'

They clink glasses and take a sip before Graham leans down for a kiss, which she accepts with gusto.

Anything to stop him from talking about moving in together.

OK, that might have been a bit harsh.

Renee snuggles down next to Graham. He wraps his arms around her and kisses the top of her head before leaning back against the pillows. She doesn't need to look at him to know he's smiling.

She realizes that she could have this life, if she gave in. Hell, she seriously considered it after the boiler gave out back at the flat that time and she stayed with him for the best part of a week. It was nice, having a place that didn't reek of mildew, with actual space to move about. She reckons Graham's living room is probably bigger than her whole flat, and there's only one of him here.

And then there's *him*. Graham. Her G, with his floppy indie-boy hair and collection of acoustic guitars. She'd laugh at him if he wasn't so damn sweet. They met in a bar in Soho, both looking as lost as each other. He wasn't usually the type of guy she'd go for – he was far too clean-cut for her tastes back then – but the helpless look they exchanged in that bar sealed the deal. He asked her if she wanted a drink. She said not really. Then he asked her if she wanted to get out of there, and yes, oh my God, yes.

So they went, had bad coffee and a shared a portion of surprisingly good chips in a run-down kebab house. And they discovered that although they really couldn't be more different, they somehow clicked, like two puzzle pieces slotting into place.

Lots of people have told her she's just being contrary. Stubborn. Childish, even. Why not make life easier? Graham's one of the good ones. He has a solid job in structural engineering – one he actually enjoys. And he clearly adores her. So why not just give in?

But that's it. That's the bit people don't get. Giving in. She's fought hard to get where she is. She doesn't come from money, and she certainly doesn't have the connections only bred-in privilege affords. Her dad's best friend can't offer her a nice internship with a complimentary car thrown in. Hell, her dad's best friend would struggle to lend her a tenner.

The first time she trained in fine dining, she realized just how alien the rich were to her. And it wasn't just the material stuff. It's the way they speak. The secret, invisible rules they abide by. The way they sound so very polite while saying the most devastating thing imaginable. It was so different to her world, where there was no sugarcoating, no false airs, and definitely no fake graces.

Graham didn't understand that. Still doesn't. As lovely and generous as he is, he's never had to sit in the dark waiting for his mum to get back from the corner shop after putting her last fiver on the leccy. He knows it happens, of course. He's protested about it. He's very vocal in his support of universal basic income. He campaigned for the Greens in the last election. But he's never lived it. It's the difference between sympathy and empathy – and it's hard to empathise without a point of reference.

'So what time is the interview?' Graham shifts so she's lying on his gym-honed-but-not-too-muscular chest.

'Ten a.m.'

'Nervous?'

'Of course. To say this opportunity would be life-changing would be an understatement.'

'Didn't NOVA get a Michelin star recently?'

'Actually, they got their second star not long ago. Gracie Fitzgerald was awarded the first two years back, and now there's rumours that a third is incoming. She's seriously talented. Like, top of her game, not-like-all-the-other-chefs talented.'

A chuckle rumbles in Graham's chest. 'Sounds like someone has a crush,' he says in a sing-song voice.

'Hey, if you paid attention, you'd know *everyone* is crushing on Gracie Fitzgerald. She's an icon. It's so hard for women to get into fine dining, even now. So for her to be up there, right at the top, having done it all by herself? She's an inspiration. I read an article about her – how Isaac Ferguson told her opening her own restaurant would be a disaster. That she needed to become a sous chef for someone with a much more prestigious history before even thinking about going solo, and you know what she did? Told him he wouldn't say that to a man. Then she told the press the only thing keeping him relevant was his misogyny. I mean, honestly. And she opened her own place anyway. Now she's about to get her third star and he's dropped off the face of the earth. I can't get over the fact that I could potentially be working for this woman.'

'OK, I get it,' Graham says, amused. 'She definitely sounds like someone you want in your corner. Everything about this sounds good.'

'No, Graham. I don't think you understand.' Renee sits up and faces him. 'It's better than good. It's everything.'

'Everything? Ren, isn't that a bit dramatic? I get this is important to you, but you have to be realistic. There's hoping for something, then there's getting those hopes up so high they end up crushing you. You need to be careful you don't put too much of yourself into this. It's just an interview.'

A spark of anger ignites within her.

'That doesn't sound supportive at all. Do you think I'm not good enough? That I'm wasting my time? Maybe I should apply to the local Wetherspoons, since that's clearly more my speed?'

'Ren, that's unfair. I'm not saying that – not at all,' Graham says, running a hand up her arm. 'I'm one hundred per cent behind this. If anyone deserves this chance, it's you. But . . . just remember, don't be too disappointed if it doesn't happen, OK? This is your first big interview in a while. And like I said – if it doesn't work out, I can help with money. Give you some time to get more applications off—'

'It's always about money with you, isn't it?' Renee doesn't mean to snap, but she can't help it. Why can't he just be excited for her? Why does he insist on trying to fix everything?

'Of course it isn't. Honey, I'm thrilled for you. But, you know – these big chefs . . . they're capricious. All I'm saying is – don't put all your eggs in one basket.'

She knows he's only trying to temper her expectations, but it still irritates her. Not because he's raining on her parade, but because she knows he's right. Her chances are slim. Even when she was one of the rising stars in the industry five years ago, this would have been a long shot. She should be grateful she has a safety net in Graham. She's pretty sure he would never let her actually fall. He's not like that.

She lies back down and lets him envelop her in his arms once again.

'I just want you to be happy,' Graham murmurs into her ear.

'I know you do. I'm lucky to have you.' She reaches up to caress his cheek and kisses him, changing the subject to something far more physical in the hope that might help distract them both, at least for a little while.

SIX

OK. You can do this.

Renee can't help but check her reflection in the windows of the shops and restaurants that flank Sloane Square. She catches a stray curl and tucks it behind her ear, lamenting the dark circles under her eyes that won't go away no matter what lotion or potion she puts on them.

There are so many big names here: The Mousetrap, Salted, La Maison de l'Escargot – all places she had once dreamed of working at. She even did part of her training at Salted. It cured her of her aversion to shellfish. No one had told her oysters could actually taste of something other than cold phlegm, and that mussels were sweet nuggets of lightly salted heaven, especially when partnered with white wine, garlic and good home-made bread to mop up the juice.

If the world was fair, she'd already be working in this neck of the woods. She could have been the next Bethany Jacobs. Hell, she could have been the next Gracie Fitzgerald. Instead, life decided to give her lemons – far too many to make lemonade – and in the end, they simply buried her.

Until now.

Please let it be until now . . .

She crosses the road and there it is, just around the corner.

NOVA.

The sign is simple: white capital letters in a plain sans serif font against a black background. In many ways it looks more like a high-end couture shop than a restaurant. Renee looks down at her feet. Maybe she should have worn the expensive shoes. They rubbed like bastards, and her feet would've been dead for the week, but they were a bit classier than her functional flats. And then there was her make-up. She wasn't one for it most of the time – she'd inherited her father's long dark lashes; the ones her mother frequently said were wasted on him – and any kind of foundation made her feel like she was suffocating. But maybe she should have tolerated it for once.

It's too late for that now. She smooths down the front of her suit, applies a slick of lip gloss and checks her hair one last time.

'You can do this,' she murmurs to herself.

As per Bethany's instructions, she presses the discreet bell next to the front door. She waits a moment, her heart crashing around her ribcage, until she spots movement in the gloom beyond. The widows are tinted, so she can't make out who it is.

She plasters a smile on her face, hoping she looks suitably keen rather than like some deranged female version of the Joker.

The door opens and a tall, slim man peers down at Renee. He's completely bald and, judging by his darker complexion and light brown eyes, he's of a similar heritage to her. For a moment, her anxiety lifts just a smidge. Maybe he'll recognize they come from alike backgrounds and the obstacles that come part and parcel of that.

But rather than show her even a sliver of solidarity, he simply regards her with a solemn air usually associated with undertakers.

'Yes?' he says.

'Uh, hi. I'm Renee Landis. I'm here for my interview with Bethany Jacobs?'

The man doesn't reply. Instead, he stands perfectly still, his intense eyes tracking their way down then up her, as if he's able to see her nerves and expose them raw. The urge to fill the uncomfortable silence bubbles up within her, and before she can stop herself, she's babbling.

'I know I'm a bit early, but like my dad always said, when it comes to interviews, ten minutes early is on time and on time is actually late . . .'

The man raises his impressive eyebrows at her. Thin and arched, they perfectly frame his clear disdain – not just for her, but possibly for life in general. The longer she holds eye contact with this man, the more Renee feels he could slice her like fillet steak without hesitation.

'Indeed. I have been informed of your interview. Follow me.' His voice is deep and resonant, and more than a little intimidating. He opens the door wide enough for Renee to slide in sideways, and she squeaks out a small 'thank you' as she slips inside.

Out of the sunshine, the restaurant feels oppressively dark. The man is dressed smartly in a sharp suit with a dark, wine-coloured tie. Renee guesses he's probably the maître d', which explains his authoritative demeanour.

'If you would follow me,' he says, turning away before she can say anything. He moves like a praying mantis as he threads his way through the empty dining area, and Renee has no doubt that nothing – and most likely no one – gets past him. No dine-ditching at NOVA. She has a feeling that if someone dared to, this man would take joy in hunting them down and skinning them alive.

Slowly, her eyes adjust to the gloom of the unlit space. Restaurants always feel a bit strange when they're unoccupied. Much like schools and shopping centres, they are places most people only visit when they are full of life. When closed to the public, they have an unsettling, backrooms feel to them.

This feeling is further compounded by NOVA's aesthetic. There is nothing homey here. From the white marble floor and walls to the austere black-and-steel furniture, it feels more like an operating theatre than a place to dine. Even the artwork hung on the white walls is minimalist, with stark white lines cutting across a black background and the occasional slash of red. To

Renee, the abstract lines form an angular and macabre Rorschach test, demanding an interpretation she isn't sure she would want to share. Her visceral reaction is that the painting looks like deep wounds carving through white fat, exposing the raw red flesh beneath. She gives herself a little shake and tears her attention away from the decor, speed-walking to catch up with the enigmatic man who is now waiting for her by the kitchen entrance. Fearing she might have angered him, she starts to whisper an apology, but it dies on her lips after he treats her to a ghost of a smile.

'Provocative, aren't they?'

'Yes,' Renee says, a little breathlessly. 'Who painted them?'

The maître d's smile is like that of a resurrected corpse.

'Who do you think?'

Before she can answer, he pushes open another door and waits for her to step through. He doesn't say anything else, just watches her as she slips past him. His dark eyes are flat and judgemental, making Renee feel like not only has she done something wrong, but that her punishment will be something dreamed up by Charles Manson or Jeffrey Dahmer.

Renee wonders if all the staff are like this. Maybe this is what happens when you work for Gracie Fitzgerald. Maybe she runs a silent kitchen, where the only sounds to be heard are the thuds of sharp knives against chopping boards. New anxieties jostle with old ones as the maître d' takes the lead again, slinking behind the pass and into the hallowed grounds of the kitchen itself.

As with all commercial kitchens, it's an homage to the neverending appeal of stainless steel. *So far, so normal.* But as Renee is led between the various prep stations, the unsettling feeling she'd experienced in the dining area rises again. It's nothing she can quite put her finger on – there's nothing about the layout, nor are there any suspicious stains that hint at bigger issues. In fact, it's the exact opposite: a disquieting air of cleanliness that makes her wonder if anyone has ever actually worked in this space before. The sinks gleam, the grill looks like it's never been used, the floor is unblemished, the huge freezer doors shine. Even in the most exclusive places, you might expect to find some blackening on the hobs or maybe a chip or stubborn stain on the floor, but there's none of that. It's like someone has gone over the place with a toothbrush, again reminding her of an operating theatre, where everything has to be sterilized following the bloodshed on the table. Goosebumps flare up her arms, and she tells herself to stop being silly. She can be overwhelmed later. Right now, she needs to focus.

On the other side of the kitchen, a woman stands reading a sheet of paper. Renee's heart rockets into her mouth, because she knows exactly who she is. Everyone does. She might not be flying as high as Gracie Fitzgerald, but Bethany Jacobs is still a legend in her own right.

Renee tries to concentrate on cultivating an air of cool confidence, all the while squealing internally like a deranged fangirl.

Bethany Jacobs!

Bethany looks over as the maître d' leads Renee towards her.

'Your . . . interviewee,' he says, in a tone you might usually reserve for finding a used tissue.

'Thank you, Q,' Bethany Jacobs says. 'Hello, Renee.'

Renee's stomach flips, and she is momentarily struck dumb. Bethany Jacobs' eyes flicker to the maître d', who sighs heavily. This galvanizes Renee; he might not like her, but she's damned if she's going to let his antipathy colour Bethany's opinion of her.

'Yes, hello, Chef Jacobs. It's an absolute honour to meet you.' She sticks out her hand and immediately regrets it, because *what the fuck, this isn't the 1950s*. Bethany regards her proffered hand for no more than a second before accepting the gesture and shaking it back.

'Nice to meet you too. And please, call me Bethany.'

SEVEN

Renee has no idea when the maître d' – Chef Jacobs called him Q, so she guesses that's what he goes by here – leaves. Her full attention is on Bethany Jacobs.

She is shorter than she seems on TV, but that does nothing to diminish her presence. She's a bit of an icon for Renee: not just because she works for Gracie Fitzgerald, but because she's also an absolute beacon for women – especially Black women – in a space that is famously pale and male. Watching Bethany on screen, Renee, as a woman of mixed heritage herself, was reassured as a young girl that she could be a chef too.

'OK, before we start, I need to tell you that Chef Fitzgerald isn't here today,' Bethany says. 'She's at a conference in Paris – something she couldn't get out of. Given I've been her sous chef for many years, and you'll probably end up working alongside me more than her, she thought it was better to get you in and see what you're about sooner rather than later. And so, with that – why did you apply for this position, Renee?'

Renee's mind goes blank.

'I, uh, I . . .'

No, no! Come on, get it together! You can do this!

Bethany holds her gaze, saying nothing.

Oh my God, she's going to ask me to leave because I can't speak.

'It's all right,' Bethany says. 'I know you're nervous. If you weren't, I'd be worried.' She chuckles, and something loosens in Renee's chest.

'I am so sorry,' Renee says, a little breathlessly. 'I'll be totally honest with you. I applied because I've always dreamed of working here. Chef Fitzgerald is an inspiration to me – to most women in the culinary world, I guess – and so are you. As a young chef I saw you and thought, "Oh my God, this is something I can do," and so when I saw the ad, my mind went straight to you only live once, and if you don't ask, you don't get.'

OK, so this isn't technically true, but she could hardly say, 'My friend pressed send before I could stop her,' could she?

'You miss one hundred per cent of the opportunities you don't apply for, after all.'

'I see. That's a good attitude to have.' Bethany glances down at her piece of paper, which Renee now realizes is her CV. A fresh surge of adrenaline makes her head swim, forcing her to take a deep breath to try to steady her nerves. 'And for that reason, I'm going to get the difficult stuff out of the way first. I can see from your CV that you were touted as a young chef to watch. You graduated top of your class at college, were awarded a full-ride scholarship to train at Le Cordon Bleu – including a six-month placement in Paris – and won Young Chef of the Year and an AAE. Then, just before you were due to start your career with a very keen Maurice Nolan at Salted, you dropped off the map. Five years later, you're applying to us with an employment history that includes a significant gap and a stint as a fry cook in a chicken shop.' She arches a perfectly sculpted eyebrow. 'I'm sure you can see why I'm curious about you. What happened?'

Renee's entire body hollows.

Shit.

It takes her a moment to gather her thoughts. Her eyes flit to one of the kitchen's high windows – odd, given they aren't in a basement – trying to figure out how she's going to re-word 'my mum was ill and the industry lost interest in me' in a way that makes her sound invested and keen rather than, well, sad.

'It was one of those things, unfortunately. Right after I completed my training, my mum fell ill. It was her heart. She and my dad live in Manchester, so I had to go back to care for her. My dad couldn't cope on his own—'

'Are you an only child?'

The abruptness of Bethany's question catches Renee even more off guard than she already is. Why does she want to know more about something so personal? Judging by the way Chef is looking at her, she gets a strange feeling she already knows the answer.

'Um, no, I have two brothers.'

'Tell me a little about them.'

Bethany folds her arms, her gaze oddly piercing with a hint of accusation. Now completely wrong-footed, Renee stutters again. This isn't how interviews are supposed to go. Interviewers are supposed to ask about the gaps in your employment then move on to figuring out whether you can actually do the job – not ask about your family tree.

'Well, I, er . . . My brother David is older than me, and Jermaine is younger.'

'Hmm. Middle child. Only daughter,' Bethany says slowly.

'Y-yeah, I suppose that's right.'

'And despite you being on the precipice of greatness, you were expected to return to look after an ailing parent?' As she raises her eyebrow, the air is thick with judgement.

'Um, yeah, I mean, you could look at it that way, but it was a difficult time for everyone. David is married and his wife had just given birth, so he had other responsibilities, and Jermaine had gone through a nasty break-up with his boyfriend and was off travelling. He'd worked like a dog to scrape the cash together to go to Thailand – he was teaching English – and my parents didn't feel like they could ask him to cut his travels short. I mean, it was hard to get hold of him, and it's not something he could have done later . . .' Renee trails off, feeling breathless from exposing so much about herself.

'So, let's recap,' Bethany says. 'You were one of the top young chefs coming up through the ranks. You proved yourself in a very difficult industry – one that, traditionally, isn't kind to women or people of colour. And despite all of that, your parents insisted that your brothers, both doing shockingly mundane, everyday things, had futures that were more important than yours, so they tore you away from what can only be described as a very promising future to play the dutiful daughter?'

Renee is at a loss for words. This isn't the first time she's told this story, but it is the first time a prospective employer has put the onus on her family rather than her. Bethany's verdict is, if anything, justification for the quiet resentment she's held towards her brothers these past few years.

Bethany sighs heavily. When the chef speaks again, Renee is surprised at the heat behind her words.

'And your brothers? Did either of them think to step up and play caregiver because their sister was on the edge of something life-changing?'

Renee can only stare at Bethany. Bloody hell, no one has ever articulated so succinctly those terrible, scratchy suspicions she harbours. Yet her family obligation is sown so deeply, she still feels the need to defend them. She was right to look after Mum and make sure Dad was OK. David has his own growing family to worry about. And Jermaine settled in New Zealand – exactly what was he supposed to do about anything when he's quite literally on the other side of the world? The only one left to step up was her. She had no choice.

'It's OK – you don't have to answer that,' Bethany says, allowing her eyebrows to settle. The tension threatening to suffocate Renee starts to dissipate. The chef purses her lips and shuffles the papers including Renee's CV in front of her. Renee didn't include any of this on it because to do so would be to sound the death knell for her career. All she put was 'working part-time at one of many low-level cooking jobs to make ends meet while caring for my sick parents'. And yes, the awards and accolades were on there, of course, but not the prospective job at Salted. That was something Bethany Jacobs – or Gracie Fitzgerald herself – would've had to dig for.

The thought that NOVA had done research on *her* has Renee feeling flattered and slightly on edge. You don't deep-dive into someone's past if you aren't interested in them. But it is unsettling. Sure, she has a LinkedIn profile like everyone else, but none of this is listed on it. And the way Bethany was asking leading questions – rippling with poorly veiled hostility towards her brothers – felt like the chef knew the answers before Renee gave them.

Red flag.

God, she's becoming paranoid. She's literally shared her challenges and misgivings on other social media platforms. It's not as if any of it is a secret, and googling prospective employees is common practice now. But unease has embedded itself into her nerves.

Renee squirms as Bethany, clearly not afraid of an uncomfortable silence, regards her for a long moment.

'Why do you want this job, Renee?' Bethany asks again, her voice dangerously low. 'The truth this time.'

Renee glances up at the high windows once more. With very little natural light filtering in, she feels trapped – like an animal cornered. The smell of cleaning products sears her sinuses to the point where the air burns in her nostrils. The kitchen no longer feels clinical. It's a crypt – a tomb where once you're in, there is no way out. Her mind keeps going back to the paintings on the walls – brutalist and archaic. Sacrificial. Lambs going to slaughter. Sons put on altars.

Her own sacrifice for her family.

Where the hell did that come from?

Bethany, silent and patient as ever, purses her lips again.

Now is not the time for weirdly ominous intrusive thoughts.

How is she going to answer? She could re-spin her last response. Crawl up the restaurant's arse, gush about how great it is. And that wouldn't be a lie. If she gets this job, she'll be working with the culinary elite. But that's not what Bethany is asking. She isn't asking Renee to pledge her undying allegiance. No – what she wants is something far more difficult to quantify.

Why she is willing to put herself through all of this?

'The truth?' she says, dismayed at how brittle her voice sounds.

Bethany nods.

You can do this. And if they don't understand, then this place isn't for you.

'I wasn't lying before,' she says. 'Working in a restaurant of this calibre is my dream. What's the point of all the hard work – the struggling, the sacrifice – if you aren't going to aim for the top? And the fact that it's run by a woman? One who's faced so much hostility, just for being strong and driven and ambitious? That's the kind of woman I want to work for. Hell, that's the kind of woman I want to *be*.'

The floodgates are not so much opened as ripped off their hinges.

'When I was training, I was minimized. I volunteered for everything, but the men on my course were repeatedly chosen over me. When that course started there was an equal number of men and women. By the end of it? There were only six women left. Six. That's it. Most of the men were still there because they were allowed to make mistakes. But the minute any of the us did the same? We were told we "didn't have what it takes". Not cut out for the competitive nature of the culinary world. There was one lecturer who saw us as eye candy. He was a big shot in the eighties and nineties – made his name by being a complete edgelord, serving his dishes off naked women—'

'Isaac Ferguson?' Bethany asks.

'Yeah. The predatory creep.' Renee realizes she probably shouldn't be this candid, but she's on a roll now. Even if she doesn't get the job, this feels *good*. 'Compared every single process to seduction and even admitted to deliberately taking on female chefs – not to train them, but to *break them in*. He said he was helping them – desensitizing them to the wider culinary culture.'

'By traumatizing them,' Bethany says with a scowl.

'Exactly. Do you know him?'

'Not personally. Let's say his reputation precedes him. If I'm honest, I'm glad Ferguson's no longer in the picture. Those women deserved every single pound of flesh they took.' Bethany drums her fingers on the countertop. Her nails are economically short and unpainted. It's a perfect chef's tell. Renee watches them, almost hypnotized. She was not expecting this interview to swing so wildly, so emotionally – for both her and Bethany Jacobs. Christ, she just slagged off a legendary chef in front of her idol, who works for a chef of mythic proportions . . . and her idol agreed with her.

Shit. This might just work.

'OK, how about this?' Bethany says. 'And I'll preface it by saying I know I'm taking a huge risk with such an offer. I'd like you to come in for a trial shift. Are you available tonight?'

Renee blinks, unable to comprehend what she's being asked.

'If you're not—'

'No, it's fine – I am. One hundred per cent. Just tell me when – I'll be here.'

At last, Bethany smiles. 'Good. It's nearly quarter to eleven. Can you be back here by five?'

The words slide off Renee's tongue as easily as they did five years ago.

'Yes, Chef.'

'Then you'd better dig your whites out. See you this evening.'

EIGHT

So . . . how did it go? Gx

Girl, don't leave me on read! Spill!

Renee reads the texts one after the other. She knows she should reply – tell them that she's been asked to do a trial shift – but she's struggling to pinpoint exactly how she feels about the whole situation. Of course, she's delighted – ecstatic, even – but she can't ignore the knot of anxiety buried deep in her chest. She can't remember the last high-end kitchen she was in. And now she has to prove she isn't a has-been. For all the stress she had over the interview, she has a sinking feeling it's going to have been the easiest part of her day.

Renee starts to reply to Graham, tapping out numerous versions of 'I think it went OK – I have a trial shift tonight' before deleting them, unable to figure out why she's so reluctant to talk to anyone about this. By the time she gets home, she still hasn't sorted it out, and is thankful that Lola's at work, allowing her space to process.

This is exactly what she's always dreamed of. No – it's *more* than she's ever dreamed of. But with it comes an avalanche of impostor syndrome. She'd given up on going back to a professional kitchen a long time ago. Sure, she can make a mean jerk, but she could do that before she studied at Le Cordon Bleu. What if she turns up tonight and Gracie Fitzgerald is there? She knows Bethany said she was in Paris, but things change. And even if

Gracie isn't there, Bethany will be. She's made it clear she's taking a huge risk with her. The last thing Renee wants to do is fail in front of a chef she admires.

Renee rummages in her wardrobe and pulls out her whites, still covered in plastic from the last time she had them cleaned. She holds them up and studies herself in the mirror hung on the back of her door. The last time she wore these, she'd been a fresh-faced student. Now, the years are starting to wear. Twenty-seven isn't exactly ancient, but it's a well-known fact that the older a chef gets, the harder the job becomes. That's why most of the good ones become executive chefs – less of the relentless pace but all the recognition. Can she keep up?

She sighs, her shoulders slumping.

OK, Renee. Stop this. Just do what you do best. If they don't like it, then it's out of your hands.

Funny how her mental pep talks always end up sounding like Granni. Probably because if there was one thing Granni didn't like, it was whining.

Feeling a little more pepped up, Renee carefully folds her whites and goes to place them in her bag. *Shit, when was the last time I put these on?* The last thing she wants on her trial shift is to be in an oppressively tight kit because she was optimistic about maintaining her barely-able-to-afford-to-eat student weight.

Shedding her interview garb, Renee shakes out her whites. They're still stiff, creases sharp. She pulls on the pair of black trousers first – ironic how they're called whites when half the uniform is black – and sighs in relief as they button up easily. Next comes the top, which is a little more snug than she remembered, especially around her upper arms, but still comfortable to move in.

It feels strange as she regards herself again. Once upon a time, this had been her everyday uniform. Now it feels like she's cosplaying. Still, at least they fit and she's not panicking, trying to figure out where to buy new ones at incredibly short notice. Yay for small victories.

The front door bangs, followed by a 'Hey, you home?' from Lola. Christ, how long has she been looking in the mirror? She got home just before one, and Lola's shift doesn't finish until half two. She's going to need to hustle if she's going to get back to NOVA by five.

'Hey, yeah, hang on,' she calls out.

Lola, forever the bull in a china shop, doesn't wait to be invited in.

'Where the hell have you been, y'bitch? Leaving me unread... oh.' Her eyes widen at the sight of Renee in her whites. Then the penny drops. 'Oh my God... Ren! Did you get the job?'

'You don't need to sound quite so surprised,' Renee says, but before she can say anything else, Lola lets out an ear-piercing screech, which is promptly met with the sound of someone thumping on the wall.

'Sorry, Mr Rahman!' Lola yells. 'Renee's got a new job.'

The thumping stops.

Thanks for the support, Mr Rahman.

'OK, before we go any further, I haven't got the job,' Renee says.

Lola's face falls a little. 'Then why are you in those?'

'I haven't got the job, but they do want me to do a trial shift. Tonight. I've got to be there at five.'

'A trial shift?'

'Yeah. It's kind of standard. It'll allow them to see if I can cut it.'

'And then they'll give you the job?'

'Well, if I succeed, then... yes?'

Lola lets out another pterodactyl screech, which is followed by more wall-thumping while Renee takes off her whites, folds them reverentially and tucks them in her bag.

'Oh, for fuck's sake,' Lola mutters, before switching back to being delighted. 'It's in the bag, then – there's no way they'll see you work and decide they don't want you.'

'That's sweet of you, but—'

'No. No buts.' Lola closes the gap between them, shaking her finger at Renee before pulling her into a hug. 'You've got this. I know it.'

Renee hugs her back, wishing she had a sliver of Lola's confidence.

'You told G yet?'

'No . . . I don't know why, but I kind of don't want to get his hopes up yet. But he keeps texting me.'

'Of course he keeps texting you,' Lola says, rolling her eyes as she pulls away. 'He wants to know how your very important interview went because he cares about you. Yeesh.'

'I know, but—'

'Oh no. We're not having this. No more self-doubt. You're going to smash this. Now get on that phone and tell him.'

'What, like, call him?'

'Ooh, steady on. No need to panic the guy. Just text him back. That should be enough. You can call him once you've got the job.'

Truthfully, this is not how Renee thought the day would turn out. Of course she'd hoped she'd get the job, but working on the same day? Not something she'd really considered. Now she's standing outside NOVA for the second time in twelve hours, the nerves are setting back in again, impostor syndrome battling it out with her desire to people-please.

She blows out a long sigh, then hits the bell. Q, the undertaker-looking maître d', is once again there to let her in. He offers no platitudes, not even a nod of his head, and this time he doesn't show her where to go either, but simply allows her to pick her way through the dining area towards the kitchen. Before she pushes the door to the pass, she pulls out her phone to sneak one last look at her texts.

OMG good luck!!!! Ur gonna smash it girl! Told u it would work out for the best in the end. I officially tell no lies! So happy for u Lxxxxx

So proud of you babe, I knew you could do it! You're going to absolutely crush this. See you later? Maybe if there's time we'll have a little celebration? See how you feel. Good luck! Xxx

Despite her nerves, Renee smiles. Lola and Graham, both their personalities writ large on the tiny screen. She switches her phone to Do Not Disturb and stuffs it in her bag.

'Right,' she whispers to herself. 'Let's do this.'

Walking into the kitchen feels like the bravest thing Renee will ever do. She pauses by the swing door and takes what feels like her millionth steadying breath of the day. Through the porthole window, she can see a small team of three chefs setting up their stations. One of them has already started their prep work.

Christ, did I get the time wrong? Not a great first impression, Ren.

Just as her panic threatens to upturn the contents of her stomach, a familiar voice floats over Renee's shoulder.

'Ah, you're here.' Renee notes how wild it is that this gentle voice belongs to the same Bethany who interrogated her earlier this morning. 'Excellent. Come with me. We've got a locker room out the back where you can change. Once you're ready, I'll introduce you to the others.'

Bethany, looking as calm and collected as ever, leads Renee into a small, dimly lit room, where Renee pulls on her whites for the second time today. There's a locker with a key stuck in it ready for her, and she quickly stashes her stuff away. Bethany gives her a nod.

'All set?'

Renee takes a beat before responding. 'I think so.'

'You'll be fine,' Bethany says, her tone soothing. Renee has a feeling the Bethany she encountered in the interview was a one-off, and that the chef's true nature is much softer. 'Just remember, you know how to do this.'

Bethany leads her into the kitchen. Earlier, it felt cavernous and clinical; now, it's still clinical, but the smell of fresh ingredients, the low chatter between the other chefs and the hum of equipment is surprisingly calming.

But that's not to say she isn't nervous as hell as the three chefs look her way. To her surprise, all of them are men. Renee had been under the impression that Gracie Fitzgerald would only want to work with other women, but that doesn't seem to be the case. Maybe she isn't the man-eating harridan the press has made her out to be.

The larger chef of the trio, with a beard swaddled in a hair net, smiles as she approaches. The chef to his left is a little more guarded. The third, who looks like a college student reluctantly on work experience, glowers.

'Right, fellas,' Bethany says. 'This is Renee. She's helping out with tonight's service – with the view to her becoming a permanent member of the team.'

'Oh, so you finally found someone for the partie position, then? Amazing! And all of a sudden, half my prep work magically disappears!' The bearded man who smiled at her entrance laughs and extends a hand. 'I'm Martin – the saucy one. I'm here to create all the juices that make NOVA flow.'

'Martin,' Bethany says with a heavy sigh, 'at least *try* to think about how that sounds out loud. For once?'

Martin bats his hands at Bethany, still grinning, clearly pleased with himself.

'Indeed, this is Martin, our saucier and general pain in the arse.' Rather than look disappointed at this description, Martin beams. 'He's been stepping up while we've been in this transition period between chefs—'

'The other one hopped it,' Martin says in a stage whisper. 'But it's OK, because while he was very good, he was also a homophobic arsehole, so Chef Fitzgerald got rid of him.'

'As you can tell, Martin has absolutely no filter, so don't tell him anything you don't want half of London knowing,' Bethany says, but it's clear even to Renee that she's fond of the young chef.

'Hi, Martin. It's, um, nice to be working with you.'

'Oh, the sentiment is entirely reciprocated. I've prepped my last pigeon, and I couldn't be happier.'

Bethany moves on to the next chef – the one who doesn't seem quite as affable. He looks older than Martin and a head shorter too, with close-cropped ginger hair and a tattooed sleeve consisting of Celtic knots, trees and other nature imagery.

'This is Roy. He's our pastry chef—'

'He's the reason I've grown this,' Martin interjects, patting his belly. 'His patisserie skills are to die for. Like, they say the best comes from Paris? No, it doesn't. It comes from this guy.'

Roy blushes a deep crimson, and Renee can't help but feel sorry for him. What was the joke about introverts? They don't make new friends, they're just adopted by an extrovert. Roy and Martin seem to prove that point.

'Martin?' There's warning in Bethany's voice.

'Oops, sorry – I know. Zip it. I'm just so excited!'

The youngest of the three snorts. 'Huh. You're *always* excited.'

'Better to be excited than miserable all the time,' Martin sings, blowing the younger chef a kiss.

'My God, it's like being at a nursery,' Bethany mutters, rolling her eyes in exasperation. 'Fellas. Enough!'

'Sorry, Miss,' Martin says playfully, but immediately turns back to his station. The younger chef doesn't say anything, just makes his displeasure known through a sullen look.

'As I was saying, this is Roy, our pâtissier. Chef Gracie found him in Paris. But he doesn't just make the desserts, he helps with prep as and when we need it.'

'Don't be afraid to ask for help if you need it,' Roy says in a soft Scottish burr. 'We're a team.'

'Thank you, Roy,' Renee says, surprised at being regarded as a team member already. 'It's great to meet you.'

Roy smiles before turning back to his board.

'And lastly, we have young Josh here.' Bethany gestures to the sulking teen. He can't be any more than nineteen – twenty at a push – and he has one of those haircuts that all the kids seem to favour but reminds Renee of broccoli. He also has tattoos – a random collection of flashes rather than the cohesive art worn by Roy. 'Josh is an aspiring chef, so Chef Gracie took him on as a commis chef to show him the ropes.'

Josh cocks his head and narrows his eyes at Renee, as if he's trying to work her out before saying anything.

'Aw'ight,' he says eventually. Renee shudders as the mockney accents of the awful men from Chickadees flash through her mind. 'They got me chopping stuff.'

'Uh, cool,' Renee says, after clearing her throat. She is not going to break on her first shift. 'Nice to meet you.'

'Likewise.'

Bethany claps her hands together.

'Right, we've wasted enough time here – we need to get on. As you all know, Chef Gracie isn't with us tonight, which isn't ideal given it's Renee's first shift, but that's the way these things go. Renee, you'll be working to the left alongside Martin—'

'Woo!' Martin does a series of little claps in front of his face.

'Martin . . .'

'Sorry, sorry!' He pantomimes contrition, then grins widely at Renee. 'So you're on the left, and I'm behind you. Any questions, you can ask either of us.'

Renee nods.

'Good. OK, we all know what we're up to—'

Except me – I don't know what I'm doing.

'So let's get to it.'

And with that, everyone turns their attention back to their stations and resumes their prep. Renee goes to follow Martin, but Bethany lightly touches her arm, startling her.

'I'll show you where everything is first. Then I'm afraid it's a mountain of prep for you. Our menu, as I'm sure you're aware, is compact, bordering on sparse, but that doesn't mean the dishes are simple. In fact, it's the opposite. We offer a limited menu because it allows us to focus on serving exquisite dishes. And all that starts with the best ingredients we can get our hands on. Come on, walk with me.'

NINE

Renee trots after Bethany, eager to display her attentiveness and willingness to learn. Bethany shows her the dry pantry, with its impressive collection of herbs and spices, oils, vinegars, flours and preserves. Whatever ingredient the recipe requires, Renee has no doubt you'd find it in here. Next to this is the cold pantry, where all the vegetables, meat and dairy products are stored.

'Fresh fruit and veg every day.' Bethany gestures at the racks bursting with everything Renee could ever need. 'It's all ordered by Chef Gracie herself. These racks are only used for fruit and veg that need to be refrigerated. Make sure you take out the stuff you're going to be using at the beginning of your shift – or at the end of your last if it needs longer to come up to room temperature.'

Renee nods. So far, so standard.

'Further in, you'll find all your dairy. Butter, cheese, yoghurt, cream – if you need it, it'll be in here. Just like the veg, Chef Gracie sources all of our ingredients from top providers, which means there isn't much wiggle room for mistakes. If you fuck a dish up, there's a good chance that will have a knock-on effect for the menu, so it's absolutely vital that you treat everything you touch with the respect it deserves. Chef employs a zero-waste policy, meaning everything gets used. Don't throw anything away. Peelings, offcuts, bones and other scraps – they can all be repurposed, even if it's just for stock.'

Bethany continues to explain, at speed, how the cold pantry is organized, with vegetables nearer the door and dairy at the back. Slowly, it all comes flooding back to Renee. No more chaotic piles of stock rammed into a fridge that probably should have been chucked away years ago; no more chest freezers that, given the chance, would swallow you whole as you dig your way through frost to retrieve the last pack of chicken carcasses. This is how it's supposed to be – how it *should* be. Squeaky clean and organized to within an inch of its life.

Heaven.

Lastly, Bethany approaches two metal doors located at the back of the kitchen. She pats the handle of one.

'Now, I'm sure you know what this is?'

Renee nods and the colour drains from her face. She knows exactly what it is, and the sight of it makes her blood run cold.

The walk-in freezer.

'Now, I don't think I have to tell you how dangerous these things can be. Even though they're supposed to be unlockable from the inside these days, accidents still happen.'

Renee offers another stiff nod. She's heard horrific tales – the dark side of this line of work that even the public would have a hard time believing. People unknowingly locking in colleagues because they thought the freezer was empty. Chefs getting stuck inside after the safety mechanisms failed. Too many stories of frozen corpses found inside them on Monday mornings, their terrible deaths written in blood as they battered themselves against the doors, knowing full well there was no way they could force them open, but breaking their bodies against cold steel just in case they were the exception that proved the rule.

They weren't, of course. And what makes it worse is that there was no intention – no malice – behind any of these tragedies. They were all down to someone not paying attention.

That is, every incident except her own.

It was her first year at culinary school, and there was a

long-standing tradition of hazing the new students. Not benign, but never anything deadly; it's how her classmates proved they could hack it in the industry. Five Finger Fillet, holding a hand over burners for as long you could, glorified games of chicken in Renee's mind. She was less concerned with being drawn into banal rituals and more focused on becoming a better cook.

The other chefs didn't like her 'arrogance'. As she was cleaning her station late one evening, she realized she hadn't grabbed her frozen Kobe for the next day's lesson. Walking into the freezer that night, she was surprised at how *immediate* the temperature drop was, ripping her breath from her throat. When she heard the freezer door click, she jerked her head to the side so quickly she felt her neck crack. Her chest constricted to the point where she had trouble feeling the rest of her body. Her extremities were rapidly going numb, legs seizing by the second. It felt like wading through sand, trying to get to the locked entrance. She slammed her fists against the doors, screaming her vocal cords raw for someone – anyone – to help. When she pressed her ear against the door, she reared back, the ice so cold it burned. Muffled laughter reached her through the heavy, sealed doors.

By the time they let her out, tears had frozen on her eyelashes and frostbite nipped at the tips of her ears. They'd kept her locked in the freezer for seventeen minutes.

Renee still has nightmares about it.

Bethany opens the door, and a waft of frigid air curls around them. Renee reluctantly peers inside. This half of the room is a chiller, with steel shelves that hold packets of pre-cut meat and fish.

'This is where we keep the stuff that either needs chilling or has been defrosted. Chef Gracie is very particular about this – things that have been defrosted go on the right, and things that are fresh go on the left. This means there's no cross-contamination between ingredients. We don't store much seafood in here – Chef prefers to get that in fresh as and when we need it. In fact, we don't tend to have a lot of fish on the menu at all, especially since Salted is just down the road. Most of our dishes are constructed around meat as the main event, and any seafood is usually supplemental to that. As you can see, all the shelves are labelled, so it's lamb here, beef there, veal next to it, pork in the corner, and then game and poultry. In the furthest corner, you'll find your offal. We tend to store offal as its own category, simply because it tends to have a shorter shelf life.'

'What's that?' Renee asks, pointing to a large bucket sitting near the offal, filled with gruesome-looking offcuts. Of everything she's seen so far, the contents of that bucket is the closest thing she's seen to what she used at Chickadees.

'That? Ah, that's something you will become very familiar with. That's our stock bucket. It's where everyone puts their scraps – the bones, sinew, fat and skin. Basically, anything you're not using in the recipe. Then, a couple of times a week, it all goes into the pressure cooker to be cooked down for stock.'

I bet people would pay money to eat the stock from here – me included.

Bethany moves further into the chiller room, towards a curtain of plastic strips. Renee has to force herself to follow as the hair on the back of her neck rises, and not just from the cold.

'This is our freezer,' Bethany says as she draws back the plastic strips. 'There's a blast chiller in the kitchen, so this is used purely for storage. This is where we keep the big cuts before they're butchered down.'

Renee swallows the panic threatening to drown her. *Focus on something else.* She notes the huge primal cuts of beef and pork suspended from vicious-looking meat hooks near the back. The air is dry and bitingly cold, with a distinct metallic tang to it – an aroma that can only be old blood. Renee shivers as Bethany points out the various chunks: the legs, ribs, shoulders, flanks – all uncermoniously impaled on hooks ready to be broken down further. And beyond them hangs a huge beef carcass that has been split in half, allowing her to count every vertebra, every rib. People often don't realize how huge a cow is, and how brutal the process is to take the still-fresh corpse and transform it from a dead animal into something that can be sold without making people feel uncomfortable.

Next to the beef are two pig carcasses. Unlike the cow, which has been beheaded and skinned, these are whole – apart from the gash along their stomachs where they've been hollowed out by the supplier. Blank eyes stare back at Renee through slitted lids, their mouths agape, revealing surprisingly human-like teeth. There's always been something about pigs that unsettles her. It's a miracle she's still upright – this is her version of hell: freezing to death with two porcine corpses for company.

'These two were only brought in yesterday,' Bethany says, slapping one of the pig carcasses. She clearly has no aversion to swine. 'But don't worry – the pork you'll be working with will already be portioned.'

'Why are they still intact?' Renee asks. 'I thought the butcher might have done that already?'

To her surprise, Bethany hesitates.

'It's a long story, and not that important . . . but since I know Martin will tell you anyway – the short version is that one of the abattoir's employees made some comments to me, and Chef Gracie demanded he be sacked on the spot. Said she'd take her business elsewhere if she ever saw him again.

'They tried to argue they were the only local distributor of small-scale organic carcasses – to which Chef said she'd cut them out completely if she had to, and buy direct. They warned her that would mean receiving whole animals, no prep – meaning no hanging, gutting, skinning, nothing. Chef just smiled and told them a little bit of blood and guts never bothered her. And if they still wanted her money – and her endorsement – they'd do as she said.'

'And did they?'

'Yeah. Never seen that guy since. Even the fellas he worked with said it was like he upped and vanished.'

'Wow,' Renee says. She'd heard that Gracie Fitzgerald was fearsome, but she hadn't expected anything like this. 'That's . . . intense.'

'She is. And the sooner you understand that, the better. The only way you'll succeed here is by doing as you're told, when you're told.'

'Oh. OK.'

Bethany smiles and rubs Renee's arm gently. 'Look, I know it seems a lot. And yes, Chef Fitzgerald is very much her own woman. But you're the kind of chef she's interested in. As long as you trust her and commit to her vision, she'll go to the ends of the earth for you.'

Renee nods, though she's not quite sure why Bethany thinks that should make her feel any better.

'Anyway, in the meantime, Chef Gracie and Martin break down the carcasses. Martin because he's a big strapping lad, and Chef because she'll never let anything stand in her way. But don't worry – you're not going to be in this section much, unless the menu calls for a particularly large cut, which isn't the norm.

'So, I think that's it.' Bethany finally leads Renee out of the freezer and shuts the door behind them. 'I'm not expecting you to remember all of that straight away, but it's a good place to start.'

'What about the other one?' Renee asks.

'The other what?' Bethany says.

'The other freezer.' Renee gestures to the second, slightly smaller walk-in, set beside the main one. For some reason, it has a padlock on it and, much like the pigs, it unsettles her.

'That one? That's nothing for you to worry about. That's

Chef Gracie's personal freezer,' Bethany says, and Renee notices a subtle change in her demeanour. It's nothing alarming, just a sudden disquiet. 'No one else uses it.'

Executive chefs often have their own spaces, Renee knows. Places to try out dishes or store newly acquired ingredients. But not many of them keep those spaces locked.

Bethany seems to sense her confusion. She lowers her voice.

'I know. It took me a while to get used to it too. But you have to trust the process. I've worked with Gracie since the beginning, and believe me, I'd walk through fire for that woman. But that doesn't mean I'm blind to her . . . idiosyncrasies. Working here means walking her path – and not asking questions along the way. I won't sugarcoat it – not everyone is cut out for this. Let's hope you are.'

TEN

When Renee rejoins her fellow chefs, it's clear that, above everything else, they know *exactly* what they're doing. With their heads down, all she can hear is the drumming of their knives on chopping boards and the whirr of kitchen appliances.

All of them, that is, apart from Josh.

He's sullenly emptying the dishwasher, clearly hating the task and wanting everyone else to know about it. Renee expects his attitude to lift once Bethany glares at him, but no; he simply glares back. She can't understand it. Most, if not *all*, new chefs would give their right eye to work in a kitchen like this. Hell, she still would.

Next to her, under her breath, Bethany murmurs, 'Saints preserve us.'

Piled on Renee's station is a massive box of peppers, onions, garlic, carrots and celery: a chef's basic arsenal. Nothing happens in a kitchen anywhere without at least three of these ingredients, which means that no matter how high you climb the ranks, you're never going to get away from the tedious business of vegetable prep.

Not that she minds. To Renee, it's almost meditative. It's clear that Bethany told no lies in terms of food quality; she doesn't even need to peel the carrots – just give them a quick scrub and they're ready. Next to her board is a list of instructions. At first, she thinks Bethany must have done this for her, but upon scanning it she realizes, with a jolt, that it's actually from Chef Gracie, outlining the recipes she's expected to prep and, later, cook. The directions are sparse – mince the garlic – but whether intentional or not, this direct communication from their reclusive leader fills her stomach with butterflies.

She cannot afford to screw this up. As she picks up the knife from the wooden board, Renee can't tell the brand, but judging by the weight and balance of the blade, it's not one found on Amazon. She selects one of the onions to test it out. With barely any pressure, the knife slides through it, leaving her a little worried that, after working with inferior blades for so long, she might cut herself if she's not careful.

A strange sensation crawls over Renee's skin – a prickling feeling that leaves her on edge. It's been five years since she set foot inside a professional kitchen of this calibre, working alongside true peers rather than someone whose main qualification is knowing how to operate a potato peeler. Being the top dog back at the chicken shop was a piece of cake; here, she's easily outclassed. A quick glance behind her and she can see Bethany effortlessly filleting Dover soles. To her right, Martin is beating aquafaba for one of his sauces. In front, Roy is perfectly segmenting oranges. There's no chatter, just a fierce focus Renee fears even a wrong look will break. She begins first peeling, then dicing, the rest of the onions. Even this proves a challenge; back at Chickadees, no one cared if the onions were chopped a little haphazardly. Everything there was about the flavour, given the majority of her food was eaten on the fly, out of a polystyrene box. Here, presentation is as important – maybe even more so – than the way it tastes, because the first taste of a dish is with the eyes. Back when she was training, you could serve a customer the finest, most amazing-tasting food they'd ever had, but if it looked like slop, you were going to fail.

'. . . smile. You know that, right?'

Renee glances over at Martin. He's grinning at her.

'Pardon?' Renee snaps back to reality with a jolt.

'I said, you're allowed to smile. It's OK. No one's going to tell you off.'

Renee offers him a self-conscious smile back.

'I know, it's just . . .' She trails off, unsure how to explain the mix of manic joy and bone-deep anxiety she's feeling right now.

Martin cocks his head to one side, studying her while he operates a small blender. He stops, lifts the lid and peers at his mixture. Seemingly happy, he goes back to his other ingredients.

'It's OK. I get it,' he says. 'Opportunities like this don't come along very often.'

'You could say that.'

'I was exactly the same,' Martin continues. 'I've been here two years now. Had an internship here, and I knew straight away that I didn't want to work anywhere else.'

'It's a prestigious place,' Renee says, aware that she's slowed down. She doesn't want to be rude to Martin, but at the same time, she really needs to get on. She can't afford to fall behind – this is her only chance to prove her skillset and demonstrate she can work as part of the team.

'It is,' Martin agrees. 'But it's not just that. There's a lot of prestigious places to work. Some have more Michelin stars than NOVA. Others have more outlandish menus. But that's the thing with Chef Fitzgerald – she doesn't need those gimmicks.'

'Are you seriously calling a Michelin star a gimmick?' Renee says with a nervous laugh.

'Oh, no, of course not – they're massive achievements, and Chef has two now, so in the eyes of everyone she's right up there with the best. I suppose what I'm trying to say is that it's more than just wanting to work somewhere held in high esteem by the Establishment. You can get into any of those places and be just as respected. It would probably be an easier time, too.'

Renee can't help but think that's an odd thing to say. It sounds like a warning.

Martin must have picked up on her confusion, because he continues in a far gentler tone.

'Ah, look, I didn't mean that in a bad way. Like, Chef Fitzgerald is the real deal. She's hard and, yeah, a bit . . . odd at times.'

'Yeah, the locked freezer kind of clued me in to that.' Renee realizes she's said that out loud and gulps. 'I mean, I—'

'It's OK. You're right. That is . . . odd. She has other policies too, but we'll get to those later. Don't want to scare you off too soon.' Martin laughs. He's clearly going for comforting, but instead hits worrying, leaving Renee with the feeling that the locked freezer is just the tip of the iceberg. 'The thing is, Chef has this ethos, and she applies it to everything. People, ingredients, recipes – you name it, everything's tied to her morality. She fought to get to the top, and now that she's up there, she fights for the rest of us. She sacked our last partie because he made homophobic comments towards me. He'd worked with her for the last four years, but she saw him harassing me, and stood up for me. For me! The saucier. I'm hardly irreplaceable – not when compared to a chef de partie. You guys are the workhorses of the team, turning your hand to whatever's needed. But she didn't care. She didn't compromise her principles because it would have been easier on her. She expects the best.'

'Wow,' Renee says, a little stunned. 'I guess the press have been wrong about her all these years.'

Martin chuckles. 'Don't get me wrong. Those stories are true, too. She can be an utter nightmare. It's Chef's way or the highway. Don't let me lull you into a sense of false security. You have to be on your toes around her. To coin a phrase: she says to jump, you say, "Yes, Chef – how high?" But you've worked in high-end kitchens before. You know how these executive chefs are.'

Renee snorts in self-derision. 'Yeah, that was a long time ago, though. I am a little rusty. In a way, I'm glad she's not here tonight. I think if she was, I might have run in the other direction.'

'Oh, you're doing fine. Look at those onions. Perfect.' Martin grins at her, and a small lump of gratitude swells in Renee. Not at his praise, but for his warmth, and his generosity with it. 'The thing with Chef Fitzgerald is she doesn't care where you come from. If you can prove yourself, she'll give you a chance.'

'You genuinely like her, don't you?'

'I do,' Martin agrees, and for once he doesn't sound like he's joking. 'I wouldn't say she's a friend, but I respect the hell out of her. Won't have a bad word said about her. But that's enough about her – how about you?' His question catches her off guard. 'Where have they been hiding you? Bethany says you were the talk of the town a few years ago. How come you're not out there, with your name in lights?'

'I . . . I don't know. There's not much to say, really.'

'Oh, the modesty of youth.'

'Hey! I've got a couple of years before they issue me my old hag card.'

Martin laughs again, and Renee loves how easily it comes to him. In too many kitchens, the chefs – be they professional or aspiring – have decided that having any kind of personality outside of intense is undesirable. Martin is a refreshing change.

'Come on, girl – spill. What's your story?'

'It's like I said – there isn't one. I did well at college. Did even better at culinary school. Won a couple of awards, did a few internships, had a job lined up at Salted . . . then my mum fell ill. I had to go back home to Manchester to look after her. She died, and when I came back, I was old news. I ended up at a chicken shop in Brixton. Chickadees.'

'I've heard of that place!' Martin says with far too much enthusiasm for a conversation about a chicken shop. 'It's supposed to be a real hidden gem. The food – that was you?'

'I suppose it was.' She knows he's only trying to make her feel better, but she appreciates it all the same.

Renee turns away to refocus on her prep. With the sofrito done, she reaches for the crate of fat red peppers while Martin moves over to the burners to sauté the lardons he's been slicing while talking to her. Before long, the kitchen is filled with the delicious scent of searing pancetta. Roy gives Renee a shy smile as he passes her bench. He goes into the cold pantry and returns with an enormous container of cream, which he pours into an oversized mixer.

Renee hones in on her peppers. They're all perfect specimens – to the point where she has to remind herself that she doesn't need to check each one for squidgy parts – and she starts to de-seed them before slicing half into strips and finely dicing the rest, as per Chef's instructions. It's only when Bethany marches by her bench with a face like thunder that she realizes something is wrong. Her heart races, worried that Bethany is going to round on her and demand she gets out of her kitchen, but instead, the sous stops by Josh. She can't make out exactly what Bethany says to him – she's too classy to yell – but it's clear she's displeased as Josh rolls his eyes like a teenager.

'All I'm saying is *this*' – he gestures to a pile of dirty bowls – 'is not why I'm here. If you want a slave, then get someone else in. I'm here to be a chef, not a fucking kitchen porter.'

Renee pretends she can't hear anything, while Roy and Martin keep themselves busy. Everyone knows that basic kitchen hygiene is an expected part of your apprenticeship, so why is Josh being so difficult? And, more importantly, why is he still here? Martin gave her the impression that Chef refuses to put up with any kind of nonsense, but Josh doesn't seem to give a toss. Maybe he's acting up because she isn't around? She's seen that before – an absolute nightmare to work with, but a complete suck-up to the boss. But then you'd think he'd be sucking up to Bethany too, not giving her a hard time. So what's his deal?

★

Just as Renee finishes with her last pepper, Bethany appears beside her with a metal tray in her hands. On it is a mound of little white lumps.

'You made short work of that lot,' she says, nodding appreciatively at the bowls of finely diced veg. 'Fancy trying something different?'

'Uh, yeah, of course – whatever you need,' Renee says, surprised at how ready for a challenge she is.

'Good. You know what these are?' Bethany places the tray in front of her. The lumps are irregular in shape and have a slight sheen, with a pink, fleshy undertone to them.

'They're sweetbreads, aren't they?'

'Nice work,' Bethany says, giving her a shrewd look. 'You ever worked with sweetbreads before?'

'I have, but it was a while ago.'

'I figured as much. These have already been soaked, so you'll just need to prep them. What are you going to do?'

Renee swallows. Of course, she knew this kind of thing was coming, but it doesn't stop the feeling of wanting desperately not to fuck up.

'First, I'm going to parboil them for about fifteen minutes, with some bay, peppercorns, a bit of salt and maybe some thyme. Then I'm going drain them and plunge them in an ice bath to stop them from going over. After that, I'll take any membrane and fatty deposits off, then cut them to the requisite size.' She looks up at Bethany, who is giving her a lopsided smile.

'OK. So maybe this is going to be a good decision after all. And with that, you're going to take on the starters for this service.'

'I am?' Renee can't help but gulp.

'Is that a problem?'

'Oh God, no – of course not. Wow. Thank you – that's a massive responsibility.' And it is. A starter is the first thing a diner will experience, setting the tone for the entire meal.

'It is. We're all about sink or swim at NOVA. All I can say is, don't mess it up.' Bethany tips Renee a wink, even though it's very clear that she's dead serious. 'We have two main starters tonight: veal sweetbreads with black pudding and walnut crumb, Madeira sauce and spiced carrot purée; and ravioli with sheep's milk ricotta, spinach, tomato sauce and basil. Now, you don't have to worry about the Madeira sauce as Martin's already made that – you'll find it in the cold pantry. Roy's already prepped the ravioli because as well as being an excellent pastry chef, he's also a dab hand at making pasta.'

Roy raises a hand then looks over his shoulder with a grin.

'I'm the only one who can make sense of the pasta-maker half the time,' he says, and Bethany chuckles.

'He's not wrong there. Usually, making pasta would be up to the commis, but . . .' She trails off.

'Say no more,' Renee says.

Bethany lowers her voice. 'It's nice to have someone in who just gets on with it, if I'm honest.'

'What else would I be doing here if I wasn't willing to just get on with it?'

'It's a shame not everyone shares your grit.'

Renee considers asking Bethany about Josh, but she's here to prove herself, not gossip about a kid, so she keeps her mouth shut.

'Anyway, back to your starters,' Bethany continues. 'Neither should give you any trouble. Just make sure you follow the recipe to the letter. Chef Gracie has spent a long time perfecting these dishes, so if it calls for a quarter teaspoon of black salt, you use a quarter teaspoon – no more, no less. I'll help you prep the plate when it's ready. I'm usually on the pass, so it'll be a good chance to show you our house plating. Once you've got the sweetbreads marinading, you can move on to the ravioli. That won't take long to prep – most of the actual cooking's done during service. Any questions?'

Renee takes the instructions from Bethany and quickly skims

them. Neither recipe looks complicated, but that doesn't mean they're easy. Uncomplicated dishes mean there's nowhere to hide. If you overcook your sweetbreads or your ravioli splits, you're in a hell of a lot of trouble.

'Any questions or issues, you know where I am.' And with that, Bethany goes back to her own bench.

Renee takes a moment to read through her recipes again, taking note of the items she'll need from each pantry. She finds everything pretty quickly – she can't find Martin's Madeira sauce initially, but that's more down to his terrible handwriting on the pot than anything else. Happy with what she's selected, she takes a moment to draw a few deep breaths.

'Everything's going to be fine,' she murmurs to herself. 'You can do this.'

She leaves the pantry with a full tray, only to walk back in on another temper tantrum.

'Fuck this, I'm going out for a vape.' There's a clatter as someone throws something metal into the sink. It's Josh, having his second strop of the evening. Impressive, given the restaurant doors haven't even opened.

Renee sets her ingredients down on her bench and glances at Martin, who just rolls his eyes in response. Then Bethany storms past, her face the picture of a woman desperately trying to hold on to her last nerve.

'There's no time for you to waltz out as and when you please, Josh,' she says through gritted teeth. 'That equipment needs to be cleaned in order for us to use it. We need those lamb cutlets trimmed. Without these things, we cannot operate this kitchen successfully.'

'Well, get her to do it,' Josh says, tipping his head towards Renee. 'She's the new girl. Fuck's sake, why does she get to play at being a chef and I get left doing the washing up? She's literally been here five minutes.'

Renee tucks her head in, feeling exposed. Maybe she should offer to stack the dishwasher. She could easily trim those cutlets. It wouldn't take her long. Anything to help lighten the atmosphere.

'She isn't expected to do those things because she is a qualified chef.' Bethany's voice is dangerously low. 'And a good one, too. I'm pretty sure that if I asked her to pitch in, she would. Because she has worked her way up from the bottom. She knows how important it is to understand every aspect of working in a kitchen – not just the bits she thinks might be fun.'

Josh snorts and covers his nose with his hand while grinning. It's a juvenile gesture and speaks of a complete lack of respect; a respect that any chef expects from a trainee. Renee can't help but be shocked. She's seen people fired for less. And at a *sous*? Bethany is basically one step down from the executive chef. She's the bridge – the one they should be able to go to if they have any issues. She's also Gracie Fitzgerald's right-hand woman and her voice when she isn't around – and as an executive chef, not being around is something she can't avoid. She puts a lot of trust in Bethany. No one should speak to her the way Josh is.

But Josh seems completely oblivious to this. He smirks as he saunters out of the kitchen, and Renee is sure she sees one of Bethany's eyes tic. She's never seen this level of entitlement before, and she's seen plenty of chefs throwing hissy fits. The difference is their tantrums were usually born out of frustration. This, however, is an expression of pure privilege.

Renee glances at Martin again, seeking a little reassurance. This time, he gives her one of those looks – one that says, 'Yeah, it's OK. I know – we all know.'

Bethany takes a deep breath, squares her shoulders and walks out after Josh.

Roy turns around and offers Renee a little shrug of apology.

'He's only been here for three months,' he says in a low voice.

'Absolute nightmare. But his uncle is one of the restaurant's financial backers, so Chef's hands are kind of tied.'

Suddenly, it all slots into place. Josh gets away with behaving terribly because there are no consequences for him. If his family has the kind of money that allows them to back NOVA, it's inevitable that he's never known hardship, never had to take responsibility for anything. He clearly decided that play-acting as a chef sounded like fun; that he could just come into a kitchen, throw some salt around and play with the burners. He has no idea what working in a kitchen is actually like.

'It's OK, though,' Martin says. 'He drives Chef Fitzgerald up the wall, too. I don't think he's going to be here for much longer. We were all sceptical at first, but she had to give him a proper go, given who his uncle is. Chef even gave him a simple recipe to follow, but it became very obvious very quickly that he doesn't know his culinary arse from his culinary elbow.'

'I remember that,' Roy says. 'What a nightmare. Thought he just had to shove meat in a pan and throw salt at it. We all ended up having to work extra hard just to cover his fuck-ups. If I'm being totally honest, I cannae wait until the day Chef locks him up in that fuckin' freezer of hers.' He tips Renee a cheeky little wink. 'You have absolutely no idea how happy we are that you're head and shoulders above that bawbag.'

'And it's even better now, because we know you're not shite,' Martin adds.

Renee grins as she gets down to sorting out her sweetbreads. God, she's missed this.

ELEVEN

Renee is surprised at how quickly the rest of the service goes by. Even with Josh's insubordination, the night runs smoothly. It's clear the team is a well-oiled machine, and even if Renee hadn't settled in and pulled her weight, they would have been absolutely fine. After so long out of this kind of environment, she's forgotten just how it feels to be part of a team like this – where excellence isn't just striven for; it's the minimum expectation. She tastes each of her dishes with relish, and yep, Bethany is right: Chef Gracie's recipes are spot-on and precise, down the last granule of salt.

Heaven.

Even Josh steps up, helping to dress Martin and Renee's plates before they're sent out to the pass to be inspected by Bethany. The intensity of the kitchen energizes her, reminding her of all the reasons she wanted to work in this field in the first place. There's nothing like that rush of adrenaline as the first orders come flooding in – three sweetbreads, one ravioli, two Dover soles, one lamb rack – on and on until it becomes a dance, a familiar beat that she feels in her bones: *you belong, you belong, you belong.*

No dishes are sent back and many compliments are paid to Chef Fitzgerald, despite her not physically being there, but no one complains or feels sidelined by that. By the time it comes to clean down their stations, Renee is hot, slightly sweaty and very tired, but also immensely satisfied. She hasn't even glanced at the clock; there has been no willing the time away, begging for the service to end so she can go home and forget about it. If anything, she wishes it could've continued, despite the exhaustion beginning to creep into her bones.

Sadly – and rather unsurprisingly – the only thorn in her otherwise perfect service is Josh. While he proved helpful when dressing plates (she'd be the first to admit, for all his faults, the kid knows how to make a plate look attractive), he's still lacking in every other aspect. It's normal for everyone to pitch in with the clean-up after service, but Renee can't help but be surprised at just how much washing up there's still left to do. Usually, the apprentice or kitchen porter would be constantly emptying and refilling the dishwasher throughout the service – a job Josh clearly hadn't bothered with. Renee can see the strain in the other chefs' faces: tightened jaws, narrowed eyes, the resentful tuts as they try to pick through the piles of crockery and pans, working out what to tackle first. The responsibility to stay on top of washing up during service should fall to the most junior member of staff.

Except Josh doesn't see it that way. In his world, chefs don't wash up.

While the others start sorting through the night's carnage, Bethany stalks over, looking thoroughly pissed off.

'Where is he?'

'He sloped off about quarter of an hour ago. Said he had a call.'

Bethany's mouth sets into a thin line.

'Right.' Her sigh signals to Renee this isn't the first time Josh has been a twat. She turns and heads back to the cooking stations.

There's a moment of quiet before an explosion of raised voices. All three chefs glance at one another: Renee concerned, both Martin and Roy angry. Still, in unspoken agreement, Martin begins unloading the industrial dishwasher and Roy fills the sink with hot, soapy water. Renee grabs the mop and starts cleaning the floor – definitely not her job, but it needs to be done, so she may as well crack on.

The next thing they know, Josh storms in, shaking his head and breathing hard. He gives Renee a hateful look and snatches the mop from her.

'You don't just take yourself outside whenever you feel like a vape break, Josh,' Bethany says. Renee is amazed at how level her voice is. 'That's never on. You need to pull your weight and work on your attitude. It's been three months. You should know this.'

Josh rolls his eyes, like Bethany's his mum berating him for coming in after curfew.

'This is fucking ridiculous. Fucking mopping. I'll tell my uncle you refuse to teach me – afraid I'll steal all your fucking secrets.'

Renee backs away and slides next to Roy. He offers her a tight little smile. She reciprocates and picks up a tea towel to help with the drying up.

'Look.' Bethany all but squares up to Josh, wagging her finger. She's not a small woman by any means, but Josh still towers over her. Bethany doesn't seem to care. She's worked with much bigger and nastier fish than this overgrown teenager. But Josh doesn't know that, and her refusal to bow down is clearly irritating him. 'Steal our secrets? You are a child. I don't care who your uncle is. You said you wanted to be a chef – this is how it goes. Every single one of us has been where you are now. If you want to work in this kitchen, you have to do as you're told, pitch in, and show us all the respect we are due – and that includes new hires. We are not here to service you.'

Josh shoots a poisonous glance at Renee, leaving her to wonder what the hell she's done to deserve that.

'We all know why she's here,' Josh says. 'Why she was chosen. Jesus Christ. I mean, look at her. Ultimate diversity hire. Who cares what she can do, as long as she ticks those boxes, eh? I bet she's a bloody lesbian as well.'

Bethany's face turns stony.

'I would think *very* carefully about what you say next, Joshua.' She takes a step towards him, fire in her eyes. 'Needless to say, I will be reporting this to Chef Fitzgerald. See how she feels about it all.'

She doesn't shout. She doesn't threaten. She speaks in a low, measured tone – one that Renee recognizes instantly, and she's once again nine years old, being told off by Granni for smashing a plate. Even Josh has the nous to look down and start mopping. Renee hopes that it's dawning on him that he's crossed a line, or else he's going to be a difficult co-worker – if she gets this job.

'You don't know how lucky you are,' Bethany continues. 'How many talented, committed young chefs would give their left foot just to spend a day working with us – with Gracie Fitzgerald. And rather than knuckle down and actually learn, you just throw a tantrum each time you're asked to do something.'

Josh moves away, his attention still fixed on the floor. There's a good chance he's never been spoken to like that, and he can't argue because no lies were told. Renee regards Bethany with genuine awe as she approaches. While there's no such thing as 'just a sous chef', the fact that Bethany hasn't struck out on her own means Chef Gracie must be utterly formidable.

'I'm really sorry about that,' Bethany murmurs. 'You shouldn't—'

'It's OK. It's his problem, not mine. I know that,' Renee says. 'And, if I'm honest, I've faced similar in the past.'

'I don't doubt you, but that's not the point. He shouldn't speak to you like that, and I hope he hasn't soured your experience here.'

Despite everything, Renee grins. 'You're safe there,' she says. 'I don't think anything could do that. I'm just grateful for the chance, and there's no way I'm going to let someone else's behaviour ruin that for me.'

'So you had fun?' Bethany asks.

'It was amazing!' Renee says, her heart leaping. 'I forgot how invigorating a kitchen can be – working with real professionals, with people who share my passion. I know it sounds a bit cliché, but I absolutely loved it.'

'Great,' Bethany says. 'What's your availability like for the rest of the week?'

It takes everything Renee has not to squeal like a child.

'Um, whenever. You tell me.'

'Would lunchtime service tomorrow be too short notice?'

'No, absolutely not. What time do you want me?'

'The others usually roll in around ten, ten thirty, ready for service at twelve. It's a lot less hectic – smaller plates, simple menu. I kind of chucked you in at the deep end today; tomorrow should be a little easier.' Bethany cocks her head, regarding Renee, who can't stop grinning. 'Now, this doesn't mean the job is instantly yours. There'll still be a trial period, mainly because Chef will want to see you in action before you're taken on. I won't lie, I wasn't convinced by your CV when Gracie first told me about you, but she has this almost supernatural ability to sniff out talent. She did it with Martin, she did it with Roy, she's done it with countless others. So, short of some kind of act-of-God-level event, I'll see you tomorrow?'

'God himself could come knocking, and I'd still be here.'

'Good. See you tomorrow at ten. You did good today. Keep it up.'

TWELVE

The flat is quiet as Renee makes her way to the living room. She barely remembers her journey home, replaying her shift over and over in her head. Lola is going to be so happy she was right about this. Renee had sent her a text but got no reply, unlike Graham, who had gushed over her, telling her he knew she'd smash it. He'd asked if she wanted to FaceTime when she got home, and she'd agreed, but she wanted time to talk to Lola first. Renee had kind of hoped she'd be waiting for her, eager to hear all the juicy details, but instead, she's welcomed by cold silence. Lola isn't working tonight. OK, she might have gone out, but surely she'd tell Renee that? Maybe she did, but Renee's phone was in her locker all night. Did she not see a text?

'SURPRISE!'

Renee's whole body jolts when she flips the light on. The shout is followed by a bang, then the sensation of something akin to cobwebs draping over her head.

Lola's laugh borders on the hysterical as she flops back onto the sofa.

'You should see your face!' she crows.

'Jesus Christ, you nearly gave me a heart attack!' Renee massages the front of her chest, hoping that might help soothe her frayed nerves.

'I know,' Lola says, a little too gleefully for Renee's liking. 'It's hilarious.'

'For you, maybe. Fuck's sake.' Renee chucks her bag into

the corner of the room and sinks down next to her flatmate on the sofa.

'Look what I've got.' Lola, still grinning, waves a bottle at her. 'To congratulate you on your first shift.' She begins unwrapping the top of a bottle of prosecco.

'That's so sweet. Thank you, girl.' And she means it. It might not be expensive champagne like the stuff Graham has, but the sentiment is the same. Plus, she prefers prosecco. 'Do you want me to do that?'

'Nope,' Lola says, struggling with the cork. 'I've got this. I can— Whoa!' The cork shoots out of the bottle and hits the ceiling as the prosecco fizzes all over the sofa.

'Oh no, no . . . hang on!' Lola shrieks, scrambling for glasses to catch the liquid.

Renee gets to them first and holds them out while Lola splashes the wine into them. By the time they share a toast, both of them are giggling, and when Lola cries out a hearty 'Cheers!', Renee enthusiastically joins in.

'So,' Lola says, 'how did it go? Did you get to meet Gracie Fitzgerald?'

'No, Chef Gracie wasn't in tonight. She's in Paris or something.' Renee takes a sip from her glass. The bubbles make her nose itch a little. 'But that didn't stop it from being just, like, amazing. I can't think of another word to use. Just amazing.'

Lola's smile turns gentler. 'I'm so proud of you. You know that, right?'

'I know,' Renee says. 'And to think, I wouldn't have this opportunity if it wasn't for you.' She holds her glass up and waits for Lola to chink hers against it.

'I know, girl. Don't you forget it.'

'I never will. If any wait staff opportunities come up, you'll be the first to know, right?'

'Ah, no. I don't think I'm cut out for proper posho dining –

Carluccio's is posh enough for me. I'd rather wrangle a kid's birthday party than deal with those stick-up-the-arses. But that's not the point. Come on, tell me everything.'

Renee doesn't need any more of an excuse. She regales Lola with all the details: about the food, the people she's working with, what the place is like – just *everything*. It all pours out of her, like a small child to their parent at the end of an exciting day, with Lola supplying gasps and 'No, he didn't!' where appropriate.

'So you're telling me you actually worked alongside Bethany Jacobs? *The* Bethany Jacobs – of *Cooking Caribbean* fame?'

'Yeah. You could say I did.'

'Well, I'm lost for words,' Lola says.

'That's a first.'

'Oh, shut up, bitch. I mean it. You've arrived.'

'Technically, I'm still in my trial period . . .'

'Psh.' Lola chases Renee's technicalities away with a flick of her wrist. 'Trial period, my arse. That job is yours now. No way anyone's going to stick you in the thick of an evening service and then say no thank you. Lunch service, yeah, I could see that, but evening? Nah. You have that job in the bag. Trust me.'

Renee wishes she could. Lola's confidence is something she's always envied. The two of them sit and drink the prosecco until Renee's phone buzzes. Who is calling her so late? The moment she picks up her phone, she gasps and slaps her hand to her head.

'Oh, shit – G. I forgot I said I'd call him.'

Lola is cackling again as Renee wrestles with the facial recognition. Finally, the phone unlocks and she answers Graham's call.

'Hey, Ren – is everything OK? I was getting worried—'

Before Renee can answer him, Lola leans over so her face fills his screen.

'Hey, G! Sorry, we have prosecco!' She waves her glass in front of her.

Renee pushes Lola down so she can see her partner.

'I'm so sorry, hun – she ambushed me with booze. Literally.'

'It was so funny,' Lola says, her voice a little muffled as she struggles to escape Renee's grip.

'For you, maybe. For me? I nearly had a heart attack.'

'Well, as long as you're all right,' Graham says, his expression softening. 'So . . . how did it go?'

The smile that creeps across Renee's face answers for her.

'It was so good. Terrifying, but—'

'So . . . you got the job?' Graham's voice is ripe with expectation.

'I haven't signed anything, but they've asked me to come in for tomorrow's lunch service, so . . .' Renee can't help feeling a little giddy every time she says this. She still can't believe it.

'That is just . . . I'm so proud of you, Renee. Congratulations!'

'Thank you, G.' And she means it.

'Look – it's late and I have to be up at six, so I'm going to go. See you tomorrow?'

'Yeah, sure. Hopefully I'll be able to give you my schedule then, too.'

'That sounds great. Love you.'

'Love you too.'

Graham ends the call.

'Love you,' Lola teases.

'Shut up.'

Lola tops up their glasses, finishing the bottle.

'G's right about one thing. I'm proud of you, too.'

Renee nods, sniffing back unexpected tears.

'I never thought I'd get there, you know? Really did think I'd missed the boat. Still might have, if I fuck up this trial period.'

'Yeah, but that's not going to happen, is it?' Lola leans over and puts her arm around Renee's shoulders. 'It won't take them long to realize you're really talented, and you've got those mad taste buds—'

'Thank you, Granni Landis.'

'Indeed – thank you, Granni Landis. What I'm trying to say is just be you. Don't try to impress them. You don't have to, because you've already got it.'

Renee bursts out laughing. 'Where did that greeting-card nonsense come from?'

'Hey, I can be deep when I want to be. The thing is – don't overthink it. I know that's one of your favourite hobbies and all, but you're going to have to try and resist for a bit, OK?'

Renee nods and drains her glass, a sudden sense of fatigue blanketing her. She doesn't know if it's the alcohol or if the adrenaline has finally worn off, but she's shattered.

'Yeah, well, I'm not going to be good for anything if I don't get any sleep, so I think I'm going to bed,' she says, barely stifling a yawn.

Lola gestures for Renee's glass.

'I'll sort these out. You go get your head down. You deserve it.'

When Renee crawls into bed, she feels happier than she has in years. It's like Lola says. She's done it.

She's *in*.

THIRTEEN

Renee wakes bright and early after the most restful sleep she's had since moving into this flat. Usually, she'd be moaning about the early start, but she jumps out of bed like a kid on the first day of the summer holidays. She's never been so excited for a new shift – then again, Chickadees wasn't exactly her dream place to work.

When she arrives, Bethany explains that Martin isn't working this shift, but he'll be there tonight. This means Roy will take over Martin's responsibilities as well as desserts, and Renee will be working directly with Bethany, focusing on both starters and mains. As promised, the menu is far simpler, but no less meticulous, and she's soon busy sautéing chicken livers to make pâté and filleting mackerel so fresh she can smell the sea air as she works. Josh, still sullen, has been left to get on with veg prep for tonight's menu. Given it's a Friday, they're fully booked, and even with the full team, they'll be tight for time unless everyone pulls their weight.

Once service is over, Renee busies herself cleaning down the work surfaces, ensuring they have that signature NOVA gleam.

Still, she can't help the sinking feeling when Bethany asks her to join her upstairs in the conference room.

Oh God. What has she done? It can't be good. If it was, she'd have said whatever it was in front of the others, right? All her previous good vibes scatter as she scuttles up the stairs, hoping for the best but mentally preparing for the worst.

The conference room mirrors the restaurant's aesthetic. Stark white walls are adorned with paintings; the table is polished stone that seems to radiate cold. Usually, art makes a place feel more welcoming, but these slashes of garish red against the pristine white walls remind Renee of a murder scene. It's clear this room hasn't been built for comfort, but for confrontation – make-or-break deals between men posturing as gods while eating NOVA's signature dishes, served to them by wait staff who probably don't even register as human in their eyes. Bethany sits by an open MacBook and gestures for Renee to sit, offering a warm smile.

'OK, Renee. You've been with us for a couple of shifts now. How do you think things are going?'

Renee squirms in her seat. She hates these kinds of questions.

'Well, I think things have gone OK,' she says.

'Just OK?' Bethany isn't giving anything away.

Time to step up your game.

'All right – better than OK. Much better. I've had an amazing time—'

Bethany holds up a hand.

'I'm not asking you how you feel about the restaurant. I'm asking you about you in this environment. How do you feel you fit in?'

Renee swallows, feeling even more flustered.

'Um, I think I've done a good job,' she says, cringing inside. This sort of thing doesn't come naturally to Renee. She'd rather let her actions speak for her. 'I've worked well with the other chefs . . . Well, maybe not Josh, but I don't think that's a me issue—'

Bethany chuckles. 'Sorry, carry on.'

'Right, OK, so . . . Martin and Roy have been really welcoming, letting me concentrate on my work instead of worrying about fitting in. I like to think that my contribution this week may have lifted some of the weight off other people's shoulders. Like, I know I'm new, but I've tried to get stuck in as much as I can.'

Bethany watches her, nodding slightly as Renee speaks. It only makes Renee more self-conscious.

But the chef says nothing, only presses a key on the MacBook. The screen flares to life – and sitting there, listening, is a woman.

Renee's chest constricts. She knows *exactly* who this is.

'Hello,' the woman says. 'And welcome to my team.'

Renee blinks – once, twice, three times – as she allows the news to sink in. She shoots Bethany a disbelieving look.

'Does this mean . . .'

Bethany nods. Gracie Fitzgerald doesn't.

'I apologize for not being there to welcome you in person, but I'm sure you understand how these things work.' Gracie's voice is low, her accent indeterminate. There's a transatlantic twang with a hint of French around her inflection, rounded off by very British vowels. 'I shall hopefully be back next week. But before I make an offer in any official capacity, I must ask you something first.'

'Of course,' Renee says. 'What do you need to know?'

'My restaurant is my world. And I don't just mean my life. I mean, it is my realm. Whatever I say goes. And whatever happens in NOVA stays in NOVA.'

'I understand,' Renee says.

'Do you? Really?'

Gracie's question catches Renee off guard. She's heard the 'this is my kitchen – do as you're told or else' spiel from nearly every chef she's ever worked for. But something about the way Chef Gracie's eyes narrow and her lips purse tells Renee this isn't the same thing. This is something else. Something more intense. Primal, even.

Renee's eyes flick to Bethany, but she's stone-faced. Behind her, the fleshy paintings look like they're pulsating.

'I-I think so,' Renee starts.

'Oh, you think so? What does that mean to you, then?'

The silence is excruciating as Renee tries to figure out what Gracie actually wants from her. Gracie raises her eyebrows and shares a quick glance with the still-stony Bethany.

'I know how things work in restaurants of NOVA's reputation. The kitchen isn't just a place to prepare food. It's the beating heart of the restaurant – the lifeblood and nervous system of NOVA.'

Gracie's eyebrows are still raised, but now she looks intrigued rather than sceptical.

'And where do I fit into all of this?' she asks, her voice devoid of emotion.

'You're the brain,' Renee says. 'The control centre. We're essential to the restaurant's function, but none of us are integral to its identity. You can replace blood with a transfusion, medicate the nerves, cut off the diseased limbs, but if you remove the brain, the restaurant is dead.'

Where the hell did that come from? Probably from all the anatomical-looking crime scene art.

Gracie lets out a long breath and taps her lips with her index finger. She shares a quick look with Bethany, then leans back in her chair, folding her arms over her chest.

'That's an interesting hypothesis. Where did it come from?'

Where did it come from? Renee wants to shrug, to say she doesn't have a clue, she was just vibing with her environment. Before she can answer, Gracie speaks again.

'It's all right. You don't need to explain. Some things are too personal. But I will say – I rather like it.'

Renee wants to thank her but doesn't. Somehow, she gets the impression it might count against her.

Silence falls again as Gracie studies her, a slight smile playing at her lips. Renee tries her hardest to look keen without seeming manic. She isn't sure if she's succeeding.

'If you wish to work with me,' Gracie says, her voice so low

Renee has to lean forward, 'I accept nothing short of perfection. You follow my instruction, always. You follow my recipes to the letter. If you make a mistake, you tell me immediately. While you are free to taste your own cooking, my signature dishes are off-limits. They are for me, and me alone. And if I see you tasting one, you will be terminated. Do I make myself clear?'

Renee feels like she's being given a dressing-down for something she hasn't actually done, rather than being on the verge of accepting a life-changing job. She nods all the same.

'Totally. One hundred per cent.'

'My whole life is NOVA. I don't let just anyone in.'

At this, Bethany screws her mouth up and stares at the ceiling, because that's not entirely true, but she lets it slide.

'I understand,' Renee says. 'Whatever Chef says, goes.'

Gracie leans toward the camera and steeples her fingers in front of her mouth, hiding what Renee suspects might be a smile. Or at the very least, a smirk.

'Excellent. You may proceed, Bethany.'

And with that, the screen goes black.

'Well,' Bethany says with a sigh. 'That's Gracie Fitzgerald.' She leans over and closes the MacBook. 'Just in case you were wondering,' she adds quietly, then laughs. 'I swear you'll get used to her. She is fabulous to work for, but she's also . . . a little highly strung. I think that's the nicest way of putting it. But anyway – congratulations. If you want the job, it's yours.' She slides a tablet towards Renee. 'Your contract. Take a break, read it through. Any questions, you know where I am. And then, if you're so inclined, sign on the dotted line, fill in all your details and we'll get everything set up for you before service tonight.'

FOURTEEN

The NOVA contract is unlike anything Renee has seen before. The basics are all there – her responsibilities, legal liabilities, holidays, sick pay, termination, redundancy, and so on – but there's a whole section on privacy, asset protection, press contact and, intriguingly, the private freezer. Renee's not sure why that specific area of the kitchen warrants its own clause, but it's not a deal-breaker for her. Still, when she comes to sign, it's with a curious mix of excitement and trepidation. She can't shake the feeling that she's signing more than a simple employment contract.

'Shame this isn't on paper,' she says, trying to alleviate the tension. 'I could sign it in blood, then.'

Bethany doesn't laugh.

The rest of the day passes in a blur. The problem with split shifts is finding somewhere to go during the few hours between them. In the end, she finds a coffee shop and treats herself to a huge slice of coffee and walnut cake – her favourite – while she texts Lola and Graham her good news. She even considers messaging her dad but decides to do that later. Her day has been overwhelming enough without adding him into the mix.

She doesn't expect a reply, knowing they're both are at work, but almost immediately, Graham texts back.

> Really? They offered you the job? Omg, that's huge! And only after 2 shifts? You've done more than smashed it. I'm so proud of you! Dinner tonight? Gxx

Renee makes an apologetic face, even though he can't see her.

Thanks G! It's so insane, I don't even know what I did for Gracie to make up her mind so easily. We'll have to call a rain check on dinner tho – I'm working again tonight. Can't let my new boss down! Rxx

And a few moments later:

Ah, that's a shame. I guess that's going to be normal now, huh? Remember, you can always come home to me if you need to. You have a key. You don't have to ask xxx

But she does have to ask. She doesn't know why she feels that compulsion, but just letting herself into someone's space without them knowing feels like a violation.

Yeah I know. Might have to later with the split shifts and all xxx

It's like I said, moving in would be easier for both of us xxx

Renee closes her eyes and takes a sip of her coffee. She'd added an extra pump of hazelnut syrup in a fit of recklessness, but now it tastes too sweet, too cloying.
A little bit like your relationship.
No. She shakes her head, cutting the thought off at the root. Graham cares, that's all. He isn't trying to trap her . . . and even if he was, would that be such a bad thing? He's a real steal by anyone's standards: good job, his own place, pension already sorted, no surprise children – the list of his perks is near endless. There's nothing wrong with him.

The problem is with her.

She stares at her phone, scrolling back through all his messages. She really doesn't deserve him. She knows his parents still hold out hope that he'll settle down with a nice Home Counties girl – someone who can ride a horse, handle a boat. You know, *their* type of people. But he doesn't care. He loves her. She should know – he says it enough. Where some might see that as a red flag or a sign of love bombing, Renee knows better. For one, he's a terrible liar: the minute even the smallest untruth passes his lips, he turns beet-red and starts stuttering. She smiles as she remembers the time he booked a weekend away in Venice – how she knew he was up to something because every time she asked what he was doing, he'd flush, stutter and continually push his floppy hair out of his face while offering terrible excuses that fooled no one.

'The problem with you, girl, is you don't like it when things go right,' she mutters to herself, and shovels a massive forkful of cake into her mouth.

She flicks over to TikTok, more for distraction than anything else. She doesn't know why, but she keeps veering between dizzying glee and stomach-cramping anxiety. She tries to tell herself it's normal. She's just taken a job in one of the most respected restaurants in the world – of course she feels conflicted. But deep down, she knows it's more than that.

Videos of pets and people baking cakes offer temporary relief. Or at least, they do for a little while.

More evidence that celebrity foodie Frank Mercer may have met 'a sticky end' – STITCH INCOMING

It starts with a news report and ends with a heavily tattooed woman with violently dyed hair, telling her followers that Frank Mercer isn't dead, wasn't murdered, and that 'the Establishment' are hiding him so he doesn't implicate anyone else in his crimes. When she was younger, Renee might have been naive enough to believe this, but now, knowing this industry, she realizes that's hardly the truth. Everyone pretends to be buddies on these shows, but it's as cutthroat as any other part of the culinary world. Sure, he might take a few down with him if he did open up, but there are plenty of sharks waiting just out of sight, ready to strike at anyone showing signs of weakness.

Still . . . it is weird. Over the years, there have been a few important men – and they are all men – who have gone AWOL. Granted, all of them vanished shortly after being exposed as predators or massively problematic in other ways – that itself isn't uncommon these days – but to disappear entirely, with no hint of staging a comeback? That's unusual. Take that Jeffrey McAdams bloke. It's only been three weeks, and he may yet resurface, but the similarities between his disappearance and Mercer's are uncanny.

Maybe there's some kind of vigilante in town, picking off awful men one by one. It makes a change. Usually, it's women who have to be careful. It's kind of refreshing, if terrifying, that it might be middle-aged arseholes this time.

Martin can barely hide his glee when he turns up for the evening shift, giving Renee a big hug as he tells her how hard it was to keep it all quiet – making her wonder if that was the real reason he didn't work the lunchtime shift. Roy, on the other hand, simply pats her on the shoulder and offers his congratulations.

'OK, right. So, we're getting some drinks in at Becky's after this shift, and before you say anything, Ren, you can't say no because you're the reason we're going. No, don't look like that – even Bethany said she'd come.'

'For one drink, Martin. Just one,' Bethany says sternly.

'Yeah, whatever – we'll see about that,' Martin continues. 'Now, Roy, you don't have a choice – Josh, you in?'

Josh gives Martin the same look someone might give the bottom of their shoe after stepping in something unpleasant.

'I don't really think it's my scene.'

'It's not about scenes, Joshua – it's about celebrating. Letting Ren knows she's welcome. Right, Roy?'

Roy offers a long-suffering yet benevolent smile in agreement.

'See? It's not about where we're going – it's about who we're going with.'

'And who is going?' Renee asks. 'Just us?'

'Oh, no – half the wait staff will be coming too. Not Q, of course. Last time I asked him, I thought I was going to disintegrate from the look he gave me. But Dean and Ruby are coming, and maybe Serge, if we can convince him.'

'Ooo, Serge,' Roy says. 'I wonder why you're keen for him to come along?'

'Shut up, Roy. This is for Ren, not for . . . Yeah, well, hopefully Serge'll come along, and maybe I'll be able to convince Danika too.'

'Who's Danika?' Renee whispers to Roy.

'Sommelier,' Roy replies.

'Oh. I didn't even realize we had a proper in-house sommelier.'

'We do. She's called Danika, she looks like a supermodel, and she's absolutely terrifying.'

'What, even more than Chef Gracie?'

Roy chuckles. 'Oh, no – Gracie's in a whole league of her own when it comes to that. Danika's more along the lines of "if you tell me to smile, I'll rip your lungs out".'

'Will you two stop it?' Martin snaps, interrupting them. 'I'm trying to organize something here.'

Roy smirks while Renee mouths 'sorry'. Before Martin can start up again, Bethany steps in.

'All right, Martin – that's enough social organization. We've still got a service to run. Let's get that out of the way first, OK?'

Martin deflates a little but knows better than to talk back to Bethany.

'Right, people – we've finally found our missing cog.' She nods at Renee. 'We all know what we're doing, so let's get this well-oiled machine on the road.'

She is answered by a chorus of 'Yes, Chef!', and by far the most enthusiastic voice belongs to Renee.

FIFTEEN

The last time Renee was in a club, she must have been twenty-one – twenty-two, at best. And even then, she'd felt like an old lady.

Going at nearly twenty-eight has her feeling like a shrivelled-up mummy.

She remembers the music being loud, but was it really this loud? And looking at the other clubbers, they must now be letting in actual children, because there's no way any of them are drink-legal – and if they are . . . yikes.

Although, if she feels like this, she can't imagine how Bethany is taking it.

Scratch that – it's perfectly obvious from the look on her face.

'Bit loud, isn't it?' Roy has to lean over and all but yell into her ear for her to hear him.

'You can say that again,' Renee yells back.

Martin rejoins them, his hands laden with glasses, a bottle of fizz under each arm. Behind him, an obscenely gorgeous French guy is equally laden. Renee guesses this is probably Serge, and from his body language, she also reckons Martin has nothing to worry about when it comes to rejection.

'How many bottles?' Bethany asks.

'We need enough for all of us,' Martin says as he begins to fill the glasses. Each one fizzes far too much, coating the already sticky table with equally sticky prosecco. 'Whoops!'

Once all the glasses are full, he and Serge hand them out to everyone present. Then Martin stands up, glass held high.

'To Ren!' he shouts. 'For joining our little team just when we need it most.'

Renee cringes as everyone looks her way and raises their glasses too.

'Uh, thank you?' She shoots Martin a look, but he's not focused on her – he's more interested in Serge.

'So you're the new chef?' The woman with the question is tall – really tall, like, nearly six feet – and has an Eastern European lilt to her voice, something Renee finds quite enchanting. She's whip-thin and incredibly beautiful, in a kind of classic, Charlize Theron way. Renee guesses this must be Danika, NOVA's sommelier.

'Yeah, that's me. Renee.'

'Danika.' She holds out an elegant hand, and Renee has to force down the urge to kiss it like she's royalty. 'You must be impressive. I've never seen anyone taken on so quickly.'

Renee's not sure how to answer that, so she just shrugs.

'I'm glad.' She takes a sip of her drink and grimaces. 'Ugh. Club fizz. Is there anything worse?'

'Corner-shop red wine,' Renee says without missing a beat.

At this, Danika throws back her head and laughs throatily.

'I think you win this one.' She raises her glass and inspects it as the pulsing coloured lights from the dance floor shine through it, making it look like a mystical elixir. 'We have such a short time on this planet. Why are we wasting it drinking trash?'

'Mainly because we can't afford the good stuff,' Renee says.

'You are so right,' Danika says. 'Always, cruelty in this life—'

She's interrupted by an already half-cut Josh, who thumps down beside Danika and throws his arm along the back of the seat behind her.

'All right, ladies – what are we doing?' He grabs a glass off the table, not really caring who it belongs to. He has a manic edge to him now – something that tells Renee he's probably spent the last ten minutes in the bathroom with a credit card and some rolled-up notes.

'Not talking to children,' Danika says, and angles her body so she may as well have her back turned against him.

'What the fuck?' Josh whines. 'Jeez, you just try to talk to people – no need to be a bitch about it.'

'I'm not. This is called setting boundaries.' Danika's tone is even yet deadly, and Renee swears she's going to do everything she can to keep this woman on her side. 'It's a radical concept, I know. One day you might get it. Renee, I'm going out for a vape – would you come with me?'

'Yes,' Renee says, relieved to have an excuse to go outside.

Josh protests as Danika stands up and walks away. For a moment, Renee thinks he might try to follow her, but even he's not that stupid. She grabs her bag and winds through groups of dancers until she's finally outside in the cool London air. She takes in a deep lungful. Much better.

'You had enough too?'

She spins around to find Roy having a cheeky cigarette with Bethany.

'Hey, I wondered where you guys were.'

'Christ, I couldn't stand another moment. I'm probably going to be off after this,' Bethany says, indicating her cigarette.

'I didn't know you smoked,' Renee says.

'I don't,' Bethany replies. 'Or at least, I'm an ex-smoker.'

Roy smirks.

'Yeah, you can shut up,' Bethany continues. 'You're supposed to be giving up too, remember?'

'Aye, aye, I know,' Roy says. 'I'm down to three a day, so I'm getting there.'

'You could replace it with a vape,' Danika says. 'That's what I did.'

'I dinnae think that would work,' Roy says, sounding a little defeated. 'My missus doesn't want anything that might pollute the house before the bairn comes. I'm not even allowed to smoke in the garden. Says it's just as dangerous as smoking indoors when it comes to babies.'

'Oh wow, is your partner pregnant?' Renee says. It's then that she realizes how little she actually knows about the people she's working with.

'Aye. Nearly six months.' Roy looks proud. 'This is my last vice, and it's definitely the hardest one to shift. But it'll be worth it. Anything for the wee bean, you know?'

Renee nods.

'Not a mother but an auntie, so yeah, I get it.'

'You want tae have kids?'

'When I was younger, I would've said no. Now? I dunno. It would be nice, I suppose, but this game isn't exactly kind to mothers. I mean, it isn't exactly kind to fathers either.'

'No, I get it. It's tough on anyone, but I wouldn't want tae be a pregnant person in this line of work. I dunno how you'd do it.'

'Mainly by having a very responsible partner who carried the baby for you, I suppose,' Bethany says.

'You've got kids?' Renee asks.

'Uh-huh. A son. He's nearly eight. Thankfully, Geraldine is an absolute super-mum.' She fishes around in her bag for her phone and shows Renee her lock screen. 'That's him, with us.' The picture shows Bethany with a beaming smile, next to an equally beaming white woman with thick ginger curls – Renee guesses this is Geraldine. Between them sits a cheeky-looking multiracial boy. His smile is so wide she can see he's still waiting for his front teeth to come in.

'He is adorable,' Renee says, and she means it. Being biracial herself, seeing another family that looks similar to her own always makes her smile.

'He is. He's also an absolute monster, but hey – kids will be kids, right?'

They all chuckle at this.

'Anyway, talking of kids . . .' Bethany takes one last drag on her cigarette before stubbing it out on the wall next to her. 'I'm offski. It's officially past my bedtime, and we've all got work tomorrow. Don't stay out too late, kids.' She winks at them before heading towards the station.

'She's got a point,' Roy says. 'My clubbing days are well over – and have been for a while.'

'Mine too,' Renee says. 'I can't keep up with this. I'm shattered. I'm only staying so I don't upset Martin.'

'I wouldn't worry too much about Martin,' Danika says. 'He has Serge to occupy his time.'

'So Roy was right? Martin likes Serge?'

'Oh, don't even.' Danika rolls her eyes. 'I just want to grab the backs of their heads and smash them together at this point. Get it over with so the rest of us can get on with work.'

Roy laughs and nods.

'So this isn't a new thing?' Renee asks.

'Not by a long shot,' Danika says. 'From the moment Serge walked in, sparks have been flying.'

'I'm surprised Martin hasn't done anything about it,' Renee says. 'He doesn't exactly come across as being backwards about coming forwards.'

'Ah, see, that's what a lot of people say,' Roy says. 'But our Martin is surprisingly sensitive. He's a good lad, though, and not just for his cookery skills. Heart of gold, that one. And a proper ride or die if he's loyal to you. If you ever need a hand, he'll be there – no questions asked.' Roy stubs out his cigarette the same way Bethany did. 'Anyway, it's time I got going. Missus won't be too pleased if I roll in at three a.m., steaming.'

'You know what? I think I'll do the same,' Renee says. 'I know it's a bit mean, given this is allegedly about me, but I'm so tired. I need to get my head down before tomorrow.'

'Amateurs,' Danika says with a smile. 'You old people, sloping off to your beds.'

'Look, we don't all have the constitution of a brick-lined elephant, Dani. Some of us need our rest.'

Danika snorts in amusement. 'It's OK,' she says in a sing-song voice. 'I shall go back inside and emasculate that young man a little more. I don't even know why he's with us. Not after all his antics.'

'I guess money talks, even when you're Gracie Fitzgerald,' Roy says. 'Anyhow, night.'

'Which way are you going?' Renee asks.

'Down to the Tube,' Roy answers.

'I'll walk with you, if that's OK?'

'Course it's OK. Come on, lass.'

After saying goodbye to Danika, they walk side by side down the dimly lit road. It's been nice, getting to know people outside of work. She chats with Roy about his plans for the baby, and he opens up about how he's a bit worried about being a good father – something Renee is quick to reassure him on.

'So . . .' Renee starts. 'Working at NOVA.'

Roy gives her a look that's both expectant and guarded.

'Aye?'

'Everything's OK? Nothing I need to know?'

'The thing you have tae understand is . . . Gracie. When people say she's not like other chefs, they mean it. There's no exaggeration there.'

'Yeah, I got that impression from Martin.'

'I'm not going tae sugarcoat it. She is hard. The kitchen's . . . easier when she's not there. But if we wanted easy all the time, we wouldn't be working there.'

'I keep hearing this, but I'm not sure I really understand what anyone means when they say that.'

'I get it. I do. I know she spoke to you today. That's how you got the job, of course. Bethany was asking us what we thought about you, so she could give our feedback to Gracie. Not that I think our opinions matter much. She walks her own path. I've worked with some absolute arses in my time with her, but she'd tolerate that so long as they did exactly what she said. But that's not to say you can be a total prick and she'll put up with it if you're talented enough. She can properly destroy a chef if they act like a cunt.' He shakes his head, fiddling with his empty cigarette packet. 'Kind of wished I'd saved m'last ciggie for now, if I'm honest.'

'Sorry – we don't have to talk about this,' Renee says, her stomach dropping a notch. Maybe this job really is too good to be true.

'No, no, it's fine. I just don't want tae give you the wrong impression, you know? In too many places everyone says they're a happy family, but I don't think that's healthy. I think the important thing for you to know is that Gracie is a true genius. Like, there are all those other chefs out there, all with amazing palates and absolutely on-point menu choices, and all of them are top-level, ten-out-of-ten chefs . . . but Gracie? There's something else going on there. While everyone else is trying to impress, it's like she wants to challenge everyone's expectations – even if that means going about her job in . . . unorthodox ways. Eating her food can sometimes feel like a dare, you know? And I don't mean playing a game of chappy – I mean like Russian roulette. When she comes in and prepares those speciality dishes of hers . . . intense isn't a strong enough word. It's like she's possessed of something. *By* something. It's hard tae explain and, honestly, I still don't understand it myself. You'll understand when you see it.'

It takes a moment for Renee to absorb that. Roy's voice at the end sounds uneasy, which is not exactly reassuring. She chews at the skin down the side of her thumb – a terrible anxious habit she's spent years trying to break.

'Ah, lass, don't look so worried. It'll be fine, I promise you. You're good – really good – and Gracie's gonna love you. If you keep your head down and follow instructions, you'll do fine.'

Yeah, not as comforting as you think, Roy. That sounds a little too close to 'just following orders' for my liking.

'Look, love, I'm gonna be late, and the missus won't let me out again if I don't get back by curfew.' Roy grins and gently nudges her arm. 'Honestly, though – well done. You should be proud of yourself.'

'Thank you.' Renee smiles. 'Just one last thing?'

'Aye?'

Renee rubs her hands together and winces a little.

'I know I probably shouldn't be asking this – but the freezer deal. What's up with that?'

To her discomfort, Roy takes a moment to answer.

Why is it that every time I ask a question, people pause like they're building in plausible deniability?

'Ah, well, that's . . . I'll be honest, I struggled with it at first. I've seen chefs be protective of their recipes and special ingredients, but with Gracie? It sounds bad, but ignorance is bliss. No one's allowed in there apart from her, so it's nothing for you to worry about. Same with the tasting thing. Taste your own food, of course – though I will say, Gracie's directions are rarely wrong when it comes to seasoning – but don't touch hers. It's the Golden Rule.'

The Tube station is surprisingly quiet, given it's a Friday night. A few people wander through the tunnels, tapping their cards on the turnstiles. As Renee and Roy pass a closed-up news stand, Roy jerks his head towards a tattered display headline.

'Still haven't found that guy,' he says.

'I saw. I reckon he either fell off his yacht, or someone made him fall off his yacht,' Renee says. 'There's that other one, too. Mercer.'

'Oh aye – that one. Another right proper bastard. You know, that McAdams guy came in about five months ago. Hired the conference room. Absolute cunt. Rude tae everyone, including Gracie. Tried to fuckin' sneak in some escorts – some of them looked barely over sixteen. Mad times. I'd lay good money that if anyone did see him off, he deserved it.'

'Crikey,' Renee says. 'That bad?'

'Ah, they all are. Bunch of bawbags the lot of 'em. Too much money, too little brains. World's better off without them, if y'ask me.'

Renee isn't sure how to respond. On one hand, she agrees. The world *is* a better place without people like that. But at the same time, she's thinking that in the confines of her mind, not saying it out loud to a virtual stranger – someone she's only known for twenty-four hours at this point. Whether these men are paragons of virtue or not, they all have families who love them. No one should have to face something like that.

'Maybe we should just tax the hell out of them,' Renee says. 'Make them do some good, even if it's only vicariously.'

'Aye, I like the way you think. In it for the common people.'

A warm puff of air signals the next train's approach, followed by a crackling voice announcing its arrival.

'Well, this one's me,' Renee says. 'Thanks for a lovely time, Roy.'

'Yeah, you too, Ren. I'll see you tomorrow. And remember – you're enough. Gracie doesn't take on just anyone.'

'Thanks. You have a good night, too. I hope your wife doesn't ground you.'

At that, Roy lets out a bark of laughter and shakes his head as Renee boards the train.

'If I'm lucky, eh?'

SIXTEEN

Despite her earlier worries, the weekend goes well, and by the time Sunday lunch rolls around, Renee is feeling much more confident. There have been no disasters, no fumbles; even Josh seems to be on his best behaviour. Maybe Bethany's lecture actually did penetrate that over-privileged skull of his after all.

Sunday lunch is always a shift every chef looks forward to, because it marks the beginning of their version of a weekend. Most restaurants of this calibre don't do a Sunday evening service, close on Mondays, and don't reopen until Tuesday evening – and NOVA is no different in that respect. They don't run lunch shifts on Wednesday either, meaning everyone has a chance to recuperate and recover.

But there is one thing that gnaws at Renee.

When is Gracie actually going to be there, in the flesh?

She's been in Paris for over a week. And while it isn't unusual for executive chefs to go away for periods of time, Renee had been under the impression that Gracie was a little more hands-on in her restaurant than most. The rules she laid out to Renee sure as hell implied that.

'I just don't know when I'm actually going to work with her,' she tells Graham over dinner. It's Monday, and she's taken up his offer to stay over so they can spend the morning together before her next shift.

'It'll happen,' he says. 'It's not as if you're in a trial period now, is it? She can't stay away for ever.'

'Good point, I guess.' Renee smiles into her wineglass as she takes a sip. Tonight's choice is a light, crisp pinot grigio – a little basic, but delicious nonetheless.

'I'm so happy for you,' Graham says, a wistful look on his face as he tilts his head to one side. 'To see you like this – you just deserve it. So much. Proud of you.'

Renee's smile turns a little awkward. She's never been good at taking compliments, and the sincerity in his voice makes her feel oddly vulnerable.

'Darling, you really have nothing to worry about.' Graham leans over the table and takes her hand. 'You know you're good. Everyone says it. When Gracie finally graces you with her presence.' He grins, making sure she catches the pun, and she rolls her eyes. 'She'll know she made the right choice. Stop second-guessing yourself.'

Renee twiddles her fork through her pasta. She made a simple seitan linguine tonight, despite Graham suggesting they get a takeaway. At the time, she'd wanted to make something simple to help her clear her head, but now she's wishing she'd just suffocated her feelings with grease instead.

'Renee, sweetheart – what's wrong?' Graham's tone subtly shifts to concerned, making Renee twist her lips in an attempt to stop her fears from tumbling out.

It doesn't work.

'There's nothing wrong with the job. Everyone's really lovely, and the environment is incredible—'

'That sounds good to me. So what is it?'

Renee can see Graham's concern is genuine, but still has to take a breath at his interruption.

'I was getting there. It's hard to explain. I'm beyond ecstatic, but after working in a more casual environment, I'd forgotten how these high-end places attract . . . characters.'

Graham nods, chewing his food thoughtfully.

'These high-status careers do tend to attract the more, shall we say, idiosyncratic people.'

'Yeah, that's what I said,' Renee replies, a little more sharply than she intended. Graham's eyes widen at her sudden bite, and she immediately shakes her head and apologizes.

'Sorry. It's just hard to explain. I've already told you about the interview and how unsettling it was, and then there's the freezer thing . . . and basically everyone who works with her says she's a bit of a nightmare – even by this industry's standards. They always qualify it by saying she's a genius and fiercely protective of her staff and everything, but . . . it's a lot, you know?'

Graham regards her for a moment.

'That makes sense, Ren. This job is a huge deal. Gracie Fitzgerald is a huge deal. And her reputation is well known. Remember all that stuff in the news when she stood up to that guy – can't remember his name – the one who was later accused of abuse?'

Renee shifts uncomfortably, because while he could be describing any number of men, she knows exactly who he's talking about.

'Isaac Ferguson.'

Graham snaps his fingers. 'That's him. Awful man. Thing is, I'd forgotten his name, even though his actions were terrible. But I remember Gracie Fitzgerald. The way she was treated – like she was the one in the wrong? All those articles about her being difficult and weird? Honestly, I think I'd be a little strange and maybe lock my freezer up too, if that was me.'

Renee tilts her head at him and smiles. This time, it's genuine. It's things like this that remind her he's a good one.

'That makes a lot of sense. Of course you're going to be protective of everything you've worked for when you've been treated badly.'

'Exactly. Once bitten, twice shy, as they say.'

'I thought that was for relationships,' Renee says playfully.

'And I thought you said food was more than just a bodily need, and that you couldn't be with someone who stood in your way.'

Renee laughs.

'I don't think I said it quite like that! I think it was more along the lines of chefs aren't just cooking, they're creating—'

'Food as an artform!' Graham lifts his hands in a dramatic flourish.

'Pack it in, pest,' Renee says. 'And it is an artform. No matter what the plebs think.'

'I'm not a pleb,' Graham says, faking offence.

'I never said you were. I said you were a pest.'

He inclines his head at her.

'Well . . . not going to argue with that one. Anyway, when's your next shift?'

'Tomorrow evening. Got to be in by five.'

'Oh. I see.' Graham makes a show of glancing at the clock on the wall. 'Would you look at that – we have the whole night to ourselves.'

'OK, lover boy. Finish your meal first. I put love into that pasta—'

'Now it's time for me to put—'

'Don't!' Renee raises a finger at him while he smirks and mops up the last of his pasta sauce with a hunk of ciabatta.

Tuesday afternoon comes way too fast for Renee's liking, and before she knows it, she's out of the shower and pulling her whites from the dryer before carefully ironing them. It doesn't matter that they'll be dirty again soon – having your whites as crisp and pristine as possible is a mark of pride. She nods at herself in the mirror.

Go get 'em, girl.

When she arrives at NOVA, she can immediately tell there's a frisson in the air; a kind of charge that hasn't been palpable since she started. As she stashes her coat away, Bethany bustles out. She doesn't look unhappy, but she doesn't look relaxed either.

'Evening, Ren.'

'Evening . . . Is everything OK?'

'Everything's fine,' Bethany says. 'I just thought it best to let you know now that Chef Gracie is in tonight.'

'What?' Renee stutters as a cloud of butterflies takes flight in her chest.

'Well, it is her restaurant.'

'Yeah, I get that, but I thought she was away?'

'She was. And now she's back again. You'll get used to that.' Bethany reaches out and fusses a little with Renee's collar. 'Q's just informed me that she'll be cooking for royalty tonight, which is the main reason she's in. It's up to us to serve the rest of the menu. All you have to do is work exactly as you have been, and if she asks you to do anything, do it. OK?'

Renee blows out a tense breath and nods.

'You're going to be fine, kid. Now get your game face on and get in there.'

Renee throws her shoulders back and tries again to settle her nerves, striding into the kitchen with what she hopes is confidence.

The change in atmosphere is even more noticeable in here. Both Martin and Roy are setting up their stations. Roy gives her a nod and Martin mouths, 'You OK?' She nods in reply.

'Where is she?' Renee whispers as she reaches for a chopping board.

'Not seen her yet,' Martin whispers back.

'Then why are we whispering?'

'It's called the Fitzgerald Effect. You'll get used to it.'

'Where's Josh?'

'Not here yet either. You know what he's like.'

And Renee does. Not having had any advance warning, he clearly thinks tonight is going to be a regular Tuesday. Poor Josh.

Renee spends a moment reading through her instructions. She doesn't want to be caught unprepared, so she gathers her ingredients from the various pantries. As always, veg prep comes first, so she busies herself with trimming the carrots. They're one of the smaller varieties, valued for their sweetness and golden, rather than orange, colour. There's also what feels like a metric ton of them, so she's going to have to really get her head down if she's going to finish on time.

No one announces Gracie Fitzgerald's arrival in the kitchen. They don't need to. The moment she strides in, the whole atmosphere noticeably shifts. The temperature in the room drops. There is no hearty 'All right, love?' from Martin; no shy smiles from Roy. Only Bethany is afforded any kind of recognition, and that's a short, tight nod.

Although Martin's right and she is *tiny* – no more than five foot three, maybe four at a push – Gracie Fitzgerald's aura is anything but. Her hair – cut short and bleached almost white – and the slash of red lipstick on her thin lips both add to her sense of ice queen supremacy. That buzz Renee felt in the air as she entered the kitchen only intensifies as Gracie prowls past them, sparing each a mere second before moving on, leaving Renee feeling as though all her nerves are raw and exposed.

To her surprise, Gracie's set-up is in the corner of the kitchen. Usually, executive chefs like to be at the centre of things so they can set the example and lead from the front. In reality, this is usually a euphemism for 'everyone can bask in my greatness', and while no one argues that watching a top-level chef working isn't worthwhile, it can feel a little bit over the top when you work with them every day.

Gracie, it would seem, is the antithesis of this, and Renee finds herself liking the chef for it. No grandstanding – and not because she isn't confident, but because she doesn't need it. She knows she's the best, and that's enough. It's a lesson a few of the more aggressive chefs choose to ignore. Plus, her set-up is right in front of her personal freezer, meaning she can grab her ingredients and work without getting in anyone's way. Renee doubts this is to do with any form of professional altruism and more to do with the chef guarding her recipes.

She watches as Gracie selects her pans and knives from what Renee guesses is her personal stash, probably locked away in her own cold pantry. The huge cleaver in particular catches Renee's attention. It looks like it belongs on a blood-soaked table in a butcher's basement rather than a top-end restaurant. It's almost as long as Gracie's forearm, but she runs it along a steel with the practised ease of someone who's sliced just about every meat there is to offer in the trade. She selects a fat white onion from a pile, tests the cleaver's weight, then brings it down sharply, slicing it in two, seemingly without effort. It takes the onion a second to fall into perfectly symmetrical halves. A slight ghost of a smile appears on the chef's lips – like she's undertaken something particularly satisfying.

Renee, mesmerized as Gracie shreds the onion so thinly it resembles a book falling open, realizes she's finally going to witness a true genius at work. A woman – no, *the* woman – who didn't so much break through the glass ceiling as smash it to smithereens, eating up her competition as if they were nothing more than an amuse-bouche and leaving no challengers in her wake. In Renee's eyes, Gracie is the living definition of a queen sitting on a well-deserved throne – only rather than being made of wood and gold, hers is made of all the men who tried to hold her back. And yet, even with what Lola would call her 'fangirling', a sting of anxiety prickles in her chest. This is it. No more hiding. She's either good enough or she isn't. This is the final test.

Everyone except Renee has their heads down, studiously attending to their assigned prep. She realizes far too late that Chef Gracie is watching her. In a slight panic, she goes back to furiously julienning what now feels like a Sisyphean amount of carrots, ready for a dish Renee doesn't fully understand yet – and maybe never will. She already knows that executive chefs are like ancient aunties: proud hoarders of secret family spice mixes that only get shared on deathbeds, and only then if the recipient promises never to tell Denzel's wife, because she insulted Granni's oxtail thirty years ago and no one has forgotten the audacity—

The soft click of kitten heels on tile breaks through Renee's thoughts. Gracie is no longer at her station. She's now behind Renee – Renee can see her reflected in the polished metal of her countertop, arms crossed, head tilted to one side. The little hairs on the back of Renee's neck stand up. She doesn't dare look over her shoulder. Instead, she keeps slicing, even faster now, to prove she is worthy. Thin slivers of yellow suddenly stain red, followed by a sharp pain. It takes Renee a couple of seconds to realize she's julienned her fingertips. Behind her, the arbiter of her entire future career sighs heavily. She braces herself for the inevitable earbashing she's about to receive.

'You'd better clean that up,' Gracie says. Her voice is soft – no histrionics, no egotistical ranting about how Renee's wasted so much food and what a fucking idiot she is. Instead, it projects a simple, quiet disappointment.

As it turns out, there are worse things than getting yelled at.

Off-kilter, Renee goes to scrape the carrots and the little curls of her own skin into the waste bin, but upon hearing a disapproving *hmm*, she stops and dares to give Gracie an enquiring look.

Chef takes a step closer, leans in and murmurs, 'These are heritage golden honey carrots. Do you know how many farms grow heritage golden honey carrots?'

Her voice is deeper than Renee remembered from the videocall, and as smooth as caramel. At first, Renee doesn't answer, thinking the question is rhetorical. But then Gracie narrows her eyes, and in a panic, Renee realizes that – oh, hell – she is indeed expecting an answer.

'Uh, not many, Chef?'

'One. Only one farm in the entire country grows them. We are their sole customer. You could go to any other restaurant in the country – no, in the world – and never taste a golden honey carrot.' She picks up a whole carrot and gives it what Renee can only describe as a loving look. 'Every single one is precious.'

Renee's gut twists, her cheeks hot with shame.

'I'm sorry, Chef. I—'

Gracie stares at her, her face passive. 'My philosophy stands.'

Blood drips from the tips of Renee's fingers, pooling on the board, collecting in the small gaps between the chopped vegetables.

'But—' she begins, unsure what Gracie means. Until it dawns on her.

Nose to tail. Nothing is wasted.

'Yes, Chef,' she whispers.

Gracie nods and glides back to her own station, where she picks up her cleaver and continues with her prep.

Renee slides her carrots into a colander. It takes everything she has to ignore her training. She knows they should be in the bin. While it is often said that chefs put their blood, sweat and tears into their creations, most people don't take that literally. No one in their right mind would serve bloodstained food. But she can't disobey Chef – not the first time she's actually working with her. She glances at Martin, then Roy, but they're both busy studiously ignoring her. Eventually, Bethany pauses her furious dicing of raw chicken livers and slides over to the sink next to Renee, pretending that she needs to wash her hands.

'Just rinse them,' she murmurs.

'What?'

'Just do it.' Bethany marches back to her bench and resumes her work.

With no other choice, Renee does as she's told. Maybe this is part of the appeal for the upper class – transgression has always been popular with the elite. They're paying through the nose for this; they'd probably find the addition of a little human blood avant-garde. Not that it makes her feel any better as she rinses the carrots, stomach rolling as she watches her shed blood turn pink as it swirls down the drain.

No time for conscience, Renee. Just do as you're told. You can have personal standards when you own one of the best restaurants on earth. Until then, shut up and wash the carrots.

The water is biting cold. She picks through the slim golden batons with her uninjured hand, making sure no incriminating slivers of skin remain on them. Her fingers throb, but the cuts are clean. There's a basic first aid kit mounted to the wall at the end of every bench and Renee scuttles over hers to grab a plaster. As she does, she notices Gracie leave her station again and head to her personal freezer. She selects a key from a small bunch hooked to her belt loop and unlocks the massive door. It opens with an audible hiss, like the whole thing is pressurized. Then she steps inside.

The door closes behind her.

Renee stops in her tracks and swallows the panic rising in her throat. She whips her head towards her fellow chefs, but none of them seem perturbed. Did Gracie really just do that? She must know the rules about walk-in freezers. But to Renee's surprise, no one rushes to re-open the door. Everyone carries on as if this is completely normal. Again, Bethany looks up and gives her a little shake of her head. Another of Chef's idiosyncrasies, then. That's her freezer, so she must know if it opens from the inside. In fact, Renee's sure she probably had it made specially. It means she can work with her personally sourced ingredients – the ones that are somehow too precious or too expensive for anyone else to touch – in peace. It's like Bethany said: no one else goes in. No one else uses those ingredients. And no one, under any circumstances, preps those dishes.

Renee is learning another important rule at NOVA: know your place.

Still, she can't help glancing nervously at the freezer, half expecting to hear Gracie's fists pounding against the inside of the door, begging for someone to let her out.

About ten minutes later, Renee is finishing up her carrot prep when Gracie finally emerges, pushing a medical-looking metal cart. On it is a slab of meat and a Pyrex bowl filled with water, a white ball floating in it. Renee doesn't recognize the cut, though the colour and fat content suggest veal. It features often on NOVA's menu, and she's had to refresh her rusty skills on it, given it wasn't really served when she was working at Chickadees. As for the pale, lumpen thing bobbing in the bowl – it kind of looks like a cauliflower? But that makes no sense. Why would Gracie soak a whole cauliflower in the cold room? It takes her a few seconds to realize exactly what the lump is after Gracie fishes it out.

It isn't a cauliflower.

It isn't any kind of vegetable at all.

It's a brain.

Renee's gorge rises. She swallows hard. No way on God's green earth is she going to puke in a Michelin-starred kitchen – especially not over an ingredient. Because that's all it is: an ingredient. Brains are considered a delicacy in some cultures. Nothing weird about eating them. Meat is meat, after all. Even offal is perfectly edible. At least that's what she tells herself.

She tries to shake off her discomfort and gets back to the vegetable prep, hoping it might distract her from what Gracie is doing.

It doesn't work.

Judging by its size, Renee doesn't think it's a calf brain. Maybe cow? Pig? That's brawn, right? She remembers her dad complaining about coming back from school to find a whole pig's head in the sink, ready for Granni to make brawn. Grampa loved it, but

Dad could never bring himself to try it – watching his mother plop the whole thing in a big pan of salted water, boil it for a good couple of hours, then split the skull and scoop out the gelatinous insides to mould into a kind of loaf she'd later slice up and put in sandwiches was enough. Back in Granni's day, no one was prepping a whole pig's head because they thought it was a prime ingredient, though. No, back then it was because it was cheap and people had a family to feed. But that's just the way it goes. A lot of 'peasant food' is now highly prized, which is why so-called cheap cuts don't exist any more . . .

Gracie looks up, as if sensing her scrutiny.

The ice in her eyes makes Renee immediately drop her gaze and start chopping furiously again. Shit. *Shit.* That's the second time Gracie has caught her staring rather than working. She still has loads of prep, and not just the carrots.

'Hey.'

Maybe if she keeps chopping, Gracie will realize that she's serious about working in this kitchen – deadly serious. That she's not a fuck-up, she's not out of her depth, she can do this. Just breathe, keep chopping and prove your worth—

'Renee?'

Balls.

'Join me. Bring the carrots with you.'

Renee dares to look up. Gracie quirks an eyebrow. Renee has no idea if this is a good sign or not.

Every eye is on her as she makes her way to Gracie's bench. She tries to read Bethany's expression as she passes, but the sous is masking too well. Clutching her colander of carrots, Renee braces herself for a dressing-down. But it doesn't come. Instead, Gracie smiles softly. Somehow, this freaks Renee out more than a scowl.

'Nervous?' she asks.

'A little, Chef,' Renee replies, her voice barely above a whisper.

'Good. Use those nerves. They will feed your hunger. Have you ever prepared brain before?'

'Uh, no,' Renee says, slightly horrified.

'Shame. People are so squeamish these days. In the past, people appreciated what they ate. Using every part of the animal is a form of respect. Plus, when prepared correctly, it's quite delicious.'

The brain sits atop her board, glistening in the harsh light. Gracie caresses it like it's her pet. For the first time since she's heard about it, Renee is starting to have positive feelings towards Gracie's 'no one tastes my food but me' policy.

'Everything within a living body is edible,' Gracie says. 'There should be no waste. All organs, muscles – even bones and teeth – have a use in the kitchen. Our ancestors understood this. In times past, the brain was prized, alongside the heart. They are, to use your words, the control centre of the body and the body's workhorse respectively. When we eat animal products, we are doing more than just consuming protein. We are allowing the energy of another to nourish us – body and soul.' She picks up her knife. 'Watch carefully.'

Renee swallows and nods, not quite trusting herself to speak. While she is getting to see one of the world's best chefs work up close, she can't help but feel this is a punishment for the carrots.

Gracie picks up a lobe of brain gently in one hand.

'This is delicate work. If you are too hasty, or use too much force, you will mangle it. Part of the joy of eating brain is its wonderful texture, so you must ensure you do everything you can to preserve it.'

Feeling a little faint, Renee watches as Gracie expertly peels away a grey-tinged membrane. Then she carefully flips the brain over. It quivers as she inspects the jellied lump, occasionally cutting out bits of it.

'You see these tubes here? You need to remove them.' Gracie

lifts her knife and, right on the tip, in a small pool of viscous liquid, a grey cylindrical structure clings. Renee wrestles with her stomach again. 'These are not pleasant to eat. They are quite rubbery and can make the dish taste a little bitter. But if they are dried, they make a pleasant seasoning. Like sumac, but a little . . . meatier.'

She finishes the rest of the brain with an ease that's almost concerning.

'Now the lobes are fully prepared, we place them in a fresh bowl of acidulated water. This helps preserve their texture and moisture before we season and cook them. They will be caramelized and eaten with an onion jus, and a julienne of heritage golden honey carrots.' Gracie straightens up, and even though Renee is taller than her, she still manages to look down her nose at her. 'Plant or animal, we must respect our ingredients. We pay them full attention.'

Renee's cheeks heat as she nods.

'Yes, Chef. I understand, Chef.'

Gracie gives her an appraising look, then leans over the bench, her voice low.

'You will get much further using this' – she gestures towards her head – 'than this.' She taps her chest, where her heart is. 'Never forget that.'

'I won't, Chef.'

'Good. Oh, and Renee?'

'Yes, Chef?'

'The carrots. Don't let your conscience eat you up. We all make mistakes. Just make sure you don't repeat them.'

'Of course, Chef. Thank you, Chef.'

Gracie dips her hand into the colander and selects a sliver of carrot. She inspects it carefully.

'Good technique,' she says.

Smiling, she pops the carrot into her mouth and chews.

SEVENTEEN

Weirdly, this service is quieter than Renee had anticipated. While Tuesdays are usually relatively soft days in the restaurant trade, it looks like Q has been selective when it comes to bookings. Renee likes to think it's so no one gets overwhelmed, but it's more likely the important guests have paid extra to ensure the randoms can't come in and gawp at them. But even though they technically have fewer covers tonight, Gracie works with such an intensity that Renee finds it hard to keep up with her.

Renee's primarily covering starters, non-signature dishes and sides this evening, alongside Martin. Bethany is, as usual, running the pass, but given she has less to supervise, she does take over a few of the mains as and when she can, if it looks like they might be swamped. Roy, forever the pastry wizard, is there to round off the night with one of his succulent desserts.

So far, so normal.

Only, it isn't. There's a rippling undercurrent of frenetic energy running between the chefs, as if they're marionettes and Gracie is pulling their strings taut by being in the kitchen. Renee can see a vein pulsating under the skin of Martin's forehead, while Bethany's foot bounces like a rabbit's in the rare moments she stands still. And no matter how hard she tries, Renee still can't get over Gracie eating the carrot. The way she'd looked at her as she did it. She knows exactly what happened to those carrots. And sure, Renee rinsed them well, but she can't shake the feeling that Gracie is testing her in some way. But what that way is, she has no idea.

Then there's Gracie's attitude to her own dishes. She isn't just overprotective, she's borderline obsessed with them. It turns out her no-tasting rule wasn't an exaggeration. In fact, it's more than that. It's not just the tasting, but the preparation of signature ingredients and dressing of plates, too. Literally everything that comes out of her personal freezer is touched by Gracie, and Gracie alone. She even deals with the scraps herself, diligently separating them into small bowls to be recycled later. Renee finds this unsettling. What's her end game? Every other chef Renee has worked under always insisted that she tasted everything, whether she was responsible for it or not. That way, she'd get a feel for the general vibe of the restaurant and know exactly what the dishes that elevate the dining experience are supposed to taste like. Every decent restaurant runs to a theme, be it classical, fusion, cultural, or even something as dumb as colour, and the chefs usually want their protégés to know their food inside and out. She once worked in a restaurant themed around the colour yellow. The head chef there was clearly trying to jump on the turmeric-is-a-superfood bandwagon and he'd insist on putting it in everything. He called it 'sunshine food', which should tell you everything you need to know about the guy. In the end, Renee only lasted a month.

The thing is, Gracie is the polar opposite of what Renee has come to expect from an executive chef. She's fine with them tasting their own dishes, made from ingredients stored in the general pantries, but every now and again she'll walk past one of them, small spoon in hand, dipping in, tasting. Renee quickly learned that if she left without saying anything, you were doing fine. However, if you weren't . . .

'Joshua.' Gracie's voice is a menacing purr. She doesn't shout. She doesn't need to. 'This is over-seasoned. I've told you before, the black salt is pungent, and you should take care with it.'

If it had been anyone else, they would murmur a quick 'yes,

Chef', and reach for something acidic to neutralize the saltiness. But not Josh.

'Oh, for fuck's sake. Who cares if it's got a little bit more salt in it than usual? Everything's salty these days. It's a thing.'

The whole kitchen falls silent. After his outburst at Renee, she thought he might keep his head down for a bit. How wrong she was.

'Oh, so what you're saying is, you know better than me?' Gracie murmurs, clasping her hands behind her back. Renee hears Bethany draw a sharp breath. 'I see.'

She takes a step towards him. Josh takes a step back, proving that while he's an arrogant little shit, he's not entirely stupid.

'Nah, nah, I'm not saying that. I'm saying, uh,' he stutters, desperately searching for an easy out and coming up empty as Gracie stands in silence, allowing him to flounder.

'There is a reason my recipes include seasoning quantities. For that amount of sauce, it needs two teaspoons. Either you do not know what a teaspoon is, or you think you know my recipe better than I do.'

Gracie's whole demeanour is one of icy calm. Josh towers over her, but her gaze just about pins him to the wall. Renee can see the cogs spinning in his head – this isn't how it usually goes – and braces herself. But rather than the inevitable outburst, Josh stares at his feet and goes back to stirring the broth.

'Renee,' Gracie says, without looking at her. 'Come here.'

Renee freezes. 'Chef?'

'Come here. Bring a spoon.'

Renee scrabbles for a teaspoon, her coordination suddenly sloppy. She swallows hard and tells herself to get it together. It's fine. It's all fine.

At last, she manages to make her hands work and picks up one of the scattered spoons, then trots over to Gracie, stealing a glance at her.

Gracie doesn't look her way, but instead continues to stare at Josh.

'Chef, would you please taste this?'

'Yes, Chef,' Renee says, her nerves spiking. She dips her teaspoon into the mixture and takes a moment to roll the sauce around her mouth.

'What do you think?'

'It's very impressive, but it is over-salted.'

'And? What makes it impressive?'

Renee glances at Josh, who is now staring at the ceiling, refusing to make eye contact with anyone.

'Um, the depth of flavour in the stock base is incredible. It's a beef-based stock, but lighter in profile, so I'm thinking maybe veal. There's a back note of thyme and rich peppercorn, plus a smooth but light red wine – not one of the heavier ones, as that would overpower the delicate flavour of the veal. Of course, if it was beef stock, it would stand up much better to a heavier wine, but this isn't about setting up ingredients to knock the diner's taste buds into submission. This is about the intricacies of the ingredients rather than their power. But it's definitely over-salted, and it lacks acidity.'

'Thank you, Chef. You may go back to your bench now.'

'Yes, Chef,' Renee all but mumbles, and scuttles back.

Gracie takes another step closer to Josh, staring up at him, challenging him to look at her. Josh tries to match her but fails miserably as he folds and blinks within seconds.

'So, Joshua. Over-salted and lacking in something. What did Renee say was lacking?'

'I dunno,' he mutters, and again Renee is sharply reminded of the boys at school dragged into the Head's office once all their bravado had fled.

'Renee?' Gracie continues to stare unblinkingly like a shark, leaving Renee wondering exactly how she learned to do that.

'Acidity, Chef,' Renee says.

'And what is the most common form of acidity used in cooking, Joshua?'

Josh shrugs again and mumbles, 'Vinegar?'

Gracie pulls the kind of face one might give a dog who has unexpectedly managed to perform a trick.

'It's a good guess. But, sadly, incorrect. Renee?'

'Lemon, Chef.'

'Indeed. Lemon.'

There is a bowl of lemons at the end of every bench, along with salt and pepper: the true chef's trinity. Gracie reaches for one. She doesn't pick up a lemon reamer, though. She doesn't even pick up a knife. Instead, she grasps the fruit in her bare hand, holds it over the cooking pot and crushes it. Juice and pulp run between her fingers as she grinds the lemon of all its innards. She then gestures for Josh to give it a stir.

At no time does she break eye contact with him before she produces another clean spoon and dips it in.

'Much more palatable.'

The whole spectacle feels like some kind of threat. Josh clearly thinks so too, given the way his Adam's apple bobs in his throat. That such a small woman could crush an entire fruit in her hand as easily as anyone else might crumple a finished crisp packet or empty Coke can? Terrifying. Impressive, yes – but mainly terrifying.

Gracie gives him one last look, then turns and returns to her station, continuing with her lesson.

'What you have to remember, young Joshua, is that my ingredients are hard to come by, whereas rich uncles and their nephews who think they might like to play at cheffing? They're a dime a dozen. Follow my recipes. Do I make myself clear?'

'Yes, Chef,' Josh mumbles.

'What was that?'

'Yes! Chef!'

'Much better.'

Gracie picks up her knife and continues with her work, and everyone begins to breathe again.

That is, until Q stalks into the room and over to Gracie, with the grace of a dancer and a face like thunder. He has a low but clearly urgent word with her. The chef, forever calm, nods, then shrugs.

'They've brought someone extra? Someone not on the list? Who?'

Q's voice is so quiet no one else can hear him, but whatever he's just said clearly amuses Gracie, who lets out a bark of laughter.

'Ha! It'll be fine. It's only one cover. I should be able to accommodate that. But they have to understand that their meal may be delayed. Poor planning on their part does not constitute an emergency on mine.'

'Of course. I shall inform them,' Q says.

'You know what to do if they make a fuss.'

Q cracks a very rare smile. 'Indeed I do.'

Renee has no idea what Q means by that, but she absolutely does not want to know what him taking care of a fussy customer looks like. There's something inherently scary about the maître d'; it isn't that he's big, or strong, or physically imposing in any way – it's more that he projects a distinct aura of not taking any shit from anyone, ever. He's a lot like Gracie in that way. Maybe that's why they've worked together for so long.

Whatever hardened them to the world clearly bonded them too, because they rarely speak but always seem to know what the other is doing – leaving Renee wondering if there's more to their relationship than just work. Not that it's any of her business, of course.

Still, she's curious.

As soon as diners arrive, the orders come flying in. Despite her being here for a blink of an eye in the grand scheme of things, Renee and Martin are in complete synchronicity – constantly checking with each other about timings, the use of utensils, even stepping around each other as if they're lifelong dance partners, never on one another's toes as they quickly cook their dishes to order. This is the bit Renee lives for: the heat; the frantic energy; the delicious scents of herbs, spice and caramelizing meat.

That is, until Gracie starts pan-frying her brains.

It's not that they smell bad. They don't. If anything, they smell sweet, with a hint of nuttiness. Much like the veal sweetbreads she had to cook on her first shift, the brains are probably more delicious than people think they are, but that still doesn't stop Renee's stomach from churning each time Gracie cooks a new portion, even though there are only two adventurous diners.

Are they adventurous, or are they forced to eat what Gracie prepares no matter what it is?

This is another thing that confuses her. Gracie's dishes aren't on the main menu. At all. So how do people choose what they want to eat? Are they sent the menu in advance, or does Gracie choose for them? And how does she decide who gets to eat the signature dishes? Not that she's questioning Gracie – whatever the system is, it clearly works for her – just wondering why and how this system came into play.

With her starters ready, Gracie takes them up to the pass but doesn't hand them over to Bethany. Instead, the wait staff are there, ready to pick up the dishes. That's when Renee notices the latest peculiarity of the night. When the waiters take Gracie's dishes, they do so wearing white cotton gloves. That might not seem weird if they wear them all the time as part of their uniform, but they don't. Until today, Renee's never seen anyone wearing gloves. What does Gracie think they're going to do – get a blob of sauce on their hand and lick it up, breaking her most sacred covenant of not tasting her dishes? As much as Renee tries to brush it off, she can't help but think that it probably is something along those lines. Not that she can dwell on it. She has four duck breasts to perfectly season, pan-fry and dress.

The breasts are fat and pink as Renee sears them skin-side down first. The slashes she made into the skin allows the thick layer of fat underneath to render, and it isn't long before they're sizzling. She knows the recipe for perfectly crisp skin is in patience and trust – too many people worry about burning the skin, so they flip the breasts over before the fat has had time to melt. She adds a few star anise, a knob of butter, and a final grind of salt and pepper into the mix while she waits for that golden moment between under- and overcooked before flipping the breasts over and sealing all the flavour in. She's surprised to find her hands shaking slightly. Renee thought her nerves from Gracie being here had calmed down, but evidently her body is telling her otherwise.

Calm down, you're doing fine.

A few minutes later, she reaches for her teaspoon. Of course, she can't sample the duck itself, but she can make a judgement from the juices in the pan. She closes her eyes, savouring the rich taste of duck fat, the sweet nuttiness of the butter and the slightly liquorice tang of the star anise before adding a final squeeze of lemon. The duck is soon ready for resting, allowing her to deglaze the pan with some wine and quickly toss in some Swiss chard. Once this is ready, Martin lays out four plates, to which he adds a good spoonful of polenta. Renee then tops it with her chard, and finally goes back to the duck, slicing it on the board to create an attractive fan.

'Well done, Ren,' Martin says. 'That duck looks perfect. Almost a shame to hide it with sauce, eh?'

Renee grins as Martin spoons his spiced plum sauce over her sliced duck.

'I don't know,' she says. 'I have a feeling I could drink that sauce.'

Martin slings a slightly sweaty arm around her neck and gives her a very quick hug.

'We are the dream team,' he says with a laugh, before turning his attention back to his next run of orders.

'Oi!' Roy says, looking back over his shoulder. 'Are y'forgetting someone?'

'Aww, you're in the dream team, too, Roy,' Martin adds.

'Aye.'

Bethany marches in.

'OK, that's two more duck, a scallop and a terrine. Roy – two apples, two ganaches. Everyone get that?'

'Yes, Chef!' they all bark in unison, while Gracie silently observes them from her station. She then picks up the meat – Renee assumes it's veal – portions it into two identical steaks, and lowers it carefully into a marinade bath. Renee notices that she has left the tiniest sliver of meat on her board and can't help but be impressed. Talk about meticulous. Although it does seem a bit odd. Why not incorporate that into the steaks, rather than waste it?

Renee shrugs to herself and refocuses on her duck. It's Gracie's kitchen; she can do what she likes. But when Renee looks up again, she notices that the sliver of meat Gracie cut is missing – and that Gracie looks as if she might be chewing.

EIGHTEEN

'Hey, who's up for a drink?'

Unsurprisingly, it's Martin asking. Both Roy and Bethany shake their heads. While the shift wasn't particularly busy, it was intense, and it's clear everyone's tired. Gracie is already long gone.

'Aww, guys . . . Ren, you wouldn't let a guy down, would you?'

'I dunno – I'm knackered.'

'Yeah, I know, but a nice little drinkie? Just the one – to let off some steam?'

He has a point. Maybe a drink is what she needs to quell the weird churning in her belly.

'OK, but hang on, I have to let my flatmate know.'

'Ask them to come!' Martin grins broadly. 'The more the merrier.'

Renee thinks about refusing, saying Lola might not be up for it, but who is she kidding? Lola is always up for anything when it comes to going out. Plus, she has a sneaking suspicion she and Martin will get on like a house on fire.

She quickly texts Lola, who doesn't disappoint. Renee tells her where they're going, and Lola informs her she'll be with them shortly. Her own shift has just ended, meaning she's not too far away.

Martin and Renee gather their stuff as Roy and Bethany bid them goodnight. Then, to their surprise, Josh hangs back.

'So where we going?' he asks.

'Uh, to Bar None?' Martin says, his confusion plain.

Anyone else might get the hint that they're not exactly welcome, but not Josh. He slings his coat on – a ridiculously puffy orange jacket that probably cost the same as her rent – and nods.

'OK, kids, come on – Mum needs to lock up,' Bethany says, jangling her keys at them. 'Out. And don't drink too much. No one likes a Tuesday Night Drunk.'

By the time Renee, Martin and Josh arrive at Bar None, Lola is already waiting. As soon as she spots Renee, she lifts her arms up and lets out a delighted bark of 'Ren!' before all but running over to her, smothering her in a huge hug.

'So, how did it go?' she asks. 'With the Big Boss, I mean.'

'Yeah, I guessed that's what you meant,' Renee replies, but before she can say anything else, Martin's there with a beaming smile. If anything, Renee's surprised he hasn't tried to get in on their hug.

'Hi! I'm Martin. You must be Lola?'

'Uh . . . yeah?' Lola says, clearly a little taken aback. 'And I'm guessing you're Martin, right? I've heard a lot about you.'

'Oh, only good stuff, I hope!' Martin says, feigning shyness.

'You're safe,' Lola says. 'Ren speaks very highly of you and your sauces.'

'Sup. I'm Josh.' Unlike Martin, Josh doesn't smile, but attempts to be cool and indifferent. Or at least, that's what Renee assumes he's aiming for. He really has no clue.

'Hey, yeah, maybe ease up on the podcasts, little man,' Lola says. Josh bristles, Martin winces and Renee just shrugs. If there's one thing Lola is good at, it's sniffing out fakes – something Josh is finding out the hard way.

People often underestimate Lola. Whether it's her East End accent or the fact that she looks like she should be on a budget version of *Love Island*, they often assume she's not that bright – something Lola uses to her advantage. Even Renee will admit that her first impression of Lola was that she was a bit of a chav, but she soon realized that appearances are misleading. In reality, Lola is a devastating combination of whip-smart and street-confident. Given Renee has already told her all about Josh . . . tonight should be entertaining, with a high possibility of Josh ending up in tears.

'Come on, then,' Lola says, clapping her hands like she's a primary school teacher chivvying a class. 'Let's get some drinks in.'

Let's get some drinks in.

It's a phrase Renee has learned to dread, because drinking with Lola only comes in two flavours: nice pint on a Sunday afternoon, and two-for-one cocktail insanity. And today isn't a Sunday . . .

'Wayhey!' Lola crows as she rejoins the three chefs with a drinks tray laden with violently coloured cocktails. 'One for you' – she passes an orange drink to Martin – 'one for the little man' – Josh scrunches his face up, but takes the proffered blue drink anyway, 'and one for my bestie, the chef extraordinaire!' She passes a pink drink to Renee, keeping the purple for herself.

'What is it?' Renee asks, having learned from bitter experience that you don't just drink something Lola gives you.

'It's a Pink Punk Fizz,' Lola says, before going back to sucking on her straw. 'God, these are a bit weak, aren't they? I could make better than this at home.'

'Why don't we do that, then? Go back to yours?' Josh says, still trying to convince everyone he's on top here.

'Sorry, no children allowed,' Lola says, holding her hand up to him.

'I don't know what this is,' Martin says, 'but it's bloody delicious. Anyway, cheers!' He raises his glass. 'To surviving another shift!'

'Hey,' Lola says, pretending to be insulted. 'What about me?'

'And to meeting Lola for the first time!' Martin adds. 'And to Ren for her first shift with Chef Fitzgerald! May there be many, many more.'

Renee chinks her glass against everyone else's. She can definitely drink to that.

At first, the night goes surprisingly well. Even Josh, while still obnoxious, isn't quite as odious as he is in the kitchen. He even buys a round for the group. For what feels like the first time in a while, Renee feels relaxed. Well, maybe not relaxed, but something bordering on it.

'And then Q says, "I don't care who you are, nor does anyone else here. If you wish to dine from the house menu, then you're more than welcome to try and book a table." And the look he gave him . . . We all thought he was going to kick off, but there was no way Q would tolerate that. He just kept staring until the guy left. It was mad.'

'And who was this?' Lola asks.

'I probably shouldn't say.' Martin leans forward, lowers his voice and replies in a juicy tone, 'Leo Frensham.'

'What – that guy from *EastEnders*? Did *I'm a Celebrity* a couple of years ago and then got upset that no one remembered him?'

Martin sits back, looking satisfied.

'That's him. Awful man. But that's why we have Q. He's not a big guy, but he's still terrifying.'

Renee giggles at that, then takes a sip of her fresh drink. She does a double take at her cocktail – this one is definitely stronger than the first.

'I honestly thought he was going to tell me to piss off when I arrived for my interview,' she says. 'What's his deal?'

'No one knows. I thought for a while that he might be, you know, with Gracie?' Martin says. 'But it's nothing like that. They're more like siblings. Or mob bosses. The phrase "thick as thieves" comes to mind, if you know what I mean.'

'So . . . he's a criminal?' Josh asks.

'No.' Martin rolls his eyes. 'I mean, he could be, but I doubt it. It's more like he'll do anything for Gracie. And not because he's in love with her or anything. It's the deepest loyalty I've ever seen – though I have no idea what goes on in his head.

'No one does,' Renee says with a smirk. 'Jesus, I need to slow down on these.'

'No, you don't,' Lola says. 'You're just a lightweight.'

'Yeah, well, you can have the rest of this. If I have any more, I'll be on track for a massive hangover tomorrow.' She pushes her drink towards her friend.

'Ah, come on, Ren. Don't be a killjoy,' Josh says.

'Look, kid, I'm older than you by more years than I feel comfortable with, and I'm going to tell you a secret. As you get older, the hangovers get more brutal, and your tolerance goes right down.'

'So what she's saying, right, is you have to work on keeping up that tolerance, or you end up a boring bitch who worries about things like hangovers,' Lola says, and Renee laughs. 'Anyway, I have something to ask you guys, right? We have this new hire—'

'Context, Lola,' Renee says when both Martin and Josh look confused.

'Oh, right. Yeah, of course.' She picks up Renee's drink and takes a gulp. 'I work at Carluccio's. I'm, like, on the wait staff there, and a couple of weeks ago we took on this new guy, and he used to work a NOVA—'

'Hang on,' Renee says. 'You never said anything about this.'

'Yeah, well, I didn't think it would help.'

'What do you mean by that?'

'Just . . . I didn't want to ruin you getting this job.'

'Ruin it? Why would you telling me about an ex-employee ruin it?'

At this, Martin pulls an uncomfortable face.

'I think I know where you're going with this,' he says. 'Is his name Levi?'

'Yeah, it is. I mean, he's a bit of a prick, if I'm honest – definitely thinks he's better than the rest of us. Keeps saying he's only taken this job as a filler until he can get back into fine dining, but . . . is it true?'

'Is what true?' Renee says. 'Guys?'

Before Martin and Josh can answer, Lola jumps in.

'He said that he was sacked cos he didn't wear these gloves when he was serving Gracie Fitzgerald's plates? He ushally . . . I mean, usually . . .' She says the word slowly, trying to hide the fact that she's now slurring – something Renee finds more than a little alarming. While she might be feeling a little tipsy after a couple of drinks, Lola can drink almost anyone under the table. 'He was a regular waiter, doing the normal stuff, but one of the others who'd been there for ages couldn't make it – family emergency or something, not important – but it meant they were one down, so he stepped up as he's had loads of exshepience.' Lola shakes her head and takes another gulp from her drink, as if that might help her clear her mind. 'And he said he was more than willing, but then they made him wear these, like, little white cotton gloves? And – and the chef, right – she was really intense with him, saying that he had to be careful – like he was gonna throw the plate across the room or something. Anyway, to cut a long story short, he took the gloves off cos they were, like, really hot, and Gracie went mental, accusing him of secretly trying to taste her food – like he was going to, I dunno, stick his finger in the gravy or something.'

'Oh, hell, yeah – I remember that,' Martin says, sounding a lot more sober than Lola. 'Gracie is really specific about these things. She makes it crystal clear that you have to follow her rules, and if you don't, you're out.'

'Yeah, but, surely that's a bit of an overreaction?' Lola says.

Her eyes are looking a little unfocused now, much to Renee's growing alarm. 'He didn't, like, steal anything, or piss in the soup. Soon as I said my mate got a job there, he said, good luck – they're mental as fuck. All of 'em. Madder than a box of frogs.'

Renee catches Martin's eye. He's bristling a little, and she doesn't blame him.

'I'm sure he only said that because he's bitter,' Renee says, hoping to smooth things over.

'It's OK,' Martin says, but then Lola sits back, blinking and bleary-eyed. Did she drink before the rest of them arrived?

'He said he got his revenge, though. Posted some shitty reviews on Glassdoor and the like. Trolled the NOVA account online. Y'know, stuff like that. Fuck me, what's in that?' She's slurring badly now, and both Renee and Martin catch her before she slumps over the table. Josh, on the other hand, just sits there, looking vaguely horrified.

'Oh, shit,' Renee says, a sharp stab of panic chasing away her own fuzziness. She'd only had one sip of that drink, but Lola's near enough finished it. 'What the hell?'

'Must have been spiked,' Martin says grimly. 'But who?'

'I don't know,' Renee says. 'Josh, you got this round in. Who served you?'

Josh shrugs. 'I dunno – that guy over there?' He points in the general direction of the bar.

'Right.' Martin balls his fists and starts to get up, clearly ready to confront the bar staff.

'No, Martin, leave it. It's not worth it,' Renee says. 'I have to get Lola home, and the last thing I need is for you to get into a fight.'

Martin blows out an angry sigh.

'OK, all right. I can call an Uber,' he says, pulling out his phone. 'Where are you going?'

Renee is about to give him her address, but the thought of

looking after Lola alone terrifies her. What if something happens? She gets worse, or chokes, or—

'I'm OK!' Lola pronounces – then slumps again.

'Oh, Christ. Um, Lennox Gardens, Chelsea.'

'Chelsea? I thought you lived in Brixton?'

'It's my boyfriend's place, and it's closer. I'm just going to ring him.' It's clear the bar staff are now beginning to look concerned, and she's in no doubt that they're on the cusp of getting kicked out. 'We need to get Lola out of here.'

Martin's jaw tightens, but rather than make a scene, he nods and slings one of Lola's arms around his shoulders. Renee picks up her phone and bag, and Josh trails behind them, looking a little annoyed.

'Look, I'm going to go,' he says. 'Hope she's OK.' He gestures to Lola.

'You could stay and help,' Martin snaps. 'She's clearly been drugged.'

'Uh, nah. I can't do sick, bro. And she looks like she's ready to hurl.'

With that, Josh takes off, never once looking back.

'Arsehole,' Martin mutters as a car pulls up.

At first, the driver argues that he doesn't want some drunk bitch in his car, but Martin's having none of that. As lovely and gentle as he usually is, he's also the very definition of a bear: huge and hairy, and, as Renee finds out, terrifying when he's riled up. In the end, the driver backs down, allowing them to manhandle Lola into the back of the cab and get her home.

NINETEEN

'What the hell happened?'

Graham is waiting on the pavement when the Uber pulls up outside his place. He does a little double take as Martin climbs out first, but doesn't question him as he helps both Lola and Renee out of the car.

Martin notices Graham's confusion and quickly introduces himself.

Graham fumbles for a reply as he focuses on looping one of Lola's arms around his shoulders to steady her.

Renee assures Martin that she's OK – he can go home. For a moment, she thinks he's going to refuse, but he then nods ruefully and bids them all goodnight. As he ducks back into the Uber, he makes Renee promise to text him in the morning.

While Lola and Graham don't always get on, his concern for her is plain. Her eyes flutter as he lifts her up, cradling her like she's a baby, and struggles upstairs to his flat. He then takes her directly into his bedroom and lays her on the bed.

'You two can stay in here tonight,' he says. 'I'll sleep in the guest room.'

'Are you sure?' Renee asks, even though she already knows the answer.

'Of course. We're going to have to make sure she isn't sick in her sleep. What did she have?'

Renee sighs heavily and sits down gently next to Lola.

'I don't know. We only had a couple. They were cocktails, but even then . . .'

Graham nods and bites his bottom lip – a sure sign he's worried. He's been out drinking with Lola before – he knows her tolerance.

'Do we need to take her to hospital?' Renee asks. 'Just to make sure?'

'I mean, we could, but in all honesty, unless she's overdosing there's not a lot they can do.'

If there's one person who knows what overdosing looks like, it's Graham. He lost his best friend to drugs, which is why he's so straight-laced now. He picks up Lola's wrist and takes her pulse.

'It's a little elevated, but her breathing seems fine.' He sits on the bed next to Renee.

'I don't get it,' Renee says, but even as she speaks, doubt gnaws at her. Because she does get it. At the time, she thought it was her own piss-poor tolerance for alcohol. Now she's hit by the cold realization that whoever did this meant to do it to her.

She recounts the night to Graham – her shift, Martin asking them all out for a drink, her contacting Lola. Everything. How she felt fine until the second cocktail. How Lola teased her and started downing Renee's drink herself.

How moments later, Lola was a total mess, unable even to hold her head up.

'Jesus. These perverts.' Graham shakes his head in disgust. 'Time to go back to only drinking from sealed bottles again.'

'Yeah. I was thinking the same. But why me? I know Lola was the one who ended up drinking it, but . . .'

'I don't think there's any logic to it,' Graham says. 'Other than two pretty women out drinking.'

'I know, but we were with Martin and Josh. The bar wasn't heaving by any standard. Why would anyone risk it?'

'Because they're animals. They don't think of anyone but themselves.'

Renee rests her head on Graham's shoulder. He reciprocates and pulls her into a hug. Tears well.

'I just wanted to have a little wind-down drink after work,' she manages to croak. 'That's all.'

'I know. It's unfair.' And he's right. It is unfair. 'How well do you know the guys you were with?'

Renee tenses. 'What do you mean?'

'No judgement, but it does sound like Martin was quite keen to go out for a drink with you.'

'No, it's nothing like that,' Renee says. 'Martin's a big bloke, but he's a complete teddy bear. I'm not kidding when I say I'd trust him with my life. Plus, he asked everyone to go. And he's gay. There's no way he would have done this. I just know it.'

'All right. He sounds like a good one. What about this Josh?'

'Josh?' A chill runs over Renee but she can't place why. 'He's the kid I told you about – the one with the rich uncle. He thinks he wants to be a chef, but doesn't want to put any of the work in.'

'And he wasn't there to help you take Lola home.'

Renee is surprised by the rage in his voice. Though Graham saying this out loud makes her shiver. In the panic of making sure Lola was safe, she hadn't been paying attention to Josh – whose first instinct, when a woman was spiked, was to leave.

'He said he was worried she was going to be sick or something.'

'Do you think the little shit did it?'

'I don't know. Look, I can't think about that right now. I just want Lola to be OK.'

But Renee's gut seems to have come to the same conclusion as Graham.

She sits up and pulls Lola's hair away from her face. It's hard to tell if Lola's pale or not, given the amount of contouring she does. She tried to teach Renee how to do it once, but Renee just couldn't master it and ended up looking like a clown. She's going to be absolutely livid when she wakes up. Lola hates people who sleep in their make-up.

'She'll be fine after some sleep,' Graham says gently. Renee knows he's trying to calm his temper for her sake. He strokes her hair, letting her curls twist around his fingertips. 'And so will you. Tomorrow is a new day.' He leans forward and kisses her. 'Try to rest.'

'Yeah. That's probably for the best. And Graham?'

'Hmm?'

'Thank you. For, you know, being there.'

'I'll always be here.' He kisses her again, and then leaves the room, pulling the door closed behind him.

Renee lies down next to her friend, feeling numb, trying to ignore her instincts screaming that Graham is right, and that Josh could be behind all of this.

The next morning dawns, and apart from a hideous headache, Lola's fine. She offers some colourful curses regarding the Bar None staff as she drinks an entire pot of coffee before thanking Graham for letting her stay then chewing out Renee for not taking her make-up off. But Renee's OK with that; she knows it's Lola's way of dealing with this. Make a joke, because jokes can't hurt, then carry on as normal.

They go back home together. Renee says Lola should call in sick, given the night they've had, but Lola just shrugs and insists she's all right. It isn't the first time something like this has happened to her. At least there were people looking out for her this time. Renee doesn't say anything about the drugged drink being intended for her. She doesn't see the point. But she's relieved when Josh fails to turn up for his shift.

She mentally adds 'predator' to the list of Josh descriptors.

Make a joke, then carry on.

'He says he has a bad stomach,' Martin says, and the way he curls his lip tells Renee all she needs to know about his opinion. Maybe he's come to the same conclusions she has.

The next service is busy, but subdued. No sign of Chef Gracie either, which she's oddly grateful for. It means she can just keep her head down and get on, hoping that, given time, last night will just become a distant memory.

Josh is back the following day, full of his usual arrogance. Maybe he did just have a bad stomach after all. Or maybe he's exactly what she suspects he is: an entitled sociopath who only needs a day to get over roofieing her best friend.

Potato, potahto.

While Gracie isn't present at every service, evidence of her coming into NOVA is everywhere. Stock changes between shifts; a note left on Bethany's bench; the lingering, slightly acrid smell of someone boiling up bones and the like for stock. She seems to prefer coming in when no one can perceive her – getting all of her jobs done on the sly rather than during the service. In a way, Renee gets it. By coming in when no one is around, Gracie is able to get on without any questions, and allowed to do her thing without having to worry about being disturbed. But that doesn't make it any less unsettling. Most chefs have a streak of the flamboyant in them, but despite being regarded as one of the best chefs in the country – if not the world – Gracie Fitzgerald borders on the truly misanthropic. Just another one of those things Renee needs to get used to, she guesses.

And she does.

Single shifts turn into days, then weeks, and before she knows it, Renee's been there a month. Her first pay cheque arrives, and she almost cries when she sees how much it is. The presence of cold, hard cash solidifies everything. It isn't a dream. It is real. Unfortunately, so are her debts, which swallow up most of the amount. Still, she manages to siphon off enough to buy herself a new pair of shoes – comfortable flats for work rather than anything extravagant – but it's the principle of the thing at the end of the day.

Gracie continues her erratic schedule throughout Renee's first month. She hardly ever tells anyone when she's going to be in, the only exception being Q, who seems to telepathically know exactly what everyone is doing at any point of the day. At this point, Renee isn't sure who's scarier – Q or Gracie.

The shifts Gracie runs are always going to be intense, but it's an intensity Renee is learning to work with. She still can't say she's completely comfortable when Chef is in, but she now feels able to get on with her own tasks without almost cutting her fingers off. What she can't get used to do, however, is the seemingly endless, ever-changing list of rules.

The Secret Freezer Bunker, as Martin calls it, is just the beginning. The no tasting rule, a mere inconvenience. There's also the cleaning products, which must come from an approved supplier; the crockery – ditto; the laundry . . . Well, the list is endless. So when one of the wait staff trips and accidentally spills some jus on herself, everyone freezes.

'I'm sorry, so sorry, Chef. I . . .' The poor girl trails off, her eyes wide and luminous in genuine fear, rich brown sauce dripping from her cotton-gloved hand.

Renee's first instinct is to tell her she's OK, it's an accident – but she doesn't. She can't. If she does that, she'll be in trouble too. That Martin is also standing stock still tells her she's made the right choice, because if there's anyone who'd lay their life on the line, it's Martin.

The kitchen falls silent. Even the sizzling pans seem muted. There is no explosion. No yelling. No profanity-laden insults hurled around, which is the usual go-to for inconvenienced chefs worldwide. Instead, Gracie just stares.

For some reason, that's worse.

A shudder chases its way up Renee's spine, and the urge to cough, sneeze – anything to break the silence – rises within her.

'Come here,' Gracie says, her voice barely above a whisper.

The girl swallows hard and takes hesitant steps towards the chef.

'What happened?'

'Uh, I didn't see the walking stick – the end of it was poking out and I didn't see it. I'm so sorry, Chef – it won't happen again—'

'Hands.'

The waiter holds out her jus-stained gloves. Even from her bench, Renee can see she's trembling. Without another word, Gracie tweezers the cuffs of the gloves between her fingers and delicately pulls them down. Then she pulls each individual finger until the gloves slide off the girl's hands.

'Wash them. Now. In here.' Gracie gestures to a nearby sink.

The waiter nods and does as she's told. It's clear to everyone that she's near to tears. Gracie makes her wash again, dissatisfied with the first attempt.

It's like she's scrubbing blood off her hands instead of jus.

The little voice in Renee's head has taken a weirdly menacing tone since starting at NOVA. The Gracie Fitzgerald Effect, apparently.

'You're now on the regular menu,' Gracie says. 'I cannot risk incompetence.'

'Yes, Chef. Thank you, Chef,' the girl all but whispers, and leaves the kitchen to get on with the service.

Renee offers her what she hopes is an encouraging smile as she walks past her bench, but she doubts the waiter saw it. She's too terrified – and probably shocked that she wasn't sacked on the spot, especially after the story Lola told Renee. Now the girl has left, Renee risks a glance back towards Gracie. She's picked up the gloves and looks like she's in the process of taking them into her freezer.

For what reason, Renee has no idea.

TWENTY

The next few weeks fly past, the shifts all blurring into one long cooking extravaganza. Even when Gracie isn't there, Renee feels more alive in NOVA's kitchen than she ever has anywhere else. As soon as one service ends, she's willing away the hours until she gets to cook again with people who are fast becoming not just friends but family to her. She's now a regular on NOVA's nights out and has started to get to know all the other people who help shape the restaurant.

The only issue is that she finds herself seeing Lola and Graham much less. By the time she rolls in after her post-shift drink, Lola's in bed, and when she gets up later that morning, Lola's either gone to work or out for the day.

It's even harder with Graham. Their respective work schedules mean it's difficult to find time for each other, and it's been a whole week of fly-by texts and just missing one another when Graham suggests that he come over Monday evening, so he can see her.

The main issue with a job as intense as cheffing is that it takes over your life. Not that you intend it to – it's just easy for things to run away with themselves, meaning you end up neglecting other parts of your life, whether you want to or not. Like relationships. She cherishes the time she spends with Graham, but she can tell that he's feeling the strain and doesn't want to let it show. It's not resentment – more of a quiet dismay that, for the time being at least, he's second place, even if Graham knows that isn't actually true. He's started going on about her moving in with him again, just so he can wake up with her. 'At least I'd get to see you every day,' he's tried to argue, 'rather than carve out time in between your shifts.'

She'd be lying if she said she hadn't considered his offer. It would make sense, after all. But then there's Lola. She's also been pushed to the back, and their new normal is a flying 'hi . . . bye!' while one of them grabs a coffee before heading out. So when Renee comes home from a gruelling lunchtime shift to find both Lola and Graham waiting for her in the living room, she can't help but feel like they're staging an intervention.

'Hello . . .' Renee says, drawing out the word, giving voice to her confusion.

'Hey, hunny,' Lola says.

'Hi, babe.'

In contrast to Lola's sunny disposition, Graham sounds almost dour, which is generally unlike him. A little concerned, Renee picks her way over to him to give him a welcoming peck.

'Everything all right?' she asks.

'Of course. Everything's fine. I just . . . don't get to see you much these days.' He smiles softly, but Renee isn't fooled. She can see the hurt behind it.

'I thought you were in the office today,' she says.

'I decided to work from home.'

'You did? Why didn't you tell me? I could have spent my time between shifts at your place.'

'Hey,' Lola says, looking miffed. 'Kind of fed up of being an afterthought, you know?'

'First of all, I did tell you,' Graham says, allowing his frustration to bleed through into his voice. 'And secondly, you live with Ren, Lola. You get to see her all the time.'

'I do not,' Lola says indignantly. 'Can't remember the last time we went out—'

'It was last week!' Graham says. He isn't quite yelling, but it's getting there. 'You went out for a drink after Ren's shift.'

'Yeah, I know, but that was with her work mates. I mean just the two of us.'

'Guys . . . Guys, please,' Renee says, feeling like a piece of meat between two hungry dogs. 'I'm flattered, but at the same time, I'm sorry. This is my new reality, and I'm sure it'll all settle down given time. Until then, I need to iron my whites for this evening and have a nice cup of tea.'

'We're still cool for next week, right?' Lola says. 'Been a long time since we went shopping for something other than groceries.'

'Yeah, of course,' Renee says. 'There isn't a lot left from my first pay cheque, but I should get paid again in the next couple of days, so it'll be nice to do something more than just window shop.'

'You got that right.' Lola beams. 'I miss you, girl. I hardly ever see you these days.'

'Well, you know how it is – new job . . . got to do everything I can to fit in, you know?'

'I guess so.'

'So you're going out with Lola next week?' Graham asks.

'Yeah, we arranged it for Monday, when I don't have to go in,' Renee says, sitting on the footstool next to the couch – their version of an armchair, as it was the only other piece of furniture that could fit in the flat.

'Oh. It's just I hoped we might go out for lunch, or something.'

'That would be nice, but—'

'Your girl made plans with me, G,' Lola says. 'You snooze, you lose.'

Although Renee knows Lola's just teasing, she notices the look Graham shoots her. Of course, she's aware that her best friend and her boyfriend don't always see eye to eye, but they'd been getting along better after the spiking incident. Renee's not sure why they've escalated from 'able to tolerate each other' to 'can I leave these two alone in a room for any significant length of time without something kicking off?'.

'It's OK,' Renee says. 'We don't run a Wednesday lunch shift, so we could have some lunch then?'

'I'm in the office Wednesday.'

'Oh. Maybe we could do the Monday after that?'

'Maybe.' Graham sighs.

Renee glances at Lola, who just shrugs. Even she realizes this isn't a good time to rib him.

'So who's coming in tonight? Any celebrity reservations?' Lola asks. 'Come on – spill.'

Now this is a subject Renee will never tire of.

'I don't think so. I mean, there could be, but if they are coming in, it won't be for Chef Gracie's special menu.'

'Special menu – oh my days,' Lola says with a smirk. 'What is all that about?'

'I don't know. I find it best to just ignore it, along with the secret bunker freezer and the no-tasting-her-stuff rules,' Renee says.

'And then there's the gloves,' Lola says. 'You can't forget the gloves. I know NOVA's, like, proper posh, but canning someone because they took their waiter gloves off? Mental.'

Inside, Renee prickles a bit. It's one thing for her to point out the idiosyncrasies of her boss. It's quite another for someone who doesn't know her to do the same. Yes, Gracie is difficult and just a bit odd, but Renee isn't sure she likes hearing Lola mock her as if she's a particularly difficult customer.

Easy, tiger. Remember it's just a job and Lola likes to talk shit.

'Although, I will say – that guy ended up being a total prick,' Lola continues. 'Thought he was better than the rest of us. No one particularly liked him, and management found out about him posting shitty things online, so I think they sacked him. Anyway, I haven't seen him for over a week.'

'Sounds like good riddance,' Renee says, shifting in her seat. 'I think Gracie probably sacked him for more than just taking his gloves off.'

'Eh, maybe. I guess he's learning the hard way that no matter what level you work at, the food world is small.'

'So, when is Gracie in next?' Graham asks, more to involve himself in the conversation than for any other reason.

'I don't know. She comes and goes as she pleases. Q seems to always know, but that's about it. The rest of us are completely in the dark until she rocks up.'

'And that doesn't strike you as strange?' Graham says.

'I mean, yeah, of course, but this is what it's like when you're working with the best. They're more like artists than cooks.'

'Delusional,' Lola says at exactly the same time Graham says, 'Temperamental.'

'OK, I know – it is weird. But this is also the best job I've ever had. So, what if the executive chef is a bit . . . quirky?'

'Mate, quirky is wearing a multicoloured hat and playing the ukulele at parties,' Lola says. 'I don't even know what category your boss falls into.'

'Not that it matters,' Graham says. 'As long as you're doing well – that's what's important.'

Lola snorts into her mug, then shakes her head, not an ounce of tact in her body.

'So, if you have no idea when the boss lady is going to be in, how do the punters know?' Lola asks, changing tack.

Renee shrugs. 'I dunno. Never really thought about it, to be honest.'

'I know. It's a sixth sense that only poshos have,' Lola says. 'They're heat-seeking missiles – except it's not heat, it's Gracie Fitzgerald.'

'Maybe she has an exclusive website,' Graham says. 'Gracie announces the days she's going to be in, so only those who are subscribed to it will know?'

'That's actually a good theory,' Renee says. 'I wonder if that's it.'

'So, like, she has a secret society thing going on,' Lola says. 'Very *Eyes Wide Shut*.'

'Well, more of a VIP list, I would assume,' Renee says. 'Like I said, we don't even know when she's going to be in, so . . .'

'I can't get over that. Isn't it hugely disruptive?' Graham asks. 'Not to mention quite unprofessional?'

'Not really,' Renee says, her hackles rising slightly. 'It's her restaurant, and she cooks a from a completely separate menu. She has her own roster of dishes that no one else can prep, works with her own ingredients – the lot. I told you – she won't even let us taste her dishes, and she'll only serve them to people she deems "suitable". You can't just walk in and ask for a signature dish. She has to make that decision.'

'Wow.' Lola pulls a face. 'So, these guys don't get to choose? They literally just have to eat what's put in front of them?'

'I guess so.' It's only when it's said out loud like this that Renee truly appreciates just how shocking the set-up at NOVA really is.

'And what happens if someone walks in and says that they want to try one of these dishes and Gracie says no?'

'That actually happened,' Renee says. 'When I worked with her last, this woman wanted to order the same as the guy she was with. I don't know who she was, but he was one of those tycoon types – big in crypto; a Silicon Valley bro. Arrogant beyond belief. Anyway, he's having the signature, and she asks if she can have it too, but Gracie said no, she wasn't going to cook for her – only him.'

'That's shitty,' Graham says. 'I thought she built her entire empire on this whole female empowerment thing?'

'Yeah, I thought it was weird too, but in the end, she had my duck and loved it, and he ate braised tripe, so . . .'

Lola all but chokes on her drink. 'I'm sorry, what?'

'You heard me. Braised tripe in red wine with sage polenta.'

Lola puffs out her cheeks, looking like she's genuinely going to be sick.

'Tripe? Isn't that, what, lungs?'

'No – stomach lining.'

'That is foul.'

'Hey, at least it wasn't brains again.'

'Again? Really?' Graham sounds genuinely outraged. 'It isn't bad enough that we unnecessarily torture then slaughter animals and their young for our consumption, but now a top-level chef feels it's appropriate to serve their brains to rich idiots? I swear, the asteroid can't come soon enough. I've said it before, but I'm going to say it again – if we're going to survive as a species, more people need to adopt a plant-based lifestyle—'

'G,' Lola says. 'Maybe not now?'

'Yes, now, Lola. It's a subject that makes a lot of people uncomfortable because they know eating meat is not only unnecessary, it's wrong – but they're too weak-willed to actually give it all up—'

'Too weak-willed?' Lola snorts. 'Oh, boy, tell me you've never been poor without actually telling me. You don't get it, do you?'

'Don't get what?' Graham snaps.

Renee can feel the argument brewing, the tension ozone-thick in the air, and she interrupts before Lola can escalate things even further.

'I get it, G. And it's a good point. I'll be honest with you – I have no idea why she serves half the stuff she does. But the punters? They go mad for it. It's like magic. She sprinkles that Gracie fairy dust over her dishes, and they can't get enough.'

'She sounds a little hard to work with, if you ask me,' Graham says, a little snottily.

'Yeah,' Renee says. 'She can be. She has a lot of rules, and most of them are completely batshit. But you go and ask anyone in that kitchen whether they'd work anywhere else, and every single one of them would say no – me included.' The need to defend Gracie is so strong now, Renee can't help herself. 'I hardly know the woman, but I can see. Feel it. There's a reason she is where she is. I'd be lying if I said anyone would call her a friend, but I have absolutely no doubt that if she asked us to ride out to battle for her, we'd fight among ourselves to lead the charge.'

'Jesus, Ren – it's a job, not a cause for war.' Lola raises her eyebrows. 'No wonder we hardly ever see you these days. Not so much of a work-to-live philosophy there, right?'

'Lola, you don't get it. This isn't just about work – about food. This is cuisine. No one works to live in this industry. Food is the life.'

'I knew it. All you chefs are nutcases drinking Gracie's Kool-Aid,' Lola says, and Renee can't really disagree with her.

TWENTY-ONE

Renee has a couple of hours before her shift begins, and she's finally managed to coax Graham and Lola into a state of semi-comfort in front of the TV that means she feels confident enough to leave them and iron her whites. She keeps the smallest ironing board ever to exist in her bedroom because, according to Lola, Carluccio's can 'kiss my arse before I iron my clothes for work', so Renee is the only one who uses it.

As she smooths out the creases with the iron, Renee takes stock of her life over the past six weeks. Working at NOVA has been simultaneously everything and nothing at all like she expected. Being back in a professional kitchen has imbued her with a confidence she hasn't felt in years. She's not *too* surprised – she was one of the best in her class, which even she can admit. And now she gets to be one of the best in the top restaurant in London—

'Shit!'

The collar of Renee's whites slips between her fingers and the iron scalds her skin, as if punishing her for even thinking like this. Renee pulls her hand away from the board and examines the damage, but the pain barely registers. A pink sear has formed next to the white scar from the night she julienned her fingers. The night she was told *by her boss* to rinse her own blood off the food being served at a Michelin-starred restaurant.

Renee has mentally added that instance to the list of Gracie's 'quirks', but refuses to tell anyone about the incident. Every time she thinks of that night, she gets a chill down her spine – not just from the health and safety aspect, but from the ease with which Gracie and Bethany handled the situation. Neither looked alarmed – especially Gracie. The chef constantly has Renee torn between feelings of awe and dread, each one fighting to outrank the other. She senses something is slowly unfurling in the kitchen – that there might be a piece to the NOVA puzzle she is close to understanding – but then Chef does something like *eat the carrot*. Renee's stomach rolls at that particular detail, so much so that she can't imagine how Graham and Lola would react.

Graham and Lola.

Shaking out her anxious thoughts, Renee unplugs the iron. She's pressed her luck leaving them alone for this long, so the half-wrinkled whites will have to do.

When she returns to the living room, she finds the pair silently doomscrolling at opposite ends of the couch. Renee can hear Lola watching a TikTok sleuth's latest theories on the McAdams disappearance. The air is so thick with resentment, Renee can almost taste it.

'Uh, is everything OK?'

They both look up at the same time, but Graham jumps in first.

'Everything's fine, babe,' he says.

She isn't stupid. It's clear something has happened. One of the more difficult things she has to balance is how different her friend and boyfriend are, and how both of them have, in private conversations, expressed that she would be better off without the other one.

'No. Everything is not fine.' She's really upset, and while Lola often plays at the dramatic, she's actually pretty chill. For something to rattle her like this . . . it's not going to be nothing.

'It doesn't matter, Lola,' Graham says. 'Ren doesn't need to worry about it right now – she has enough on her plate.'

'There you go again!' Lola explodes. 'Always diminishing her, treating her like she's a kid.'

'I'm not treating her like she's a kid,' Graham shoots back. 'If anything, I'm the one who wants her to fully embrace actual adulthood, rather than keeping her in this state of perpetual teenagedom—'

'Hey, hey, hey, what's all this?' Renee says. 'What's going on?'

'Mr Responsibility here thinks you need to move out.'

'Graham?'

He doesn't even have the decency to look a little bit sheepish. In fact, if anything, he looks annoyed.

'I'm not the bad guy in this,' he says. 'All I want is what's best for Renee.'

'Which is basically me out of her life?'

'Pardon?' Renee focuses on Graham. 'What's she on about?'

'She's taken something and blown it all out of proportion—'

'No, no – say it with your chest now that Ren's here. He thinks you should move out and live with him, because it's more *appropriate* now you're working somewhere posh.'

'I didn't say that,' Graham snaps. 'I said it's unfair that now she has a good job, she has to continue living like she's still a student.'

'Now she has a good job? The job at the chicken shop wasn't bad, and it paid the bills. She did well there, too. My God, I swear, you posh twats are all the same. Life comes so easy to you, all you do is judge the rest of us.'

'That's unfair!' Graham is now shouting. 'And this isn't about me.'

Lola pulls a face and snorts at him. Renee watches on in horror, trying to work out how she might jump in and defuse this situation, but every time she tries to interrupt, one of them starts shouting again.

'Renee is a talented, exceptional person, and to be perfectly honest, there are times when I can't figure out why she tolerates you – the way you've latched yourself on to her.'

'Latched? What the fuck are you jabbering on about?' Lola is now on her feet – always a danger sign. 'There's no latching here, bro. She's my friend. We got a good thing here. We're doing it ourselves, without handouts from Daddy, working our way up – something you'll never understand.'

'Lola . . .' Renee says.

'Oh, you siding with him?'

'No! No, I'm just . . . this . . . None of this helps,' Her mind races as she tries to sift through every diplomatic option she has at her disposal. 'I mean, Graham has a point. We're going to have to sort this out eventually – we can't be roommates for ever—'

'Oh, right. So this is how you tell me?'

'Lola, no – I'm not saying that.'

'What I mean is—' Graham begins, but Renee shushes him.

'No, you need to be quiet. You're not helping.'

Graham folds his arms over his chest.

'So I'm not allowed to defend myself any more? Because I'm not part of the sacred sisterhood you two have?'

'Sacred sisterhood – oh my days,' Lola says. 'I swear to God, I have never, ever met anyone with less of a clue than you, bro.'

'Don't call me bro.' Graham jabs a warning finger in Lola's direction.

'Whatever, bro,' Lola snaps back.

'OK, this is not how I wanted to spend my free time before my next shift, which I now need to leave for in less than an hour. This all needs to stop,' Renee says, a little more forcefully than she intended. 'Graham, I think you should go home.'

'What? You're kicking me out?' Graham looks aggrieved; Lola, triumphant.

'No, of course not. We can talk about this later, OK? But right now, I am not in the right headspace to be dealing with you two squabbling. At the end of the day, what I decide to do is up to me – not up to you two. I'm not a kid in a custody battle. I've got to leave in a minute—'

'Your shift doesn't start until five!'

'I know. But I've still got to get ready, get myself mentally prepared. I don't just rock up and start chopping stuff, you know. It's a little more taxing than that. So right now, I need some peace, and given Lola lives here, I don't think chucking her out of her own flat is going to make any of this better.' She holds out her hand. At first she thinks he might argue with her but, after a moment, Graham reluctantly takes it and allows Renee to haul him up off the sofa. She leads him out of the room, towards their front door.

'Renee, please. You need to listen. I can't . . . It's her! She's—'

Renee silences him with a kiss.

'Not now,' she says. 'Please. We'll talk about it later. Promise.'

'You always say that, but we never do. If you don't want to be with me, you just have to say.'

'Graham, it's not like that, and you know it. I love you, but I've been through a lot, and I need to do things in my own way, at my own pace.'

He lets out a long sigh and visibly deflates.

'I know. I do. And I respect that. How about a compromise? Why don't you stay at mine tonight? After your shift? No strings, just a nice night together?'

'OK, that does sound nice. I should be finished by half ten – eleven at the very latest. I'll text you.'

'Cool. I'll see you later, then. Have a good shift.'

'See you later. Love you.'

'Love you more.'

He ducks down for another kiss, then leaves. Once he's gone, Renee leans back against the front door and lets out a huge sigh.

Lola appears in the doorway, looking hurt.

'I'm not leaving,' Renee says, matter-of-factly.

'He said I'm not good enough to be your friend.' Lola is clearly upset. 'That I'm just a waitress. That I drag you down.'

'What? He actually said that?' Renee knows Lola is telling her the truth, because when she nods, her eyes glitter with unshed tears.

'Oh, honey, no.' Renee approaches her, arms held out. Lola steps in and allows herself to be drawn into a hug. 'That's not right. You're my bestie. I love you.'

'I know,' Lola says, sniffling. 'I'm very loveable.'

'Yes, you are. You're a fucking delight.'

Lola laughs and wipes her eyes with her fingers. Renee, never one for acrylic nails, has absolutely no idea how she manages to do it with her talons, but Lola's a pro.

'I really am, aren't I?'

'Yes, you really are. And anyone who says any different is either an idiot or a liar.'

'They are complete imbeciles.'

'I agree. So . . . what started all that?'

Lola sighs heavily, wanders back into the living room and sits down heavily on the couch.

'It's been a thing for a while now,' she says. 'He says he's only looking out for you, but it feels like you belong to him – and not in a good way. He said you deserve better.'

Renee purses her lips and shakes her head.

'He doesn't get it,' she says. 'He's never lived a life like ours.' She looks up at the clock. It's nearly four. 'Oh, hell – I've got to go to work soon, and I said I'd go to his afterwards. But tomorrow afternoon – me and you, all right? Like old times.'

She holds out her pinky finger. Lola laughs, and hooks hers around it.

'Pinky swear,' Lola says.

'Pinky swear. And you know what happens when those get broken.'

'Yeah. Nothing. But it's the thought that counts.' Lola sighs heavily. 'He's right though, isn't he? We can't live like this for ever.'

'No, we can't. But we'll worry about that later.'

'Yay for later,' Lola says, sounding tired.

TWENTY-TWO

It's another week before Gracie's in again. As soon as Renee steps into the kitchen, she feels it – that strange frisson, like the beginning of a relationship, when things are still delicate but also exciting and, honestly, terrifying.

When Gracie calls Renee over to her bench, she walks with a heavy mixture of excitement and trepidation churning inside. For the longest moment, the chef simply stares at her, her gaze penetrating to Renee's bones. Just as Renee's trepidation begins to dominate and sour to dread, Gracie speaks.

'I have decided to put you in charge of the starters today. Don't make me regret it.'

She doesn't wait for Renee to reply, simply hands her a sheet of paper and turns away, getting on with her own prep.

Both Roy and Martin give a stunned Renee secret smiles and thumbs-up as she rejoins them, because this only means one thing.

Gracie trusts her.

Gracie Fitzgerald *trusts* her!

Renee settles at her station and reads the list of ingredients. There are no surprises, just the standard Thursday night menu, which instantly boosts her confidence.

She can do this.

What is surprising, though, is when Gracie announces that she'll be taking on the fish main tonight.

'I'm in the mood to cook,' she says. 'And I only have one

customer worthy of one of my signature dishes tonight. Plus, it's been a while since I have indulged in fish cookery, and I know we have some John Dory in our cold pantry, ready for my filleting knife.'

Even Josh seems enthusiastic tonight, which is a first. Although it doesn't take long for Renee to realize why.

'Is he going to be here? Like, tonight?'

'Yes,' Bethany says, exasperated.

'Who's going to be here?' Renee asks, a little confused.

'Troy Fisk,' Martin says, and pulls a face – one she readily returns.

'Troy Fisk? Really? Here?'

'I know, man! It's sick,' Josh says, clearly not reading the room. 'Man tells it like it is, you get me? Got his finger on the pulse. He doesn't cater to the woke feminist agenda. You try telling him to do the washing up and he'd beat your arse.'

'Yes, well, that's all very informative,' Bethany says. 'But whether you or he likes it or not, you still have washing up to do. I suggest you get on with it before Chef Gracie sees you slacking off. Again.'

Josh screws his face into an ugly pout, and there's a tense moment when Renee thinks he might bite back, but then, almost on cue, Gracie strides back out of her freezer, carrying a tray with some very suspicious-looking organs on it.

There's no way . . .

'Is everything all right, Joshua?' Even though it's an innocuous enough question, there's no doubt she heard everything Josh said. Renee forces her gaze away from the tray to look at her head chef. All it takes is a raised eyebrow from Gracie for Josh to retreat back to the sink. 'Remember, as soon as the dishwasher is on, we need those shallots diced.'

'Yes, Chef,' Josh mumbles.

Gracie unloads her personal ingredients on her bench,

plopping each of the suspicious-looking organs into a bowl of ice water. As she does this, Martin's eyes widen so much that Renee wonders if he's thinking the same thing she is about tonight's special dish.

'Are you all right?' Renee murmurs.

'Oh my God . . . she wouldn't,' Martin says, a curious mixture of disgust and admiration colouring his voice. 'Is that why she has me making hollandaise? It has to be. *Frivolités*.'

'I was hoping my instincts were wrong. I guess not,' she says, shocked.

Martin grins gleefully.

'I guess Mr Is-It-Gay-To-Touch-Your-Own-Arsehole is going to have some balls in his mouth whether he likes it or not.'

Stifling a laugh, Renee goes back to her starter prep. Yes, it's unethical. Repugnant, even. Everyone should know what they're about to put in their bodies. But even so, she can't help but find the irony particularly delicious, given everything this man embodies. Because Gracie Fitzgerald, in her infinite wisdom – and, it seems, her infinite capacity for incredibly dark humour – has decided to serve the influencer Josh so admires *frivolités à la hollandaise* with tender asparagus, crispy black kale and a beetroot espuma.

It would take someone with a heart made of flint not to find it at least a little funny.

As an influencer who has made his name in the so-called manosphere, Troy Fisk famously likes getting free things, especially when it's a woman serving him. Renee guesses that, in this instance, he doesn't actually know what these 'free things' are, and he's too arrogant to look it up.

But she does.

Frivolités is a French word for grilled testicles, usually either lamb or calf. That Gracie is pairing this dish with hollandaise might be considered a little on the nose – visually and texture-wise – but to then hammer her actual feelings home with tiny, dainty spears of soft asparagus, black slivers of crisped kale and an almost blood-red espuma? It's something out of Greek tragedy, but rather than serving him his own sons, she's making him eat his own hubris.

Gracie: 1; professional misogynist: 0

The dishes Renee has been asked to prepare are as complicated as ever, requiring meticulous attention to detail. But that doesn't stop her from glancing over towards Gracie, who is currently *peeling the testicles like eggs*. Renee swallows the bile that has crept up the back of her throat. She can't take her eyes away, disgusted and horrifically fascinated at the same time. The testicles are large, which is unusual for French cuisine, which tends to favour the younger, more delicate organs from very juvenile lambs and calves. Watching Gracie take one of the peeled balls and then dice it roughly is revolting and oddly satisfying, as with every *thunk* of Gracie's cleaver against the wooden chopping board, her smirk only intensifies. This woman knows exactly what she is doing.

As Renee begins prepping a mustard panna cotta, she can't help but wonder how many times Gracie has done this to her customers. Is that why she is so insistent on being the only one who tastes her food? Because she's serving items that people usually find disgusting? She thinks back to the kind of people Gracie cooks her signature meals for. Are they all men? They're definitely all rich – that kind of comes with the territory if you want to dine here in the first place, let alone eat from Gracie's menu.

Renee isn't sure how much her dishes go for, but it isn't going to be cheap. That she's serving these out-of-touch wealthy types ingredients most people would chuck away is fiendishly clever and definitely a little immoral . . . but when did these types ever worry about morality? In a way, she can now see why Gracie told her to wash the carrots the first time they worked together. They were going to be served with brain – and given the foodie name for brains is *cervelles*, they probably wouldn't have realized this at the time – so what is a little diluted blood when you're eating that?

Renee surprises herself at how easily she can rationalize this behaviour. *It's not like I'm the one doing it.* She turns back to her station, not wanting to follow that particularly sticky line of thinking. With her mixture simmering at the correct temperature, Renee takes the pan off the heat and adds the gelatine. It's funny – people eat gelatine all the time, and no one questions it. But what is gelatine? Boiled-up bone, skin and cartilage. Renee reckons that there would be a lot less call for it if people knew how it was created. In fact, a lot of the ingredients people use come from what most would think of as barbaric practices. Even ethically sourced meat starts with killing something, after all.

Her panna cotta made, Renee leaves it to set in the chiller and switches her attention to the pickled beetroot. This isn't the kind of pickled beetroot you'd get out of a jar – this is the kind you make from scratch, full of delicate aromatics that mustn't be overpowered by the pickling liquor, a feat which requires careful tasting at each stage to ensure the result is a sharp yet sweet foil for the richness of both the panna cotta and the goat's cheese crumble. Renee's other dishes are less intensive timewise, but a lot riskier, as most of the work is done to order – the main component is a tartare of tuna that can't be made up ahead of time, and the seaweed crisps will go soggy if made too early.

By the time service starts, Renee feels that now-familiar surge: a heady mix of nerves and excitement. She's always thought you should never become too comfortable in the kitchen, especially at this level. Comfort means you've stopped taking risks, and that only leads to boring dishes. And if there's something she never wants to do, it's serve boring food.

The tartare is proving popular, meaning Renee spends most of her time dicing tuna, adding pickled ginger and coriander seeds to taste. Out of the corner of her eye, she can see Gracie working flat out, filleting John Dory and rinsing shellfish for the non-speciality main. She can't help but be impressed. Too many executive chefs would find a regular service demeaning, but not her. Even though these aren't her signature dishes, it's still all her own food – she's responsible for it. That she takes such a hands-on approach is something Renee finds inspirational, to the point where she often finds herself asking 'What would Gracie do?' when she faces her own culinary challenges.

Every now and again, Q will walk in and have a quiet word with Chef. Renee doesn't bat an eye at this any more – she simply accepts that Q would rather deal with Gracie and Gracie alone, and that's fine. But when he marches in now, his face is like cracked granite.

'He's brought an entourage.'

No one has to clarify who 'he' is.

Usually, Gracie won't entertain influencers, so everyone was kind of surprised she agreed to this one, especially given the recent scandals. The accusations of human trafficking may or may not be true, but that doesn't stop Troy Fisk from being a spectacular prick of the very highest order. But then Renee remembers the dish Gracie is going to serve, and smiles. Because whether he realizes it or not, he's going to get a massive comeuppance.

Other chefs might explode into a sweary outburst at this kind of news, but not Gracie. She sets down her knife, her gaze level.

'Unless his entourage wants to order from the main menu – at full price, of course – they can wait outside. And if he complains, just remind him of the contract he signed in order to dine here. He wanted to sample a signature dish. And he will. No one else. If he makes a scene, you know the protocol.'

Q nods, a slow smile breaking through the stone.

'Of course, Chef. I shall inform him post-haste.'

'No . . . take a little break. Let him stew. The more he acts out, the more people will see him for who he is. Let him make a fool of himself. I don't think he appreciates that our clientele aren't the sort to be impressed by lavish performances of cuntery.'

Renee almost chokes on the sample pickling liquor she was tasting when Gracie drops this bomb. Next to her, Martin snorts then shakes his head in amusement – a gesture that screams 'that's our Chef'.

Gracie finishes the plate she is working on, then slips into her freezer to gather her already prepared *frivolités*. As per her suggestion, Q goes over to the corner where they prepare drinks and fetches himself a bottle of water. He doesn't gulp it but instead takes demure sips, as if he's enjoying a nice gin and tonic. Josh, whose station is nearest to the refreshment area, gives a bark of laughter.

'God, you drink like an old lady, bro.'

Q slides his attention towards Josh, then pointedly ignores him and continues to sip his water.

'What's she serving him, anyway?' Josh continues, addressing the entire kitchen. All four chefs and Q share a cackle. 'Nah, really – what is it?'

'Balls, Josh,' Martin says.

'Balls? Like, what? Chicken balls?'

'Last time I checked, chickens dinnae have balls – eh, Renee?' Roy says, making her laugh. Because no, chickens do not have balls. She should know.

'Guys . . .' Bethany says, a slight hint of warning in her voice. 'Focus.'

'Sorry, Chef,' everyone bar Josh choruses back.

'Hang on.' From his expression, it's clear something is dawning on Josh. 'Do you mean actual balls? Like, man balls?'

'Yeah, Josh. Actual balls,' Martin says, rolling his eyes. 'Although those are probably bull balls or something.'

'You mean we're gonna feed him actual balls?' Josh crumples his tea towel into a wad and throws it to the floor. 'That's disrespect. Nah. I'm not gonna have that. I'm gonna tell him.'

He tries to storm out, but Q gracefully blocks his path.

'No, you aren't,' Q says. Like Gracie, he doesn't shout, but he still makes his point abundantly clear. 'You are going to go back to your sink and behave like a professional.'

'Fuck that. Fuck all of you. You all go on about fairness, and how women and Blacks and the pronoun mafia have it so hard, but mocking my man Troy? That's OK? Just cos he's a white man and he speaks the truth?' It's clear that Josh feels emboldened – not just because Gracie isn't in the kitchen but because his hero is in the other room and he wants to get the man's attention.

'But I suppose that's what you get when you hire by tick-box. Fucking DEI. Gotta have your quotas of women and gays – not to mention the sheer amount of fucking minorities. I mean, two mongrels, a welfare queen and a fag, all in a kitchen of what – seven people? And the only other white guy is a fucking Jock. It's fucking nuts.'

The whole kitchen draws a sharp breath and holds it, the silence that follows smothering all other sound. Renee feels like someone's wrapped a plastic bag around her head. Of course she's heard this all before, but that's been from strangers: customers, people in bars, on the street. And while none of it's acceptable, this feels horribly personal. It's clear Josh has been harbouring these thoughts for a while, and even though he's doing this for attention, she has no doubt this is exactly how he feels inside. She glances at Martin, his jaw tightening even under his thick beard, then at Bethany, who looks as floored as she feels. But Josh isn't done.

'Back in the day, people got things by merit. Look at my man outside. He worked hard, made a name for himself, but all the cucks tried to get him cancelled. He wouldn't stand for this shit. He'd be telling all you bitches to do as you're told. And you know what? You'd do it, too. Because you know it's the natural order of things. He's the alpha. A high-value male. All you need to do these days is show up and present your triggers.' He starts pantomiming what he thinks is distress, waving his hands around in mock panic.

'Ooh, you owe me because your ancestors put mine on a boat. Boohoo,' he whines. 'Like it matters any more. Fuck off. It's all an excuse. You can't say anything because if you do it's "he's a racist" or "he's a misogynist" or "he's so homophobic." It's like my man Fisk says – everyone's so scared of upsetting the BLM, feminazi and the alphabet mafia these days, no one will say it like it is— What? Don't fucking look at me like that.'

All through Josh's rant, Q stands ramrod straight, the epitome of poise and grace. He then raises a hand to his lips, gives a polite cough and looks pointedly towards the other end of the kitchen.

Everyone turns.

Gracie has stepped out of the freezer. Her expression is unreadable.

Finally, Josh shuts up.

He stares at Gracie, a mixture of defiance and *oh shit*.

'Have you quite finished?' Gracie asks. Again, she doesn't yell, doesn't growl. If anything, her tone is silkier than ever.

Because he's young and incredibly stupid, Josh chooses to go with defiance.

'Finished what? Telling the truth? So fucking sick of the disrespect I get round here.' Then, to everyone's horror, he marches over and knocks the tray out of Gracie's hands, sending her prepared ingredients flying.

Everyone stares, their eyes ghoulishly wide, at the testicles splatted on the floor. Everyone, that is, except Gracie, who narrows hers, laser-focused on Josh.

'Now, that was very foolish, wasn't it?' Her voice is barely above a murmur, but she may as well have screamed it for the effect it has on her kitchen staff. 'Pick them up.'

'What?' Josh manages to choke out. 'No! You do it.'

Gracie says nothing. Renee wants to hide behind her counter and, judging by the way both Roy and Martin are all but cowering, they'd probably join her.

'What?' Josh continues, but there's a crack to his voice now as uncertainty creeps in. 'I'm not touching them.'

'Yes, you are.' Gracie's glare never wavers. 'Pick. Them. Up.'

Josh glances around wildly, looking for allies, but finds none. 'Nah. I, I—' he stammers. 'I'm gonna tell my uncle—'

'Tell your uncle what, exactly?' There's a slightly more venomous note to Gracie's voice now. 'That you disrespected my staff? That you violently ruined a classic French dish because you don't actually understand cuisine? That you decided you, a mere child, know better than I do – me, a chef your dear uncle invested seven million pounds in – all so you could try to impress a borderline paederast with a middling YouTube channel?' By the end, Gracie is shouting, her voice deep and booming – a sound someone as small as her shouldn't be able to make. And then, in the blink of an eye, it drops down again to a mere notch above a murmur. 'Go on. Tell him. Please. *I dare you.*'

She steps towards Josh, and Renee swears she sees him flinch. Gracie gets so close, she could kiss him if she wanted.

Instead, she leans in and whispers something in his ear.

Josh's eyes bulge in their sockets.

Gracie nods at him once, never blinking.

Renee has no idea what she's said to him, but as soon as Gracie turns and stalks back to her bench, Josh hunkers down and picks up the organs, then places them back on their tray. Just as he's about to set the tray down on the steel table, Gracie barks, 'Rinse them!' so loudly everyone jumps. Josh looks like he might protest again, but the needle-sharp glare Gracie shoots him has him scuttling over to the sink.

'All right, people,' Gracie says in a calm but authoritative manner. 'We've had enough drama tonight, and we've just lost precious minutes to our schedule. Eyes down.'

TWENTY-THREE

As predicted, Troy Fisk does indeed try to make a scene. Not about the meal, but about his entourage. He doesn't succeed, though. The three men he's with slope off when Gracie herself comes out and tells him that she will refuse him entrance, let alone service, if he disrupts her restaurant's valued ambience any further, and he can refer back to the contract he signed if he wants to get funny about it.

He starts to get shirty – a perfect mirror of Josh's tantrum – but in the end gives up in the face of Gracie's sheer indifference. It's clear that his attempts to intimidate her fail spectacularly. He even tells her she needs to 'submit', which only results in a raised eyebrow and a head tilt – two gestures that have had scarier men than Troy Fisk running for the hills. In the end, she shuts him down by taking a step towards him and telling him he's more than welcome to try to 'sort her out'.

By now, the entire restaurant – guests and staff – are watching, and it's clear Fisk has absolutely no idea how to handle someone who simply doesn't care about him or his reputation on any level. If it wasn't for NOVA's house rules around phones, Renee reckons this scene would have gone viral in a hot minute. In fact, people outside *are* recording – something Troy Fisk looks a little worried about. Physically, he is imposing, and Gracie just isn't, and even with his limited intellectual capacity, he can see this isn't a good look for him no matter which way you slice it.

Rather than back down and leave, he turns to his goons and

has a quiet word with them. This worries Renee. Is he planning on jumping Gracie after service? Not that he'd succeed – they'd have to go through both kitchen and front of house to get to her, judging by the way everyone has set their jaws. But they leave without a fuss. With the goons dispatched, he meekly follows Gracie towards a single-occupancy table in the furthest corner of the restaurant, just to make her opinion of him bare.

He doesn't complain.

She nods towards the bar, and Danika strides out – all six feet two of her. Stripped of his cheerleaders, at last it seems to dawn on this idiot that he's going to have to behave. He resigns himself to ordering a drink and being a good little boy. When the time comes for Gracie to serve him her signature dish, everyone is watching with a sense of delighted, almost predatory relish. Except Josh, who is, of course, still sulking.

Fisk pokes at his meal before taking a nibble. His eyes widen, and he tucks in with gusto.

Suppressing a smirk of pure schadenfreude, everyone goes back to the kitchen to continue the service.

Everyone, that is, except for Gracie, who continues to watch the jumped-up little dick, with what can only be described as carnivorous glee.

After the heat of the kitchen, the cool night air is a balm to Renee. As much as she loves her job, if there's one thing she could change about it – apart from the endless onion prep, of course – it would be for someone to invent air conditioning that could actually cool a kitchen mid-service.

She pulls out her phone and brings up Graham's number. Usually, she texts him to tell him she's finished and on her way home – so he knows she's safe – but tonight she's feeling a little wired and wonders if he might like to go out for a drink. Just the two of them.

Because as much as she enjoyed this evening, it also left her feeling... conflicted.

Was Gracie right?

Of course, Fisk deserved everything he had coming. Josh, too, to be honest. But at the same time, deserving or not, it was clear that her boss had enjoyed every minute of it. She hadn't just served the meal as a form of ritual humiliation (although that was definitely a part of it); there was a sadistic element that just didn't sit right with Renee. Who else has Gracie done this to? Is that the true purpose of her special menu – to punish people she doesn't like?

Then there was the episode with Josh. Of course, she's happy Gracie took him to task. He one hundred per cent needed it. She's never seen a boss dress down an employee in front of the whole team like that. These things usually end up being dealt with quietly in an office, followed by a subdued meeting the next day informing the staff that the perpetrator has 'decided to move on', like they've done them a favour rather than sacked them.

In fact, she's a bit surprised Gracie didn't demand that Josh leave the kitchen there and then, but she guesses making him stay and face the entire kitchen's disdain was more of a punishment than sending him home. In a way, she's more surprised he didn't walk out. Whatever Gracie said to him must have been something personal, because he looked like she'd threatened to skin him alive afterwards. He didn't say much for the rest of the service, even when Fisk was making a massive scene – just kept shooting resentful looks at them all.

But not at Gracie.

He didn't dare look at her once.

Graham answers Renee's call promptly, which Renee takes as a good sign that he wasn't in bed.

'Hey, G – I've just finished—'

'Uh, hi, Ren. Look, I know you were supposed to come back

here after work but I'm going to have to say no tonight. Sorry.'

'Oh.' Renee's stomach sinks. 'Are you all right?'

'Me? Yeah, I'm fine. It's not about me. It's – well, something weird is going on outside.'

'Weird?'

'They've shut my road. The police—'

'The police?' Renee can't help the worry that infects her voice. 'Has there been an accident?'

'No. At least, I don't think so. I didn't hear anything. But there's an ambulance outside, so maybe? They knocked on my door about an hour ago, asking everyone to stay inside. They haven't told us why, but I went on the NextDoor app, and the woman from number thirty-two says they've put up a cordon around a manhole cover in front of her house, and she's heard mention of human remains being found.'

'Christ, that's not good.'

'I know, right? Nothing's been confirmed, but it does sound a bit suspicious. There's lots of blue lights, and the entire road's been sealed off.'

Renee hears the clack of blinds being moved in the background.

'There's a lot of people in uniforms outside, so it must be serious,' Graham finishes.

'Wow. I hope it isn't too bad. Are you going to be all right?'

'I'm fine. I'm supposed to be going to Croydon tomorrow – a site visit – so we'll see if that happens.'

'I'm sure you'll be able to postpone it a day or two, given the circumstances.'

'Yeah, hopefully. Where are you now?'

'Well, now you're indisposed, I guess I'm heading towards the Tube.'

Graham falls silent. 'Look,' he says after a moment, 'I know this is going to sound a bit mad, but I'm going to call you an Uber,

OK? This whole situation has shaken me up a bit, and I don't really want you on the Tube this late at night.'

Renee laughs. 'Graham, I've been doing it for ever. I'll be fine.'

'I know – you're more than capable, but . . . please. Indulge me. For once. It just feels like this area's been in the news way too often, you know?'

Now he mentions it, Renee realizes he has a point.

'OK – for you. Let me order it, though, and I'll just head back to NOVA – makes it easier for the driver.'

Graham sighs. 'Thank you. I'll send you the money for it. I know I'm probably just being paranoid, but if anything happened . . .'

'I get it. I feel the same way.'

Renee turns and begins retracing her steps back to the restaurant as she toggles between apps, staying on the call as much for her comfort as for his.

'Did you have a good shift?'

Anxiety rekindles in Renee's belly.

'It was pretty great,' she says. 'I was in charge of starters because Gracie was in, and she was doing some of the mains.'

'So lots of super-secret signature dishes being served tonight?'

'No . . . she was working off the main menu. There was only one signature dish – for that idiot who likes to tell young boys that girls are inferior and they should know it.'

'Ugh, which one? There are so many these days.'

Renee smiles at this. Even if he can be a bit clueless, Graham is definitely a good one.

'I know, right? Anyway, it was Troy Fisk.'

'I *hate* that guy.'

'Me too. And I hate him even more now. He comes in like he owns the place, demanding that his – and I quote – "boys" are served as well, but Gracie wasn't having any of it. She's pretty fearsome when she gets going.'

'Did she refuse to serve him?'

'No, that's the weird thing. She refused to serve his entourage but was happy to feed him.'

'That doesn't sound like something Gracie would tolerate,' Graham says.

'Normally I'd be with you, but there's more to it than that. You see, she knew he was coming in, so she prepared a dish especially for him. *Frivolités*.'

'*Frivolités*?' She can hear the cogs turning in Graham's head. 'Hang on . . . isn't that the French testicle dish? I remember my dad ordering it for me as a joke.'

'Yes, it is – and what the hell, Neil?'

Graham laughs. 'Just another in a long line of reasons why I went vegetarian at a young age.'

'Yeah, not surprised. And I wouldn't be surprised if this idiot goes down a similar path when he works out what he was served.'

'Oh. She pulled a Neil, then?'

'Yup. I mean, I will admit it was funny – especially when he all but licked his plate clean – but at the same time, it was a bit, I dunno, cruel?'

'Well, you know what they say – never piss off the people who are going to serve you food. You never know what they're doing to it.'

'That's a very good point.'

'I wouldn't worry too much about it. You said it yourself – he enjoyed the meal, and there's no shame in that. So what if they were indeed testicles. It's not illegal to eat them. In fact, the only place you'll get them these days is in high-end dining. He should consider himself lucky to be served what's considered a delicacy in other parts of the world. Surely there's some kind of twisted machismo-esque street cred in eating something so off the wall, too?'

Renee sighs. This is why she loves him. He's so reasonable – always trying to see the best in any given situation.

'I guess so. It's not so much the food – more the blow to his ego when he finds out what it was.'

'And that's his problem to deal with, not yours.'

'Yeah. Still . . .'

'I know, but he's a jackass and you're too good for this world, Ren.'

If anyone else had said that to her, she'd laugh in their face. But not Graham. He truly means it.

She turns the corner, and there is NOVA – just over the road.

'OK, I'm here now. Looks like everything's locked up.'

'I can stay on the line if you like?'

'No, I'll be fine. My phone just dinged, so that's probably my Uber on its way. Keep me updated on the madness, OK?'

'As long as you're sure.'

'About the madness?'

'No, dummy,' Graham says with a chuckle. 'About leaving you there.'

'Ah, you know me. Street as fuck.'

'Says the girl who hid at her own birthday party.'

'Shut up. We can't all be social butterflies—'

A scraping sound coming from the entrance to the alley behind the restaurant cuts short Renee's gentle teasing. She turns and spots something moving in the dark.

'Ren? You still there?'

'Yeah. Just . . . hang on . . .' She lowers her phone but doesn't end the call. 'Hello?' she shouts down the alley.

No one answers.

'Must be a cat,' Renee mutters to herself. She goes back to her call.

'Is everything all right?'

'Yep, everything's fine. Just heard something out the back

of the restaurant. Probably a cat trying to get into the bins again—'

A low moan emanates from the gloom.

'Oh shit,' she breathes, blood roaring in her ears as she steps away from the alley entrance.

'Oh shit what? Renee? What's going on?'

'You didn't hear that?'

'Didn't hear what?'

But Renee isn't listening to him. She's straining her hearing, trying to work out what might be down there. She doesn't think it's a cat. Could it be a fox? They're everywhere, and they do make disturbing noises. Although she's never heard a fox make a sound like that before. It was too low, too drawn out. If anything, it sounded more like a person in pain.

'Wait there, G. Something's going on behind the restaurant.'

'What?' Graham's tone immediately drips with worry. 'Ren, whatever it is, leave it alone.'

'But someone could be hurt.'

'Yeah, and it could also be some crackhead rummaging through NOVA's bins.'

As if on cue, another moan seeps out of the alley, ending in a wheezing gurgle.

'Oh God, I honestly think someone might be hurt,' Renee says, creeping forwards. 'Hello?' she calls out for a second time. 'Are you OK?'

Silence.

Her phone dings again above Graham's increasingly frantic demands for her to leave this be. It's her Uber arriving.

'OK, the Uber's here, so I'm going to go.'

'Just get home safe.'

'Yeah, but what if someone needs help?'

'Ren, love – please.'

'Yeah. You're right. Better safe than sorry. I'll text you when

I'm home. Love you.' She ends the call as she climbs into the back of the car.

'You all right?' the Uber driver asks. 'You look like you've seen a ghost.'

'Yeah. I just . . .' She glances back towards the alley, but everything is still. 'Yeah, it's nothing. Hard shift, that's all.'

TWENTY-FOUR

Over the next few weeks, the glorious summer weather gives way to never-ending drizzle, and this morning is no different. Renee groans. Of course it's raining. It's September now – the month where you either drown or swelter. Nothing in between. Oh well. At least it means she won't have to water the plants on her balcony. Small mercies.

She sends Graham a quick text as part of her morning routine, feeling a little guilty that she hasn't seen him in person since last Monday night. Sadly, this remains a bit of a thing. Shift working isn't exactly conducive to normal relationship patterns, and while she knows Graham doesn't exactly blame her for it, it's proving to be a recurring source of tension between them.

The text is nothing special – just a good morning. Usually, he just sends the same sentiment back, leaving her happy that he replied but also a bit guilty for neglecting him. Like the plants on her balcony.

But not this morning.

This morning, he calls her.

'Uh, hey, G. Is everything OK?' she says, her stomach bottoming out. No one calls anyone this early in the morning unless it's bad news. Or they've won the lottery. But Graham doesn't play that, so . . .

'Everything's fine. Why do you ask?'

'Thank God for that,' Renee says, blowing out a sigh of relief. 'You know I immediately think something terrible has happened when you call me like this, right?'

'Yeah, I know – I'm sorry, but I really needed to talk to you. I didn't want to do this over text.'

Renee sits down, her stomach sinking again. No good conversation ever starts with 'I don't want to do this over text'.

'OK . . . and why is that?'

'No, Ren – it's nothing bad,' Graham says, quickly reassuring her. 'It's fine. Nothing's happened – no sudden deaths or anything like that.'

'Phew,' Renee says. 'So, what's up?'

'I've been thinking . . .' Graham starts.

'Dangerous . . . but go on.'

Graham chuckles. 'Cheeky, but I'll let it slide. I've been thinking that we haven't had much of an opportunity to spend any quality time together recently. We snatch hours here and there as we can, and that's fine – I know you're busy – but I wanted to treat you. To treat *us*. To something a little extra.'

There's a fizz of excitement in his words now, but Renee can't help being a little wary. This is going to be about her moving in again – she can just tell. He has a habit of springing things on her without thinking – like sending her huge bouquets of flowers, which is lovely – but without considering the little things – like how she's going to get them home.

'OK, hit me.'

'Right. I was thinking about how busy you are, and how much you deserve a break, so I thought I'd book us both into the Guerlin Spa for a weekend. Not this weekend, of course, but in a couple of weeks. I thought about maybe whisking you off to Paris or somewhere, but then I thought you'd probably prefer to stay local so we wouldn't have to worry about travelling and the like—'

'What?' Renee says, interrupting him.

'I've booked us into a spa.'

'A spa?'

'Yes.'

'When?'

'Weekend after this. I've done it all – you don't have to worry about anything—'

Renee closes her eyes and rubs the bridge of her nose with her free hand.

'OK, so that's very nice of you and I love your generosity, but there's no way I'll be able to go anywhere for a weekend – let alone at such short notice.'

'If you're worried about paying for it, it's no problem,' Graham says. 'I've already paid for it all. I keep saying, you don't need to worry about that. As for getting time off, I'm sure I can push it all back a couple of weeks . . .'

Renee lets the phone dangle from her hand and sighs heavily. This again. She's tried being kind. She's tried being understanding. She's tried to explain that he can't just pay to make things better. That money isn't part of why they're together. But he won't listen. For a so-called progressive, he still thinks money can solve basically everything. He really doesn't get it.

'Graham, babe, I'm not sure how I can break this down so you understand. Whether I can afford it or not isn't the issue. It's not the point. I work weekends. And, for the record, I'm going to be working weekends for the foreseeable future. Because I work in a restaurant. You know – the place people famously tend to flock to on the weekend. Which means I'm not going to have a weekend available any time soon.'

'But . . . how does that work? Legally, you're entitled to leave—'

'Yes, of course I am. But with chefs, they have to jostle things around to make sure everything's covered. I can't let Gracie down. I'm her chef de partie. I'm part of the team.'

'But that's not your problem. Surely Gracie has contingency plans if, say, someone goes off sick?'

'I'm not pulling a sickie, Graham. Not now, not ever.'

'I'm not suggesting you should. I'm just saying that legally, you're entitled to leave, and it's not your problem to ensure your shifts are covered.'

'Graham . . . I know it's an adjustment, and I really do appreciate your patience, but that's just not how it works in my field. I'm not just *at work*. This is my career. My dream. I'm finally doing everything I wanted to do with my life – and more.'

'So . . . what? Are you saying you prefer to be at work than with me?'

Rather than sounding hurt, Graham is growing increasingly defensive – as if Renee is deliberately trying to be difficult.

'Graham, I'm not saying anything like that.'

'So what are you saying? That your job is more important than spending time with me? I hardly ever see you these days. For the last couple of months, you've been a ghost. I only really get to see you when you stay over, and that's becoming a rarity. And I'm sorry, but I'm feeling a bit hurt by it all, if I'm honest. Like I'm no longer one of your priorities.'

Renee reels a little.

'What do you mean, priorities? Oh, like when your job meant that you had to go and live in Germany for a month? Because if we're talking about not seeing each other for a long period of time—'

'That was for business. It wasn't a holiday.'

'And what do you think I'm doing? Sitting by the pool drinking piña coladas?' She takes a breath to steady her voice, hoping to keep this from becoming a full-blown argument. 'This has been my dream since I was a kid. I've wanted to be a chef far longer than I've been with you – and I'm sorry, but I need you to understand that you're going to have to take a backseat for a while. At least until I get myself established.'

Graham doesn't respond, but she can hear him breathing. It's heavy and a little erratic, telling her she's crossed a line.

'And how long is that going to take?' he manages to say.

'I don't know. Look, love, I'm sorry. I'm tired and under a lot of stress—'

'No, it's fine. I understand.'

'Do you?'

'Of course I do!'

It's easy to say that. To say you get it – 'Everyone goes through it. Suck it up, buttercup.' But it's a cop-out phrase – an easy win. What makes it worse is that Renee reckons he doesn't understand any of it – not really. Mainly because he hasn't had to. He doesn't get being poor. He's never been there – not even when he was a student. Doesn't know what it's like to strive for something, only for it to be ripped away by forces out of your control. He doesn't understand having to take a job – any job – just to make ends meet. Or what it's like to be a classically trained chef working in a fucking chicken shop because that's all you could get. And now – at last! – someone has thrown her a bone. A bone that she has to hang on to for dear life. Because there are a lot of other chefs snapping at her heels, ready to take that bone off her the moment she slips up. No, he doesn't understand any of it.

'Babe, I'm not saying no. I'm just saying not yet.'

'It's OK, Renee. It's fine. I'll cancel the booking. Not sure what I'll do about the deposit, but that's my problem, not yours.'

'Graham . . .'

This is another thing she's noticed. It doesn't matter what any of their arguments are about, she's always the one who feels like she needs to apologize. It doesn't matter if she started it or not, nor if she's actually right or not – the mere existence of her disagreement is enough for her to be in the wrong.

'No it's fine. I have a busy day ahead of me, and I'm sure you do too, so I'll speak to you later, OK?'

'G, wait—'

He ends the call.

Renee stares at her phone in disbelief.

TWENTY-FIVE

Say what you want about high-end cuisine, but there's nothing better than a full English at the smallest greasy spoon cafe you can find. Renee and Lola are lucky enough to live right round the corner from one, and it's as much of an experience as eating at NOVA – only at the other end of the spectrum.

This one is called the Breakfast Cafe, which pretty much sums up its whole vibe. People are often surprised to find out that it's run by a Malaysian couple, but they've had the place for years, and while the menu is a little labyrinthine, it's worth the time to learn how to navigate it.

On the surface, it's simple: full English large, full English small, full English vegetable. Toast. Tea. Coffee. Cold cans. But if you're local, you know that's not where the menu ends. If you're local, you know that Minnie (Renee learned her given name is Maeena, but she thought customers would find 'Minnie' easier to say) and her husband (no one knows his name, as Minnie does all the talking, all the time) are spice wizards, and will incorporate all manner of fusion twists into the food, but only if you know what to ask for – and only then if Minnie likes you.

Thankfully, Minnie likes Lola and Renee.

She hails them as they walk in. There are no names for the fusion dishes, but both Renee and Lola know exactly what to ask for: full English large with *roti* and *telur dada* instead of toast and fried eggs, with a cup of pulled tea each. Once their orders are taken, the pair sit at their favourite table – the small round one in the window with mismatched chairs. Lola immediately starts their catch-up with her most recent Hinge disaster, lamenting that all the men she matches with are either arseholes or looking for a new mummy. This one, it turns out, was an arsehole who *also* wanted a new mummy.

'So he was the complete package, huh?' Renee says.

'Oh yeah, he subscribed to every single one of the broken-man channels. But it's OK, I'm not going to be seeing him again – fuck, no. Shame, cos he had a cute dog. Maybe I should date the dog?'

Renee can't help but laugh.

'You know what, if we ever get out of Mandem Towers, we should totally get a place that allows pets, so we could get a dog.' Lola pauses. 'Or a cat. No, I think I'd prefer a dog.'

'Ah, but should we get a big dog or a little one?'

'Little one. Actually . . . scratch that. Let's get a big one – like a staffie or something.'

'Staffies aren't big dogs,' Renee says. 'I was thinking more along the lines of a rottie.'

'Jeez, girl, you're talking about big big dogs, which are a big big no for me.'

'Aww, I don't know. I think they're cute.'

'Yeah, right up until it rips someone's face off.'

'They don't do that. If they're trained properly, they're nice dogs. My brother's got one. His kids ride it like a horse.' She picks up her phone and scrolls through her photos. 'See?'

'OK, that is kinda cute. But that's enough about dogs. I couldn't help but overhear a certain . . . altercation this morning. Everything all right?'

Renee blows out a long sigh.

'Yeah . . . I think so. G's just being so . . . pfft.' Renee mimes her head blowing up. 'Like, I get it – we're not seeing each other as much as we used to, and that's a shame, but I can't help it. I have responsibilities now. An actual career that might go somewhere. But he doesn't get it. He kept going on and on about it.'

'Hey, what about me? I hardly see you either. He can get in line,' Lola says. 'I come first.'

'If you say sistas before mistas,' Renee says, 'I'm going to throw that bottle of ketchup at you.'

Lola cackles and sips at her tea.

'So what set him off? He's usually Mr Rocksteady. Why's he kicking off first thing?'

'He said he's booked us a spa session at the Guerlian for the weekend after next.'

'What? And you're complaining about that?'

'Well, no, but—'

'Cos where I come from, we say "thank you very much, yes please" to things like that. We don't start arguments.'

'No, Lola – you don't get it. It's not the spa trip that's the issue. It's that he did it without asking me.'

'Yeah, Ren – there's this thing, right? I dunno if you've heard of it, but it's called a surprise, and people generally do things like that when they really love you and want to spend some quality time with you.'

'Oh, yeah, very funny,' Renee says, her back stiffening. 'It's not the surprise that bothers me. It's that he knows I can't do a weekend. I'm working. Then he started going on about me taking leave for it – like that's easy. Honestly, you'd think he'd have caught on to the fact that I work shifts by now. Not everyone has the privilege of working nine-to-five with two days at home.'

Lola gives Renee a long look as Minnie sets down their breakfast plates. As usual, the food looks brown and uninteresting, but it smells divine. Both of them dig in, suddenly starving.

'I don't know, Renee,' Lola says through a mouthful of *roti*. 'Quite honestly, if I had a guy book me a spa break just because he wants to spend some time with me, I don't think I'd be complaining about it. Shit's expensive. Let him pamper you.'

Renee pauses, a forkful of *telur dada* halfway to her mouth.

'What, you're taking his side?'

'Hey, I'm not taking anyone's side. All I'm saying is – and it pains me to admit this – you could do a lot worse than G. He might be a bit of a dork, but at least he genuinely loves you. Better than the losers I'm having to wade through right now, that's for sure.'

'Yeah, I know, but . . . it's always on his terms. He wants to pay for everything, says all of my problems could be solved if I just let him help me . . . Hell, you know he's still expecting me to move in with him now I'm working at NOVA, right? He keeps going on about how it makes sense, that he lives closer, and now I've got this job maybe I won't feel so sensitive about the money thing, but . . . I don't know.'

Renee was hoping Lola might pick up the slack and start agreeing with her, but instead Lola sighs.

'Honey, I don't know what you want me to say. That time he told me that I was holding you back? That was him being a prick. But he did apologize. Said it was selfish of him, but he can't help that he wants to build a life with you. And I can't lie, if I had a man as devoted and rock-solid as G, who was willing to let me live with him in his fancy-arse flat in Chelsea, I don't think I'd hesitate. I'd be in there like a rat up a pipe. Sorry, but that's the way it is.'

Renee sits back in her seat, stunned and miffed.

'So you *are* taking his side on this?'

'Ren, there are no sides when it comes to these things. Would I be upset if you moved in with him? Yes, of course I would. I'd miss you like hell. But at the same time, I'd understand. That's how life works. When it comes down to it, I don't think your boyfriend wanting to pamper you and look after you makes him a bad guy. You should cut him some slack.'

'Yeah, but . . .' Renee pauses to take a sip of her drink, because she can't think of a way to rebut that. 'It's not that he wants to treat me well. It's more that he didn't even ask if I was working. He just assumes.'

'And? He doesn't work in food. No one outside the industry really knows how it's run. If you lived with him, maybe he'd have a better idea, but you don't – so you can't kick the boy for trying.'

Renee takes a moment to register what Lola is saying. That if their roles were reversed, she'd likely already be gone, taking every single advantage of her wealthy partner. It was like no one understood her stance – her plight.

That's a little self-indulgent, even for me.

She was trying her very best, but everyone around her seemed to just want to belittle her achievements. Everyone, that is, except Gracie. Gracie saw her talent. Saw her dedication and fire. Gracie encourages her. Challenges her. Makes her hungry to learn. To grow. Renee's appetite flees. She doesn't need this right now. She doesn't need them. If she has to, she'll go her own way – carve her own path. That's what Gracie did, and look where it took her.

Renee sets her knife and fork down on her plate and gathers up her bag.

'Hey, where are you going?' Lola says.

'I've just noticed the time – I have to get to work.'

'Have to get to . . . Ren, it's half past nine. You've got ages before you have to think about that.'

'Yeah, well, that may be the case in a franchise restaurant, but when you're in a top-end establishment, they expect a little bit more from you.'

'Hey,' Lola says, clearly hurt, and Renee regrets her last comment. 'I know you're a bit stressed out and all, but that doesn't make you better than me.'

'OK, look, I'm sorry. I didn't mean that.'

'Yes, you did. Otherwise you wouldn't have said it. Renee – and I say this with all the love in the world – you've got to get your priorities sorted. I know you're excited about NOVA, but at the end of the day, it's still just a job.'

'Work to live rather than live to work,' Renee says, mimicking Graham. She meant it as sarcasm, but when Lola grins, she knows that's not how it's been taken.

'That's exactly it,' Lola says. 'You need to live a little. Chill a little.'

'Yeah, Graham said something similar.'

'Then maybe you should be listening – because him and me, we rarely see eye to eye, but it sounds like we're both pretty solid on this one.'

Renee stands up and shoulders her bag as a sudden urge to cry swells within her.

'I've got to go.'

And before Lola can say anything else, Renee scuttles out of the Breakfast Cafe, not looking back.

TWENTY-SIX

After catching the Tube, Renee wanders around for a while, feeling lost. She's achieved her career goals, but at what cost? It seems as if life likes to play balancing games: Oh, you have the greatest best friend and a boyfriend who loves you, but your job is shitty and sucking the life out of you? Well, we have a solution for that! Here's your dream job, served to you on a fucking platter, but if you accept it, then we're going to make your roommate and partner distance themselves from you. Because if there's one thing life doesn't like, it's for people to be happy.

Is that actually the way it is or am I spiralling?

Renee wends her way closer to NOVA, walking past the top of Graham's road. She considers dropping in on him, but decides that'd probably be a bad idea, given the mood she's in. Police tape flutters from a lamppost, reminding her of the night he told her he couldn't meet up after her shift. Did they ever sort that out? They said it was human remains – she knows that much – and the media covered it for a few days afterwards, but they soon forgot all about it with the next news cycle. She spends a moment wondering who it might have been, and what they'd done to end up in a sewer.

As the time ticks past ten, she starts heading over to NOVA. At least this part is straightforward. She's a little early, but as always, Q is there to let her in. She smiles and nods, saying 'thank you' as he holds the door for her, but he doesn't crack. In many ways, he remains almost as much of a mystery to her as Gracie is. He rarely comes into the kitchen if Gracie isn't working, and when he does, he usually speaks to Bethany – which makes sense, given she runs the pass, but even so. She doesn't even know his last name. Like Prince, or Madonna.

In the kitchen, Renee isn't surprised to see Bethany's already there. She *is* a little surprised to see Roy and Martin, though. She checks her phone to make sure she isn't late, but it's only just gone a quarter past ten. Why is everyone here so early?

Maybe they've all had arguments with their loved ones and come in to take a break, too.

When they spot her, they welcome her with a chorus of 'Hey, how you doing?' and 'You all right?'. Martin even holds his arms out and grins, enveloping Renee in a hug, but only after she smiles and steps towards him.

The one thing that is strange is there's no sign of Josh.

'You know what he's been like ever since Gracie took him to task when that influencer was in. Maybe he's decided he can't stand the disrespect any longer,' Roy says, sipping from a mug of coffee.

'I don't know,' Bethany says. 'The boy's delusional if he thinks that. If word gets out, no one will have him – no matter who his uncle is.'

'That's the problem with these nepo babies,' Martin says. 'They've never had to work for anything, so just do stuff on a whim. Everyone thinks working in a kitchen is easy until they actually have to do it. I'm surprised he lasted as long as he did, if I'm honest.'

They continue to chat while they set up their stations. The conversation drifts between Josh's no-show and the expectations for the day's service, leaving Renee feeling more at home here than anywhere else. Here, no one here judges her, nor do they make unreasonable demands of her. Here, she is valued. Appreciated. Regarded as an equal.

Respected.

Closer to eleven, and they're thick in their prep work when Gracie strides into the kitchen. Renee's heart skips. They haven't seen much of her over the last couple of weeks, and her presence has been missed. That she's in again really boosts Renee's mood, because if there's one person who doesn't stand for nonsense, it's Gracie. At least she can trust her to tell it straight, not manipulate her, not twist her words.

Chef greets everyone in the kitchen with a curt nod. She doesn't say anything about Josh's absence but instead talks quietly to Bethany at the back of the kitchen. If she's angry about Josh dropping them in it, she doesn't betray that. Every single part of her is the picture of serenity – completely at odds with her harridan reputation.

They all look over when the door that leads to the pass is wrenched open and an unnaturally stressed-looking Q enters, making a beeline for Gracie. They share a few looks and even fewer words, utilizing that strange telepathy only available to people who've known each other for years. But where Q looks concerned, Gracie just laughs.

'Let him come,' she says, loud enough for everyone to hear. 'It'll be fun.'

'Are you sure?' Q sounds genuinely concerned. 'Especially after last time—'

'Of course. And, just like last time, I will prepare one of my signature dishes for him.'

Q's expression flits from stressed to something far more vicious.

'Of course, Chef,' he says, and for a moment, Renee thinks he might bow before her. 'I shall go and inform him.'

'Right,' Gracie says, addressing the team as Q leaves. 'It looks like we're in for yet more fun today. With one no-show employee we were already going to have to be on our toes, but I have just been informed that the supposedly retired food critic Preston Walls has decided to grace NOVA with his presence yet again.'

No one actually gasps, but Renee can tell from the way everyone's eyes widen that this is something of a curveball.

'So, in light of this new information, as you heard, I will be serving Mr Walls one of my signature dishes. As usual, this will not be part of the wider menu, and so I will need you all to keep on top of things without me – at least until Mr Walls is done with us.' Then, to Renee's complete and utter shock, Gracie looks her dead in the eye. 'Renee. Please join me.'

It takes a moment for Renee's brain to catch up with her ears.

'Uh, yes, Chef,' she says, stunned. What is she doing? Surely she's going to be needed to keep on top of the other courses? She looks around awkwardly before scuttling over to Gracie's bench. Crap. What has she done? Why has she been singled out? *Fuck.* She thinks back over the last few shifts, trying to remember if anything she'd done could be perceived as wrong – if she'd undercooked or, God forbid, overcooked something – but she comes up blank. As far as she's concerned, everything's been going well. Maybe she's wrong. Maybe Gracie has decided she's made a massive mistake and needs to get rid of her.

'Why do you look so worried?' Gracie says softly, breaking through Renee's panicked train of thought. 'I don't bite, I promise.'

'Of course not, Chef. I wouldn't even dream—'

'Renee, calm yourself. Don't make me regret this.' Gracie holds her gaze, leaving her feeling like a mouse caught in the sights of a particularly adept cat. 'Ever since that first shift, I've seen something in you. I can't tell you exactly what it is, because it is rare. It isn't talent, but something . . . deeper, more visceral. And to that end, I've decided that you're going to assist me today on this dish. I want to challenge you. It's up to you how you take this.'

TWENTY-SEVEN

Renee stares at Gracie in disbelief.

'W-what? Oh, sorry. I didn't mean to sound rude, but—'

Gracie's expression doesn't change.

'Renee, by doubting yourself, you are doubting me, and I don't appreciate that.'

'No, sorry, Chef. Of course. I'm just really honoured.'

'Yes, yes, that's all very nice, but nice doesn't get you anywhere in this industry. You are clearly talented, and I think you have been criminally overlooked, but you need to toughen up. You should be out there, knocking them dead, making my life an absolute nightmare. But instead, fate has thrown us together, and I want you to have the experience I didn't.'

Renee has no idea what she means by that, but she can't really focus on it right now, because Gracie Fitzgerald – *the* Gracie Fitzgerald – wants to mentor her for a whole shift. *A whole shift!* A sense of pride swells within her, so big she feels she might burst.

'Thank you, Chef. Thank you so much—'

'That's enough of that,' Gracie says. 'Don't make me regret my decision.'

'Of course not. Sorry.'

'And you can stop doing that too. As I've already told you – don't apologize. Never apologize. Take up space, and don't let anyone say you don't deserve it.' Gracie thrusts a knife into Renee's hand. 'As always, we start with vegetable prep. I'm going to get my . . . personal ingredients while you fetch me everything else.'

'Personal ingredients?' Renee asks, sensing an opportunity to find out what's actually in Gracie's freezer of mystery. It can't all be brains and testicles and endless cuts of veal.

Gracie scrutinizes her for a good long while – enough to make Renee feel uncomfortable. But just as she thinks Gracie is going to brush her off, the chef shrugs.

'As I'm sure you are well aware, my restaurant sources the finest of ingredients for our dishes, yes?'

Renee nods but doesn't say anything. Who knows when Gracie will be in such a generous mood again?

'There are some ingredients that I source that are mine, and mine alone. They are used only in my signature dishes. They are prepped by me, tasted by me. These dishes are a personal communication between myself and the diner. This is why I don't allow others to taste these creations when I am here. When I come into my kitchen, these dishes need to meet my standards, and no one else's. My chefs understand this. If they don't, they can seek employment elsewhere. Do I make myself clear?'

'Of course, Chef. One hundred per cent.'

Gracie smiles at her again, but it doesn't relax Renee. If anything, it only increases the tension. It's not as if the smile is off – it reaches her eyes – but it doesn't come across as happiness, or even satisfaction. There's a slyness to it, almost bordering on smug, and it unnerves Renee.

The dish, Gracie explains, is an example of classic haute cuisine, but with her own twists. It celebrates veal, which comes as no surprise to Renee. Gracie is always about the veal, and Renee is under no illusion that is because it's the one meat that gets under people's skin. If anything, she's relieved Gracie's picked a relatively normal ingredient for once. As funny as the testicle thing was, she's not sure she needs a lesson in how to prepare them.

First, Gracie tells her what she needs to gather from the dry pantry: fat white onions, olive oil, fresh tarragon and balsamic vinegar. Then, from the cold pantry: a bowl of fresh oysters still in their shells, morels, butter and eggs – carefully piling them so she doesn't drop them. By the time she hauls everything back to Gracie's bench, the chef is already there with what looks like the most succulent joint of veal Renee has ever seen. It's a perfectly cylindrical cut of the fillet, clearly butchered by an expert. Next to it are some bones, steeping in a bowl of salted water.

'Now, you know what this is?'

'Yes,' Renee says with as much confidence as she can muster. 'It's a veal fillet.'

Gracie again holds her gaze a little longer than necessary, and when she looks away, the strange smile is back.

'Good. Have you worked with this cut before?'

'I have, although not as often as other types of meat.'

'That is often the case,' Gracie says. 'Pork, beef and lamb fillet are much more common. But don't worry. I'll lead you by the nose through this, OK?'

Renee nods, trying to ignore the slightly repellent turn of phrase.

'Firstly, as you can already see, I select my cut. I'm not going to be preparing two – this cut is incredibly hard to get hold of, and I never make mistakes.'

Renee watches as Gracie picks up a long, impossibly sharp filleting knife and slices through the fillet in one long sweep. The meat teeters before falling, oozing a little myoglobin as it does so.

'Right. What we have here,' Gracie continues, 'is what would be called a filet mignon if this were beef – but it isn't, so it is just a fillet. A small thing, but small things matter. It is the small things that make you stand out from the competition. Looking after the small things is what sets you apart.'

Renee nods enthusiastically, not daring to speak as Gracie places the rest of the fillet on the back bench. Next, Chef removes the bones from their salted water bath. 'I prepped these last night.'

She did? But she wasn't in last night. Not for service, at least. Did she come in after they'd all gone home? But why leave it that late?

'Are you all right?' Gracie asks sharply. Renee realizes she's frowning and immediately smooths her expression to something more passive.

'Yes, of course I am. I'm just . . . it's nothing. Just my concentrating face.'

Again, Gracie studies her, dragging the moment out just a bit too long. Then she makes a little *hmm* noise before continuing.

'I always try to make sure I have bone marrow to hand. An amazing ingredient that many baulk at, for some reason. Much like other offal cuts, people are so squeamish. It's such a shame. There is so much wonderful flavour in it.'

One by one, she takes the bones and chops the joints off the top with a hard, practised swing of her cleaver. She then swaps it for a long, thin-bladed knife and scoops out the marrow, which she collects in a glass bowl. It isn't long before she has a sizeable, quivering mass of yellowish jelly.

Renee has prepared bone marrow before – of course she has; all chefs learn how to do this – but she's never worked with veal bones before. At least, she guesses they're veal. They're definitely not beef bones, which are much thicker and denser – there's no way you could crack those open with a cleaver, no matter how experienced you are. But she can't shake the suspicion that these bones are too long to be from calves. Although, saying that . . . calves are very leggy, so . . .

She feels a little pang deep inside her stomach. That must be it. The bones only look longer because they're thinner and less dense – a result of the animals being so young when they are slaughtered.

She forces herself to focus on the task at hand, ignoring how fast her heart is beating.

'Once the marrow has been removed, we will blanch it in a pan of boiling water. The kettle is over there.' Gracie gestures to the other side of the bench and Renee almost trips as she darts over, keen not to waste the opportunity to be involved. Once the water is boiled, she pours it into a saucepan and watches as Gracie carefully slides the marrow into it.

'Now, we don't season at this stage,' Gracie explains, 'because salt will toughen the marrow. We just need it to solidify. It usually takes about ten minutes, so while it's firming up, we shall use that time to prepare our onions. I'm going to let you do this. Select the best one, then quarter it.'

Renee carefully selects the fattest onion and places it on a fresh board. Beside her, the little round slab of veal glistens. The meat is a darker shade of pink, with a delicate marbling of fat running through it, telling her that this isn't rose veal, which tends to be lighter in colour.

At least that's something.

While Renee preps the onion, Gracie puts the larger fillet away. Renee can't resist glancing back when she hears the hiss of the freezer door, followed by a gust of frigid air curling up the backs of her legs. She doesn't see much – just a cold steel interior with shelves bolted to the walls – and observes Gracie set her tray on a middle shelf. Suddenly, the chef turns, as if she can sense that she's being watched. Renee's pulse quickens as she whips her attention back to the onion, hoping Gracie hasn't seen her staring. If she has, Gracie doesn't say anything. Renee refocuses.

The task is ridiculously easy – literally quarter the onion and then separate the layers to resemble pearly petals – but for a split second, Renee isn't sure if she can do it.

Come on, Renee. Get it together. A child could do this. You've been cutting onions all your life. She takes a deep breath and, with two deft slices, she has four neat quarters.

'There,' says Gracie, returning to the bench. 'That wasn't so hard, was it?'

Renee doesn't reply, unsure if Gracie is joking or not. Seemingly oblivious to her discomfort, Gracie continues her lesson.

'Now we check on the marrow.' She pokes the mass with a slotted spoon, breaking off the tiniest piece and holding it up for Renee to inspect. 'See how it's solidifying? We don't want to take it too far, or it becomes too firm.' She then picks the blob of marrow from the spoon and pops it into her mouth, closing her eyes as she savours the flavour. 'People don't know what they're missing. So rich, so meaty . . . Simply a wonderful ingredient.'

A bowl of iced water magically appears – Gracie must have prepared it in her cold room. She uses the slotted spoon to fish the rest of the firm marrow out of the saucepan and plunges it into the iced water.

'We now wait for it to cool. It won't take long. Once it is cold, we remove it from the water and pat it dry. The last thing we want is to spoil our marrow. Good marrow like this is a devil to come by.'

The marrow now dealt with, Gracie moves on to the other aspects of her dish. She puts the onions in a pan along with the balsamic vinegar and olive oil. Leaving that to sweat, she moves on to the morels – strange-looking mushrooms that have always made Renee uncomfortable. There's just something about the way they look, with their strange, folded caps that resemble tiny brains, that make her cringe. Still, they're highly prized in kitchens worldwide, so she suppresses her reaction. The last thing she needs is Gracie knowing she's a bit funny about fungus.

After giving them a once-over with a soft brush, Gracie quickly blanches the morels in boiling water, then strains them, reserving the resulting liquid for the next step – the oyster sabayon. Renee's made plenty of sabayons before, but never with oysters. It feels oddly barbaric, tipping the freshly shucked oysters straight into a blender. Not that it seems to worry Gracie. If anything, she seems to relish the act as she turns the machine on, transforming the lumpen, slimy creatures into a thick, greyish paste. At least their deaths were quick, Renee reasons.

Gracie marches back over to her freezer and places the blender jug on a shelf near the door. That's when Renee realizes Gracie isn't furtively going into her secret pantry like some burglar in the night. She's quite blatant and doesn't make any effort to block Renee's view before shutting the door again. It's almost as if she wants Renee to look.

'OK.' Gracie dusts her hands off. 'That's our basic prep done. Now we ask Bethany where we are with the starter, so we know how long we have until the actual magic begins.'

TWENTY-EIGHT

As soon as Bethany signals she's ready, Gracie's whole demeanour hardens. No longer is she Gracie the mentor; now, she's Gracie the executive chef. She works at a terrifying pace, first making the sabayon, then turning her attention to the veal and mushrooms. The marrow is chopped and mixed with the tarragon, which she adds to the sautéing morels. Finally, she pays attention to the meat, handling it with a respect that verges on reverential.

'Can you please give those morels a stir?' she asks, probably because she's aware that Renee has done nothing other than watch.

Renee nods eagerly and tosses the pan. The smell coming off it is incredible, with the bone marrow caramelizing the edges of the mushrooms to a perfect nutty brown. Without thinking, she leans over for a spoon – tasting really is second nature in a kitchen – but before she can put the smallest of morsels into her mouth to ascertain the seasoning, Gracie barks out a sharp *'No!'*

The rest of the kitchen falls silent as everyone turns to find out exactly what has upset their executive chef so much.

Gracie snatches the spoon from Renee's unresisting hand and throws it in the sink. She glares at Renee, her mouth a thin, taut line, the tendons in her jaw flashing.

'I'm so sorry, Chef. I was so caught up in everything, I wasn't thinking—'

'Be quiet,' Gracie hisses.

Although the other chefs have gone back to their own tasks, Renee knows they are listening.

'Yes, Chef,' Renee whispers. 'I'm sorry, Chef.'

'Maybe you're not ready for this after all.'

'No! I mean, I am – one hundred per cent. It was just a momentary lapse of judgement—'

'All it takes to ruin a dish is a momentary lapse of judgement. All it takes to lose all respect is a momentary lapse of judgement. Do you understand?'

'Yes, Chef,' Renee whispers, her attention squarely on her feet. Her heart is beating so loud she's shocked no one else in the kitchen can hear it. She can feel Gracie's eyes on her, burrowing into her just as her knife did with the marrow, agonizingly drawing out the moment. Renee dares to look up and sees Gracie's eyes flashing with a quiet rage.

I'll be lucky to get out of here alive, let alone with my job intact.

When Gracie leans over towards her, it takes everything she has not to flinch.

'If I ever see that again,' Gracie murmurs, her lip mere centimetres from her ear, 'you will be gone. Do I make myself clear?'

'Yes, Chef.'

'Good. Now attend to the morels. I can't risk them burning.'

And with that, Gracie turns back to her veal.

Renee's hand shakes as she picks up her spatula, clumsily turning the mushrooms over in the thick, gelatinous marrow. Thankfully, they don't look ruined, but she reduces the heat, just in case. A moment later, Gracie turns back to her, picks up a clean teaspoon and dips it into the mushrooms. She scoops up the tiniest amount, closing her eyes and smiling like someone has just given her a taste of manna from heaven.

'Delicious,' she says. 'Perfection, as always. Now we must complete the dish.'

It's like the previous few minutes never happened.

Feeling whiplashed, Renee can only watch as Gracie finishes off the veal, setting it aside so it can rest before being plated. The fillet has a gloriously caramelized exterior; Gracie demonstrates how she knows it is still soft inside by pressing it with one finger. Renee was taught that the best way to judge the status of your steak was by pressing on it, then pressing on various parts of your face to see how well it was done: soft cheek was rare – the most common request. Judging by the way the meat bounces back, it's clear this is perfectly cooked.

'One of my instructors told me the best way to check how well a steak is cooked was by touching my cheek and comparing,' Renee says, desperate to re-establish her connection with her mentor.

It's something she immediately regrets when Gracie looks at her, one eyebrow raised.

'Interesting. I was taught the same,' Gracie says, much to Renee's surprise. She was so sure she was going to be told to shut up again. 'Was it Isaac Ferguson? I trained under him.'

'Really? Yes, it was him. He was working as a lecturer at Le Cordon Bleu. I guess the culinary world is smaller than we think.'

'Indeed,' Gracie says. 'He was a . . . character.'

'That's one way of putting it, I suppose.'

'And what would be another?' Gracie tilts her head and watches Renee through slitted eyes. Again, Renee wishes she'd just kept her mouth shut.

'Uh, I don't—'

'Yes, you do. Say it.'

'I would rather not.'

'Why?' Gracie's stark questioning has Renee backed into a corner, where the only response she can give is a helpless shrug.

To her surprise, Gracie smiles.

'The man was a monster,' Gracie says. 'Sexist pig. At least by the time you came across him, he was using the cheek on your face. When I trained under him, he was telling students that the best way to test how well their steaks were done was by, and I quote, "touching a young lady's bottom".'

'Oh. That's . . . vile.' Renee is disgusted.

'Indeed it is.'

'How did he get away with it?' Renee asks quietly.

Gracie's smile turns predatory. 'I don't think he did. Where is he now? No one knows. No one cares. But we must get back to my dish. This meat has been rested enough, and judging by the empty plate that has just come back, Mr Walls has finished his starter, which means we have a dish to plate.'

Gracie works so fast it's almost impossible to follow. Usually, a filet mignon is served whole so it doesn't dry out, but Gracie has sliced hers into three pieces, revealing perfectly cooked meat inside. She dots the morels around the veal, then carefully stands one cleaned piece of femur upright beside it. She fills the cavity with oyster sabayon, then dresses the plate with fresh tarragon and a pinch of something from an unmarked tub.

'My own secret mixture. A puzzle others would kill for,' she says, grinning wolfishly.

Rather than calling for service, she picks up the plate herself. As always, she will serve her signature dish in person – like it's a piece of art. This is how she built her career: she dared to do what no female chef ever had. Rather than beg people to come into her restaurant and eat her food, she *challenged* them to come, and then she judged if they were worthy of her food. Not the other way round.

And it worked.

Gracie turns to Renee, a glimmer in her eye as she marches out of the kitchen.

'Are you coming?' she says. 'I'd like you to see this.'

TWENTY-NINE

Preston Walls.

He was once a big name in food. A *very* big name. If Walls liked your food, you were set for life. At least, that was the case until he decided to turn his acerbic wit on Gracie Fitzgerald.

Renee watches from the door to the pass as Gracie stalks over to him, plate held aloft like a sacrifice. To an outsider, it might look like she is happy with this arrangement, but Renee knows better. Like the proverbial elephant, Gracie Fitzgerald never forgets. This guy tried to tear her down – something she didn't take without a fight. When it comes to reviews, received wisdom is to shut up and deal. Don't respond. Don't complain. Just take your licks and hope it doesn't happen again.

But not Gracie.

She didn't so much clap back as annihilate Walls. And she didn't do it by throwing a tantrum or slinging insults. She did it by proving him wrong. Rather than crumble under the weight of his scrutiny, Gracie Fitzgerald used the pressure to harden herself, like carbon. She continued to serve her own food, without changing anything, and won her first Michelin star. People started to really take notice then – and, more importantly, question why Walls didn't see the obvious potential in her. The scrutiny reflected, he slunk off in shame, and his once prestigious name became a byword for not keeping up with the times. As Lola might say, Gracie ate and left absolutely no crumbs.

Renee thought she'd seen Gracie at her most lethal with Troy

Fisk, but this is another level. It's like she's witnessing an assassination in slow motion.

This time, it's personal.

Walls offers Gracie an insincere smile as she sets the plate in front of him. Without so much as a thank you, he picks it up and begins to inspect it from every angle.

'You do realize it's best eaten warm, yes?' The restaurant is quiet enough that Renee overhears them comfortably. 'I don't like it when people mess with my creations.'

Walls clears his throat, unable to hide his embarrassment as he puts the plate down. Renee can't help but smile. He should have known better. Gracie isn't one to mince her words.

Gracie retreats towards the bar. She's pretending to talk to Danika, but is actually watching Walls interrogate her dish. Renee knows she should get back into the kitchen and take some of the pressure off the others, but she can't tear herself away. Her eyes flick between Gracie and Walls like she's watching two lions circle a carcass.

Who will win?

The smart money is on Gracie.

Only, Renee isn't sure *how* she wins.

What she is sure of is there's a pattern to the dishes Gracie selects for these kinds of guests. Her choice of meat seems to mirror her opinion of the person dining. It's common knowledge that the minor royal who came in during Renee's first week isn't considered the brightest star in the sky, so she fed him brains. Troy Fisk? That doesn't take much figuring out. She served up heart to a bigshot in the city, and incorporated tripe for a dodgy journalist. But Walls? Walls she can't puzzle out. Gracie's served him a sumptuous meal by anyone's standards, and by all accounts, she absolutely despises him. Surely she'd make him something awful, too?

Or maybe this is the revenge. Maybe showing off her immense

skill is the perfect culinary fuck you. She's now top of the league, while he's barely scraped into the regionals.

That does sound satisfying.

Walls pulls out one of the slices of meat and tests its succulence by pressing down on it with the flat of his knife. Juice oozes, mixing with the marrow-dressed mushrooms. Renee sees Gracie smirk as he makes a surprised little moue, like he wants to find fault but can't, and that annoys him.

He then lifts the bone and the oyster sabayon floods out. There's just enough of it to enhance but not smother the dish. Another surprised little noise. Then he cuts into one of the pieces of veal and drags it through the sabayon. Gracie watches him like a thirsty man might regard a glass of water – her lips slightly parted and a look of immense satisfaction gleaming in her narrowed eyes.

Walls inspects his first forkful, then pops it into his mouth and chews.

Renee has almost given up on watching the critic; she's far more interested in her boss's reaction. She's never seen a chef act like this. Most retreat to the kitchen to continue working the pass, but Gracie is acting like this is some kind of performance art.

Preston Walls eats like a pig: smacking his lips and grunting as he roots through his meal. Every now and again, he'll stop and chew with his eyes closed, as if relishing every morsel. At last, he scrapes the final piece of meat through the last of the sabayon, spears a morel, pops it in his mouth. Renee wonders if he might actually lick his plate clean before he lays his cutlery down, indicating he is finished. Gracie gives him a moment, then saunters over.

Renee has never seen anyone look quite so satisfied.

Gracie doesn't say anything as she approaches.

'Well,' Walls says with a little sigh. 'That was an experience.'

Gracie smiles graciously, still silent.

'You've been causing quite a stir over the last few years, haven't you?'

'Since you last reviewed my food? Yes. I have.' Her voice is now silky smooth – a dangerous sign.

Walls harumphs and lets out a discreet burp.

'Come now. Let bygones be bygones. That was magnificent. I don't think I've ever tasted veal quite like that.'

'You're too kind,' Gracie says. 'I butchered it myself.'

'You . . . what?' Walls is taken aback.

He's not the only one. Is that why she has her own freezer? Because she buys the carcasses whole? Sure, it could make sense for quality control, but when does she find the time? Butchery like that is incredibly labour-intensive. That's why chefs employ butchers. And she does use butchers, because Renee's seen them bringing in NOVA's regular meat orders. The larger carcasses – beef, pork, lamb and the like – are, if not dressed, then at least cut down so they're easier to work with.

But then again . . . those deliveries are always taken to the communal cold pantry. Martin usually helps with that job, because he's the strongest out of all of them, but even he would struggle to carry an entire side of beef by himself, let alone carve it up. And if Martin would struggle, then it would be near enough impossible for Gracie to do it on her own.

So why hasn't Renee ever seen anyone deliver meat to Gracie's freezer?

'Usually veal filet is quite tasteless, but that bone marrow really intensified the flavour,' Wells says pompously, speaking loud enough for everyone to hear him praise Gracie. Even Renee knows what he's trying to do.

This, it seems, is his attempt at a comeback.

'The caramelization, too . . . it almost had a pancetta-like quality to it,' Walls continues. 'Did you maybe use pork caul?'

'Oh, come now, Preston. You know I can't share my secrets.'

That's . . . odd, because while Renee doesn't know all of Gracie's secrets, she knows enough to say there's no pork in that recipe. Unless . . . that little sprinkle of seasoning at the end? But he said it was in the caramelization, and the only thing Gracie used for that is butter.

'Well, secret or not, that was fabulous,' Walls says, patting his ample stomach. 'I'm almost aggrieved to say that in all my years, I've never eaten anything quite like it.'

'I take it it's more to your taste than the last time you were here. What was it you accused me of?' Gracie pantomimes thinking, as if the memory escapes her. 'Ah, yes – that I served you a "posh roast dinner, more suited to a Toby Carvery than a high-end restaurant".'

'Oh, come now, Gracie. That was a long time ago, when dunking on chefs was all the rage. If you weren't being a snarky bastard, no one would read your articles. The public, they love cruelty, but we're no longer allowed to throw people to the lions, so we threw chefs under the bus instead. It was nothing personal. Until you made it so, of course.' There's a hint of condescension now, a sour edge betraying a sense of embarrassment born purely out of his own entitlement.

'All I did was defend myself.'

'And all I did was do my job. But please, let's not let the past ruin this. I'm going to say it loud and clear – that was incredible. You could be my comeback, kid.' He leers at Gracie, and Renee knows that if she were standing any closer, he'd have nudged her in the ribs like they were old pals.

'So, a good review?'

'Definitely. I'll tell you a little secret.' Walls beckons Gracie closer and whispers something to her. Renee expects her to rear back in horror and demand that he get out of her restaurant, but instead, she smiles, all saccharine sweetness.

'Aww, that's nice. And since you've shared a secret with me, I'll share one with you.'

Gracie's eyes sparkle with vicious glee as she glances over to the pass and briefly meets Renee's gaze. Then she hunkers down, right up to Walls's ear. Renee instinctively leans forward, as if that might help her hear, despite the distance between them. Of course, she can't make out a thing.

Walls's eyes widen. His cheeks flare bright crimson before all the blood drains from his face. Gracie straightens up, folds her arms and quirks an eyebrow at him, like she's just laid down a dare.

But Walls isn't laughing. If anything, he looks like he's going to be sick.

'You . . . no. You can't have – you—'

His sentence is cut off as he dry heaves. Renee glances around the restaurant – there aren't many diners, but still, isn't Gracie worried about her reputation? This is much worse than the tantrum Fisk threw. The last thing she needs is a food critic throwing up all over his table.

Gracie, however, looks entirely unbothered. In fact, she looks happier than ever.

'I'll ruin you!' Walls spits. 'Just you wait!'

'Like last time? Because that went so well for you.'

Walls blusters as he wrenches himself out of his seat. His previous florid complexion is now deathly white and, for a moment, Renee wonders if they're going to have to call an ambulance. Luckily, he manages to stagger out, somehow looking both furious and terrified at once.

'Goodbye, Preston!' Gracie calls after him, looking so unhinged Renee takes two steps back from the chef. 'I wish you luck with your impending comeback.'

THIRTY

Renee ducks back into the kitchen, feeling sick. She got to live her dream training under her idol tonight, but what she just witnessed in the dining room? That disturbed her. Hell, it went beyond just being disturbed. It was horrifying.

That was not how these things usually went.

Judging by the rattled look on Bethany's face, it's clear she's feeling the same way. When Gracie strides back into the kitchen, the sous chef dares to take her aside for a moment, whispering worriedly to her boss.

'Oh, stop it,' Gracie says. She almost sounds drunk. 'It'll be fine. No one listens to him anyway. I made sure of that.' Then she points at Renee and beckons her over with a crooked finger. Bethany shoots first Gracie, then Renee, an apprehensive look.

Gracie ignores her and walks Renee back to her station. Her aura of cold yet calm authority has been replaced by one of electrifying elation.

'So how are you enjoying your shift?'

'Um, it's been great,' Renee responds shakily. 'I've learned so much.'

Gracie steps back so she can appraise her newest hire. Renee self-consciously clasps her hands in front of her, unsure of what is coming next.

'I don't usually warm to chefs until they've been working with me for some time, but you . . . I don't know what it is about you, but you're different. You did really well today, Renee. You should be very proud of yourself. Keep it up, and I may end up leaving NOVA to you when I finally retire.'

Renee's laughs nervously. 'Well, ha-ha, that's—'

Gracie's expression turns stony. 'Did I say something funny?'

The nervous giggle dies on Renee's lips. 'No, no, of course not,' she whispers. 'I just . . . I mean, you're kidding, right?'

'Do I come across as someone who *kids* people?' Gracie now looks almost affronted, making Renee shrink back from her. 'I am deadly serious. Under my guidance, you might reach greatness. You may even become spectacular. You have a talent, Renee, and I'm not about to let you hide it so men as small as Preston Walls feel comfortable enough to use you as a prop in their futile attempts at rousing their zombie careers. The time for women to reduce themselves to near invisibility so men can feel comfortable is over as far as I am concerned. Make a noise. Fill up that space. You have more talent in your little finger than half the chefs out there begging to train under me, and don't let anyone tell you otherwise.'

Renee is lost for words. A lump swells in her throat – a mixture of fear and glee. No, scratch that – it isn't glee, it's *pride*; the only emotion, along with anger, that men have taken ownership of.

'Thank you, Chef,' Renee manages to croak out.

'Don't thank me. Just don't let me down. What you don't understand is that I spent the early years of my career trying to please. Trying to fit in, to know my place. I realized later that was why I was being treated badly. Men like Preston Walls and Isaac Ferguson – they don't want to teach, they want to punish. They want to torture you for even daring to try. Realizing that there was no pleasing these men, and that in reducing myself I was not only allowing them to feel superior, but was instead actively encouraging it, was a revelation. One I'm now hopefully passing on to you. If you follow my instruction, internalize my philosophies, allow me to guide you, you will be unstoppable.'

'But . . . aren't you worried?' Renee can't help blurting out. 'About what happened out there? People saw—'

Gracie lets out a short, sharp bark of laughter.

'They saw a food critic having a tantrum. And a washed-up food critic at that. I destroyed him last time he tried to mess with me. I'll obliterate him now. I'm nobody's tool, Renee. I'm not going to adjust my principles just because he wants to rouse his flaccid career.' Gracie is growing more passionate with everything she says, and it's infectious. The sense of pride that she is stoking within Renee inflates, stamping down her reservations until she feels like she could quite possibly walk on air. Gracie Fitzgerald isn't just an amazing chef, she has opened Renee's eyes to a world she didn't even know existed. For far too long, making sure men felt comfortable was the only path to success. Don't rock the boat. Don't scare the horses. Now she can see there's another way. By being unapologetically authentic, Gracie has risen head and shoulders above her competition. She's put herself in a place where men can't reach her. And now she's offering to do the same for Renee.

She'd be a fool to pass it by.

As if sensing her shift in attitude, Gracie offers her a conspiratorial smile.

'That's more like it. Together we'll make those men bleat.'

The rest of the service passes in a blur for Renee. The unease she experienced during the Preston Walls incident has been swallowed by Gracie's infectious drive. The chef's approval has boosted her confidence to even loftier heights, meaning she is less hesitant, not second-guessing herself, and by the time the last plate goes out, Renee is looking forward to the evening shift so much that she decides to hang around the restaurant rather than go home for the afternoon. She doesn't need respite; she needs *action*.

She needs NOVA.

At the end of her shift, she catches up on her messages. There's a couple from Lola, the first one from a couple of hours ago.

Ren r u ok, we should talk Lxx

Then, about an hour ago:

Have u seen TikTok?

And five minutes after that:

Omg, what happened?

Lola's attached a video, but Renee doesn't watch it. She's too excited to worry about memes right now.

When Bethany realizes Renee's still there, she tells her to go home and put her feet up for a couple of hours. But she's too wired for that. Instead, Renee busies herself with cleaning, hoping that might catch Gracie's attention by the time the evening shift rolls round.

To her disappointment, Gracie isn't in the kitchen this evening, and she's taken that frisson – that sense of *danger* – with her, making the shift feel sedate. Boring, even. Everyone is just as lovely as they've always been to her, except Josh, who is still MIA, but no one's missing him. In fact, everyone seems much, *much* happier that he's decided to haul his entitled arse off somewhere else – but that doesn't stop Renee from craving *more*.

More of what, though . . . she isn't quite sure.

By the time she's ready to head home, the buzz is beginning to wear off, and the exhaustion that only comes after an adrenaline high sets in. She decides to spring for an Uber, because she can't face the Tube. When she pulls up at the flat, she sees that the lights are on, meaning Lola's home. After all the excitement, it feels like she hasn't seen her in weeks rather than hours.

She can't *wait* to tell her about the day she's had.

Lola is in the living room, eating fried chicken out of a

cardboard bucket. She's in her sweats, hair up in a messy bun. Once upon a time, Renee was the one who brought home fried chicken for her. Was that really only a couple of months ago? It doesn't feel like it. In fact, her memories of working at Chickadees are so distant now, they feel alien to her.

'Hey,' Lola says as Renee enters the room and makes herself comfy on the couch. Lola picks up the carton and offers it to her. 'You want some? I got extra, just in case you were hungry after your shift.'

She isn't. One of the perks of working in a restaurant is that you often get the leftovers at the end of service, and tonight Renee ate pretty well. But she takes a drumstick – more as an acceptance of this peace offering than anything else.

'You OK?' Renee asks.

'Yeah. You?'

'Yeah.'

They stare at the TV for a moment. It's one of those awful reality shows where impossibly beautiful people are terrible to each other while holidaying in a luxury beach resort. It's literal chewing gum for the brain, and just what Renee needs after such a hectic day.

'Look,' Lola says as Renee reaches for a handful of fries. She may have eaten well, but Michelin-starred restaurants rarely make fries, and sometimes, that's all a girl wants. 'I'm sorry.'

'No, Lola, I'm sorry. I shouldn't have snapped at you.'

'No, no . . . I should have realized how much this job means to you. I guess I've not really seen professional Renee before. I just thought G's idea was a nice gesture. I wish someone would do that for me.'

'Maybe you should go in my place,' Renee says, joking.

Lola snorts. 'Yeah, like that'll work.'

'It could be funny.'

'I could kill him.'

Renee giggles at that, despite how inappropriate it is.

'So . . .' Lola says, shifting in her seat so she can lean closer to Renee. 'Did you watch that video I sent?'

'No, sorry, I was busy. You won't believe what happened today. Oh my God—'

'So you know?'

This catches Renee a little off-kilter.

'What do you mean?'

'The video. You know about it?'

'No – what? I think we've got some crossed wires here.'

'Well, what were you going to tell me?' Lola asks. For some reason, she seems concerned.

'I was going to tell you that I had the most amazing shift today.' Renee feels that now-familiar plume of excitement whenever anyone mentions the restaurant. 'Lunchtime, it was just . . . I can't even begin to tell you. Like, Gracie, she actually singled me out to cook one of her signature meals with her. Me! Can you believe that! And she said I'm *different*. I think she sees promise in me. Even said she'd leave the restaurant to me when she retired. Sure, I know she's not serious, but even so! She sees my potential, Lola. I can't believe it's all coming together like this.'

Lola doesn't respond immediately. Instead, she pulls out her phone and starts scrolling.

A little spark of annoyance flickers in Renee. She thought Lola would be delighted for her, but instead, she's ignoring her.

Is she . . . jealous?

But before she can say anything, Lola thrusts her phone into Renee's face.

'Watch this.'

'What, why – is that the video you sent me? Look, I'm really not in the mood for . . .'

Renee trails off as the footage starts playing.

She doesn't know the person recording the video, but that

doesn't matter. She instantly recognizes the location, and the man outside it.

It's NOVA, and Preston Walls is outside shouting about how he's going to ruin Gracie Fitzgerald for good this time.

Renee cradles Lola's phone in her hands, increasing the volume so she can try to work out what Walls is actually saying, but it's hard. Every time he tries to verbalize what's bothering him, he gags. A small crowd has started to gather, and then Q steps into the frame. He glares at the people recording, tells them to stop it or he'll be seeking legal advice. Then he tries to lead Walls away – not back into the restaurant, but towards a waiting taxi. Only, he can't, because Walls darts away, disappearing into the little alley that leads to the back of the kitchen. Q is in hot pursuit, and by the time the amateur videographers have worked out what's going on, Q is blocking their view, telling everyone to leave in his firmest, most severe voice. But the person recording doesn't stop, so Q lunges for them. There's a scuffle, then the phone sails through the air, landing on the pavement behind them. The picture blurs, probably as the screen cracks. A moment later, the phone's owner can be seen running over and scooping up their phone, ending the footage.

It takes Renee a moment to process what she's seen.

'What's going on there?' Lola asks. 'People are saying he was really angry. Like, proper furious. And that he kept on gagging. They're saying he's poisoned or something. There's a rumour that he stuck his fingers down his throat to make himself sick.'

'No, no – he wasn't poisoned. Of course he wasn't.'

'Yeah, but how can you be sure? I mean – Secret Bunker Freezer, right?' Lola raises her eyebrows and sucks in her lips, discomfort written all over her face.

'That's ridiculous,' Renee says. 'I helped prepare his food. I was literally mentored by Gracie herself today.'

'Did you taste anything?'

'Well, no, but that's only because of her kitchen policy. I saw her taste it. Why would she poison something she's going to eat herself?' As soon as the words are out of her mouth, Renee remembers the 'special ingredient' Gracie sprinkled on Walls's plate before she served it.

Her stomach twists.

'All I'm saying is that man was not impressed, and he looked awful. The optics aren't good, Ren. People are going to ask questions.'

'And Gracie will answer them. You don't understand – that guy is Preston Walls. He used to be a food critic for a bunch of newspapers back in the day. He tried to mock Gracie early on in her career, but she wouldn't stand for it. And he lost. Big time. He was in NOVA today hoping to use Gracie as his big comeback, but she refused to engage. She let him eat, watched him recant his own words and admit that she's really talented, and he didn't like that. Gracie told him . . . She . . . she said . . .'

Renee shakes her head, blinking rapidly.

No. This is ridiculous. Walls was just angry that Gracie had refused to play his game. That's all. What did she say to him, though? He was fine until she shared that so-called secret of hers. What could make him react like that?

'It doesn't matter. He was angry. Gracie didn't give him what he wanted.'

'Come on, Ren. Do people storm out of places because they can't get their own way? Yes, of course they do. But he doesn't look angry. He looks like someone just tried to feed him his own dog or something. What did he actually eat?'

'Veal fillet with morels sautéed in bone marrow and an oyster sabayon,' Renee says almost automatically.

'A what in a what? Look, it doesn't matter—'

'It's regular restaurant food,' Renee says, a little defensively. 'It's not as if she was even using any out-there ingredients.'

'Like the time she fed that arsehole Fisk testicles without telling him?'

'That was pure justice—'

'Honey, that was bullying via food. I hate Fisk as much as the next normal person, but what Gracie did to him? That was next level.'

'You laughed!'

'Yeah. I did. Because on the face of it, it's funny. But then you think about it for a bit, and you realize just how . . . immoral it is—'

Renee snorts in derision and shakes her head again, as if that might dislodge the doubts Lola is trying to sow in her mind.

'Lola, it's not that deep. Preston Walls is a massive diva. That's it. He just wants people to pay attention to him.'

'Watch the footage again, Ren. Does that look like a guy who only wants attention? Yeah, he's angry, but he also looks . . . disturbed. Scared, even. And people are talking about it.'

'Let them talk. Gracie doesn't care.'

But Bethany does. Again, doubt worms its way into her thoughts.

'I don't think it matters if Gracie cares or not. You know what people are like these days. If Gracie gets cancelled—'

'Oh, come off it, Lola. Why would that happen? She hasn't done anything wrong!'

'Oh my God . . .' Lola massages her temples. 'Renee, please – look at the facts. I'm not saying that NOVA is bad, or your job is bad or anything, but . . . Don't look at me like that.'

Renee can't help it.

'NOVA is the best place I have ever worked.'

'You say that, but you've only been there, what, a couple of months?'

'And?'

'Just . . .' Lola is clearly struggling to find her next words. 'Right, I'm just going to come out with it, because I don't do pussyfooting. NOVA's vibe . . . it's *off.*'

Renee tenses. 'What do you mean, *off*?'

Lola pauses, chewing on her lip. It's clear she knows exactly what she wants to say but she's unwilling to voice her concerns. Taking a leaf out of Gracie's playbook, Renee holds her silence and just stares. It works. Lola begins confessing, her words coming out in fits and starts.

'Just . . . before . . . I mean . . . Recently, you've been . . .'

'I've been what? Go on, Lola – tell me. What have I been? Happy? Driven? Ambitious? Proud? Yes. I have been all these things, and more. NOVA has allowed me to flourish. It's like I was fated to get that job.'

'And I'm proud of you for succeeding. Or I would be, if I ever saw you.'

'You see me near enough every day!'

'No, I don't. I see Renee the chef. I haven't seen Ren my flatmate for a while now.'

Renee leans away from Lola, her eyes wide as genuine shock renders her momentarily speechless. Lola sniffs, and Renee realizes she's on the verge of tears.

'Ren the flatmate was never me,' Renee says. 'This is me. I am a chef. A proper one. And in order to become a proper chef, you have to be dedicated. I've told you before, this isn't something you do just to get by. It's a vocation—'

'Spare me the fucking lecture,' Lola snaps. 'I work in the same industry.'

'Yeah. As a waitress. In a chain restaurant.'

'What? Are you saying that you're better than me?'

'No. I'm just saying that your customer base is middle managers in local businesses thinking Carluccio's is a step up from Wetherspoons. Whereas I cook for celebrities. Fuck, I cook for royalty. Our establishments, our experiences, are not the same.'

'I wish I never saw that job advert,' Lola mutters.

'So you'd be much happier if I was still the lowest of the low?

Is that what you're saying? That it was better when you were the one working for a more *prestigious'* – the word drips with sarcasm and derision – 'establishment? I think I know what this is. This isn't about that video, because let's face it – it isn't the first and it won't be the last. This is about me working in a top-end restaurant under a genius chef who isn't afraid to stick to her vision, and you're still stuck waiting tables and singing "Happy Birthday" to sixteen-year-olds being taken out for their first "posh" meal. Sure, Carluccio's is a step up from working at Chickadees, but we're hardly in the same league.'

Lola's mouth flaps open and closed a few times before she can speak.

'You arrogant little shit,' she finally manages. 'I couldn't give a toss about where either of us works. You could be serving the fucking King and Prime Minister personally, and I'd feel nothing but pride for you. This isn't about what NOVA is. It's what NOVA is doing to you. What Gracie's doing to you. You've developed this cruel edge recently – towards me, towards Graham—'

'Don't you even think about bringing him into this,' Renee snaps. 'You don't like him. You've never liked him. Maybe he actually did have a point. You're only saying this because you're jealous.'

'Oh, fuck off with all this!' Lola sits back, a hand on her chest, her eyes wide. 'Jealous? Jealous of what? I got nothing to be jealous of, Renee. At least I work in a place where the manager doesn't upset the diners so much they end up screaming outside the premises and making themselves sick after eating there.'

'That's just a rumour. You said it yourself.'

'Not the point!' Lola is yelling now and, on cue, there's a bang on the wall from next door. She closes her eyes and takes a deep breath. 'Look. Please, honey. I am not trying to sabotage this for you. I know you're excited about everything. I know that NOVA is everything you've ever wanted, but I can't stay silent. Something's not right there, Ren.' She lowers her voice to an almost-whisper. 'That place . . . that *woman* . . . My spidey-senses are screaming at me. It's not just the video. It's everything else. These so-called special dishes? They aren't chef's specials. The personal freezer, the not-tasting stuff, the secrecy and the weird ingredients . . . It's revenge. Even I can see she only serves these things to people everyone hates. And while I'm with her on thinking these people need to be taken down a peg or two, I'm not sure if it's healthy to be around someone who treats their entire career as a weapon.'

'And so what if she does? So what if she upsets some rich bastard, or humiliates men who've treated her badly in the past?' Renee's voice rises. 'You know what I think? I think she had dirt on him and told him as much, and he didn't like it, so he had a tantrum outside. You don't know Gracie. She's unapologetic. She said it's about time these men were humbled. They need to recognize that they can't keep belittling and harassing us – that we are their equals—'

'So she's a feminist, is she? Standing up for the girlies? Come on, Renee – you're not stupid. This isn't about a woman taking a stand. She wants to torture people.'

'No, she just wants them to feel uncomfortable – just like they've made women feel.'

'Ren . . . I don't know what to say.' Lola sighs heavily, looking defeated. 'I know you're keen. I know you want to succeed, but I can't lie – it feels like you've joined some kind of cult. All you ever talk about is the restaurant. It's Gracie this, Gracie that. Gracie, Gracie, Gracie. It's like she's the most important person in your life right now. I'd even put money on that being the reason Graham wanted to take you away for the weekend. To get you away from NOVA. Away from *her*. That's why I don't blame him. It feels like you're slipping away from us, Ren. It's like Gracie is trying to body-snatch you or something – turn you into her clone.'

'I can't believe this.' Renee throws her hands up. 'I just can't. This is what fine dining looks like, Lola. Chefs of Gracie's calibre? They don't usually look twice at people like me. Yes, she's intense. Yes, she has some odd habits. But that comes with the territory. There's a reason they are where they are. They don't get up there by bowing down and being nice to people.'

'Renee . . . I don't know what else to say. I knew you were in deep, but I didn't realize you'd gone this far. Are you seriously saying that you'd pick Gracie over your friends? Over your boyfriend?'

'At the moment? Yes. Yes, I would. Because Gracie wants me to succeed. She wants me to push myself – to become something I thought was just a pipe dream. She said that I have it. She can see it in me. She said I impressed her. Do you know how many people would give their right eye for Gracie Fitzgerald to even look at them, let alone say something like that? You should be happy for me. Proud of me. But no, you just want to drag me back down—'

Lola snatches up her phone and jumps off the couch, scattering discarded chicken bones over their coffee table. She makes to storm off, but before she leaves the room, she turns and points at Renee.

'This isn't good, you know. You're going to lose yourself completely if you keep working with that woman. I'm only trying to look out for you.'

'Yeah, well, maybe I can look out for myself. Did you ever think of that?'

Lola doesn't answer as she stomps away towards her bedroom. She slams the door closed, which only infuriates Renee further. They're adults, for fuck's sake – not teenagers.

Leaving the chicken bones on the coffee table – Lola did it, so she can clear them up – Renee retreats to her own bedroom. It's small and not very tidy, mainly because she hasn't had time to do anything other than change and sleep in here. Still fuming, she pulls off her clothes and gets into her pyjamas. She'd intended to have a shower, but now she can't be bothered. Instead, she lies on her bed and calls the only other person who has any idea what she's going through.

Graham answers almost immediately.

'Babe? What's up?'

As soon as she hears his voice, her throat constricts.

'Hey, G . . . everything's OK. Well, no. Everything's not OK – it's not OK at all.'

'Ren? Are you all right?' Graham asks. 'Are you still upset about last night? You don't need to worry about that. I've had a think and you might have had a point. It is unfair to expect you to ask for leave when you're still new in the position. As soon as you're ready, I'll rebook it. How does that sound?'

In all honesty, Renee had all but forgotten their tiff. After everything that's happened today, it feels like a lifetime ago.

'Yeah, I mean, that sounds good. I guess I was being a bit self-absorbed, but things – they're just really hectic at the moment. And Lola's now mad at me just because I had a really good day at work. Gracie wanted me to work directly with her and she never does that, and then this guy came in and—'

'Ren? Can you slow down a bit? I don't really get what you're saying. Something about Lola and Gracie?'

Renee takes a deep breath, tears of frustration and exhaustion running down her cheeks.

'Yeah, sorry. Um, hang on.' She pauses, trying to sort her thoughts into something that vaguely resembles a coherent narrative. 'I had a really good day at work today. It was basically life-changing. Gracie asked me to work directly with her, assisting her with one of her dishes. This food critic had come in, you see, so she wanted to serve him something special because he gave her a bad review in the past.'

'But that's good, isn't it? That's what you wanted?'

'I know. And I did. I still do. She served him and he really enjoyed the meal, but then Gracie said something that really upset him. He ended up going outside and causing a scene. I didn't know about it until Lola showed me the footage on TikTok.'

'Wow, that sounds . . . dramatic,' Graham says.

'I know, right? Only problem is, Lola's now convinced herself that NOVA is the Bad Place, and that Gracie is basically the devil. She literally believed some anonymous TikTok account over me. I told her exactly what happened, but she won't have it. She says she's worried about me, but I think she's angry because I'm doing well now, and she knows that I'm going to move out of here at some point—'

'Really? You're thinking about moving out?' Graham says, sounding hopeful.

'Yeah, of course. I'm not going to be drawing my pension here, am I?'

'Babe, you know you have a place here – with me. We could do it tomorrow if you wanted.'

Renee can't help but laugh at that, marvelling at how they could have the worst kind of argument, and he'd still want her to move in with him.

'I know. You've only told me that a few times before,' Renee says, sniffing back her tears and rolling onto her back. 'I just don't understand. I don't get why Lola's being like this. I get one good thing, and everything else starts falling apart.'

'Ren, love – nothing is falling apart. This is just a period of readjustment. And some people don't always cope with that very well. I'm sure Lola didn't mean to upset you. She's just scared she's going to lose her friend.'

'Yeah . . . she said something like that. I just don't understand why she can't be happy for me.'

'She *is* happy for you. But she's only known Chicken Shop

Renee. She's now meeting Professional Renee. She just needs time. Look, how about we have a night out? Your choice this time. No strings, no deadlines. You tell me, OK?'

The backs of Renee's eyes prickle again. She really doesn't deserve him.

'OK. I'm flat out for the next couple of weeks, but I'm sure I can ask for a night if I give them enough notice.'

'Oh, so next week's probably not going to be on the cards?'

'More like next month, maybe. I'm sorry, love – I just have so much going on.'

'No, it's OK. Adjustment period, remember? It's not a big deal. I'm not going anywhere.'

'Do you really mean that?'

'Of course I do. Have a think and let me know – when and where.'

'Thank you, G. I love you.'

'I love you too.'

Renee's breath catches, and the tears flow freely again.

'Hey . . . Are you sure you're all right?'

'Yeah, of course I am.' Renee wipes her tears away with her fingertips. 'I'm just tired.'

'In that case, I'll leave you. Sleep tight.'

'Love you, Graham.'

'Love you more.'

He rings off.

Renee lies back on her bed, stretching her body out, hoping it might release the tension she's holding inside.

Maybe she should take the plunge. Move in with him.

But Lola . . .

Nope, you are not in the right headspace to deal with this right now, girl. The only thing you need to do is sleep. Everything'll be better in the morning. You just need to get some sleep.

Or so she hopes, at least.

THIRTY-ONE

Renee doesn't see much of Lola over the next couple of weeks. She has mixed feelings about that. On one hand, she's sad that her friend seems to be avoiding her. On the other, no more complaining or insulting her mentor. Because whether Lola likes it or not, that's what Gracie is now.

Renee takes every shift she can. No breaks, no days off. She can't get enough of NOVA, immersing herself in every single aspect of it. And Gracie largely lets her. Renee's learning about all the ins and outs of running a restaurant of NOVA's pedigree, from the kitchen to the bar to who Gracie hires to deep-cleaning the ovens once a week. She even tags along when Gracie visits her suppliers: farms and markets, beekeepers and slaughterhouses. No matter where Gracie goes, Renee is her shadow, learning all she can about every aspect of the culinary process.

Well . . . almost every aspect.

There's only one real bastion of secrecy left to explore.

Gracie's freezer.

'When you're ready, I will let you in,' Gracie says when Renee finally plucks up the courage to ask her about it. 'But I have to be sure. There is no going back. That is my legacy – my mission in life. I need to be one hundred per cent positive that you will carry my torch without question. And I won't lie – I am hoping that will be soon. You're shaping up to be a fine chef. You remind me so much of myself.'

'Yes, Chef,' is all Renee can say, her chest fizzing with excitement and pride.

But even the keenest protégés can take things too far and burn out.

'I think it's time for you to maybe take a night off,' Bethany says, peering at the dark circles around Renee's eyes. 'You look tired, love. And tired people make mistakes. Remember, you have to look after yourself as well as this place.'

'No, Chef. I'm fine, really.'

'Ren, listen to me.' Bethany folds her arms over her chest. 'You need to take some time for yourself. I know you love NOVA, but taking a bit of a break isn't a betrayal. I'll talk to Gracie for you – get you something sorted.'

'Honestly—'

'No.' Bethany raises a hand. 'You're going to do as you're told for once.' She grins, letting Renee know she's being teased. 'I'll let you know.'

Renee wasn't sure what to expect, but it isn't this. When Gracie first enters, the way she studies Renee makes her feel like she's done something wrong.

'I've spoken to Bethany,' Gracie says.

Renee's heart rate spikes. 'Honestly, if it isn't convenient—'

Gracie holds up one hand, and Renee falls silent.

'You've been at every service since you joined us, yes?'

'Um, yes, I think so.'

'And I know so. And I think Bethany is right. A night off once in a while is good for you. But I want to extend the offer. Let me feed you.'

'W-what?' Renee says, not really understanding what her boss is saying.

Is she suggesting . . . a signature dish?

Given Gracie's pattern of settling scores with her dishes, Renee isn't sure if this is a good or bad thing.

'Come to NOVA. Experience it as a diner. No cost to you.'

'Oh my God . . . really?'

'Yes, of course. It'll be my treat. It's your birthday soon, isn't it? Consider it a gift. Bring that man of yours. I want to check him out – make sure he's good enough for you.'

Tonight is the night.

There are some who might think that Renee wouldn't want to eat at the restaurant where she spends the majority of her time. That she might like to go elsewhere, experience something new. That in knowing the recipes inside out, she might find them a little boring.

Of course, those people are free to think all these things. But they'd be wrong.

And there are those who might think that Renee would feel a little nonchalant walking through NOVA's doors, and that the glitz of the place might be wasted on her.

They'd be wrong, too.

Adrenaline fizzes in Renee's belly as Graham opens the restaurant door for her. Although she's been in the dining room many times, she's never really experienced it like this – at peak hours. When they're busy, the chefs are usually stuck in the kitchen doing what they do best. To be here as a diner is a completely different deal altogether.

She smiles at Q as they approach the maître d'. He doesn't smile back.

Typical.

'Hi, Q,' she says. 'Table for two under the name Murphy, please!' She grins impishly, first at Graham, then back at Q, who sighs and gives his head a little shake. Whether it's in disdain or affectionate exasperation, Renee doesn't know and, quite honestly, she doesn't care.

'If Madam and Sir would follow me,' Q says, forever the professional.

Renee and Graham follow Q as he snakes past tables full of diners. Theirs is in the corner near the pass, but Renee is fine with that. She always prefers a less conspicuous location to being out in the middle of the room, where everyone can see you. Plus, being closer to the pass means your food gets to you quicker, or at least that's what she tells herself. Q pulls her chair out and indicates for her to sit down as Graham settles opposite her. She giggles at the ridiculousness of it all, but at the same time, she's delighted. This is the most fun she's had in months – maybe even years.

'Is Gracie in tonight?' Renee asks.

Q purses his lips and hands her a wine list. 'She is, but she isn't cooking this evening,' he says.

'She's not?'

'No. Something came up. Don't ask me what, because I don't know.'

He gives them both a little head bow and glides away, back to his host stand where yet more diners are waiting.

'You weren't wrong,' Graham says. 'He's a . . . character?'

'That's Q for you. He's worked with Gracie for years. He's a bit prickly, but he's OK.'

Graham picks up the drinks menu and starts to peruse it.

'Gosh, you weren't kidding when you said it was posh here. Look at these wine prices. Even my dad would raise his eyebrows at these. Are you sure this is all on the house?'

A shot of anxiety breaks through Renee's elation.

'Uh, yeah, that's what Gracie said. We could get the house wine, just in case. Don't worry – it's a good wine. The sommelier here is excellent. In fact . . .' She spots Danika and gives her a little wave, trying to catch her attention. When Danika sees her, she looks delighted and strides over.

'Ren! Gracie said you were in tonight. It's your birthday soon, right? Please, let me get the best wine I have.'

'Oh, Christ, no . . . Danika, that's too much.'

'Pfft.' Danika chases Renee's worries away with a flick of her wrists. 'This is my gift to you. Now, do you have a preference?'

'Actually, only one.' She smiles at Graham. 'Do you have any vegan wines?'

Danika chuckles. 'Do I have any vegan wines? Only the best vegan wines on the market. Do you prefer red or white?'

Renee nods at Graham, but he simply shrugs.

'It's your gift. You decide.'

'OK . . . Maybe a nice red? There's never a huge amount of fish on the menu, so . . .'

'We can wait until you've ordered, if you'd prefer?' offers Danika.

'No, no – it's fine. Honestly, I prefer red – white always seems to give me heartburn.'

Danika frowns playfully and gives her a little smile. 'None of my whites would ever do that, I can assure you, but I have an incredible vegan red nonetheless – a Tommasi Ca' Florian Amarone della Valpolicella Classico Riserva. An excellent wine, from the Ca' Florian Cru vineyard in Italy. It's full-bodied with gorgeous garnet highlights, and on the nose it's an elegant bouquet with notes of ripe red fruits along with spicy nuances of liquorice and cocoa, and a long, fresh finish. How does that tickle those amazing taste buds of yours?'

'Wow, that sounds . . . complicated,' Renee says with a laugh. 'But I trust you. Graham? Are you happy with that?'

'I'm happy with it if you are.'

Renee smiles at Danika, who nods then leaves to fetch their wine.

'She's so good,' Renee says. 'Like, excellent at her job. But, then again, Gracie only tolerates the best— Why are you looking at me like that?'

'Nothing.' Graham smiles at her wistfully. 'You said it yourself – Gracie only tolerates the best.'

'Oh, no, I didn't mean that. I—'

'Ren, take the compliment.'

Danika returns, bearing an expensive-looking bottle, and pours a splash into both their glasses. Graham takes his sip first and rolls it around his mouth like he does this all the time. Renee copies him, and though she never swills the fiver bottle from the corner shop around this way, even she can tell that this is some serious wine.

'Gosh, that's very good,' Graham says as Danika tops up both their glasses.

'Yes, vegan winemaking really has come a long way – to the point where I'm wondering if the industry as a whole may adopt their techniques. Of course, there are people worrying about how the old ways might be forgotten . . . but then you have to ask yourself, what's better? Good wine on a more humane planet, or holding tight to the old ways, no matter how unnecessary they are?'

'This is exactly what I've been saying!' Graham gushes. He's quite animated now, clearly happy to be speaking with someone who understands his language. 'It's going to get harder and harder to justify the current culinary culture, especially with climate breakdown and half the world's population going hungry . . .'

Renee takes another sip of the wine, starting to wish Danika hadn't said anything. Once Graham finds his feet, there's no shutting him up when it comes to his passions. Danika must have noticed her subtle change in demeanour, as she tactfully disentangles herself from Graham's enthusiastic monologue.

'It has been a pleasure meeting you,' she says. 'But I have other guests to see. I'm sure you understand.'

'Of course,' Graham says, and once Danika is a few tables away, he adds, 'What a nice person.'

'Danika's lovely,' Renee agrees. 'I don't always get to catch up with her, which is a shame.'

'Good evening, and welcome to NOVA,' a young man says as he approaches their table.

He's smartly dressed in a crisp white shirt, black trousers, and a navy blue waistcoat with a black dickie bow. Renee vaguely recognizes him, and she gets the same impression that he feels the same way about her as he very briefly narrows his eyes at her. She doesn't blame him for not remembering her. She looks very different when she's working, with minimal make-up and her curly hair tied back in a messy bun, her chef whites half obscured by a similar navy blue apron. Tonight, she's made an effort, and it isn't all for Graham's benefit. She's been secretly hoping Gracie might come out and see her, even if she isn't cooking. She wants Gracie to see that she's got class as well as talent.

'Hello, there,' Graham says. He's clearly more comfortable in this kind of setting than she can even pretend to be.

'If you would like to peruse the menu?' the waiter asks.

'Yes, please,' Renee says, enchanted at the novelty of being on this side of the table for once.

The waiter nods and hands them both menus printed on heavy vellum.

'Just one thing before we start – what are your vegan options?' Graham asks. 'I take it you do provide vegan dishes?'

Renee glances at the waiter, hoping he might take that as an apology.

'I'm sure we will be able to accommodate your dietary needs. If I may enquire, is this due to any allergies?' the waiter says, his voice pure silk.

'No, it's a lifestyle choice.' A hint of suspicion infects Graham's voice, making Renee want to nudge him under the table. *Not here. Please.* 'But that doesn't mean—'

'Of course, sir – it's fine. Many of our dishes can be altered to accommodate a plant-based diet. You simply have to ask.'

They can?

Renee can't remember the last time anyone had to adjust anything – except that time a diner asked for peanuts to be removed, which was fine because there wasn't anything on the menu that day involving peanuts. Plus, the menu is limited, so there's not a great deal of wiggle room. But then again, the kind of people who eat at NOVA aren't like Graham. After all, Gracie is famous for her magic with meat, and that's what usually attracts diners. They don't want a cauliflower steak, or hay-baked carrots. They want something that bleeds – something that was sacrificed to them, and their money.

Maybe I shouldn't have brought Graham here after all.

As the waiter informs Graham of some of the substitutions NOVA can accommodate, Renee can't help but feel sorry for Martin, given he's the most likely candidate for making them. That boy loves his butter, so asking him to substitute it for oil is going to hurt.

In the end, Graham chooses a starter of charred oyster mushrooms with tamarind and fennel, and a main of spiced roasted cauliflower with a baba ganoush purée, crispy kale, roasted hazelnuts and a tahini drizzle. Renee chooses the scallop ceviche with sea lettuce, lovage oil and a horseradish foam, followed by the roasted quail served with chestnuts, confit parsnip, a port jus and cranberries.

Renee uses the time before their first course arrives to talk about the menu, explaining to Graham exactly what dishes she works on, and what she has to do in terms of techniques. Graham is an attentive audience, and while she has absolutely no doubt that he's only humouring her, she's pleased to do it. Finally, Graham can see what she does, and why it's such a big deal to her. They both enjoy the wine, and so, by the time their starters arrive, she's feeling a bit warm in the cheeks.

Her scallops are perfect. She didn't doubt they would be anything other than flawless, but she hadn't realized just how incredible it would be tasting them as a guest. And judging by the way he's attacking his charred mushroom skewers, Graham is enjoying his food too.

'Wow, what is in this goo?' Graham says, dipping his mushroom in a sauce the consistency and colour of tar, a blissful expression on his face.

Renee leans over and dabs a little on the tines of her fork. She takes a moment to savour it – it's delicious, full of umami flavour and a sour kick, with a hint of sweetness.

'Martin's knocked this out of the park,' Renee says. 'He's replaced the oyster sauce with mushroom ketchup, and it really works. It also enhances the natural umami of the mushrooms and the sour tamarind without overpowering them.'

Graham shakes his head, still smiling. 'You're incredible, you know.'

'Of course I do.' Renee blushes.

They finish up their starters and the waiter comes back to collect their plates. While they're waiting for their main courses they make small talk: Graham's work, Renee's opportunities, whether they should catch a movie afterwards – everyday things that don't run the risk of sparking an argument.

When their mains arrive, there's no sign of the waiter. Instead, it's—

'Martin?' Renee can barely keep the confusion out of her voice. The chefs don't wait tables.

'Ren, love!' He holds his arms out and Renee obliges by standing up and giving him a great big hug. 'What, you think I wouldn't come out and say hi to our guest of honour?'

'Oh, stop it,' Renee says, feeling a little giddy.

'Hey, you're Ren's partner, aren't you?' Martin says, turning to Graham. 'We met in passing after the spiking disaster.' He pulls an awkward oh-my-God-what-was-that-all-about face.

'Right, yeah, sorry,' says Ren. 'You didn't get a proper

introduction, did you? Martin, this is Graham. Graham, this is Martin—'

'Her partner in crime,' Martin butts in, waggling his eyebrows in jest.

'Nice to meet you again, Martin. I've heard all about you, and I wanted to thank you properly for taking care of Ren and Lola that awful night.'

'It's what any decent human would do,' Martin says brightly. 'Something that little twat Josh wouldn't understand,' he adds.

'I agree with you there. But Ren said you made the sauce on those mushrooms? God, I could drink a bucket of it.' Graham holds out his hand, and Martin shakes it enthusiastically.

'Thank you – that's the nicest thing anyone's said to me all day. And it's great to see you under much calmer circumstances.'

'Q says Gracie's in but not cooking?' Renee asks.

'That's right,' Martin says. 'But keep that under your hat. If people knew she was here . . . Pandemonium.' He rolls his eyes.

'I can imagine,' Renee says. 'Say hi to everyone from me, will you?'

'I thought you'd want to go backstage and say it yourself,' Martin says. He winks at Graham. 'You've got a right little firecracker here. Only been here five minutes and already working with the Boss! We're all so pleased she's here. Looks like those pricks at the chicken shop did her a favour in the end, right, Ren?'

Renee's eyes widen, and all good vibes evaporate. She never got round to telling Graham exactly why she left Chickadees. When Graham looks confused, Martin glances down at Renee, his expression fading to one of puzzlement.

'Well, you enjoy,' Martin says quickly, swiftly changing the subject. 'The tahini drizzle is my invention, but don't tell anyone,' he says in a mock whisper before raising his voice again. 'Anyway, I've got to get back to the grindstone. Unless you fancy coming in and doing some washing up, Ren?'

He laughs as he leaves.

Neither Graham nor Renee laughs with him.

'What was that about?' Graham asks.

'Oh, it's just Martin. He's lovely, and you don't have to worry about him – I told you he's gay, remember?'

'That's not what I'm talking about.'

'It's nothing,' Renee says. 'I don't really want to talk about it here. Let's eat up. Letting food go cold at NOVA is a hanging offence.'

She tucks into her quail. Juicy meat, crisped skin, a fresh burst of cranberry that counterbalances the sweetness of the jus . . . it's an absolute masterclass on how to cook a notoriously difficult bird.

'This is delicious,' she says, hoping that Graham will realize she wants to talk about the present, not the past.

'Yes, it is,' he says stiffly. On the surface he looks like he's enjoying his food, but Renee's been with him long enough to know he isn't going to let this go.

She sighs inwardly. 'OK, I handed in my notice at Chickadees before I got the NOVA job. I know it was a risk—'

'That's not what I'm talking about.'

'I don't understand.'

'Yes, you do.' Graham says this more to his plate as he saws through his cauliflower steak, making Renee wonder what the vegetable's done to hurt him so. 'Your friend Martin said "those pricks". What did he mean by that?'

Renee lays her cutlery down, wedges her elbows on the table (she can hear Granni shrieking through the ether, but chooses to ignore her) and tents her fingers in front of her, like a crime boss.

'He didn't mean anything. It was just the last straw at Chickadees. Clive didn't handle something very well, and I decided that enough was enough.'

'Clive? I knew it. I knew he was bad news. What did he do?'

Graham is all riled up now, and it dawns on Renee exactly what he's thinking.

'Oh God, no – it was nothing like that, I promise.' She takes a deep breath and picks up her cutlery again. 'There was a bunch of lads eating outside – you know, posh boys slumming it – and they gave me a hard time. That in itself isn't unusual, but one of them touched me and pulled me onto his lap, so I slapped him. Clive didn't defend me, which was kind of the last straw—'

Graham snorts into his baba ganoush. 'Is that it? Why didn't you tell me?'

Renee blinks. 'Uh, excuse me? You know that counts as sexual assault, right? I could have pressed charges against that guy.'

'But you slapped him instead, which is actual assault. I think you got the better deal there, Ren.'

'What the fuck are you talking about?' Renee hisses, aware that some of the other diners are starting to glance their way.

'He just pulled you onto his lap. Was that appropriate? No. But it's hardly dragging you into an alleyway—'

'Wow. *Wow*. I didn't tell you because I thought you might go after those guys, and I didn't need that. What I wasn't expecting was for you to minimize what happened to me.'

'Ren, please – I'm not. All I'm saying is he was probably just showing off. More than likely drunk and therefore not completely in command of all his faculties.'

'That's not an excuse!' Renee can feel her anger rising. 'He touched me inappropriately. The others were making misogynistic comments. I have the same right as anyone else to not feel objectified and intimidated at work – even if it was just in a crappy chicken shop.'

'Of course you do,' Graham says.

He's trying to placate her, switching to his low, soothing voice, but rather than calming Renee down, it makes her even more furious. She's not a toddler who needs a verbal lollipop. She's an adult who experienced something sadly not uncommon, but still incredibly shitty.

'But at the same time, you're always going to have to deal with arseholes,' Graham continues. 'And you hit him? You're lucky he didn't come after you for assault. This is the problem, Ren – things get blown out of proportion. Instead of just telling him to stop it, you used violence, and that's when things go wrong.'

Renee just stares at him, and so do half the diners around them. They're clearly enjoying the drama, eagerly watching to see where this goes next. She can't believe the words coming out of his mouth.

He's supposed to be a good one.

'I can't believe you just said that,' Renee manages to say. 'We can't win. When we brush these things off, we're blamed for our inaction. When we defend ourselves, we're taking it too far and need to stop being so sensitive.'

'That's not what I'm saying at all, and I don't appreciate your insinuations,' Graham says. His faux-soothing tone is gone and he now sounds like her father telling her off for leaving her shoes in the middle of the living room after school. 'I'm just saying you overreacted a bit. You could have refused to serve him and got Clive to kick him out.'

'Oh, that's right – I forgot you're an expert in women being harassed at work and what they need to do about it. When was the last time you had your arse pinched, Graham? Had someone leer down your top? Made insinuations about your body?'

'I appreciate that, but from a legal standpoint—'

'Fuck legal standpoints! I'm your girlfriend and you should *be on my side.*' She shakes her head. 'Anyway, it doesn't matter any more, because I'm here now. This place is heaven compared to Chickadees. Gracie would never let anyone get away with something like that. She'd deal with it straight away. No skirting around the issue. Gracie would've grabbed him by the balls and told him— What?' Renee stops mid-rant, because Graham is very obviously rolling his eyes at her. 'I'm sorry, am I boring you?'

'Honestly? Yes. You are. I hardly see you these days, and when I do, all I hear is NOVA this, and Gracie that. It's like you're consumed by this place. I hoped the novelty would wear off, but if anything, it's getting worse. And no, I don't get it. It's not a religion. It's just a job. I wanted a nice date – to get you *away* from it all. But no. You bounce in and tell me we've got a table booked here. A place that doesn't even have a proper plant-based dish on the menu. It's not exactly suitable for me.'

'What are you on about? You've been given amazing food, cooked by the very best chefs in the business, in a Michelin-starred restaurant.'

'There you go again. NOVA, NOVA, *NOVA*. I want you to *get away* from this place when you're not working. Not spend your free time here too!'

Renee goes to bite back, but the entire dining room is now openly watching them. Her cheeks burn with shame. Graham has made a scene in such an important place – her *place of work* – in front of people she respects. She can see Bethany on the pass, looking concerned.

It wasn't meant to be like this.

Graham was supposed to enjoy himself tonight. See where she worked. See the expertise of the other chefs who work here. *Appreciate how far she has come.* But he doesn't get it. At all. How he can sit here, eating NOVA's food, and not understand why she's so excited – so *dedicated* – not only to this restaurant but also to Gracie?

He's a lost cause.

She takes a deep breath and lets it out slowly in an attempt to calm herself. She'll be damned if she's making any more of a scene.

'Graham,' she says, quietly but firmly. 'I think you should

leave. You're embarrassing me in front of people I respect, and you're embarrassing yourself.'

'Renee—'

'No. I'm not listening to your excuses. Not here. You've made it quite clear how you feel about my career choices, and honestly, I think the best thing you can do right now is walk away.'

It looks like he's going to argue with her, but instead, he slams his chair back and marches to the exit, where Q is already waiting with his jacket. It's almost funny – Q clearly read the situation and knew *exactly* what was coming. Graham spares her a glance over his shoulder, expecting her to run after him and apologize, but she stays where she is. When it becomes clear she isn't going to play the Good Little Girlfriend, he turns and stalks off into the night.

The restaurant falls cave-silent for a split second – then everyone turns to their own tables and starts talking, all at once, trying to pretend they didn't see what just happened.

Renee sinks in her chair, wishing the ground would swallow her.

Out of the corner of her eye, she catches movement – it's Martin, looking worried. She thinks he might be coming over to comfort her, but instead, he gives her a sympathetic grimace and hands her a note.

It's from Gracie.

Wait until close, then come to my office for a drink. It looks like you could do with one.

THIRTY-TWO

If there's one thing everyone knows about Gracie Fitzgerald, it's that she likes her privacy. She's always said that her food will speak for her – and it has. Everyone talks about Gracie Fitzgerald the chef. No one talks about Gracie Fitzgerald the human being.

Is she married? Does she have any children? Any family at all? Where does she live? What does she like to do in her spare time?

How old is she, really?

All of these things remain a mystery to just about everyone. Renee thinks that maybe Bethany knows a thing or two, and Q might know more, given how long he's worked with her. But even then, Renee suspects Gracie has only shared what she *wants* them to know.

Outside the culinary world, Gracie is a ghost.

Renee is in the kitchen, scrolling on her phone. She offered to help with the service, but Bethany shooed her off to a corner, where she now sits, feeling a little awkward.

She hasn't heard anything from Graham. She doesn't know if that's a bad or good thing. Is it even a thing at all? She thought they'd be happier now she has a better job, but it seems that since accepting her role at NOVA, all she and Graham do is fight.

*Human Remains Found in Chelsea: Cracked and
Polished Bone 'Hints at Possible Serial Killer'*

Renee snorts in disbelief. Really? There's nothing sensationalist about that. They found disarticulated skeletal remains in the sewer. Surely that's what did all the damage? Rolling through muck and filth under London, being gnawed on by rats, stuck in fatbergs . . . Surely that's got to do a lot of damage to a corpse? Still, anything for a headline.

She clicks out of the article and continues scrolling.

There's been no mention of Preston Walls in the mainstream media, which doesn't surprise her. Most of the fallout is confined to TikTok, and much of the content is nothing short of mocking. Lots of reaction videos from young people treating Walls as yet another boomer having a meltdown.

The culinary world, meanwhile, is notable for its total silence.

The last order of the evening goes out and the chefs begin their clean-down. It's always an odd time. Relief that the stress of service is done with, but also disappointment that the high is over and won't return until your next shift. Renee emerges and, despite Bethany's good-natured scolding, helps wipe down the counters and empty the last load of crockery, still hot from the dishwasher.

With everything clean and the staff getting ready to leave, Renee bids them goodnight and makes her way up to Gracie's office – an almost imperceptible space located at the back of the conference room where Renee had her interview. The door is barely distinguishable from the wall it's set into –deliberately so, Renee suspects.

An easy place for Gracie to hide. Lucky her.

Renee has never actually been in Gracie's office before, and if it wasn't for the door being cracked open, she reckons she probably wouldn't have found it. Gracie sure does love her mystique.

Even though the door is ajar, Renee still knocks.

'Come in.'

Renee enters slowly, like she's crossing onto holy ground.

'Hi, Renee.' There's a clear hint of amusement in Gracie's voice. 'Come in and take a seat.'

The executive chef gestures to the space next to her on an expensive-looking leather couch. Gracie herself also looks different out of her whites – she's wearing palazzo trousers with a bold print of red hibiscus on a black background, and a simple black top. She could be mistaken for a primary school teacher, if it weren't for that aura of hers.

An aura that envelops Renee like fog.

She sits primly beside her mentor and tries to take in the room. It isn't very big, but it is very full. The entire ethos of the restaurant seems to stop at the door: outside it's clean and clinical, whereas in here it's all warm oak, old leather and an ornate desk carved with flowers and scrollwork. Scores – maybe hundreds – of accolades cover the walls or stand proud on shelves: certificates, awards, statuettes . . . If it can be won, Gracie has won it. The sheer enormity of who Gracie is – and what she has achieved – hits Renee again, leaving her breathless.

Gracie doesn't say anything. Instead, she stands up, saunters over to an oak cabinet, and retrieves two heavy-bottomed crystal tumblers and a bottle. She doesn't even ask if Renee wants a drink – she just pours one and hands it to her.

'You look like you could do with it,' Gracie says.

Renee accepts the glass and cradles it in her hands. Gracie sits down next to her again and sprawls back.

'This profession takes no prisoners,' Gracie says, after taking a sip of her drink. 'People think it's easy, or unimportant, because food is fundamental to the human experience. It's why some find it so hard to lose weight, for example. Get addicted to heroin? Come off it and never touch it again. But get addicted to food? Good luck with that.'

Renee isn't sure what point Gracie is making, so she politely drinks. She knows it's strong even before it hits her lips – and nearly coughs when she swallows.

'Mind yourself,' Gracie says, amused. 'That cognac is more expensive than you are.'

'Really?' Renee says.

'In a hotel bar, a single measure will set you back about four hundred pounds.'

Renee actually laughs when she hears the amount.

'Four hundred quid? And I thought the wine was expensive. Are you serious?'

'Absolutely. I'm always serious – especially when it comes to cognac.' Gracie holds her glass up to the light and inspects its amber depths. 'Others wax lyrical about the merits of the single malt scotch, but I always found it a rather uncouth drink. Too raw, too eager to make itself known. Good for cooking, I'll give it that, but as a drink? I much prefer this. Silk over steel, I suppose you might say.' She brings the glass to her lips and takes another sip before regarding Renee. 'What do you think?'

Renee has no idea how to reply but feels compelled to say something. She doesn't know why Gracie has called her up here either, but it feels like some kind of test.

'I don't have much experience of cognac,' she says. 'Outside of cooking, I mean.'

Gracie is now watching her intently, her bright eyes narrow, almost challenging. Renee was going to tell her she likes it, but now she realizes that's the wrong approach. Gracie doesn't want to be pleased or flattered; she values honesty and confidence. She *likes* to be challenged.

'I'm not sure yet,' Renee says. 'Now the alcohol burn has dissipated, I can taste orange. And wood smoke. There are floral notes.' She takes another sip – not because she wants more, but because she wants to impress Gracie with her palate. 'There's something sweet in there too. I think it's honey.'

Gracie raises an eyebrow. 'I know I've said this before, but I knew hiring you was a good idea. You have a good palate. It's such a shame you dropped off the map for so long. It may not surprise you, but I vet my applicants meticulously. I want to see what they're about. Where they've worked. What they've achieved. And you' – she tilts her glass to Renee – 'you intrigued me.'

'Is that why you interviewed me?'

'This is where I am supposed to say no. But I didn't get where I am today by doing that, so I'll be honest. Yes. I wanted to know what happened to you. Why you'd all but given up, despite your qualifications.'

'I hadn't given up—' Renee starts.

'Hadn't you? I don't remember seeing your CV on my desk before.'

'To be fair,' Renee says, the alcohol in her system emboldening her, 'I don't remember seeing an advert for any positions until recently.'

'I see. So, you were willing to let a little thing like permission stop you from trying? What's the phrase – it's easier to beg for forgiveness than ask for permission?'

'That's not what they taught us at college.'

'And that's why most chefs don't succeed. If you want something, you have to be unapologetic. Take no prisoners.'

'If you were so intrigued, why did you get Bethany to interview me?'

Renee is impressed by how easily she's keeping up this back-and-forth. *Must be the alcohol.*

'Isn't it obvious? Bethany is a far more approachable person than I am. She might be TV-famous and a big deal in her own right, but she's not me.' Gracie isn't boasting – just stating a fact. 'I learned long ago that if I interview, applicants behave in one of two ways. I'm sad to say, it's usually along gender lines.

'The men become grandiose, puffing up their chests and

showing me how fast they can chop. To them, the interview is a contest – the job a prize that can be won. The women, though . . . They tend to diminish their successes. They want to please me, to make me like them. This is unhelpful when trying to select someone who might fit into my team. I don't care that you're strong and can dice twenty kilos of carrots in ten minutes. I don't want to be flattered either, nor shown how meek you can be – how agreeable you are. I only want to know if you can cook. And you, Renee, can cook.'

Renee feels her cheeks warm, and she swallows down more of the cognac. The more she drinks, the nicer she finds it.

Ha. A bit like Gracie.

'I saw your little tiff,' Gracie continues after draining her glass. She holds out her hand for Renee's and returns to the drinks cabinet. This time, she brings the bottle with her and sets it on the low table in front of the couch before pouring two generous measures. 'These times call for more than just one glass.'

Gracie hands the drink back to Renee then chinks her own glass against it.

'I won't lie. I hoped you might have missed that,' Renee says.

'You should know I'm fully aware of anything and everything that happens in my kitchen, at all times.' Gracie sinks back into the couch. 'I have to be. If I don't, things go wrong.'

'Like what?' Renee asks, further emboldened.

Gracie lets out a long sigh.

'Where to start?' she murmurs against the side of her glass, then shifts the subject. 'That man – the one you were with. Was that your partner?'

'Yes, that was Graham,' Renee says, unsure where this is going. 'We've been together about three years.'

'Hmm. Interesting. So he's never really experienced you working in a professional kitchen before. This can cause issues. Do you think you're both strong enough to weather it?'

Renee sighs, suddenly feeling very tired. She could lie, say everything is fine, but she knows Gracie will be able to sniff that out in an instant. The only option here is honesty – however painful.

'A little while ago, I'd have said yes. But lately . . . I'm not so sure.'

Gracie nods sagely. 'The culinary world can be incredibly hard for people outside of it to understand. Sadly, it's one of the reasons most high-end chefs are male. It's simply down to the fact that they usually have someone at home taking care of business – a mother, a wife, a girlfriend. Notice how they're all women? In actual fact, a lot of the female chefs I come across are lesbians. I don't think I need to explain why.'

Gracie sighs and goes for another sip of her drink. For such a small woman, she can certainly put it away. 'We are all told the same lie when we're small: women are naturally nurturing. We *want* to care. We *want* to neglect our own ambitions to prop up the men in our lives. So when men come up against a woman with true ambition, they insult her. Say she is too masculine. Bossy. Outspoken. Aggressive. They'll do anything they can to humiliate her. Anything to put her back in her place.'

'I don't think Graham's quite like that,' Renee says, the urge to defend him strong. 'He's always been very supportive of me.'

'Renee, he started a heated argument in one of London's top restaurants, which also happened to be your place of work. He could have left it until you were home, but he didn't. He didn't because men expect subservience. They expect obedience. And when you don't comply, they'll go out of their way to make a fool out of you.'

Renee blinks in the face of Gracie's blunt honesty, trying to think of a comeback – some way to refute her claims. But she can't, because Gracie's right. Graham *could* have waited until they got home. He didn't have to make such a scene.

But he did.

'He demanded vegan food, didn't he?' Gracie asks.

'Yeah – he's been vegan for the last two years. I'm grateful that you accommodated him. I didn't even think about it when you made your offer. Not many high-end restaurants would adjust their menus like that. Thank you.'

Gracie snorts in what Renee hopes is amusement.

'We're all having to do it, one way or another. And that's fine. If your organic, grass-fed boyfriend wants to deny himself meat, that's up to him. But it still doesn't give him the right to humiliate you.'

Renee shrugs and sips her cognac. She imagines not many people see this version of Gracie Fitzgerald.

She has no idea why she's seeing it now.

'I wasn't too different from you when I started,' Gracie says. 'Keen. Talented, clearly. Eager to please and desperate to prove myself. I learned so many lessons the hard way . . . I expect you have too.'

Renee doesn't reply, and they both lapse into silence. Because she has. Forget Graham's outburst – that was nothing compared to Isaac Ferguson propositioning her at culinary school. He ended up being the first in a long line of powerful men trying to exploit her with the promise of an *easier path*. She never took it, though. For a while, she'd even lamented that. Thought that if only she'd accepted their offers . . . What was her dignity if it meant a glittering career?

But if she'd done that, she wasn't sure she'd be able to live with herself. It's easy to imagine the what-ifs when you don't have to face yourself in the mirror afterwards.

Plus, if she'd done that, she would never have met Gracie.

'It was the nineteen nineties,' Gracie says. 'In many ways, it was a simpler time. No mobile phones. No social media. If you did something wrong, you weathered the storm. No one was going to upload your shame to the internet. You just had to wait for people to forget. And people are surprisingly good at that. You won't believe the things people are willing to forget.' Her gaze is fixed not on Renee, but on a blank section of wall behind the door to her office – a patch of slightly mismatched plaster where the handle might strike if the door were flung open.

And for the first time, Renee witnesses Gracie displaying real vulnerability.

'He said it was the opportunity of a lifetime. A chance to experience true innovation – true *transgression*. I know I said the nineties were simpler, but they also had this strange anarchic streak. Not like today, where everyone wants everything to be safely labelled, crying foul if something doesn't align with their own sensibilities. No, back then, people craved danger. Everyone wanted to shock or be shocked. Body modification was a huge trend. All of a sudden, everyone had something pierced. Some were even beginning to experiment with scarification, tongue-splitting, flesh-carving. There was a real sense of wanting to push the boundaries, to break long-held taboos, to *transgress*.'

She emphasizes that word – transgress – like she's trying to ensure Renee understands something fundamental about the time period – and about her.

'In the food world, that meant pushing taste to its limits. And I don't mean making dishes with ever-growing levels of spiciness – although that did happen. This was a time when the world was opening up. New culinary traditions and delicacies from different cultures were being thrust into the spotlight. Looking back, it was all incredibly disrespectful. Just because we don't eat eggs marinated in the urine of small boys here doesn't mean it's an oddity to exploit. To the people who do consume it, it's part of their culture. Many Indians are absolutely appalled at our beef consumption – cows are sacred to them. The British are disgusted by the eating of horse meat, but in France it's as normal as picking up a pound of sausages. The thing is, as a species, we are very inventive when it comes to feeding ourselves. But despite all of that, there is one ingredient that remains taboo across the board.' She fixes Renee with a piercing stare. 'What do you think that might be?'

Renee takes a fortifying gulp of cognac before shrugging.

'I-I don't know,' she says. 'People?'

'Bingo.' Gracie tops up her glass yet again, her eyes shining now.

Renee wants to tell her she's OK, she's had enough, but Gracie's on a roll.

'People. Cannibalism. An act so transgressive whole myths have sprung up around it. Did you know that cannibalism isn't technically illegal? You can consume human flesh and commit no actual crime. The act of killing someone is, of course, murder and illegal. But eating them afterwards? Unless you're caught in the act, it's hard to prove.'

Renee squirms in her chair. Her head's beginning to feel a little foggy, and Gracie's story has taken a very uncomfortable turn.

If Gracie notices Renee's discomfort, she doesn't acknowledge it.

In fact, she's smiling.

THIRTY-THREE

1997

The BodyWorks Project

The BodyWorks Project. Even the name sounds horribly pretentious – made even worse by the slogan 'flesh is flesh'.

I give myself a shake. I'm lucky to be here. Ferguson could have brought anyone to this, but he didn't. Despite my mistakes – despite not being, as he so regularly reminds me, his 'top student' – he brought me.

The only thing I know about the project is that it's the brainchild of Jasper Etherington, also known as the Vegetable King. He's one of those hippy types who refuses to use animal products in his dishes, so God only knows what this is all about. Nut roasts in the shape of internal organs, or maybe baby animals to remind us how cruel we all are for working with meat.

I'm only here because Ferguson has told me doing this would make my path easier if I went with him. And I'd be lying if I said I didn't know what he means by that. Of course I know. Isaac Ferguson is considered a champion in the arena of shitty bosses, and legendary when it comes to lechery. But he's also one of the biggest names in the culinary world, and it's times like his when the only thing you can do is grit your teeth and get on with it. Because what else is a girl going to do? Take on the entire system just because your boss likes to feel you up once in a while? Ha.

Like that's going to get you anywhere, especially when it comes to exclusive events like this.

The BodyWorks Project is by invitation only, and we've all had to sign waivers and non-disclosure agreements to attend. I've been told to wear something nice, which is probably code for something revealing, but instead, I pick a sensible cocktail dress – something one might wear to the opening of a new establishment, or maybe a book launch. I know I've made a mistake the moment Ferguson looks me up and down, a judgmental frown creasing his brow, but he doesn't say anything. Given he's in a simple dress suit, it's not like he can complain.

The venue is a nondescript industrial building in Shadwell. This is deliberate, of course – the grunginess of the surroundings is undoubtedly meant to reflect the depravity of our usual trade. We're greeted at the door by some large young men who look more like club bouncers. If it weren't for the other guests in their stuffy suits, I might be able to kid myself I was at an illegal rave rather than whatever the hell this all is.

Inside, the lights are low, and a haze of cigarette smoke drifts to the ceiling, deepening the nightclub ambience. I take a quick glance around, hoping to see someone I recognize – and I do. I recognize a lot of the men here. Every single one of them is right up there at the top of their game.

What I don't see is many other women.

In fact, there are only three, including myself.

My stomach drops a notch. Women develop senses men could only dream of when it comes to discerning danger, and every single one of mine is shrieking at me to get out, get out *now*. But I know that if I walk away, Ferguson will never forgive me and I'll never work in this industry again.

I also know why he's brought me here instead of one of his other mentees.

'Oh, Isaac, how are you doing, old chap?' The voice is

unctuous and instantly recognizable. Charles Wakefield of *Food and Drink* – also known as 'the housewives' choice'. Ferguson grasps his proffered hand and shakes it far too vigorously – the way men do when trying to dominate each other.

'Charles, it's been a while,' Ferguson says. He's smiling, but his eyes are flat and predatory. It always fascinates me how often this happens – the wider the smile, the deader the eyes. He really must hate Wakefield if this is his reaction to him.

'Been busy, old boy. Out in the sticks. Or as the peasants call it – Thailand.'

'Shooting?'

'In all senses of the word.' Wakefield waggles his eyebrows, and I feel a little bit of my soul wither away, because I know *exactly* what he means. 'How about you?'

'Me? Just showing the girl the ropes, if you catch my drift.' Ferguson gestures towards me, like I'm nothing more than a piece of meat.

'Oh, hello. You're rather delicious, aren't you?' He holds out his hand. Naively, I take it, thinking he means to shake it. Instead, he grabs it and raises it to his lips, planting an unpleasantly moist kiss on my knuckles. 'What's your name?'

'Grace,' I say, my entire body creeping. I try to snatch my hand away, but he's got my fingertips pinned under his meaty thumb.

'Well, isn't that delectable?' he says, giving Ferguson a knowing look. 'Charles Wakefield. You must be very, very good at your job if this old goat has brought you here.'

'She's learning,' Ferguson says. 'Not there yet, if you know what I mean.'

'Indeed? An unbroken filly? How delightful.'

I'm used to old men being disgusting in this industry, but this particular specimen is on a whole new level. I'm finding it hard to steady my breathing as I continue to prise my fingers out of his sweaty grasp, but the more I wriggle them, the tighter he holds on. Just as I'm plucking up the courage to say something, a gong rings out. Everyone falls silent and turns towards the far end of the room. I use this distraction to snatch my hand back as three figures emerge from behind a red screen.

In the middle stands a man in a simple black robe. Flanking him are two women wearing collars and nothing else. From each collar runs a length of chain, which the man holds in each hand.

The women don't look at the crowd. Their attention is fixed firmly on their feet while the man raises his hands like a preacher about to deliver a sermon.

'*The BodyWorks Project* is the culmination of half a decade's work. This is my gift to you. Please, enter at your own risk, and remember what you have promised.'

The man lowers his hands and steps back behind the screen, the two naked women in tow.

'Bravo,' Ferguson murmurs beside me. 'Say what you like about Jasper Etherington, he knows how to put on a good show.'

I should have left the minute those women walked in. Should have seen it for the warning it was.

But I didn't.

I stayed. I stayed because my desire to please – and therefore succeed – overrode every sense I possessed. Because I knew that if I left, my career would be over. If I said anything, I would be out. Not just from this nightmare, but from the industry as a whole.

The first thing that hit me was the smell. Cigarettes, meat and sweat. I've never been to a strip club, but this is exactly how I imagine one might smell. I braced myself for the worst – waiting for poles, waiting for dancers – completely oblivious to just how innocent I really was.

The first time I spotted them, it took me a moment to understand what I was seeing. I thought they were mannequins.

But then one of them twitched.

Women – no, *girls* – laid out like platters, staring at the ceiling while chefs pluck hors d'oeuvres from their naked bodies. Jasper Etherington is mingling, inviting us to try everything. Ferguson approaches one blonde with gusto.

It's all I can do to stop myself from being sick.

There's a commotion at the other side of the room. One of the chefs is arguing with a fully dressed member of staff, claiming he was only 'interacting with the exhibits'. A few people are muttering among themselves, shooting him distasteful looks, but more are smirking, clearly thinking this guy is a legend. I don't know exactly what happened, but I can guess.

The poor girl in question is young – my age, at most. Probably a student trying to earn a bit of extra cash. She's clearly been instructed not to move, and she's doing her best. She still has some tiny pastries on her stomach, but all the ones covering her breasts and genitals are gone. There's a suspicious smear of sauce on both. As she lies there, she silently weeps. No one tells her she can stop. No one tells her it's OK. The men just keep taking morsels of food – food that probably cost more than her rent – off her flesh, as though she's nothing more than a piece of furniture.

I desperately want to go to her. To cover her up. To tell her it's OK, she doesn't have to do this . . . But I don't, because I'm outnumbered. I can't even see the other two young female chefs that have been dragged along to this awful stunt. I'm guessing they're doing the same as me: hiding in the shadows, wishing they could disappear. If only there were more of us here. If only I'd smuggled in a camera.

If only . . .

I sigh. It's pointless. There are six women-platters, plus the two women-slaves still flanking Etherington. With the three of us female chefs, that makes eleven women in the room. Sure, we're still outnumbered three to one, but we could try. In an ideal world, we could make a scene. Band together. Defend each other.

Sadly, we don't live in an ideal world.

Sadly, even if we succeeded, no one would believe us. All we'd have done is destroy our own futures.

So I stay in the shadows, sucking it up, and hating myself for it.

In many ways, it's just a normal day in the kitchen.

THIRTY-FOUR

1997

Flesh Is Flesh

It isn't long before the novelty of young female flesh wears off for Ferguson and Wakefield, and another gong is rung. Etherington raises his arms and beckons for everyone to follow him through a set of industrial double doors into a large, clinically cold room.

Everything is white, except for the table, which is made of brushed steel. It's chilly to the touch, like the inside of a fridge, and roughly cut in the shape of a human body. We're invited to sit by the still-silent women, who are now acting as our wait staff. I offer the one near me what I hope is an understanding smile. She doesn't return it.

While the atmosphere had been raucous for the hors d'oeuvres, in here it's the complete opposite. Everyone is nervously fiddling with things, glancing around the room like naughty children waiting for their fathers to get home from work. Everyone, that is, except Ferguson. He's watching me, his expression unreadable.

'What?' I mouth.

He simply shrugs and looks away.

The actual meal comes in the form of a tasting menu, all served by those poor girls. They're still naked as they place the dishes on the table, leaning in between the guest chefs so they can ogle them anew. Thankfully, they leave; I don't think I could stomach them in the room, watching us eat with their disassociated gazes and stiff, uncomfortable posture.

Not that their presence is needed to make the room feel unnerving.

The dishes look and smell incredible. Of course they do – Etherington is, after all, a respected chef. But he's also a staunch vegan . . . so why do these dishes look like they contain meat?

The dish in front of me could be veal, served with a wild mushroom polenta. The portion is small, but that's what you'd expect from a tasting menu. It's not meant to be a full meal, just a showcase of the chef's talent. I glance around the table, waiting for someone else to tuck in.

No one does.

Chefs aren't usually shy when it comes to tasting food. Usually, the hard part is stopping them from grabbing a teaspoon and digging in. But here, everyone is hesitant, exchanging nervous glances.

'Go on,' Ferguson murmurs to me. 'This is why we're here.'

'But—'

'Come on. You wanted to be here. Don't embarrass me.'

I bite down on my retort – that I *don't* really want to be here, that he was the one who said it would do me good – and I do as I'm told. I dig my fork into my portion, and the meat falls apart in perfect, gelatinous ribbons – clearly cooked long and slow. As I lift it to my mouth, I realize all eyes are on now me. A second later, the meat is in my mouth. It's perfectly cooked: meltingly tender and full of rich, umami flavour. Now I've tasted it, I'm revising my initial guess of veal to pig cheek. Maybe that's what this is all about – championing inferior cuts, raising awareness of the waste in the system? I chew appreciatively, feigning confidence.

'How is it?' Ferguson asks as I swallow.

'It's good. Well cooked. Very tender. I think it might be pork, but it's a little *gamier* than that. Maybe boar?'

My mentor smiles – a horrible, wolfish expression.

'Try a little more. See if you can guess.'

So, not boar.

I take another forkful.

The room is silent. A few of the chefs are now prodding at their dishes, as if they've never seen food before. Two of them are actively staring at me, their expressions caught between revulsion and fascination. I thought I'd felt uncomfortable before, but that was nothing compared to the scrutiny I'm facing now.

Then one of the chefs tentatively pokes out his tongue and laps at his forkful of meat.

'Oh, it's surprisingly palatable,' he announces. 'Although it resembles veal, it's definitely more pork-like in both texture and taste. Fascinating.' He looks over at me, like I've pulled off some kind of trick. 'Brave of you, girl. I wasn't going to be able to bring myself to try it, but in the face of your fearlessness—' He shovels the rest into his mouth.

One by one, the other chefs take a tentative taste of the dish in front of them. Some of them announce that's it – they've hit their limit, they can't do anything beyond that one taste.

A couple of them, however, chow right down. No one refrains entirely.

Confused, I turn to Ferguson, who still hasn't tasted anything.

'What's going on?' I ask him.

And with a shit-eating grin, he tells me what this is all about. What I've just consumed.

'It's human meat, darling. You're eating someone's flesh.'

It doesn't register at first. A laugh bubbles up within me.

'Very funny,' I say. 'It can't be. That would be illegal . . . wouldn't it?'

'Oh, no,' Ferguson says. He's enjoying this far too much. 'It's perfectly above board. Donor meat, you see. Some chap was in a motorbike accident. Had his arm and leg amputated. Donated it to *The BodyWorks Project*. Etherington calls it "ethical meat consumption". Which is rather ironic, when you think about it. After being told for centuries that cannibalism is wrong, one chef comes along and proves it might actually be morally better than slaughtering animals. Nothing had to die. The meat was literally a waste product. So rather than incinerate it, why not eat it? Like you said yourself – it's good.'

The room tunnels around me and begins to spin as I dig around the backs of my teeth with my tongue, finding strings of flesh still clinging to them. My breathing turns erratic and I try to stand up. I need to get away – to escape this place, rinse my mouth and purge it of the sin I've just unknowingly committed.

But Ferguson has other ideas.

He grabs my wrist and gives it a vicious twist, pulling me back into my seat.

'Sit down,' he hisses. 'You are not going to embarrass me. Remember who we're with.'

But I can't help it. Bile surges up my throat, hot and acidic, and when it floods my mouth, there's no way I'm going to swallow it back down. It's like my body has to purge itself of this humiliation, this desecration.

The room falls silent again. Then someone else gags. And another. And another. One by one, people struggle with their stomachs. Some manage to hold it. Some don't.

I don't wait to see how it all ends.

As soon as I can breathe, I run. And I don't stop until I'm back outside, taking in huge lungfuls of the night air.

THIRTY-FIVE

By the time Gracie has finished, Renee feels like she's inside a fever dream. Even though she wasn't there, she can feel it. Hell, she can almost *taste* it. All of a sudden, everything about Gracie makes much more sense. Her refusal to be brought down. Her fierce fight against a patriarchal industry. Her private freezer and need to butcher the carcasses herself. Her mentor, who had broken her trust so completely, to the point where she truly believes the only person she can rely on is herself. If anything, it makes her sharing her expertise all the more poignant. Now Renee understands, their eyes lock; it's almost as if Gracie is transmitting her story telepathically.

'He fired me after that,' Gracie continues. 'Said I'd embarrassed him. That he never should have taken me with him. Like it was *my* fault.' She spits out the last sentence, as if she can't stand to have it in her mouth. 'These men who think themselves gods but are nothing more than the pigs we so readily slaughter, squirming in the mud of their own self-satisfaction, not realizing that they aren't just part of the problem – they are the *whole* problem.

'In a way, I'm grateful to Etherington. Because he was right. Meat is meat. These holier-than-thou chefs, saying they embrace local produce but still import vanilla and saffron over vast distances. Saying they abhor cruelty, but still serve foie gras as a *luxury*. Saying they advocate a nose-to-tail philosophy, but only if it's a socially acceptable animal killed purely for our consumption.

In the grand scheme of things, what is the difference? Dressed up in a fancy sauce and given an edgy name, they all ate the human meat. They all *consumed*. And yet *I* was the embarrassment. *I* was the problem. Too delicate. Too close-minded. Too *female* – unable to understand the artistic merit of Etherington's work.

'But I showed them. It took me a while, but I fought my way back. And this time, I came back with a cleaver in my hand. One by one, I showed them *exactly* what a female chef is capable of. These once-proud men, so sure of their supremacy, bleating like sheep as I tore through their ranks. That is why I will never compromise my principles. And neither should you, Renee. You mustn't let them get in your way, no matter how succulent they may seem. They will try to bring you down in any way they can, because even if they don't realize it, they have been conditioned to believe that their egos are more important than you. Even if your man says he's a feminist – and you don't have to look at me like that, I know the type – underneath, he's like all the others. He's a feminist when he wants a pat on the back. But when it counts – when he is asked to move aside or take the longer route – he'll be there with the rest of the swine, squealing that it's not fair should you ask him to give up one ounce of his privilege.'

Gracie settles back in her seat, chest rising and falling rapidly while she works her jaw. Renee is lost for words. She'd guessed that some deep trauma drove Gracie, but *this*? This was on a whole different level. It was unhinged. Complete and utter, tried-and-tested, organically grown insanity.

But that doesn't mean Renee doesn't understand. Despite it being the most mental story she has ever been told, she believes it happened. In fact, she's sure of it. No one speaks like this unless they've suffered something so heinous it's scarred their very soul.

Gracie's success wasn't by chance. No, it was something far more calculated, far more personal than that.

Everything she does, every move she makes.

It's revenge, pure and simple.

By the time Renee leaves the restaurant, it's pitch dark outside and she's quite drunk. After Gracie revealed her past, she'd topped their glasses back up and moved into far more pleasant waters – talking about NOVA, her vision, and exactly how Renee might fit into this. Renee had never seen Gracie this animated before, her love for her restaurant tumbling out of her. How she'd been looking for someone to train up and mould in her image but had been disappointed by the lack of real talent out there; how, yet again, the industry favoured genitals over ability, and that she'd been close to giving up until she came across Renee's CV. Renee could barely keep up; the alcohol and pivot to non-cannibal conversations left her with vertigo.

'I knew it was a risk,' Gracie had said, raising her glass to her. 'But if there's one thing I'm not afraid of, it's risk. Sometimes, it doesn't pay off. Sometimes, it can make things worse. But then there are the times when it doesn't just pay off – it changes everything.'

Renee had blushed at that, unsure of how to react. Gracie then told her to stop being modest, revel in her own excellence, and have another drink.

So she had.

Renee checks her phone – it's nearly one a.m. Jesus, how long had she been in there? She takes a few deep lungfuls of air in the hopes of sobering up a bit. It doesn't work.

In the end, she crawls into the back of an Uber and lets the driver take her home.

She doesn't check to see if Lola's up, just heads straight for bed and falls asleep in her make-up.

It feels strange, going back to work like nothing has happened. Like Gracie hadn't just let Renee in, confided in her, told her everything. That she now knows more about her enigmatic boss than anyone else.

She doesn't let it affect her work, though. She can't. If anything, she feels even more of a responsibility towards NOVA now, even more invested. Now, it isn't about the prestige of working at the top. It's personal. Now she knows Gracie's intentions, she has to prove that she's worthy of her trust.

Sadly, she can't say the same about life on the home front.

Graham and Lola have definitely been speaking. Their efforts are far too coordinated for it to be any other way. Every time she sees either of them, they look at her like she's dying, or treat her like she's made of porcelain. They're both convinced she's heading for some kind of breakdown, which is ridiculous, because she's never felt stronger.

That is, until the police turn up.

Thankfully, they arrive at NOVA just as service is winding down, asking if Ms Fitzgerald is in. Bethany nods and, as if by magic, Gracie appears. This is becoming a thing, and Renee realized a while ago that the executive chef is in her restaurant more often than not, watching from her office. Once, she might have found that odd, but now she knows better than to question Gracie's motives. The police officers introduce themselves and Gracie takes them up to the conference room while the chefs continue their clean-down, sharing apprehensive glances as they do so.

After a short while, they are each called up, one by one, starting with Bethany and ending with Renee.

'If you would take a seat,' the female officer says, gesturing to the chair across from her. Renee looks around nervously. 'I'm PC Cosh, and this is PC Colebrook.' The taller, male officer inclines his head. 'We're investigating the disappearance of Joshua Armitage, who we understand used to work here?'

'Um, yeah?' Renee says, unsure of what they want from her.

'I didn't really know him all that well – I hadn't been here long before he legged it.'

'So you're under the impression that he just left?'

'Well, yes. He threatened to do it all the time. He wasn't happy here.'

'I see. In what way wasn't he happy?'

'I'm sorry, but do you think someone in the restaurant had something to do with him going off?'

'Going off? Why do you say that?'

'I don't like to speak ill of people who can't defend themselves, but he was . . . difficult. He came from money and was used to getting what he wanted. He was quite rude to us – very rude actually – causing Chef Fitzgerald to reprimand him. He didn't like that. That's why he never came back. Or, at least, that's what we thought.'

'I see.' The officer scribbles something down on a pad. 'So, would you describe Joshua's relationships with his fellow employees as strained?'

'I suppose. He was a . . . challenge to get along with sometimes. He was very entitled.'

'And why do you think Chef Fitzgerald put up with his behaviour?'

'Because his uncle is one of NOVA's financial backers.'

'These things are always more complicated when money's involved.'

Unsure of what they're getting at, Renee doesn't answer.

'I think he tried to spike my drink once,' she says, then immediately regrets it when the officers share a look.

'He did? Why do you think he did that?'

'I don't know. Well, I think I do, but . . .' Renee stops and tries to gather her thoughts. 'He wasn't happy about my employment. He thought it was unfair – that he should have been made chef de partie, despite not having the experience or qualifications for the role. He was under the impression that just being there was enough, and that I'd cheated him out of something.'

'So he spiked your drink?'

'It was either him or the bartender, and I don't think it was the bartender. I just . . . He thought I would make a fool of myself, or that I might not turn up for work – something along those lines. He wanted to humiliate me.'

'So it was a revenge thing?'

'I think so. And then, after his rant, and Gracie chewing him out . . . I don't think his ego could take it, and he bounced.'

'Is that why no one reported him missing?'

'Why would we report him missing? We're not his family.'

'True.' PC Cosh takes a moment to read over her notes. 'OK. I think that's everything. Thank you, Ms Landis. You've been very helpful.'

Renee, however, is not so sure.

'This is serious, isn't it?' Martin says, dejected. He's only saying what everyone else is thinking, given the way they share a collective sigh.

'It is, but we have to keep it together.' Bethany, forever the den mother, is in the process of making everyone a cup of coffee. She passes everyone a mug, followed by a tin of home-made biscotti.

The thing is, none of them had given Josh's absence a second thought. They'd all assumed he was just being his difficult, entitled self, and not without reason. But now . . .

'We should have said something,' Martin says.

'Like what?' Roy says, always the realist. 'For all we know, Gracie fired him. Told him not to come back.'

'She would have told us,' Martin counters.

'Would she? She didn't tell us about that waiter. Renee's friend was the one who told you about him. She's a law unto herself when it comes to these things. We all know that.'

That Bethany doesn't dispute this speaks volumes of its truth.

'So what now?' Renee says.

Bethany shrugs.

'Probably nothing. We've all given our statements, told them what happened. What else can we do?'

'What I want to know is, why has it taken his family and the police this long to come to talk to us?'

Martin has a point.

'I don't know, and quite frankly, there's no point speculating. At the end of the day, apart from working with him, what did we really know about him?'

'He tried to spike my drink,' Renee says.

'He did what?' Bethany looks shocked.

Renee shares a look with Martin.

'When I first joined. He got a round in. I thought I was just being a lightweight, so I gave mine to my mate Lola. She's far more hardened in the arena of drink than I am, but it was clear something was seriously wrong when she basically passed out after finishing it off. Me and Martin took her home. At the time I wondered if it'd been one of the bar staff, but then Josh started with that weird hostility towards me . . . I think he was trying to make a fool out of me. Maybe hoping that might make Gracie sack me in favour of him, or something. I mean, I'm just speculating – it might not have been him, but . . .'

'Sounds suspicious,' Roy finishes.

'Yeah. I decided not to make a fuss, because it wasn't worth it. I didn't have any proof, and going up against his family's kind of money? That was never going to end well.'

'Shit,' Bethany says. 'I'm sorry, Ren. Missing or not, that's not right.'

'I know, but it's in the past now. I still hope they find him safe and sound. He might be a prick, but there's always the chance he'll grow out of it.'

The other chefs share a grimace, telling Renee that they're not so sure.

'OK, people,' Bethany says, draining her coffee. 'We have service tonight and it's going to be a busy one. We've got a couple hours, so let's go home, chill out for a bit, and come back as refreshed as we can, all right?'

THIRTY-SIX

The kitchen is subdued when everyone returns for the evening service. Even Martin, whose exuberant nature often compensates for the others when they're not feeling it, is quiet. Renee has been assigned mains tonight, but the thrill she normally gets when looking at Gracie's notes is missing.

There will be three mains: braised pork shoulder, rack of lamb and pan-fried duck breast. The recipes all call for a range of seasonings, all designed to complement the various meats. In this case, Renee is noticing a sweet-leaning flavour profile, but that's not surprising – pork, lamb and duck all have characteristics that lend themselves to sweeter dishes. Even in her sombre state, Renee appreciates Gracie's instincts. While all the recipes are unique, they use similar ingredients so, rather than having to make up three wildly complicated marinades, she can create a base and add additional flavours as needed.

In the dry pantry, Renee piles what she needs onto a tray and carries it back to her bench. Then, as she makes her way over to the cold pantry, she notices something odd on Gracie's station.

A small bunch of keys.

Is she in? Renee had been under the impression that she wasn't. But if that's the case, why the keys? And why hasn't anyone noticed them? They can't be hers. Must be someone else's.

She goes to call out and ask if they belong to anyone, but the other chefs are so busy she is loath to disrupt their flow. If they do belong to someone in the kitchen, they'll notice soon enough.

Still . . . if they are Gracie's, it's a strange lapse for someone so obsessed with control – especially given she isn't here.

At least . . . she hasn't told anyone she's here.

Renee thinks back to the night she joined her in her office, and how Gracie said there's nothing she doesn't know when it comes to her restaurant. She could very well be up there now, and none of them would know.

Watching.

Ignoring the keys for now, Renee shivers as she enters the cold pantry, her breath frosty as she searches for her meat. Nothing in here is actually frozen – that's the job of the horrendous walk-in freezer – but that doesn't stop it from being chilly. She gathers the racks of lamb, then a tray of fat duck breasts. They've been left right at the top of their shelves, making them easy to spot.

The same can't be said for the pork.

The cut on the top of the pork shelf is a vacuum-packed portion of ribs. Delicious, but not what she's looking for. She needs a shoulder, which is usually a staple in a kitchen of this size. Renee continues searching, thinking someone might have accidentally buried it. She pulls out vacuum-packed parcels, one by one, finding loin and chops, belly and hocks . . . but no shoulder.

Renee frowns and looks again, hoping she simply missed it, but even after she's unpacked half the shelf, there's no pork shoulder to be found.

Now, this *is* weird. For Gracie to assign her the mains, but then forget to order the cut? Impossible. If it had been anyone else, she might have put it down to absent-mindedness.

The keys left on Gracie's bench. That was also weird. Also dismissed as absent-mindedness.

Gracie Fitzgerald. The least absent-minded person in the world. Being absent-minded not once, but twice?

No. There's something more to this.

It could be a test. A way for Gracie to see how she handles an emergency like this. What will she do? Who will she pick? Who is more important: the diner or the chef? Her initial reaction is to say Gracie, of course, but why would Gracie ask her to run the mains only to risk sabotaging it all, just to test her loyalty? It's preposterous.

So maybe she did just forget to order in the pork after all.

But that also goes against everything Renee knows about Chef. She wouldn't do something as crass as forget to order a cut for her own restaurant. It's ridiculous to even consider it.

But then why? Gracie's so protective over her ingredients. Why would she decide to change that now, without speaking to Renee first? Especially when pork shoulder isn't a difficult cut to source.

Renee looks one final time, just to be sure she's not going mad, then leaves the cold pantry with her trays of lamb racks and duck breasts. She eyes the keys on the table, her mind made up. There's no way Gracie would have left them there by accident, which means she left them there on purpose. But was it a test of Renee's loyalty to her carefully guarded privacy? Or did she leave them as an initiative test, to see if Renee would break the rules in order to run a successful service?

She glances around the rest of the kitchen. Everyone else is working, their heads bowed in deep concentration. She could ask if anyone knows where the pork shoulder went. Maybe Bethany put it out earlier. But why would she do that? To be nice? As lovely as Bethany is, she doesn't do that for anyone else, so why do it for Renee?

She snatches up the keys. One way or another, she's going to run a successful service. That's what Gracie would do.

She's sure of it.

That doesn't stop her hands from trembling as she selects the correct key and slides it into the lock. It turns with an easy click. Renee peeks over her shoulder, her heart racing, waiting for a furious Gracie to swoop down on her and demand to know what the hell she thinks she's doing . . . but the kitchen remains unchanged. No one even looks up.

Renee slips inside.

It turns out, Gracie's Secret Pantry of Mysteries is just another cold pantry, and not a very big one. As before, when she caught a glimpse inside, there are stainless steel shelves holding various ingredients – but, surprisingly, no meat. There's milk and butter, cream and eggs, but nothing else. It's almost as if Gracie has cleared the shelves ahead of time.

Renee sighs in frustration.

Has she just violated her boss's one rule for nothing? Does this mean she's failed the test?

No. There has to be more to this.

Especially given there's another door, tucked away at the back of the pantry.

This is definitely not standard practice. But given that nothing about Gracie is standard practice, Renee stalks over and tries this door, just in case she keeps her meat in a separate storage area behind this one.

It's locked.

Renee frowns as pure unease squirms in her belly. She looks at the keys in her hand. There are two. One is for the main pantry door . . .

She selects the other and pushes it into the lock. It fits.

Renee holds her breath as she turns it.

It clicks.

'And one for the secret door,' Renee breathes to herself.

She had no idea what she'd been expecting as she pulls the door open. A meat locker, maybe? That would make the most sense, given the circumstances.

But a set of stairs? That wasn't even in the top ten.

Eight white-tiled steps with a black anti-slip bar descend into a cold, dark room. For some reason, their clinical appearance feels wrong; everyone knows that secret stairs behind secret doors should be crumbling brick or creaking wood with slats that allows some terrible monster to grab your ankle as you go down them. These look like every single set of stairs she's ever seen in a hospitality setting – meaning that even if they are hidden, they were still built with purpose, and in accordance with building regulations.

Renee hesitates. It's not too late. She could turn back, leave the freezer, lock up, pretend she's never been in here.

But the pork . . .

'Fuck,' she hisses, and begins creeping down the stairs.

It's dark down here. Like, proper, bottom-of-a-well dark. She fumbles around the wall near the entrance, hoping to find a light switch, but comes up empty, which is odd. But then again, maybe it isn't. If no one but Gracie comes down here, then she can put her light switch wherever she wants.

Except . . . why would she put it anywhere else?

The suspicion that Gracie is hiding something sinister rears its ugly head again.

Renee blinks, willing her eyes to adjust to the gloom. She can now make out basic shapes and realizes that, as in the room above, there are stainless steel shelves lining white-tiled walls, with various cuts of meat on them. Excellent – so this is just Gracie's meat storage after all. Nothing sinister or weird about it, just a traumatized chef making sure absolutely no one can tamper with her cuts. One who left her keys out for her trusted employee to use if she needed to.

Or, at least, that's what Renee's telling herself.

She peers carefully at the shelves, but none of them are labelled. Again – of course not. They don't need to be when only one person is using them. So she focuses on the cuts, selecting one that that looks like it might be a shoulder.

Something is written on its packaging.

Young Pig.

She smiles to herself. Success.

She picks it up and goes to leave, but as she turns, a flutter of movement in the corner of her eye freezes her in place.

A blinking green light at the opposite side of the room turns on.

'What the hell . . .' Renee mutters, as a whirring sound starts up, followed by a gust of cool air. She blows out a shaking breath.

It's OK. Must be the cooling system kicking in.

A soft clack on the tiles interrupts her panicky thoughts.

Is someone else in here?

Oh God, it's Gracie, Renee thinks, racking her brain for an excuse as to why she's down here. Of course – this is an initiative test. She's watching her, waiting to see what she does, how she might justify herself.

Except . . . if it is Gracie, surely she would have revealed herself by now?

The room falls silent again.

Then, a few seconds later, a scraping *creak*.

Renee's heart beats in her throat as she peers ahead of her, trying to make out the various shapes in the now green-tinged gloom.

Whatever they are, they're large.

And one of them is swinging, ever so slightly.

Her immediate reaction is to freeze, her eyes wide.

'They're just carcasses,' she whispers. 'Just carcasses. Nothing else.'

Creak.

She takes a step back.

'OK, time to leave,' she says to herself. She's sure there's a perfectly innocent explanation for all of this, but right now, she's too wound up to think straight. She hustles up the stairs and relocks the doubly secret door, leaving Gracie's private space for good, all sense of curiosity replaced with a deep sense of dread.

THIRTY-SEVEN

For the first time in a very long time, Renee feels genuinely uncomfortable in NOVA's kitchen.

She's unpacking her meat, stripping each cut of its plastic wrapping – leaving the pork until last. No matter how much she tells herself she's being silly, she can't shake the feeling it's tainted in some way.

Test or not, she shouldn't have gone into that freezer.

Well, it's too late for regrets now. Either she's going to cook a cracking main with it and Gracie will forgive her, or she'll get sacked. All or nothing.

A bit like Gracie herself.

'You all right there, love?' Martin gives her a concerned look.

'Yeah, I'm fine. I was panicking a bit because I couldn't find something, but it's all right now.'

Thankfully, Martin doesn't press further.

After scoring the duck breasts and placing them in their marinade, she can't put it off any longer.

It's time to tackle the pork.

She suppresses a shudder as she slices open the packaging and inspects the shoulder. Normally, she prefers working with this cut; once, while prepping belly, she came across a nipple. Of course she knows pigs have nipples, but usually the butcher removes them before delivery. Being faced with one in the kitchen felt strangely obscene. There's no harm in eating it, technically, but it's as if society has universally agreed that nipples are off the menu. Coming face to face with one was a disconcerting and surprisingly visceral reminder that the meat was once a living, breathing animal.

To this day, she's still a little bit funny about pork.

Renee places the slab of meat on her board. It's already been boned, so all she needs to do is score the skin and season it before placing it in the pressure cooker. She picks up her knife, strokes the flesh to decide where to start, then hesitates.

The skin is unusually smooth, bordering on soft. Far smoother and softer than she's used to. Of course, this pig must have been spoiled rotten before its little holiday to the abattoir; you don't find meat of this quality in supermarkets. It would have come from a bespoke farm catering only to the upper echelons of fine dining. But the skin isn't just softer; it's thinner too, and the hairs that remain on it are lighter and sparser than the coarse bristles you'd typically find on this type of cut. Exactly how young might this pig have been? She's only worked with suckling pig a handful of times, and never had to prep one, but anyone could see that this cut is too large for a piglet.

Right on the edge of the slab is some kind of stamp – most likely a slap-mark for identification purposes. It's more intricate than usual, but then again, the place this pig came from probably has a bespoke logo to ensure no one tries to pass off inferior meat as their own.

Still, the apprehension kindled in Gracie's freezer deepens. Renee peers at the mark, trying to make out what it might have said. Normally these things are a hastily printed set of numbers and maybe letters, but this is different. It's more like a picture, with something written through it.

'. . . o . . . ear?' She frowns. *O ear?* Could that be how they label batches? Maybe that's why it looks familiar – she's seen it on paperwork, or on other cuts Gracie's been preparing. She gives herself a mental shake. Whatever it is, it doesn't matter. This shoulder should have gone in ten minutes ago – if she doesn't get it on pronto, she'll be late for the pass.

'Hello, Renee.'

Her heart stutters and begins to race as Gracie appears beside her.

The chef makes a show of studying the slab of meat in Renee's hands.

Oh my God, she knows. She knows I went into her freezer. Oh fuck, fuck, fuck—

But Gracie doesn't say anything. Not at first, anyway.

She just smiles.

After what feels like an age, Gracie leans over and murmurs directly into her ear.

'Have you been exploring?'

'I-I, uh, um. I mean, I was—'

Gracie spins her keys on one finger, her smile even wider. It's not a pleasant smile. It doesn't even inch towards nice. There's a cruel edge to it, sparking a light in Gracie's eyes that Renee has seen far too many times before.

Renee freezes. She has no idea what to do, or what to say, except brace herself for the inevitable dressing-down. But it doesn't come. Instead, Gracie runs her fingertips over the meat's skin – gently, like a lover might do to their partner's stomach.

'You know what?' Gracie says. Her voice is like clotted cream and honey – thick and sweet and unctuous. 'I'll take over this one, so we don't fall behind. You focus on the lamb and the duck.'

'Gracie, look. I'm sorry – I really am. I can—'

'I'm sure you can,' Gracie purrs. 'But I'm in the mood to cook. I wasn't earlier, but I am now. And I do so love this dish.' She leans a little closer to Renee and whispers, 'If you're good, I might even let you taste it.'

A few days ago, Renee would have been jumping for joy.

Now she's beginning to think that might not be the privilege she once thought it was.

Despite Renee's unease, the rest of the prep work goes smoothly. She trims the fat from the lamb rack, then spends a while scraping the bones clean of meat and sinew before bathing it in the marinade. She then preps her veg and checks with Martin that her sauces are ready.

Gracie's eyes stay pinned on her the whole time.

Again, a sense of intense foreboding steals over her, but this time it isn't driven by a fear of making mistakes. No, this is something different. Something more unnerving. It has her looking over her shoulder more than a few times, but she can't pinpoint the reason. It's almost as if she's been forced to play a game whose rules she doesn't understand.

Eventually, just before the doors open, Gracie beckons her over.

'Renee, you've proven yourself a real asset,' She pauses while Bethany makes her way to the pass. 'And as I said before, I see great things in you. Your hunger . . . your expertise . . . I can't help but wonder what great heights you'll reach. You're already climbing, but that only makes me want to help you – to *push* you on to even greater things, so you can realize and seize your full potential.'

Pride swells within Renee, mingling with the discomfort she's felt since entering the private freezer. This is what she's always wanted: not only a mentor who can teach her, but a mentor who believes in her.

'Thank you, Chef,' Renee murmurs.

'To that end, I now trust you enough to taste this signature dish.' Gracie smiles, but again, there's a slyness to it – something bordering on sadistic. She may say she believes in Renee, but this feels more like she's playing with her. 'I trust you. And only you.'

'Oh. Gosh. That's . . . Thank you, Chef.'

'You are most welcome, Renee.'

Gracie jabs her fork into the now-cooked pork. Martin has prepared the sauce, but Gracie hasn't yet added it, so for now the meat sits there: an undressed, pink, wobbling lump. She twists her fork, easily pulling off a chunk. The morsel steams as Gracie holds the laden fork, its almost-jellified fibres dribbling a greasy liquor that drips down Renee's chin as Gracie feeds her like an infant.

Renee closes her eyes as she accepts the meat into her mouth, but instead of the flavour explosion she was anticipating, she has to stop herself from gagging.

Did Gracie forget to add something? Or maybe the meat wasn't stored correctly and she's been sold a dud. Because this doesn't taste right – not at all. She'd been under the impression she was tasting a slow-cooked pork shoulder – the chef's version of humble pulled pork, something she's eaten plenty of times in her life. But this is like no pulled pork she's ever tasted. Yes, the meat is superficially pork-like in flavour profile, but there's an unpleasant gaminess to it – an acrid tang that clings to the back of her throat. Normally, that metallic gamey taste would come from blood being left in a carcass that's since gone rancid – a mistake many an amateur cook has made. The sour notes could come from the animal being stressed during the slaughtering process. It's well known that if an animal is afraid, it releases adrenaline, causing its muscle fibres to tense, resulting in tough, bitter meat.

Maybe her assumptions that Gracie's meat suppliers are at the top of their game was a mistake, but that seems very unlikely. Renee's visited some of these places, seen how they work, and they treat their livestock like royalty before slaughter. And she hasn't noticed anything off in the other meat dishes she'd prepared and tasted. She couldn't even put it down to not liking the choice of sauce, because Gracie hasn't added that yet.

This is . . . wrong.

Gracie looks at her expectantly as she chews, which Renee does slowly, hoping it might stop her from retching.

'Hmm.' Renee nods. The meat squelches as she pushes it into her cheek, the fibres wrapping themselves around her back teeth like they never want to leave. 'Lovely.'

Gracie sighs blissfully and scoops up a forkful for herself, which she eats with a reverence usually reserved for religious communions. She chews it slowly, clearly revelling in the taste.

Renee uses the moment to surreptitiously spit her mouthful into her hand.

'So *delicious*,' Gracie breathes. 'It's almost a shame we have to add anything else to it, really. Unfortunately, people expect *pizzazz* when they come to NOVA, so serving plain braised shoulder just wouldn't work.' She gives the wobbling lump of flesh in her pan an almost loving look, then sighs and pours over the sauce Martin prepared earlier. '*C'est la vie.*'

'Yes, Chef. Thank you, Chef. I'd better get back to my own dishes now, Chef.'

Gracie narrows her eyes. For a split second, Renee fears she's going to ask what's in her hand.

Or worse, insist she taste the meat again, now with the sauce.

Instead, Gracie just nods and turns back to her own dish, leaving Renee to wonder what the hell that was all about.

THIRTY-EIGHT

FINANCIER'S NEPHEW REPORTED MISSING: Joshua Armitage, nephew of multi-millionaire Neil Armitage, was last seen on 8 August. Police are asking for any witnesses who might have seen him in the Chelsea area around midnight. The family have released a statement expressing that 'Although he has run away before, we are still desperately worried.'

Renee scans the rest of the article on her phone, not really taking it in.

So, it's official. Another name to add to the ever-growing list of missing wealthy men.

Hopefully, this is just a case of crossed wires, and Josh has decided to go and find himself in Thailand after Gracie's dressing-down.

Except . . . if that were true, surely there'd be receipts? Credit cards. Phones being accessed. Internet activity. It's hard to truly disappear these days. Every device tracks your every move, whether you like it or not. Something's always pinging your location, logging every key stroke, remembering every Google search. And Josh doesn't strike her as the type to worry about any of that. Most people don't.

But if not that, then what? An accident? Maybe he fell into a hole, like the skeletal remains of the person they found in the sewers beneath Graham's flat. The police are currently running with the theory that the bones' owner probably stumbled into an uncovered manhole – finally tamping down the wild serial killer rumours – which would explain why his body hadn't turned up until now. Maybe something similar happened to Josh.

Yeah, right. Because there are so many uncovered manholes in London, the newspapers are practically bursting with stories of people falling down them. But she understands why people come up with such theories. Humans like things to fit into neat little boxes.

Renee puts down her phone. It's Sunday night. Usually, she has a different kind of Sunday Scaries. While everyone else dreads the return to work after the weekend, Renee is usually lamenting the break, eager to get back into the kitchen she loves so much.

But not tonight. Tonight, she just feels sick.

Since she went into Gracie's freezer, something has changed. She can't quite put her finger on it, but she can't get rid of the heaviness at the bottom of her stomach. A worry. No, it's stronger than that. An *anxiety* she hasn't felt in years, but it's not the usual kind – about work or bills or forgetting something. It's deeper – something you don't just feel in your skin, but also in your bones.

Something is very, very wrong.

'You all right?'

Lola is giving her a concerned look. Lola's giving her a lot of concerned looks these days. She's tiptoeing around Renee, like she might explode – something so uncharacteristic Renee can't help but worry more.

'Yeah.'

What else can I say? I think you might be right?

'You sure? You look a bit . . . peaky.'

'I do feel like I might be coming down with something,' Renee says, seizing the bone Lola's just thrown her.

'You are working quite hard. When did you last have some proper time off?'

'Uh . . .'

They lapse back into silence, leaving Renee with her spiralling thoughts.

Granni always told Renee to trust her gut. She claimed that it had never steered her wrong, and that most disasters happen because people ignore that sinking feeling, thinking their heads know better.

Heads are easily befuddled. You can't befuddle a gut. That's deep down in you, where your instincts live, and we got 'em for a reason, girl, so use 'em.

She takes a breath. Holds it. Then lets it out again. Repeats it a few times, hoping to feel some of the tension drain out of her, but the tight, spiky tangle of unknowns has lodged itself so far down in her chest she can barely breathe.

It's not working because you know there's something wrong. And it won't feel right until you do something about it.

Renee stands up. 'I'm going to bed.'

'You are? But it's only half eight.'

'I'm really tired.'

'OK. Sleep well. If you need anything, just shout.'

Lola's eyes bore into her back as she leaves.

In her bedroom, Renee sits on her bed, ramrod straight. She reaches over to her nightstand and takes a gulp from her water bottle. It's been days, and she still can't get the taste of that awful pork out of her mouth. It doesn't matter how often she brushes her teeth, or how much Listerine she gargles, it's like it's bonded itself to the insides of her cheeks, her gums, her tongue – plaguing her with visions of the wet lump of jellified meat, fresh out of the pot.

She sucks in another deep breath in a desperate attempt to steady herself.

The image warps, taking her back in time to when the shoulder was raw. When it was just a mound of glistening flesh, slightly damp and oozing myoglobin into the tray. She remembers how the pink fluid stretched, then snapped, like thin rubber bands as she lifted it to rinse it before scoring. She dismissed the thought at the time, but now she can't help but dwell on how little fat it had – especially for pork. It's one of the reasons people often struggle to cook it right. The meat may look lovely and caramelized on the surface, but if you don't time it right, the middle stays raw, the fat inside still tough and chewy. It's a dense meat, which is why it benefits from a long, slow and low approach. You need to loosen those fibres. Melt that fat.

But there was hardly any fat. Plus, the skin felt wrong. Too thin. Hairless. No bristles.

And half a tattoo.

'It was a brand,' Renee whispers to herself. 'A slap-mark.'

We've been over this. When have you ever seen a slap-mark that intricate?

'I don't know. Maybe that's what bespoke butchers use—'

Come on, Renee. When was the last time you saw anyone branding pigs with a tribal design that looks for all the world like it had the words 'No Fear' in the middle of it?

'No. It didn't. It was just a brand,' Renee whispers.

So tribal tattoos and trite slogans are not only for insecure dudebros now, but pig farmers too?

Renee's gorge rises. A hot lump forces its way up her oesophagus, scorching the delicate flesh of her throat. There's no way she can swallow it back down – it's all she can do not to vomit in her bed. She staggers to the bathroom and purges herself clean.

'Ren?' Lola calls out. Renee hates how worried she sounds. 'Oh my God. OK, um, let's get you to bed.'

Another wave of nausea rips through her, causing Renee to see stars. Lola rubs her back, murmuring platitudes. Once her stomach is empty, she straightens herself up, wiping her mouth and eyes. She glances down into the toilet bowl and her heart jolts – enough to make her fall back into Lola in horror – but quickly she realizes there aren't human fingers among the chunks, just her lunch from earlier this afternoon.

'I need . . . I need to lie down.'

She allows Lola to guide her back to bed.

'It's OK, babe. I'll just get you a basin – maybe you ate something bad or picked up a bug or something . . .'

Renee swallows the manic laughter rising inside. Because she definitely did eat something she shouldn't have—

No, Renee – get a fucking grip.

Life isn't a movie. These things don't happen in the real world. NOVA is a restaurant of worldwide acclaim. If there was anything dodgy about it, everyone would know. Gracie Fitzgerald isn't just a highly regarded chef, she's also a widely despised woman. There's no way she'd risk her entire career, and for what? Petty revenge? No, it's all nonsense. She's just tired. Tired and stressed. It's been ages since she's had time off – no wonder she's feeling so awful. What she needs is a good night's sleep. A proper rest. She's been neglecting herself recently. Time for some self-care. See Graham. Reforge those links.

Just in case.

Lola returns with a basin from the kitchen. It's old and stained, but it's the only thing they've got, and it's weirdly comforting because it reminds her of home, when her mum would use something similar whenever she was ill. Lola places it by the side of her bed and makes to leave, but Renee stops her.

'Lola . . .'

'Yeah?'

'I'm sorry, OK? Really sorry.' She struggles up into a sitting position. 'I've been so wrapped up with the restaurant, I've completely forgotten about anything else. And that's not right. I've treated you so badly. And I'm sorry. I really am.' She reaches out for her friend, placing her hand on her arm, unsure if Lola's ready to hug her, even though that's all she wants right now.

They regard each other, a little warily at first, but that soon crumbles away. Lola nods. Renee's throat constricts. She doesn't want to cry, but it's too late now.

'Come here,' Lola says, and wraps Renee in a hug. It's warm and generous and everything Renee needs right now.

'Look, you get your head down, OK? Do you want me to text G – let him know?'

'No, it's OK – I'll do that.'

'As long as you're sure.'

'I am.'

Lola gets up, pausing by the door. 'I know I probably shouldn't say this, but I'm worried about you, Ren. I know you say you're happy but . . .'

'I know. I just want to sleep.'

'OK. We'll talk in the morning. Try and get some rest.'

She doesn't.

It doesn't matter how hard she tries, Renee can't sleep. Music, podcasts, breathing exercises, cute animal TikToks – you name it, she's tried it. In the end, she gives up and makes herself a cup of tea. Even though it's five a.m., she pings a text off to Graham.

He replies five minutes later.

Hey . . . you OK? Xx

Yeah. Can't sleep. Sorry if I disturbed you xx

It's OK. I was getting up – want to be at the gym by 6

Renee smiles, despite everything.

Goody Two Shoes

Yeah, I gotta keep it up, how else am I going to be a trophy husband, eh?

Oh, husband? Anything you want to tell me?

Maybe . . . 😊

It was something they'd discussed in the past but had decided to shelve. Or, at least, Renee had decided to shelve.

Maybe it was time to revisit it?

She doesn't say anything about her worries. There's no point. In the cold light of day, she's not even sure if she believes them herself. Plus, they've only just rebuilt things after the incident at NOVA, and she doesn't want anything to ruin that. There aren't many guys out there who'd have been willing to talk things through after a blow-up like that.

It isn't long before he has to go. Before leaving, he reminds her that he won't be in tonight – he's out with some of his architect buddies to celebrate a new contract. And once again, Renee is left alone with her thoughts.

She does her best to fill the day. Lola told her to stay in bed before heading to work, but Renee needs to get out of the house. She thinks about seeing if Martin's free but decides against it. He's still firmly caught up in the magic of NOVA. Same goes for Roy and Bethany.

She's going to have to sort this out by herself.

Josh's disappearance is all over the news now, naturally. He's young, could be considered attractive – if you're into that gymcel kind of look – and, most importantly, comes from money. At the moment, the theories are vague, but already the odd podcast is mentioning that he worked at NOVA. It's only a matter of time before someone starts looking into that connection more seriously.

Then there's the remains found in the sewers under Chelsea.

Bones Show Signs of 'Being Disturbed', Experts Claim

It can't be real. It just can't. It's too insane.

But the tattoo—

'Shut up.'

Renee sits on the sofa, her arms wrapped around her knees, staring at her phone. She's been doing this for over an hour now. She knows it's not healthy, but she can't help it.

She has to be wrong.

She hears keys turn in the front door, and Lola calls out, 'Honey, I'm home!' before stomping into the living room. She chucks her bags in the corner and sits down heavily on the sofa beside Renee.

'Fuck me, what a shift,' she says. 'You should count yourself lucky that you get Monday nights off, because . . . Are you OK? Still feeling rough?'

Renee offers her a one-shouldered shrug and continues staring at her phone.

'What are you watching?' Lola prises the device from her hand. 'Crap, yeah, I was going to ask you about this. Is this the same guy? The one who went out with us the night I got spiked?'

Renee nods. She never told Lola her suspicions about Josh. Didn't see the point. She just made sure the two of them never crossed paths again – and never trusted him to buy her a drink.

Not that it matters now.

'Shit. That's heavy.'

'The police came in to talk to us,' Renee says.

'They did? When?'

'A while ago.'

'Why didn't you say something?'

'Dunno.'

But she does know.

The tattoo—

'Have you eaten today?'

Another one-shouldered shrug is all Renee can manage.

'Renee, what's wrong?' Lola says. 'I know you're not feeling well, but there's something else going on. Spill.'

Renee starts to shake her head, but her bottom lip betrays her.

'What's happened?' The wariness is back, but this time with a side order of genuine concern.

It takes Renee a moment to speak.

'I don't know. I mean, I *do* know, but I don't . . . I can't. It's—'

'Complicated?'

'Just a bit,' Renee whispers.

'Right.' Lola rubs her hands together, clearly uncomfortable. 'I think we need to get a nice big pot of tea on, and maybe make us some mug cakes. Now, I know they're cheap and no Michelin-starred chef would ever dare sully themselves in such a way, but if you put enough sugar in it, everything tastes good.'

Despite everything, this raises a smile.

'See? Told you. Even the thought of it makes you feel better. You sit tight, I'll be back in a minute.'

When the tea is made and the mug cakes are out of the microwave, Lola settles on the sofa and drags a blanket over the two of them, like they used to before Renee started at the restaurant. At first, Renee has no idea where to begin, but Lola doesn't interrupt as she meanders through disjointed apologies, fragments of what Gracie told her and flashes of that last service – though crucially she leaves out her suspicions about Josh and the pork. Even she's not sure she believes that quite yet.

Finally, she grinds to a halt. Her tea sits untouched, her mug cake slowly congealing under a melted layer of ice cream.

'OK.' Lola stretches the word out, clearly trying to muddle her way through Renee's confessional, careful not to say anything that might make things worse. 'Let's try and get this straight. Fuck, I feel like I need to write this down. Hang on.' She rummages in her bag and, after a minute or two, pulls out a battered notebook and a half-chewed biro.

'So,' Lola begins, flipping to a fresh page, pen in hand. 'Let's start with something – not easier, but maybe . . . simpler?'

'I am so sorry,' Renee says. 'I just want to say that again. I'm just . . . sorry.'

'Oh, honey, it's OK. I overreacted too. You've been through a lot. Settling into a new job – especially one as intense as yours – it takes a toll, you know? I get it. I really do. Remember when I started at Carluccio's? You may sniff, but after Chickadees, that was a huge jump. Going from a chicken shop to a proper franchise? Terrifying. You jumped even further, even higher. Of course you're going to feel strange. Now you've got your feet under the table, the high of landing your dream job wears off, and what's left is the pressure to live up to it. Which is what might be happening now? You've taken every shift they've thrown at you, plus more. Ren, you're one of life's all-or-nothing types. Even if it takes a while, you're not going to settle for less.' Lola gives her a cheeky grin. 'Apart from G. I mean, girl, I know he's got money, but that boy was at the back of the queue when they were handing out aura.'

Renee can't help but laugh at that – because yeah. Graham is a sweetie, but his game is practically non-existent. But then again, that's why she went out with him. It was refreshing to date a guy who wasn't gym-obsessed or fretted over your body count. She'd take kind over slick any day of the week.

'That's right. That's what we need,' Lola says. 'Smile, girl. You deserve it. So – we're going to draw a line under all this?'

'Yeah,' Renee says. 'I want to go back to the good old days.'

'Right, so we can cross that one off the agenda.' Lola makes an exaggerated flourish as she ticks the first point. 'Which leads me to . . . whatever the fuck that other stuff is.'

Renee takes a moment to compose herself. Her thoughts are a jumble – a mad riot of emotional highs and lows. She has no idea where to start, nor how to get Lola to understand her suspicions. She's not even sure 'suspicions' is the right word. One weirdly cooked pork shoulder doesn't prove anything. Rich people will eat all manner of disgusting things and tell you it's fabulous, simply because it's expensive and being served by the right person. They're almost like small children in that regard: if a toddler falls down, you distract them with dinosaurs – 'Oooh, look! *Tyrannosaurus rex!*' – and they forget to cry. Except instead of dinosaurs, it's peasant meals with a thousand per cent mark-up – 'Oooh, look! Oxtail!'

'I think the easiest way is to start with the small stuff,' Lola suggests. 'Then go from there?'

Renee nods. But soon comes to regret it, because once Lola starts listing it all on paper, all that small stuff sure adds up to a hell of a lot of red flags.

The private freezer. Not tasting Gracie's dishes. Gracie personally serving certain customers. Gracie taking revenge on people she doesn't like by serving them things designed to disgust. Gracie's control-freakery in general. Asking a new employee to come upstairs, plying them with cognac and then telling them the most bizarre story they've ever heard. Then telling that employee how wonderful she is and how Gracie wants to bequeath her restaurant to her at some undetermined point in the future.

Once Renee has finished, Lola puffs out her cheeks, eyebrows raised.

'OK, so when you said it was complicated, I didn't realize it was going to be *complicated* complicated. You do know you wouldn't have gone along with any of that if Gracie was a man, right?' Lola asks. 'That you'd have seen all of this as an entire forest of massive red flags?'

Renee can't deny it – because Lola's right. She would have been at least suspicious. She learned long ago never to go anywhere private with a man who has even a sliver of power and privilege over you – and even if they don't, it's still probably not a great idea. She'd never dream of accepting a drink from someone like Isaac Ferguson, and for good reason. He was – and possibly still is, wherever he may be – a predator. Renee let her guard down simply because Gracie is a woman.

'But she didn't, you know, *do* anything,' Renee says, still feeling an inexplicable need to defend Gracie. *When is that going to stop?* 'There was a point when I wondered if she might have . . . other intentions, but I don't think stuff like that is important to her. I get the impression everything goes into her cooking. She kept topping up my glass, but she never, you know, made a move. It was more like she wanted to check I was OK after my argument with Graham. Like she wanted to make sure he wasn't hurting me. But then she started telling me this weird story from her past, and how it's made her who she is today.'

'And dare I ask what that story was?'

'Umm,' Renee hesitates, unsure whether to share something clearly so personal to a woman she had, until incredibly recently, considered God.

'If it makes you feel better, I won't tell anyone.' Lola holds up three fingers. 'Brownie's honour.'

'You were never a Brownie,' Renee scoffs.

'Fuck off, I was. For far too long. I wanted to leave, but my Brown Owl was a mental old lady who wouldn't let me, and my mum said I'd pestered her so much to join that I had to see it through to the end. I was thirteen by the time she let me go. I'm surprised Operation Yewtree didn't come knocking – my Brownie uniform was so tight.'

'And that actually happened?'

'Yeah, it did. So don't try me. I've got my own skeletons.'

Renee can't help but snort.

'OK, what do you want – the long or short version?'

'Hmm.' Lola taps her lips with a long fingernail painted neon pink and studded with tiny rhinestones. 'Short version first. Then maybe the long one if it's as mental as you're making it sound.'

'All right. Don't say I didn't warn you.'

'Give me some credit. I once saw some desperate dudebro swallow a live frog to impress his mates. It can't be worse than that.'

'You say that now, but . . .' Renee blows out a sigh and shifts in her seat, unsure how to lay it out. 'Short version is, early in her career, Gracie was tricked into eating human meat in front of a bunch of high-ranking chefs. And please don't look at me like that.'

Lola's jaw is hanging, her eyebrows trying to become one with her hairline.

'Excuse me, what? Run that by me again?'

'Gracie was tricked into eating human flesh. In front of a load of other chefs. She said it was the nineties, and people did stuff like that back then. Or something.'

'I'm sorry, but what in the absolute *Requiem for a Dream* dystopian bullshit is that? *How*? And *why*?'

'Allegedly, her mentor wanted to humiliate her. Or, at least, that's what she suspects. As for the *how* – give us a moment.' Renee picks up her phone and googles *The BodyWorks Project* before handing it to Lola.

Lola reads in silence, her expression changing from scepticism, to surprise, to horror. Finally, she lands on full-body disgust.

'Fuck me, those boomers got issues,' she mutters, handing the phone back. 'And who the hell lets a chef have their amputated limb to cook it up for canapés? Shit's messed up. And we think it's bad now. At least no one's cruising the hospitals hoping to rustle up some medical waste.'

'I know, right? The things people will do for notoriety,' Renee says.

'Made even funnier cos I've never heard of this Etherington bloke. Really made a name for himself, didn't he?'

It's a good point.

'So that was awful,' Lola says, 'but what's it got to do with you?'

'I don't know,' Renee says. 'I thought she told me because she feels like she can trust me. She keeps saying I remind her of her younger self, and how she wants to mentor me in her image. But what that has to with *that* story, I'm not really sure.'

'Yeah, well, you can do all that without spinning some yarn about eating some bro's leg. You can just say, "You're promising. Let's get you trained up." You know, like a *normal* person.'

'I guess I hadn't really looked at it that way . . . It is weird, isn't it?'

'Girl, this has left "weird" by the door and gallivanted into the far fields of "what the actual fuck".'

'Brace yourself, then,' Renee says with a wince.

It's Lola's turn to blow out a huge sigh. 'I'll be honest, I don't really know how you're going to top eating an amputated leg off some rando, but go on, surprise me.'

Renee pauses, wondering exactly how she's going to convey it all without Lola calling the local psych unit.

'OK. So that was weird, but it was just a story. Whereas the last shift I worked—'

'Actually, you know what – hang on.' Lola gets up and disappears from the living room, only to return two minutes later with a bottle. 'I have a feeling I'm going to need this.'

'Vodka?' Renee asks.

'Yeah. Now pass me your mug. I know you've been sick, but I've already heard enough nonsense to know we're both going to need something more fortifying than tea by the end of this.'

Renee reckons she's not wrong.

THIRTY-NINE

Lola doesn't say a word as Renee recounts her last shift. She doesn't have to – her facial expressions tell Renee everything she needs to know. When it comes to Josh, though, Renee can't bring herself to make that connection – at least not out loud. Even in her own head, the thought sounds unhinged. It's just a coincidence.

It has to be.

When Renee's finished, Lola eschews her mug and takes a good gulp of vodka straight from the bottle. Then she hands it wordlessly to Renee. Renee doesn't usually drink spirits – maybe the odd gin and tonic in summer; she's more of a wine girl – but she accepts the bottle and takes a gulp of her own. She almost gags when the burn of the alcohol hits the back of her throat.

'Jesus, where did you get this? Tastes like it was distilled in someone's bathroom.'

'Hey, I won't hear anyone bad-mouthing convenience-store vodka. This stuff got me through college, I'll have you know.' It's clear Lola's still processing everything Renee has told her, and her almost pathological need to turn distress into humour is clearly in overdrive.

'So . . . what do you think?' Renee asks, her voice still a little hoarse.

Lola takes the bottle back, asks Renee to wait by holding one finger up, and takes another hit.

'OK,' she says eventually. 'I'm going to need some time to

process this.' She takes yet another swig, then sits in silence for a moment. 'You've already told me about the mysterious secret bunker freezer, and how she won't let anyone taste what she cooks from it, so that in itself is nothing new.'

'Right.'

'But today, she breaks her own rule. She tells you to make one of her recipes – and the joint of meat you need isn't in the regular freezer.'

'Cold pantry,' Renee says, automatically.

'Yeah, whatever. I think we have bigger and weirder things to worry about than storage semantics.'

'Sorry.'

'It's OK.' Lola pauses, trying to remember where they'd got to. 'Right, so secret bunker pantry, or whatever it is, is always locked, but today Gracie leaves her keys on her bench.'

'Yes. Which is very unusual because she's usually so careful and organized,' Renee says.

'I mean, we've all been there. Even control freaks leave their keys lying around sometimes.'

'And usually I'd agree with you,' Renee says. 'But don't you think the timing's a bit too convenient? She just happens to leave her keys on the bench, allowing me to get what I need out of her secret service freezer. Something she usually fires people for even looking at? I mean, remember that guy who worked at your place? She sacked him for taking his gloves off.'

'OK, that's true. But – and please don't take this as me not believing you – I'm just going to play devil's advocate, OK? As much for my sanity as yours. I totally get why you're a bit freaked out, but have you considered all the other things Gracie's said to you?'

'What, about eating people?'

'No, Ren – not about eating people. I honestly think she just made that up because she gets a kick out of telling twisted stories.

I mean, all the stuff about seeing herself in you. She's made it pretty clear that she likes you. I'd say you're more at risk of her, you know . . .' Lola gives her a slightly disgusted, knowing look.

'At risk of what?' Renee says.

'Oh for God's sake, Renee – sexual assault. Grooming, maybe. I know you said she isn't like that, but have you considered she might be attracted to you?'

'That? I don't think so. I mean, she knows about Graham—'

'Yeah, I get the impression she probably doesn't care about that, Ren,' Lola says.

'I don't know. We've all been operating under the assumption she's most likely asexual. Martin says she's never been seen with anyone – not even close. She never talks about relationships. He says all she seems interested in is her restaurant and her food.'

'Foodiesexual.' Lola grins.

'Stop it.'

'Sorry.' Lola fakes looking suitably chastised. 'But you have to agree, if she were a man, you'd be calling HR, right?'

Renee sighs, closes her eyes and nods. Lola's right. If a male chef had behaved the way Gracie has towards her, you wouldn't see her for dust. Because as complimentary as Gracie is, she's also crossed a few boundaries. Not in any sexual way, but . . . it's still there.

That nagging feeling that she has been violated.

'Everything she's doing smacks of grooming,' Lola says, serious now. 'I think she wanted you to find those keys. She probably didn't tell you where to get the meat for her recipe because she assumed you'd go into her pantry to get it. They were literally left for you to use. I don't think it was an accident. I think this was her way of . . . inviting you in, if that makes sense?'

'Yeah, sure. But what about the meat itself? It was . . . wrong. Kind of like pork but – I don't know . . . denser. Less fat. You don't need me to tell you how important fat content is in a decent cut. And the skin was thin. More like lamb's skin than thick pork rind.'

'I'll admit, that is weird. But again – devil's advocate – have you ever worked with Kobe beef?'

'A bit.' She smothers the memory of how cold the culinary school freezer was. 'We looked at luxury meats in college, but the industry trends more toward local, seasonal produce these days. Hardly anyone imports it now, and those who do are kind of looked down on in a weird way, like they're cheating. I mean, how can you make a Kobe steak taste bad? You can't. It's cooking on easy mode – something celebrity chefs or influencers might do – but anyone with real skill will tell you British beef is top quality, as long as you know your suppliers.'

'Dear Lord above, I do love you, but you're a nerd, you know that? My point is, maybe pork has an equivalent? Really high-end luxury pigs bred specifically to have more delicate skin and less fat?'

'But that still doesn't make sense,' Renee says. 'Kobe beef is that way due to its higher fat content. You need fat for moisture and flavour.'

'Look, I dunno,' Lola says, holding her hands up. 'I'm just throwing out ideas.'

'I know. And I appreciate it. It's hard to get across just how bizarre it all was. You go in there expecting to find what you want, but then – no. There's another locked door, and behind that it's like a small basement, or something. No automatic lights. No lights at all – at least, I couldn't find them. Unlabelled shelves. A packet of pork was marked as "young pig". Who does that?'

'Weirdo nerd chefs who have no life?'

'Lola, I'm being serious. In that basement freezer room . . . I don't know. It just felt wrong. Like I was stepping into a place I really shouldn't have. It's all so secretive, and it felt kind of – I don't know – *criminal*. That's the closest I can describe it. It felt like a crime scene, or a place where bad things happen.'

'Huh. Maybe the restaurant is a mafia front.'

'Lola . . .' Renee warns.

'What? I'm not joking. It wouldn't be the first place. You said it yourself – she kind of came out of nowhere. Maybe some of the money that's backing her is a little south of legit.'

'What, you think she might be hiding stuff in there for someone?'

'Why not? If you think about it, it's the perfect place. Why would anyone look in chef's freezer for evidence of a crime?'

She has a point. A horribly plausible one. Maybe NOVA isn't as squeaky clean as she thought. Maybe that's why no one really knows anything about Gracie. It would also explain why she keeps her kitchen staff small and her bookings exclusive. Then there's Q – where does he fit into all this? Maybe that's why he looks down on her: because he thinks Gracie is making a mistake, trying to bring Renee into all of it.

All of a sudden, Lola's grooming theory doesn't sound so implausible. Grooming doesn't always have to have a sexual motive.

Maybe Gracie wants to ingratiate her into some kind of crime syndicate situation?

Even as she thinks this, she knows it's a step too far. Sure, it's more believable than the cannibalism stuff, but it's still out there. No, there has to be another explanation.

But whatever that might be, Renee has no clue.

And then there's the brand. That was the most damning thing about it all. Which then swings her back to . . .

'. . . cannibalism.'

Renee blinks. She hadn't been listening to Lola, and the word coming out of her mouth catches her off guard.

'Sorry, what was that?'

Lola rolls her eyes. She's wobbling a bit now – the vodka is clearly kicking in.

'What I'm saying is crime – like, money stuff – that's more believable than cannibalism. Where is she getting the meat, for one thing? I can't see her going around snatching homeless people from the streets so she can Sweeney Todd them in her posh-arse restaurant. And even if she was, someone would have noticed. There'd be reports about them disappearing, but there isn't.'

'But there have been reports of disappearances, though, haven't there? That hotelier guy in the news. That guy off the TV.' *Josh*. 'The chef, Isaac Ferguson – he vanished a couple of years ago. Everyone assumed he'd gone into hiding after those rape allegations, but what if that's not it? And then there were those remains found in the sewer under Graham's road. The police said they looked suspicious – like they'd been sliced.'

'OK, I'll give you that one,' Lola says. 'But if they are the remains of a man-meal someone cooked up, they're not going to be local. They'd have been dumped far away from the actual crime scene. The thing is – why? Why would you risk it? For what end? Someone someday is going to break ranks and say something tasted weird, or they'll try to recreate the recipe and it won't go right . . . What I'm saying is . . . What was I saying?'

'That it's implausible for a restaurateur to risk using human meat in their dishes.'

'Exactly that.' Lola goes to take another glug of vodka, but Renee stops her. They've already made their way through nearly a third of the bottle, and only one swig of that was Renee's. 'Hey, what are you doing?'

'I'm being the boring nerd, here to tell you that I think you've had enough,' Renee says.

'Lies and slander.' Lola shifts so she's lying down, her head in Renee's lap. 'Why do you say such terrible things to me?'

'Yeah, well, I'm going to say something else terrible. It's gone past midnight and you have work tomorrow.'

Lola groans. 'You're evil. Burn her – she's a witch.'

Renee can't help but laugh. 'That's right. I'll turn you into a newt if you're not careful.'

Lola giggles at this, and closes her eyes. 'I miss this,' she says.

'What, getting drunk?'

'No! Us. Here. Shootin' the shit.'

'Drinking all the vodka.'

'Shut up, bitch. You know what I mean. I know you weren't happy at Chickadees, and that you thought you were wasting your life, but we had time for each other back then. Now all you do is work, work, work. I miss those times.'

Renee can only agree. She misses it too.

'I get it,' Lola continues. 'You've got so much talent . . . you should be working in the kind of place you are working. But those people . . . all the cheffy-chefs and poshos that go to eat there? They're not our type of people. You could stew up an old boot, and as long as it comes from the right kitchen, they'd say it was delicious and can they have another portion, please?' She reaches up and grabs Renee's cheeks, pushing her mouth into a pout like aunties did when she was younger. 'You know why that meat tasted so rank? Because it's rich-people food. Not proper food. That – and your mad spidey-sense taste buds.'

In a way, it's a nice thought. A nice, forgiving interpretation of everything. It's weird and wrong because it's rich-people shit. Tiny slivers of nonsense covered in a foam of fucking acorns or whatever, served on a silver platter. Not only does the emperor have no clothes – he also doesn't have any actual food half the time, either.

But deep down, she knows that isn't the case.

Something is wrong.

More than wrong.

It's . . . rotten.

FORTY

The night is another restless one. Despite being absolutely shattered, Renee's mind won't quit. It insists on replaying everything over and over, making connections where there might not be any, forcing her to check her phone every half an hour until the sky lightens to a dull grey.

How the hell am I going to work today?

On the outside, everything looks normal. Renee gets up, showers, eats a small breakfast, texts Graham and thinks about going to the gym. But as the day progresses, she's back in her own head again, second-guessing everything.

She could call in sick. No one would question her, and even if they did, she genuinely looks as rough as she feels. She checks her phone for the thousandth time. Still nothing from Graham. It's been a couple of hours now. She'd meant to call him last night, but she'd forgotten after her confessional with Lola. She'd pinged a text off to him in the early hours, but he hasn't replied, which is unusual. He'd usually respond promptly, even if they'd been arguing.

With all the other weirdness going on around her, she decides to call him. Even though she knows he's busy during the day, she needs to hear his voice. But he doesn't pick up. It rings and rings until his voicemail eventually kicks is.

'Hey, it's Graham. Leave a message and I'll get back to you.'

Short but sweet, warm but functional. Sums him up perfectly.

'Hey, G, it's me . . . I'm sorry I didn't call last night – I was with

Lola. I know you're probably busy, but please, pick up. I just need to hear your voice. Love you.'

With nothing else to do, Renee decides she needs a distraction. She pops to the bakery round the corner and picks up one of their greasy mystery meat pies and a jam doughnut the size of a hubcap. She also picks up a takeaway frappé with a mountain of whipped cream from the cafe opposite to try to cheer herself up.

Back home, she makes herself a nest, arranges her treats on the coffee table and starts surfing Netflix. She's already seen most of what's on offer, and the few things she and Lola haven't watched is stuff they'd dismissed as sheer trash.

Today, sheer trash is exactly what she needs.

Settling back, she covers herself with a blanket and picks at her pie. The pastry is soaked with gravy and the chef in her laments its soggy bottom, but the northerner in her drools. Just because it isn't perfect doesn't make it wrong. Sometimes, wrong is exactly what you need.

It's only once she's finished the lid that she delves into the filling, but the sight of the globules of mystery meat swimming in sludgy, equally mysterious gravy turns her stomach. The memory of that forkful of quivering, greasy flesh rears its head like it had been waiting all along, and once again her mouth is filled with the taste of that rancid meat, her tongue coated with its juices. She closes her eyes and sets the pie down on the coffee table, its filling untouched.

Hell, maybe it's time to join Graham and go vegan after all. No such thing as a mystery vegetable.

She takes a long swallow of her frappé, which is delicious, but she doesn't really enjoy it. It's like her doubts over Gracie have sucked all the flavour out of everything. She puts the half-finished iced coffee down and lies back, phone in hand.

As soon as she brings up Bethany's number, adrenaline surges within her, making her feel sick. By the time it rings, she's on the verge of bolting for the bathroom.

When Bethany answers, Renee doesn't have to fake sounding ill.

'Hey, Ren. Is everything OK?'

'Hi, Bethany . . . No, not really. I'm so sorry. I was hoping I'd be OK, but I've been sick – like properly throwing up – since yesterday.'

'Oh no, that's awful, you poor thing. Hope it's not norovirus. Make sure you keep yourself hydrated, and you can't come back in until you're forty-eight hours clear, so I'll adjust the schedule for tomorrow as well. If you're still being sick tomorrow, let me know because I'll have to think about getting in some agency staff for the end of the week. But don't let that worry you. You just get better, OK?'

'OK,' Renee manages to croak as guilt caves in her insides.

'Thanks for letting me know.'

'Hopefully see you on Thursday.'

'Hopefully. Bye.'

Bethany rings off. Renee stares at the ceiling, tears sliding down the sides of her cheeks, the guilt festering with her anxiety into a nasty, pulpy mess that settles low in her chest.

She checks the time. Just gone twelve. Nearly lunchtime.

She brings up Graham's number and calls him again.

Still no answer.

On any other day, she'd dismiss this as him simply being busy. But today . . . it feels off.

Very off.

He usually works from home on Tuesdays, so she could go straight round to his flat. He'd ask questions, but she's fine with that. She just needs to see him. Make sure he's OK. Shut up that sinking feeling in her gut that something is wrong. She doesn't even care if someone from the restaurant spots her. She can always say she was going to the doctor.

★

The tape around the end of Graham's road is long gone. She trudges up the steps and presses the buzzer for Graham's flat.

And she waits.

And waits . . . and waits.

She blows out a long sigh. Maybe he's on a call. She presses the buzzer again. Still no reply.

She rummages in her bag for Graham's spare key. She never really felt all that comfortable taking it. Sure, it made sense for her to have it, but she almost never uses it. She isn't sure why it makes her feel uneasy. Maybe it's down to Graham's insistence that she should move in with him – using his key to enter unannounced would feel like giving in. Giving in to what, though? Renee doesn't really know. It's not that she's shy of commitment – they've been together long enough to prove that isn't the case – but for some reason it felt like having a safety net she hadn't really earned.

The key turns easily in the lock, unlike her own front door. The lobby is silent and smells vaguely of polish. Up the stairs, and she's by Graham's door. She knocks.

No answer.

She uses the second key to let herself into the flat.

'Graham? Are you in?'

She's met with silence.

Beyond the short entryway is the main room of the flat – an airy living-room-slash-kitchen. As she enters, Renee can tell that something isn't right. The air is stuffy, and the whole flat has that dull, almost echoey quality that only happens when a place has been empty for at least a day.

She goes over to the sink. There's a dirty coffee mug in it, with a thick, congealed layer of brown sludge at the bottom. She then turns her attention to the houseplants on the kitchen windowsill. They're beginning to wilt – something Graham would never allow. Renee always teased him about how much he doted on his peace lily in particular; there's no way he would neglect it.

'Graham?' she calls out, just in case.

Again, no reply.

Renee checks his bedroom and bathroom, but they too are empty. Completely at a loss as to what to do next, she makes a coffee and settles on the sofa, phone in hand. She dashes off a quick message.

At yours, where are you? Rxx

A few minutes later, her phone buzzes.

It's Graham.

Her heart jolts and begins to race. Thank fuck for that. He's fine. He's just out.

I am busy. Will be away for a few days. I need to clear my head. Gx

Renee's heart stutters.

What does he mean, he's gone away for a few days? And why is he being so short with her?

G, please, where are you? I just want to talk.

Again, a few tense minutes pass. Then:

No. I don't love you any more. It's over.

Renee stares at her phone in shocked disbelief. He . . . wants to break everything off? After everything they've been through? And over text?

Her initial instinct is to be angry. How dare he. Three whole years, ended with a fucking text message? Oh no, that's not happening. If he wants to ditch her, he can do it in person.

What the fuck, Graham? Where are you?

She waits.

The seconds slip by.

Then a minute.

And another.

She stares at her phone, willing it to show her a new message.

But it doesn't.

Graham is silent.

Ten minutes after sending her text, Renee's anger beings to drain away and the unease returns – that awful, nagging feeling that something is horribly, horribly wrong.

She twiddles a lock of her hair, unsure what to do next.

If he'd gone away, there would be signs of it, right? Like, his suitcase would be gone, he would have packed some clothes – that kind of stuff. Renee jumps up, filled with hot, nervous energy, and marches into his bedroom.

At a glance, everything looks normal. The bed, meticulously made. The book he's reading, dutifully on his nightstand, a bookmark poking out of the top of it. Absolutely *nothing* is out of place.

Even his wardrobe looks untouched.

As in, there's his suitcase and all his clothes, hung neatly, organized by item. Trousers and jeans to the left, shirts to the right, jackets and blazers in between.

It's the same story with his chest of drawers. T-shirts, neatly folded. A full drawer of socks and boxer shorts.

His passport, hidden beneath them.

Renee swallows, struggling to keep a lid on her growing panic.

OK, I'm going to check the bathroom, and then . . .

She can't finish that thought. Call the police? 'Sorry, my boyfriend broke up with me over text and I haven't seen him in nearly a week, so I went to his flat to see where he is, but he's out and his clothes are still here, therefore I think something is wrong.' Get a grip. At best, they'd laugh her off the line. At worst, they'd send someone to detain her for being a delusional stalker.

No, she has to work out what's going on by herself.

She sits on Graham's bed and reads the last couple of texts again. They're very short. Formal. And, most importantly, totally unlike any of his other messages. Totally unlike *him*. He's always been a talk-it-out kind of guy. Even if he did want to finish things, he'd explain why, in detail, whether she liked it or not.

Then it hits her.

Find My Phone.

Graham had added her to his phone, and she'd done the same. They'd been separated at too many pubs, music venues and supermarkets. It didn't always work – mainly because it just said they were both in the same location – but at other times it had been a godsend.

It was worth a try.

Her hands are trembling as she opens the app. At first, she's dismayed when there's nothing on it. But then it refreshes, and a blue dot appears on the screen.

Renee frowns, her heart pounding.

There he is. Except . . . why is he there? He knows she isn't there.

It's closed Tuesday lunchtimes.

According to the app, Graham is at NOVA.

A prickling sense of creeping dread crawls over Renee's skin. She's the only reason he'd go there, and after the spa debacle, he'd asked for her schedule. So why is he there? Or at least, why is his phone there?

It takes a couple of minutes for Renee to regain her composure. She doesn't have a clue what any of this means, but her gut is telling her that whatever it is, it isn't good.

She needs to get to NOVA, and fast.

FORTY-ONE

It was all there. Gracie never hid any of it from her.

The secret freezer. Not letting anyone taste her food. Her absolute hatred of men she thinks have slighted her. Calling them pigs. Serving Troy Fisk testicles without telling him. Whatever she whispered to Josh that terrified him so much, then him disappearing shortly afterwards. The joke about Graham being grass-fed and organic. Even Preston Walls's reaction to his meal – unusual for someone with his ego – was, with hindsight, exactly the kind Renee imagined from someone who'd not only been tricked into eating human flesh, but had enjoyed it. It wasn't just disgusting – it was a violation.

A violation Gracie herself had experienced.

Was she trying to punish the critic for what happened to her, even though he wasn't directly involved? Had Gracie told him what he was really eating, knowing full well that if he went public, no one would believe him? She is the current titan of the culinary world, even with her cutthroat reputation, and he's a washed-up critic, after all.

But come on!

Her mind rebels, unable to accept the enormity – the sheer ridiculous insanity – of the situation.

It's stupid. Nonsense. The kind of thing that only happens in movies, and bad ones at that.

But no matter how hard her head tries to convince her to drop it, her gut insists she's right. It's the only thing that ticks all the boxes.

Dread sours to terror in her belly.

Gracie saw Graham and Renee having an argument. Spoke to Renee about their relationship. And now Graham is missing.

Did Gracie see Graham as nothing more than an obstacle to overcome in her indoctrination of Renee?

Shit.

Is all this her fault?

For the first time, Renee wishes NOVA was further away from Graham's flat – to give her more time to think.

More time to talk herself out of whatever she's going to do next.

She passes a newsagent on the way to the restaurant. More headlines about that missing hotelier. About Frank Mercer. About Josh's disappearance. And the media are starting to speculate. Make connections.

But they're still too far away from the truth to do anything with their suspicions.

Then there's that partial skeleton. The one the forensic people say bore evidence of being butchered. Was that Gracie too?

How long has she been at this?

Renee takes a long, shaky breath. It could all be a misunderstanding. All the so-called evidence is circumstantial at best.

But the tattoo . . .

She closes her eyes and wills her overactive mind to just shut the fuck up—

'Hey!'

The yell is angry, momentarily jolting her out of her own head. A man on a bike is in front of her. She glances down at her feet. She's managed to wander onto the cycle path.

'I'm sorry – I was a million miles away.'

'You need to look where you're going,' the man snaps. He's wearing bright green lycra, which isn't as flattering as he thinks it is. 'Stupid bitch.'

He glowers as he cycles off. Renee watches as he then runs a red light, almost mowing down a pedestrian trying to cross the road. The pedestrian doesn't call him a stupid bitch. She doesn't call him anything. Instead, she scuttles to the other side of the road before the traffic starts up again. The light turns amber, and someone beeps.

I'll take 'That Was a Man' for £500.

Renee peers through one of NOVA's front windows, just to see if she can spy any signs of life inside, but it's as silent as the grave.

Good thing she knows the code to the supply doors.

There are people around, but she feels like she's doing something clandestine, scuttling down the narrow alley that leads to the back of the restaurant. It isn't the same as a bustling Friday night, when people flock to this area – not because they're hungry, but to flash their cash and eat for the experience. That was something Granni never understood. *Why would you want to feed those who aren't hungry, Renee? Those who just want to consume the world because they can afford it?* She'd been angry at Granni for that remark; for years, those words were branded on her heart, pushing her to achieve greatness. *Because food is an art, Granni*, she'd said. *It isn't just about filling your belly. It's an experience. An adventure. You take people on a ride to places they've never been before.*

Granni had then sucked at her teeth and given Renee the stink eye.

So you want to help the rich eat like kings when there are mothers out there who can't feed their babies? One day you will learn, Renee. One day, you will see.

'Sorry, Granni,' Renee mutters under her breath as she keys in the code.

The lock on the smaller door clicks, allowing her to pull it open. She glances up at the sky, one hand placed on her chest, and offers a silent prayer to whomever may be listening. She can feel her heart thrumming against her palm, the adrenaline coursing through her body, making her feel sick yet wired.

You can always turn back. You don't have to do this. It's insane. He can't be here. Why would he be here? He's probably just at work.

'But if that's the case, why is his phone here? And why did I get those texts?'

Her inner voice goes silent.

'Exactly.'

Inside the loading area of the restaurant, everything is as it should be. Empty crates are stacked by the entrance, ready to be taken away by the delivery driver the next time they pay NOVA a visit. A pair of work gloves has been left on a ladder. There's even a dirty mug set down in one corner.

Whoever left that is going to be in trouble if Gracie sees it.

Renee knows she's stalling. Knows she's trying to put off the horribly inevitable truth.

The side door from the loading area to the actual kitchen is unlocked. There are no lights on, which lifts Renee a little. Maybe no one is here after all. But then she checks the Find My Phone app again, and yep, there's Graham's phone – now in the same place as hers.

'Where are you?' she mutters under her breath.

She knows she should turn on the lights, allow herself to search properly, but she can't. Because that would make everything real, and right now, she's still able to kid herself into thinking that maybe she's overreacting – maybe she's having some kind of nervous breakdown.

She stops wandering the kitchen. Her heart is in her mouth.

Gracie's freezer is open.

It's just a crack, but it's enough.

Gracie, who is the most anal-retentive person Renee has ever met, has left it unguarded for the second time in less than a week.

Once could be put down to a genuine mistake. But twice? That's deliberate.

Renee should leave. Call the police. Hell, call Martin, Roy, Bethany – even Q. She doesn't have Q's number, but she's sure she could find it here somehow. They could go in as a pack, finally expose the insanity.

But she doesn't. She doesn't because it *is* insanity. And if nothing is here – if Gracie is innocent – then she's out of a job, and Gracie is influential enough to ensure she'll never work in food ever again. Even the chicken shops would shun her.

She has to do this alone; face the consequences alone.

The cold pantry is dark and empty. Renee feels stupid for not realizing earlier that this is a front, just in case someone manages to get inside. No, the real freezer is the one beyond the other door, down the stairs.

The one she had to go into to retrieve the meat.

Renee swallows and shakes her arms, hoping that might help disperse the panic that has her legs shaking with every step she takes. She wants to run, flee, curse this place and never look back. But if there's even a tiny chance Graham might be down there . . .

She starts towards the door but checks herself. She's seen the movies. You don't go down into the creepy freezer basement without taking a weapon of some kind. This is a kitchen; it's full of knives and heavy things that could knock someone out. While she's hoping against all hope that she won't have to use it, she picks up a chef's steel. It's heavy enough to make someone think twice, but not as deadly as a knife.

Steel in hand, she creeps back to the secret door, hoping it's unlocked – and praying it isn't.

The handle is ice-cold as she pulls. The door opens. Renee's head swims.

Too late to turn back now.

Again, she descends the pristine white stairs into the dark.

It's bitingly cold down here, the frigid air making her lungs ache after the balmy air of the outside world. Renee flicks on the torch function of her phone and sweeps it around the room, searching for the light switch she couldn't find last time. She moves cautiously, the surrounding space no different than it was a few days ago. Neat packages of vacuum-sealed meat are piled on the shelves, labelled 'pig', 'bull', 'offal' and, most disconcertingly, 'misc.'. She dares to peer at one. It's filled with packs of various offcuts she can't quite make out – or maybe her mind is refusing to see the truth, because at first glance, one of the packets looks like it contains a human ear.

Wrestling with the urge to turn tail and flee, she closes her eyes and counts back from fifty. She gets to thirty-seven before she feels able to carry on.

Where the fuck is the light switch? Why isn't it by the door? Renee keeps running the feeble beam of her phone around the room – it has to be here somewhere. Even if Gracie knows every inch of her freezer, she still needs light to work.

God, I hope she needs light to work.

The plastic strips isolating the rear part of the freezer stir. Already on edge, Renee skitters back, ready to bolt for the stairs. She doesn't care if Gracie sacks her for being down here without her permission. She doesn't care if she never works in food again. She just wants to get out of here, away from this cursed Rob fucking Zombie hellscape.

'Hello?' Her voice shakes. She clears her throat, hoping it'll make her sound more confident than she actually feels, and adjusts her grip on the steel. 'Who's there?'

As soon as the question leaves her mouth, Renee regrets it. Because unless it's Graham, she doesn't want to know.

She spends a few precious seconds convincing herself that she's OK. Everything's fine. No one is going to jump out of the shadows with a bone saw and chop her up into cutlets.

She thinks. She hopes.

If only she could find the bastard light switch.

She ventures further into the freezer, closer to the plastic sheeting at the back.

Like last time, a very faint, dull green light gives off just enough illumination to enhance the shadows rather than reveal anything. As she inches closer, she can make out its shape. Closer still, and she knows exactly what it is.

A vacuum-pack machine. A large one. And next to it . . .

'Thank fuck.'

Renee flips the switch. The whole freezer lights up, banishing the deep shadows and confirming there is no one lying in wait. In fact, now she can see properly, she realizes it's a carbon copy of the other cold pantry: clinically white, with stainless steel shelving units stacked with trays of vacuum-packed meat, ready to be used.

What she can't see is Graham's phone. She quickly inspects the shelves again, just so she can convince herself she hasn't missed anything.

OK, can we now get the fuck out of here?

She wishes she could convince herself the answer is yes, but she can't. Because while she's given this part of the room a good going-over, there's a place she hasn't looked.

A place she's had a bad feeling about from the moment she first came down here.

The heavy-duty plastic strips hanging from the ceiling are the same kind you'd find at any abattoir. Which makes sense – if what Gracie said to Preston Walls is true, she butchers her carcasses herself. Back then, Renee thought that was something to be proud of: a true nose-to-tail philosophy, ensuring nothing goes to waste. But now? Now she realizes it's ridiculous. Who has time to cut down beef carcasses? They're massive. And heavy. Who's going to heave one down here? And now she's thinking about it – would a beef carcass even fit through the door? Then there are the stairs. There's no way Gracie could manoeuvre a whole cow down here by herself, even if it was gutted. It's nonsense. In fact, it's even worse than that – it's downright stupid. And yet, as far as Renee knows, no one has challenged her about it. Everyone's just accepted it, like it's a normal part of working in a kitchen.

Renee knows she has to go behind those curtains. Knows she has to at least take a cursory look. Because if the worst has happened, where is the likeliest place she'd find Graham? All she can do now is hope she's wrong. Because if she isn't . . .

The heavy plastic strips are frosted, so she can't see anything through them in any detail. She braces herself and gingerly draws back one of the strips using the steel.

At first, she can't see anything. Much like the rest of the freezer before she found the light switch, it's inky-dark in there. Using her phone again, she checks the walls near the plastic sheeting. This time, she finds exactly what she's looking for and flips the switch.

It takes her a long moment to comprehend what she's seeing. Not because it's a complicated scene, but because it's an impossible one. Her mind, already on high alert, is now in overdrive, physically unable to process what's right in front of her.

Because she's right.

About *everything*.

She staggers back, her hand over her mouth, her eyes wide.

Hanging from two meat hooks suspended on chains bolted into the stainless steel ceiling is the perfectly bisected, headless corpse of Josh Armitage.

She knows it's him by his tattoos.

Well, most of his tattoos. One of his shoulders has been removed, neatly cutting the largest one in half.

A panic so deep and primal races through Renee, she forgets

how to breathe. She wants to scream, but can only manage a low, animal moan. She wants to tear her eyes away from the ruin that was once Josh, but she can't – the sheer horror of the scene is hypnotic, her vision tunnelling so the corpse is the only thing she can see. If she wanted to, Renee could count every one of Josh's vertebrae, inspect his ribs, his pelvis. The cavity where his heart used to be. The hole where his organs used to nestle. Her eyes roll in their sockets as she notices horrific little details: the bucket of blood set down in the corner; Josh's head, leering down at her from a tray on a shelf, his jaw slack, his eyes staring.

A pair of shoes, poking out behind him.

For a moment, Renee can't process it. A pair of shoes? In here? Sure, Gracie has to strip her victims down somewhere, but surely her neat-freak ways wouldn't allow a filthy pair of shoes in her pristine slaughterhouse?

But then her mind catches up with her. She recognizes those shoes.

Her scream is thin and scratchy, like a part of her is still aware she needs to be quiet – more than ever now.

'Graham?'

She stumbles forward on pure adrenaline. The world around her feels floaty and soft, turning in on itself, her limbs not her own, her mind softly splintering. Aware that she's going to pass out if she's not careful, she tries to steady her breathing. Fainting here could be the death of her – either from hypothermia, or from Gracie discovering her. She tries to edge past Josh's split carcass, but misjudges where it is in relation to herself, and ends up brushing past his partially carved arm, sending that half of him swinging. She lets out a high-pitched shriek as the body spins back into her. His flesh is cold and horribly pliant as it collides with her, leaving a foul, metallic-smelling streak of coagulated myoglobin across her shirt.

Renee drops to the floor. It's all she can manage. Tears stream down her face. She has no idea when she started crying, but now she's sobbing, trying to form thoughts and words. Instead, there's only a jumble of stark terror. She wants to curl into a ball and cry for her parents, like she's a child and this is just a horrible nightmare.

This is real, this is real, THIS IS REAL.

She gulps down air and forces herself to crawl under Josh's blood-streaked feet, over to the shoes. Initially, she's relieved to see they're just shoes, with no accompanying feet in them. But as she crawls closer, that meagre solace is shattered.

Graham is slumped against the side of the freezer wall, stripped down to his underwear. His clothes are folded in a neat pile next to his shoes.

Above his head, two large meat hooks dangle.

Thankfully, there's no blood, nor any other indication that Gracie has tried to butcher him. From this angle, Renee can see a large gash on the back of his head, which makes a horrible kind of sense. Taking him by surprise and knocking him out from behind meant he couldn't fight back. It was also practical from a meat production point of view. Stressed livestock leads to sour flesh.

'No, no, no . . . Graham . . . Come on, G . . . Let's get you up.' Renee tries to hook her arms under his armpits and haul him to his feet, but he's a dead weight. She can't help but wonder how Gracie got him down here in the first place. She must have lured him, because there's no way she'd be able to lift him by herself.

Unless . . .

Did she have help? Are they all in on it? Is this entire enterprise run and staffed by people who are as far down the rabbit hole as Gracie clearly is? Martin, with his good humour and even better hugs? Roy, with his soft eyes, who always remembers exactly how everyone takes their coffee? Bethany, their kitchen mother – always there, ready to lend a hand or a shoulder to cry on, depending on what you need?

She can't even begin to contemplate any of them being involved in something as barbaric as this. And if they are involved, why would Gracie insist on being the only one tasting her *special* dishes? Like the one she allowed Renee to sample. The one that is . . . that was . . .

No. She isn't going to think about that now, because it's not important. She can fall apart later – quietly, and within the comfort of her own home. Right now, she needs to focus on Graham and getting them both out of there.

'Hang on, Graham – I'm going to see if I've got a signal.' She unhooks her arms from his and pulls out her phone. She realizes too late that she's forgotten to turn off the torch function, leaving her with only twelve per cent battery. It also doesn't help that the signal is terrible – no 4G, let alone 5, and absolutely no bars to speak of. Still, she tries to dial 999, but even the emergency call setting isn't working. Which makes her wonder: was this by design?

'I'm going to go back upstairs and call the police, OK?' she says to Graham's slumbering form. She picks up his clothes and tries to wrap what she can around him, hoping it makes a difference, no matter how small. 'I'll be back in a second. I promise.'

She pulls back the heavy plastic curtain, but before she can rush towards the stairs, she hears the sharp click of heels on tile.

She freezes as a small figure descends.

FORTY-TWO

There's nowhere to hide.

Renee backs up, retreating towards the plastic curtain, hoping that Gracie hasn't spotted her. But it's too late.

'Renee, I know you're in here,' Gracie says, her tone as thick and sickly sweet as treacle. 'It's OK. I'm not mad. Not in the slightest.'

Behind the curtain, Renee remains silent, her eyes squeezed shut in desperate prayer. Maybe Gracie's just assuming she's down here. Maybe she hasn't actually seen her.

The curtain twitches, then parts.

Gracie smiles at her and holds her arms out, like she's asking for a hug.

'You don't need to be worried,' Gracie says. 'I'm not angry. How could I be? In fact, I'm delighted.'

Renee's eyes bulge in her skull as a mounting pressure builds. She tries to speak – to ask her mentor what the fuck she's playing at – but instead, she lets out a thin whine, like an injured dog.

'Oh, come now, Ren,' Gracie says, pulling a coy expression. 'You're a smart girl. So very, very smart.' She reaches over to stroke Renee's cheek. 'I was hoping you'd put the pieces together eventually. It's not like I've been hiding it from you – not really.'

'But, but—' The rest of her sentence comes out as a sob, and all she can do is gesture towards Josh's corpse.

'Oh, sweetie,' Gracie says. 'I know. It's a shock. It always is, at first. But believe me, it gets easier – with time and experience.

You know it yourself. You've told me as much. This industry, it chews women up and spits them out as mangled wrecks. And if we say anything, we're blamed for our own wrecking.'

She takes a step closer. Her voice is calm.

'I've told you before: men don't want us here. They don't want us to be successful. To thrive without them. Look at the discourse these days – they throw the single cat-lady scenario at us, even when all we're asking is to be treated like regular human beings, not some crude mash-up of mother, child and whore.'

Gracie's voice tightens.

'If anything, they do it to themselves. They're quick to question us – to *blame* us – when we're attacked by them. What were you wearing? Why did you walk that way? What did you do to provoke him? If you'd just given him a chance, he wouldn't have done this to you. Every – single – day' – Gracie punctuates her words by striking her palm with the edge of her hand, like a knife – 'society gives mediocre men a pass – whether it's at work, at play, outside, at home. We bend over backwards to accommodate their shortcomings, and when they succeed they tell themselves it's because of invisible quotas. That the whole world is against them. That it's not their fault – it's because women and minorities have rigged the game.' Gracie's eyes bore into Renee, as if she's trying to force her to see – to believe – that her way is the correct way.

And Renee can't argue with her. Because she's right. It's all true. She's experienced it first hand. Always having to work harder, play harder. Be an expert, but also an innocent. Be confident, but not *too* confident. Don't usurp the men; only facilitate them. But that's not a good enough reason to *eat them*.

Gracie nods, a satisfied smile spreading across her face.

'You know I'm right. I can see it in your eyes. It's wonderful when you decide not to conform. When you stop consenting to be prey, and instead become the predator. They hate it. Strong women terrify them. That's why they go to such lengths to destroy us. To keep us small. "Barefoot and pregnant" isn't just a saying – it's a universal truth for women worldwide. They tell us our biology is confusing. That we're making up our pain. But they can't cope with even a fraction of that pain when it's theirs. So I decided to own my pain in the most taboo way. I used it to set myself free. You can, too, Ren. I promise. You'll feel so much better when you see men as the animals they truly are.'

'But . . . but *why*?' Renee asks, finally able to find her voice. 'Why butcher them? Why consume them? Surely there are other ways to fight back. You don't need to kill people to make a point.'

'Ha! Oh, you really are deep in the sauce, aren't you? I mean, not as deep as young Joshua found himself.' Gracie laughs, as if she's telling a light-hearted joke and not describing a man she killed and then ate. 'He was a stupid little boy, throwing around words he didn't understand. Not caring who he hurt, who he belittled. Only thinking of himself and his wounded privilege.'

Gracie holds Renee's gaze so intensely it feels like hypnosis. 'I promise you – you *will* see things my way. Once you realize how much good you can do with it. These men – they have nothing to offer society except hatred, violence and division. They're seen as powerful simply because they crush others under their heels. And so I decided it was time for someone to crush back. Someone to give them a taste of their own medicine, so to speak. Women have been victims for too long. I'm proposing that maybe it's time to turn the tables – in the most delicious way possible.'

'But . . . but what about the legality of it all?' Renee asks, clinging to the last threads of her sanity – and whatever may be left of the chef's. Not because what Gracie is doing appals her, but because she makes a horrific kind of sense. Men have been consuming women – body and soul – for too long. 'You're going to be caught. You can't kill powerful men and expect no one to pay attention.'

Gracie makes a pantomime of stroking her chin, then pins Renee with one of her intense glares.

'I'm almost insulted,' she says. 'I thought you were smart. Of course someone would notice if I was killing aimlessly. Like a man. But I don't. I plan everything. Meticulously. Most of the time, people think the victims are somewhere else. And if the law does come sniffing around – well, I'm just a small woman trying to play in the big leagues. I'm not scary. I couldn't possibly lift a corpse. I certainly couldn't overpower a big strong police officer. See how their pride blinds them? They dismiss me out of hand. I think I could go in for a police interview in a bloody butcher's apron, wielding a cleaver, and they'd still think me innocent. Their arrogance won't – *can't* – let them see any different.'

'But . . . Gracie . . . this can't last for ever,' Renee says. She's shivering, both from the cold and from shock. 'You're too close to Josh. His family are looking for him. The police have already been here. They've already interviewed us all—'

'Why are you acting like I don't know this?' Gracie snaps. 'Have they been back? What makes you think they have the faintest clue?' She leans in closer, as if she's about to share a particularly delicious secret. 'The thing is, when you're known for being a spoilt brat, people will just assume that whatever has happened to you is down to you being, well, *you*. When his uncle came in, I told him his precious nephew had been a racist, misogynistic little shit one too many times, and that he couldn't handle me taking him to task over it, so he bounced.'

She pulls a concerned face and alters her voice to something lower and more soothing. 'I'm so sorry, Mr Armitage. I'm worried too. I hope he's all right. If you hear anything, please let me know. We may have had our differences, but I still cared for the boy.'

Gracie drops the act with a sneer. 'See? That's how you do it. You perform a version of femininity men respond to – in this case, worry and nurture. And the best bit? His idiot uncle *thanked* me for being so caring, then apologized for his nephew's behaviour.' Gracie closes her eyes, inhaling like she's caught the scent of some divine fragrance rather than the rancid coppery tang of old blood and offal. 'That, Renee, is power.'

'Someone's going to join the dots. You can't do this for ever.' Renee doesn't know what else to say. As terrible as Gracie is, Renee can't help but have a sick, reluctant appreciation for her grit. If this were a movie, she'd be cheering Gracie's character on. She's tapped so perfectly into the deepest, darkest desires of every woman on this earth: the desire to make them pay for what we have endured.

But this isn't a film and you need to figure a way out, now.

'Maybe. One day,' Gracie says, inspecting her fingernails. 'But they haven't yet. Tell me, what happened to Isaac Ferguson? What was the conclusion after his retreat from public life?'

'Uh, he retired? After the whole MeToo thing, he basically went into hiding.'

Gracie grins wolfishly. 'Indeed, that's what they say. But it's not true. I know *exactly* where Isaac Ferguson is. Would you like to see?'

'W-what do you mean? Did you . . . You couldn't have . . .'

Gracie's grin widens as she crooks a finger, beckoning Renee to follow her over to one of the deep freezers. She lifts the lid and, from under piles of frozen meat – *just how many men has she slaughtered?* – she pulls out a package. When Renee realizes what it is, she gasps and covers her mouth with both hands.

'It's not very big,' Gracie says, exaggerating an expression of disgust. 'Especially after the frostbite got to it. I don't know how he had the confidence to keep waving it at young women, but he did. For so long, I thought it was just me – the humiliation, the shame, the guilt. Funny how women always carry the burden, isn't it? It's never their fault. Always ours.'

She throws the severed penis back into the freezer. 'Ultimately, I had the last laugh. I actually took that off before I killed him. The look on his face when I held it up . . . that alone healed a lot of my wounds. To see the fear, the disgust, and the sheer disbelief that the mouse had caught the cat, and that the mouse would treat his most sacred object with such disrespect. He made a delicious ragù, by the way.'

'Isaac. Ferguson,' Renee says, unable to take in the enormity of it all. 'You killed Isaac Ferguson?'

'Yes. I did. And I didn't just do it for myself. I did it for all the women he hurt. Women like *you*, Renee.'

And there it is. The chink in her armour. Because Renee is in no doubt – Isaac Ferguson deserved his ignominious end in every single way.

'You may have noticed,' Gracie continues, 'I only feed awful men my special dishes. 'Feeding Ferguson to Preston Walls the first time he came into my restaurant was particularly delicious. I was just starting out then, making a name for myself. Human flesh, while superficially like pork, has more in common with game, I find. There's a depth of flavour there, similar to older meat. It's why humans largely prefer the taste and texture of lamb and veal. The animals are so young, they haven't been exposed to things like cortisol. Their meat's naturally tender. But humans? You need careful preparation, and at that point in my career, I hadn't completely mastered the art of making human meat palatable. Now, of course, I'm a master. Or should I say, a mistress.'

'Is that what you told Preston Walls when he came in? Is that why he stormed out?'

Gracie laughs.

'Oh my, that was funny, wasn't it? I asked him if he enjoyed his meal, and then told him that was the second time he'd eaten someone. The look on his face . . . he couldn't believe it. Was I joking? Was I being serious? Or was I simply messing with him? He had no idea. And what was he going to do? Go to the police, tell them that he'd eaten a delicious meal – quite literally licked his plate – and then the executive chef joked about serving him people? Even if they did come to interview me, all I have to say is that he was looking for headlines. Everyone knows he's washed up, and they also know that he hates me. He'd say anything to trash my reputation again. Even accuse me of serving him braised boy.' Gracie barks out a laugh. 'Oh my God, you have no idea how good this feels. That I can finally share all of this with someone. Someone who gets it. Someone I can trust.'

'I don't understand,' Renee says, confused both by the cold and by Gracie's whiplash emotions.

Gracie steps forward and cups Renee's face in her hands. Renee instinctively flinches. Gracie's fingers are cold against her cheeks as she forces Renee to meet her gaze. Her eyes are dark and as flat as a shark's – devoid of all emotion, except an animalistic malice.

'I never had children. I don't really care for them. If I'm honest, I don't really care for humans in general. But you. You are the daughter I would have wished for, had I been so inclined. As soon as I saw you . . . I knew. When Bethany was interviewing you, I was watching. I've installed cameras throughout my establishment, so I know exactly what everyone is up to when I'm not here. I heard what you said. And my God, I knew. Here was a young woman, no older than I was when I was ritually humiliated by a man, talking about her own shameful treatment. And yet – there she was, still standing, still fighting. I saw so much of my younger self in you . . . So much potential. You are my protégée, Renee. My *legacy*. Imagine what we can do together – what we can *achieve*. We'll be unstoppable. We will *rule*.'

The intensity of Gracie's gaze is mesmerizing. Her words, as insane as they are, tempt Renee. She could be the next big thing.

Being trained and endorsed by Gracie Fitzgerald would open doors to places Renee has only dreamt of.

She could have it all.

Gracie lets go of Renee's cheeks, breaking eye contact. Renee gasps, as though surfacing from deep water. She watches as Gracie picks up a knife and wanders over to Josh's suspended, headless corpse.

'There's only one more thing you need to do for me,' Gracie says. She slices two slivers of flesh from Josh's thigh. The meat is pink, with a nice layer of white fat. Not too much that it becomes a flabby mouthful; not too little that the meat is dry and tough. If he'd been a pig, this would have been a fine piece of pork – good for curing, maybe even an exotic form of prosciutto. Much better than shoulder. 'Just one last test to prove your dedication to my cause.'

She holds out one of the slivers of meat to Renee and smiles.

FORTY-THREE

Renee stares at Gracie's hand. It's only a tiny slice of meat. A tiny sacrifice. Just a small piece of flesh for an even smaller part of her soul.

Except, it's not a small part. It's a big part. Maybe even all of it. The entirety of her soul, for a minuscule scrap of cold flesh.

That she is tempted revolts her, even as she realizes – she can't do this. It's not only amoral, it's insane.

Gracie Fitzgerald is insane.

But geniuses often are. They dance that fine line between innovation and madness, testing boundaries, teasing the edges of what's considered acceptable. Gracie took the broken pieces of herself and stitched them back together in a way that allowed her to use her trauma to become the best version of herself – and if that meant a few horrible men met their end at her hands, so what? She only fed the horrible men to other horrible men, via her special dishes. A kind of closed circuit. Shit feeding shit.

Except it wasn't just horrible men, was it? She'd fed Renee too. It had only been a taste, but she'd still subjected her to it, and in exactly the same way Gracie had been introduced to it. Through deception. Watching Gracie slice another sliver of flesh off Josh and eat it like prime carpaccio turns Renee's stomach. Maybe she'd hoped Renee would have the same epiphany she did – unknowingly consume human flesh, then somehow come to crave it?

Renee recalls the greasy mass Gracie had pushed into her mouth. The way it fell apart, wrapping tendrils of muscle fibre around her teeth like a parasitic worm seeking a host. The way she'd known something was wrong. That this wasn't what Gracie had made it out to be.

And the way Gracie had relished that moment, thinking she'd successfully moulded Renee into her very image.

No.

No, because she wasn't Gracie. She didn't live alone. She had friends, family – *Graham*. Gracie's demented performance had distracted her from getting him out. He must be freezing, sitting there in his underwear. She glances past Gracie. Even from here, she can see his skin has taken on a nasty bluish tint. If she's lucky, she might still be able to get him to a hospital where they could treat him for hypothermia.

If not . . .

She locks eyes with Gracie again. Smiling, Gracie offers up the scrap of meat.

Renee realizes this is her bargaining chip. She can deal with the insanity later. Right now, she just needs to get out alive.

'OK,' Renee says. 'But I have one condition.'

Gracie tilts her head, frowning.

'Really? And what might that be?' Her tone is bordering on mockery. She truly believes she has every angle covered.

'Let me take Graham home. Get him medical treatment. If I don't do it now, he's going to die . . .' Renee trails off as Gracie starts laughing.

'Oh, my dearest, darling girl. You still think he's alive? Look at him.' She gestures at Graham's body – at the mottled skin and the fact that he is clearly not breathing. 'Although it's cute that you thought covering him back up might revive him. But it's OK. You'll soon learn – humans are infinitely more fragile than cows or pigs. Their skin is thin, their bones easy to crack. Even the larger ones are no trouble. Not when you've been trained to break down cattle carcasses.'

Whatever spell Gracie has been weaving around Renee finally shatters. She barges past her, past Josh, and drops to her knees in front of Graham. She reaches out and touches him. He's ice-cold.

'Come on, G – wake up. Please.'

Her tearful entreaties are met with stone-cold silence.

'Darling, it's too late,' Gracie says, standing behind her, her voice soft, almost comforting. 'Believe me, it's better this way. I saw how he treated you. I heard the things he said. There was absolutely no way I was going to let that slide. Even the so-called nice ones are tainted in the end.'

Tainted.

She thought Graham was one of the 'horrible' ones. When all he ever did was love and support me. Sure, he made mistakes – everyone does. It's called 'being human'.

Being human. The complete opposite of whatever this psycho has metamorphosed into.

Renee takes everything – the fear, the disgust, the worry, the heartache – and pounds it into rage.

Because Gracie has no right. Who made her judge, jury and executioner? Sure, Renee was never going to mourn the death of Isaac Ferguson – no woman was, except maybe his mother – but Graham? He was loved. Hell, even Josh. He was young. He had time to learn and change.

She raises her hand and tilts Graham's head back. His blue eyes have turned an icy grey in death. The knot on his head is more pronounced now she can see all of it, and there's a deep cut to his throat. Renee finally understands the nearby bucket of blood. No mess, no fuss – Gracie simply knocked him out and bled him like a pig in a slaughterhouse, with an expertise that sends convulsions of terror and fury through her.

Ignoring Gracie, she looks up.

They're still there.

Good.

Renee lunges to her feet, snatching up one of the meat hooks Gracie had intended for Graham. It's heavy and sharp, and the cold of the metal bites into her hand. As she turns, she swings it at Gracie. She isn't sure whether she means to hurt her or just frighten her. But in the end, the choice is taken out of her hands.

The meat hook, so sharp and so heavy, pierces Gracie's side. Bright blood blooms immediately, staining her chef's whites a deep crimson. She grimaces and gives Renee a confused look, but then smiles, exposing blood-stained teeth.

'Oh, Renee. I always knew you had it in you.' Her voice is hoarse, her throat already bubbling with blood. 'I—'

Her words are cut off as Renee drags the hook through her stomach, emptying her guts onto the floor in steaming piles.

FORTY-FOUR

Renee sits on the floor opposite Gracie, once-hot blood pooling around her, cooling and thickening to the consistency of syrup.

She knows she should move, but she can't.

'Well, G – what are we going to do now?' she says, before holding up her gore-streaked hand and coughing. Her throat is raw from all the bile she's made herself swallow.

Gracie, once so vibrant, so inspirational, is lying on her side. She's not quite dead, but she soon will be. Her intestines, a stinking pile of red and purple rope, are spilled across the tiles. But that isn't what disturbs Renee. No – the real horror is the almost beatific smile gracing her face.

Heh.

Gracing. Gracie. The woman who graced Renee with her time, her expertise and her deepest, darkest secrets.

Renee crawls through the blood to sit beside her mentor. The only things Gracie can still move are her eyes, and they track Renee's progress with her usual unnerving intensity. A wine-red foam bubbles from her mouth as her breath turns to a wheeze.

She's trying to speak.

Renee hunkers down, her ear as close as she can get it to Gracie's lips, but she can't make out what she's trying to say. Only one word is audible.

You.

With a final gasp, Gracie's eyes lock onto Renee's, then fix in a perpetual stare.

Renee sits up. She isn't unaware of the irony. That Gracie once killed her own mentor for tricking her into eating human flesh, only to be killed by her protégée for unknowingly feeding her the same. In a way, it's almost amusing. Like a modern Greek tragedy, or something Shakespeare might write.

In trying to recreate Renee in her own image, Gracie had sealed her fate.

Renee laughs.

It isn't a nice laugh. It starts as a smirk, then builds to a shrieking crescendo that echoes off the tiled walls in a great cacophony of madness that reflects back to her. The splintering that began when she first entered the freezer is now complete.

Once, there had been a part of Renee that would have pushed back against these thoughts. Headed them off at the pass. Refused to entertain them for a second. Everyone has them, these thoughts. The *if I just place the knife here and lean against it, how would that feel?* thoughts. The *if I just squeezed that little bit harder, what might happen?* and *if I jumped off, how long would it take for me to hit the ground?* musings. Those nasty, intrusive little thoughts.

Now, even the sound of footsteps on tile doesn't worry her.

A hand draws back the frosted plastic strips, and Q steps in. He doesn't scream. He doesn't shout. He doesn't swear, gasp or cry.

Instead, he simply locks eyes with Renee and nods.

'I see.'

'She passed on her legacy, I guess,' Renee says.

'Indeed she did.' He checks his watch. 'Service begins in less than three hours. I understand you called in sick.'

'I did. I did do that.'

'Then I suggest I take you somewhere and get you cleaned up.'

'You've done this before, haven't you?' Renee asks. She feels drunk.

Q doesn't answer her.

'I shall be back in a moment,' he says, then turns and leaves.

Renee leans over Gracie. She's still holding the sliver of Josh in her hand. After studying it, Renee plucks it from her fingers.

'Meat is meat,' she mutters.

She pops the slice of flesh into her mouth and chews.

ACKNOWLEDGEMENTS

First things first: it isn't an exaggeration to say that this book has had a dream team behind it from day one, and I thank the dark gods that conspired to connect Nicole and Sandra that day.

To my amazing agent, Sandra Sawicka, who has stuck with me through thick and thin, even when things get a bit weird and disgusting (and, let's face it, a hell of a lot of fun). I know you said 'no cannibals', but I'm really glad you decided to go back on that one! Your support, guidance and belief in me is a constant source of inspiration, and every single day I thank you for your patience, especially when things go a bit off piste (or indeed extra-dimensional).

Then there's Nicole Witmer, the editor who said 'See what you can come up with', and I came up with brains. And, bless her, the moment she said 'Yes, brains!' rather than 'Oh, dear Lord, are you all right?' I knew everything was going to be OK. It's not often in my life that people say 'Don't hold back' and actually mean it – the fun I have had! Thank you, Nicole, for taking this chance, and trusting me with so much. It has been a complete honour and an utter pleasure to work with you (even if I did get lost the first time we met).

And speaking of pleasures to work with – the same goes for everyone else at Bantam/Transworld. No book is an island, and my thanks go to everyone from copyeditor Rebecca Wright and proofreader Alan Heal, to illustrator Scarlett Yang and designer Beci Kelly for their amazing cover, and to Nina Lewis for her enthusiasm for this project.

I would also like to mention two people from my past: Paddy and Eddy, who used to run the restaurant at the Sailing Club in Bosham. I worked in the kitchen for four years as a teenager in the early nineties (when employing random teenagers and giving them knives as long as their arms was considered perfectly fine), and it is to these two semi-retired chefs that I ascribe my love of food (plus, being a Taurus. Never met a Taurus who didn't love a good dinner). They were both in their sixties, so the chances are they're both long gone now, but I remember them fondly (and with a small measure of terror): Paddy, a mixture of Mary Berry and Prue Leith, a whizz at desserts, her lemon silk crunch still haunting my dreams thirty years later; Eddy, Gordon Ramsay on a bad day, an even more genial Keith Floyd on a good, who taught me so many things: basic knife skills beyond massacring an onion; that you can't say you don't like something until you try it (you can say no to brains, though. That's fine), which led me to liking tapenade, skate wings with brown butter and capers, haggis, mussels, scallops and black pudding (but not mushrooms – that was the one thing I could never stomach, and still can't); and most importantly, how to make perfect Yorkshire puddings. If it wasn't for Eddy, my toad in the hole wouldn't be legendary, and I wouldn't be known as the the Toad Queen among my friends, a title I take very seriously. So Paddy, Eddy and all the members of Bosham Sailing Club circa 1991–95 (including Sandy, who just happened to be the late Sir John Forster 'Sandy' Woodward, GBE, KCB, but I didn't know that because I was just a dumb kid and he was just a nice old man to me) – if you're still around, you won't remember me, but I remember you. I washed your pots, prepped your veg, made your starters and learned a few culinary tricks that ultimately helped me write this book. Thank you.

Then there's my family, especially my husband, whose expertise saved my life when a third of the first draft was corrupted. Being a software engineer, he was able to do magic and get into the file and extract the raw text (don't ask me how; for all I know he put milk in his slippers and the computer elves did it for him because he knows the sorcery of the magic White Text on the Black Background), allowing me to save my precious words, if not my precious formatting. Let this be a lesson: back your stuff up. Like, often. And be nice to the nerds in your life. You never know when you're going to need them.

Also, my daughters, Lucy and Emily, who are surprisingly chill about their mother's increasingly unhinged Google searches, and my cats, Hiccup and Tifa, who offer amazing cuddles, but also like to wander across my keyboard and add their own, nonsensical chains of miscellaneous letters and characters, because the corrupted files weren't exciting enough, apparently.

And lastly, to my mother, whose cooking is legendary. Where the question 'what's in this?' is met with 'it doesn't matter', and we didn't so much have 'meat pies' as 'hunt the meat pies' (much to my father's eternal chagrin). Nothing was ever wasted, everything went into a stew, if you had to ask what it was you weren't hungry enough, and if I brought it home from the restaurant 'for the dog', you'd better believe we were having that for dinner the next day (not that I blame her, those were prime leftovers!). She taught herself to cook; her fish pie is to die for, her Yorkshire puddings are more fit for roof tiles, and I'm not sure what part of Italy her pizza is from but wherever it is Rome excommunicated it long ago and I still crave it from time to time. Oh, and if she offers you a pickled onion, take one. You shall not be disappointed. You might not be able to breathe for about twenty minutes afterwards, but you'll be happy nevertheless.

ABOUT THE AUTHOR

Ellie Graves has always been drawn to the darker side of life, in human psychology and the supernatural. She has had a lifelong love affair with the written word, through writing, reading and teaching. She has lived in and around Portsmouth all her life, and lives there now with her family. She can't imagine living anywhere else; the sea is in her bones. She likes to collect rocks, draw fantastical creatures and watch horror movies. Ellie also writes psychological thrillers under the name Claire Lunn.